Antoine Henri Jomini

Life of Napoleon

Vol. 2

SALZWASSER
VERLAG

Antoine Henri Jomini

Life of Napoleon

Vol. 2

Reprint of the original, first published in 1864.

1st Edition 2022 | ISBN: 978-3-75259-247-4

Verlag (Publisher): Salzwasser Verlag GmbH, Zeilweg 44, 60439 Frankfurt, Deutschland
Vertretungsberechtigt (Authorized to represent): E. Roepke, Zeilweg 44, 60439 Frankfurt, Deutschland
Druck (Print): Books on Demand GmbH, In de Tarpen 42, 22848 Norderstedt, Deutschland

LIFE OF NAPOLEON.

VOLUME II.

LIFE

OF

NAPOLEON.

By BARON JOMINI,

GENERAL-IN-CHIEF AND AID-DE-CAMP TO THE EMPEROR OF RUSSIA.

"Je fus ambitieux; tout homme l'est, sans doute;
Mais jamais roi, pontife, ou chef, ou citoyen,
Ne conçut un projet aussi grand que le mien."
VOLTAIRE, *Mahomet.*

TRANSLATED FROM THE FRENCH.

WITH NOTES,

By H. W. HALLECK, LL.D

IN FOUR VOLUMES.—WITH AN ATLAS.

VOL. II.

NEW YORK

1864.

a 2

CONTENTS.

VOL. II.

CHAPTER VII.

CAMPAIGNS FROM 1802 TO 1804.

FROM THE RUPTURE OF THE PEACE OF AMIENS TO THE ESTABLISHMENT OF THE EMPIRE.

PAGE

Internal Affairs of France—New Difficulties with England—Mission of Lord Whitworth—His Conference with Napoleon—Hostile Declaration of George III.—Napoleon's violent Language to the English Minister—English Ultimatum rejected—Military Occupation of Naples—Invasion of Hanover—Effect of these Operations on the rest of Europe—New Relations with Spain—She declares War against England—Portugal purchases her Neutrality—The English in India—Chances of a Descent into England—Preparations for this Descent—Plots against the Life of Napoleon—The Duke d'Enghein—An hereditary and stable Government necessary to France—Establishment of the French Empire—Impossibility of restoring the Bourbons—Effects of this Establishment of the Empire—General State of Europe—Difficulty with Russia—She refuses to recognize the French Empire—It is recognized by Austria—Indecision of the Porte—The Pope at Paris—Napoleon's pacific Declaration—He offers Peace to England—Organization of the Grand Army—It prepares to embark—Napoleon's Project compared with that of Cæsar—Concerted Movements of the French Fleets—The Fleet of Rochefort—The Toulon Squadron—The Brest Squadron—Nelson sails for Egypt—Villeneuve at the Antilles—He returns to Europe—Nelson also returns to England.... 13

CHAPTER VIII.

CAMPAIGN OF 1805.

FROM THE FORMATION OF THE THIRD COALITION TO THE TREATIES OF VIENNA AND PRESBURG.

PAGE

Origin of a new Coalition against France—Pitt's Project to reduce her to the Limits of 1792—He negotiates with Russia—Napoleon assumes the Iron Crown of Italy—Alliance between Russia and England—Hesitation of Austria—Napoleon in Italy—His Fortifications and Camps of Manœuvre there—His Coronation at Milan—Return of the French Fleets to Europe—Villeneuve at Ferrol and Cadiz—Consequences of his multiplied Faults—Austria accedes to the new Coalition—Mission of Nowosiltzof—First Project of the Allies—Their Definitive Plan—Their Efforts to induce Germany to join the Coalition—The Austrians enter Bavaria—The French march from the Coast of the Channel to the Danube—Organization of the Grand Army—Passage of the Rhine—Direction of the French Masses on Donawerth—Mack awaits them on the Danube—Napoleon turns his Right and falls upon his Rear—His Confusion—Napoleon manœuvres to cut him off from Bohemia—Murat's Faults—Mack attempts to Escape—Combat of Haslach—Napoleon returns to the Danube—Operations of the Austrians—They burn the Bridge of Elchingen—Ney's Operations—Battle of Elchingen—Investment of Ulm—Ney's Attack—Murat pursues Werneck—Mack summoned to surrender Ulm—Conditional Capitulation—Defeat of Werneck—He surrenders—Surrender of Mack—Fate of the Wreck of Mack's Army—Russia threatens to join the Coalition—Napoleon directs his Forces on the Inn—Passage of the Inn, the Salza, and the Traun—Remarks on Napoleon's March on Vienna—The Emperor Alexander at Berlin—Massena's Operations in Italy—His Instructions—Passage of the Adige, and Battle of Caldiero—Retreat of the Archduke Charles—Napoleon at Lintz—Propositions for an Armistice—Operations of Murat and Davoust—Kutusof passes the Danube at Krems—Affair of Dirnstein—Napoleon approaches Vienna—State of that City—Murat captures the Bridge on the Danube—Critical Situation of Kutusof—Unskillfulness of Murat—Combat of Hollabrun—Kutusof effects his Junction—Napoleon at Schoenbrun—General Plan of Campaign—The French Army at Brunn—Operations in the Tyrol—New Attempts at Negotiations—Movements of the Allies—Napoleon's Disposition for their Reception—The Allies' Plan of Battle—Napoleon's grand Attack on their Centre—Soult's Success—Check of the Enemy's Left—Success at the Centre and French Left—Napoleon and Soult attack the Enemy's Left—He is cut off from Olmutz and thrown on Hungary—Interview between Napoleon and the Emperor Francis—Remarks on the Battle of Austerlitz—Napoleon returns to

PAGE

Vienna—Treats with Prussia—Also with Austria—Operations in Hanover—The Dynasty of Naples ceases to reign—Napoleon's Orders to Villeneuve—Nelson returns before Cadiz—Mutiny of the two Fleets—Battle of Trafalgar.................................... 62

CHAPTER IX.

CAMPAIGN OF 1806.

FROM THE RUPTURE OF THE PEACE OF PRESBURG TO THE DESTRUCTION OF THE PRUSSIAN ARMY.

Napoleon returns to France—Crisis of the Bank—Relations with England—Progress of the English Power in India—Disastrous Maritime Expedition of the French—Continental Means of opposing England—Difficulty of forming Alliances with the Great Powers—System of Federate States—Reasons for the successive Additions to the French Empire—Death of Pitt—Blockade of Ports by a mere British Order in Council—New Difficulties with Prussia—The Cabinet of Berlin perverts the Treaty of Vienna—Motives for this Step—Negotiations of Haugwitz—A New Treaty—Discussions with Austria, for Cattaro and Wurtzbourg—A Federation substituted in place of the German Empire—Napoleon crowns the different Members of his Family—Joseph, King of Naples—Louis, of Holland—Eugene, Heir to the Throne of Lombardy—Murat, Grand Duke of Berg—Military Operations in Naples—Siege of Gaeta—Diversion in Calabria—Confederation of the Rhine, with Napoleon as Protector—Francis abdicates the Crown of Germany, and is proclaimed Emperor of Austria—Sensation at Berlin—Prussia entitled to the Presidency of the Confederation—Interior State of the French Empire—Mechanism of Napoleon's Government—The Public Credit restored—Conscription regulated—Monuments—Internal Improvements—Military and Maritime Works—State of Prussia—Negotiations with England—Treaty signed, but not ratified, with Russia—Mission of Sebastiani to Constantinople—Attack of the English on Buenos-Ayres—Rupture of the Negotiations with England—Prussia abruptly decides on War—Her extraordinary Ultimatum—First Movements of the French Army—The Position and Plan of Operations of the Prussians—Napoleon's Plan of Operations—Faults of the Prussians—Their Generals—Views of the Duke of Brunswick—Napoleon cuts off their Communications—His decisive Manœuvre—Battle of Jena—Battle of Auerstadt—Extraordinary Results of these two Victories—Combat of Halle—March on Potsdam and Berlin—Visit to the Cabinet of the Great Frederick—Entrance into Berlin—Operations of Hohenlohe—Fall of Spandau—Dispositions against Hohenlohe—Combat and Capitulation of Prenzlow—

PAGE

Fall of Stettin—Blucher retires on Mecklenbourg—Capitulation of Custrin—Measures for taking Possession of the Country between the Rhine and the Oder—Armistice with the Saxons—Blucher driven to Lubeck—Fall of Lubeck—Capitulation of Blucher—Taking of Magdebourg—Napoleon at Berlin—The celebrated Berlin Decree—British Orders in Council—Armistice with Prussia, not ratified—Napoleon advances to the Vistula—Immense Results of this Seven Weeks' War............ 154

CHAPTER X.

CAMPAIGN OF 1807.

FROM THE ARRIVAL OF THE RUSSIANS ON THE VISTULA TO THE TREATY OF TILSIT.

Condition of the Enemy's Forces—Poland—Napoleon's Measure for securing his Rear—The King of Prussia rejects the Armistice—The Russian Army—Invasion of Moldavia—Position of the two Armies—Napoleon takes the Offensive—Combat of Pultusk—Napoleon prepares for Winter-quarters—Measures for securing his Position—Continuation of the War between Russia and Turkey—Benningsen takes Command of the Russian Army—Affairs of Silesia—Benningsen attacks Napoleon's Left—Movements of the Latter—His Project accidently discovered by the Russians—Soult fights at Bergfried—Combat of Landsberg—Combat of Liebstadt—Battle of Eylau—The French Army resumes its Winter-quarters—Combat of Ostrolenka—Embarrassment of Napoleon's Position—Menaces of Spain—Austria offers her Intervention for Peace—The English threaten Constantinople—Passage of the Dardanelles—Sebastiani rouses the Turks to defend themselves—Retreat of the English—Napoleon's Firmness—Negotiations at the Camp of Finkenstein—Negotiations with England broken off by Perceval—Treaty of Triple-Alliance at Bartenstein—Operations in Pomerania—Negotiations with Sweden—Army of Observation on the Elbe—English Expediton into Egypt—Sieges in Silesia—Siege and Fall of Dantzic—Resumption of Hostilities—Danger and Escape of Ney—Napoleon Marches to his Assistance—Favorable Changes of Napoleon's Position—Battle of Heilsberg—Operations of Benningsen—Battle of Friedland—The Russians recross the Niemen—They propose Peace—Interview of the Emperors at Tilsit—The Peace signed—Prussia—Conditions of the Treaty of Tilsit—Revolution at Constantinople—Projects on Turkey—Special Stipulations at Tilsit..... 244

CHAPTER XI.

CAMPAIGN OF 1808.

FROM THE TREATY OF TILSIT TO THE INVASION OF PORTUGAL.

PAGE

Results of the Campaigns of 1806 and 1807—Origin of the Continental System—Its general Plan—Its Influence on Commerce—On Industry—This System leads to War—Its Influence on State Policy—On Maritime Relations—Measures requisite for its Execution—Mediation offered by Russia to England—English Expedition against Denmark—Preparations of the Danes for Defense—Capture of Copenhagen and the Danish Fleet—Brune takes Stralsund and Rugen—Russia declares War against the English—Intercession of Austria—Negotiations respecting Turkey—Distribution of new Titles of Nobility—Suppression of the Tribunat... 326

CHAPTER XII.

PENINSULAR CAMPAIGNS OF 1807 AND 1808.

FROM THE INVASION OF PORTUGAL TO THE TREATY OF EVACUATION.

Affairs of Spain—Napoleon decides to occupy Portugal—Treaty of Fontainebleau—Junot occupies Portugal—Dissensions in the Royal Family—Talleyrand urges a War with Spain—Affairs of Italy—Napoleon's Interview with Lucien—The Milan Decree—Difficulties with the Pope—Napoleon's vast Designs in Italy—Projected Transfer of the Holy See to Paris—Occupation of Rome—Annexation of Tuscany to France—Difficulties in the Royal Family of Spain—The French occupy the Spanish Fortifications—Alarm of the Spanish Court—The pretended Project of removing it to Mexico—Political Explosion in Spain—The Revolution of Aranjuez—Murat enters Madrid—Napoleon's Instruction—Interview with the Spanish Court at Bayonne—He resolves to place a new Dynasty on the Throne—Objections to Napoleon's Plans—His Reasons for adopting them—Operations of Murat—Insurrection of the Second of May—Spanish Junta convoked at Bayonne—Napoleon's Conduct toward Ferdinand VII.—General Insurrection in Spain—Moncey driven from Valencia—Insurrection in Aragon—The Army of Galicia advances on Valladolid—Joseph proclaimed King of Spain—Dupont capitulates at Baylen—Beginning of the Siege of Saragossa—Retreat from Madrid—Romana flies from Denmark—Errors of the

PAGE

Campaign—Junot's Position in Portugal—General Interests of this Country—Sacrifices imposed on the Portuguese—General Insurrection in Portugal—Landing of Wellington and the English Army—Junot evacuates Portugal—Military Operations in the North of Europe....... 350

CHAPTER XIII.

NAPOLEON'S CAMPAIGN OF 1808 IN SPAIN.

FROM THE EVACUATION OF PORTUGAL TO ITS RE-INVASION BY SOULT.

French Reverses in Spain—Military Preparations of Austria—Difficulties and Chances of Napoleon's Position—Conference of Erfurth—Napoleon goes to Spain—Supreme Junta—Position of the Spanish Forces—Napoleon at Vittoria—Character of the War—Plan of Operations—Affair of Burgos—Defeat of Blake at Espinosa—Battle of Tudela—Battle of Sommo-Sierra—Napoleon enters Madrid—The English advance from Portugal—Napoleon marches against them—Moore retires on Coruña and Romana on Orense—Battle of Coruña, and Embarkation of the English—Lefebvre on the Tagus—Victor defeats Infantado at Ucles—Operations in Catalonia—St.-Cyr recaptures Rosas and succors Barcelona—Affair of Cordedeu—Victory of Molino-del-Rey—Victories of Cappellados and Walsch—Second Siege of Saragossa—Soult sent to Portugal—Departure of Napoleon for Paris—Intrigues of Talleyrand...... 411

LIST OF MAPS

TO ILLUSTRATE

JOMINI'S LIFE OF NAPOLEON.

VOL. II.

12. MAP OF THE OPERATIONS, WHICH LED TO THE CAPITULATION OF ULM, in October, 1805.

13. BATTLE OF AUSTERLITZ, 2d October, 1805.

14. MAP OF PRUSSIA AND POLAND, to illustrate the Campaigns of 1806, etc.

15. BATTLE OF JENA, 14th October, 1806.

16. BATTLE OF AUERSTEDT, 14th October, 1806.

17. BATTLE OF PULTUSK, 20th December, 1806.

18. BATTLE OF PREUSS-EYLAU, 1st Sheet, Evening or 7th February, 1807

19. BATTLE OF PREUSS-EYLAU, 2d Sheet, 8th February, 1807.

20. BATTLE OF HEILSBERG, 10th June, 1807.

21. BATTLE OF FRIEDLAND, 14th June, 1807.

22. MAP OF SPAIN AND PORTUGAL, to illustrate the Campaigns of 1808, etc.

CHAPTER VII.

CAMPAIGNS FROM 1802 TO 1804; FROM THE RUPTURE OF THE PEACE OF AMIENS TO THE ESTABLISHMENT OF THE EMPIRE.

Internal Affairs of France—New Difficulties with England—Mission of Lord Whitworth—His Conference with Napoleon—Hostile Declaration of George III.—Napoleon's violent Language to the English Minister—English Ultimatum rejected—Military Occupation of Naples—Invasion of Hanover—Effect of these Operations on the rest of Europe—New Relations with Spain—She declares War against England—Portugal purchases her Neutrality—The English in India—Chances of a Descent into England—Preparations for this Descent—Plots against the Life of Napoleon—The Duke d'Enghein—An hereditary and stable Government necessary to France—Establishment of the French Empire—Impossibility of restoring the Bourbons—Effects of this Establishment of the Empire—General State of Europe—Difficulty with Russia—She refuses to recognize the French Empire—It is recognized by Austria—Indecision of the Porte—The Pope at Paris—Napoleon's pacific Declaration—He offers Peace to England—Organization of the Grand Army—It prepares to embark—Napoleon's Project compared with that of Cæsar—Concerted Movements of the French Fleets—The Fleet of Rochefort—The Toulon Squadron—The Brest Squadron—Nelson sails for Egypt—Villeneuve at the Antilles—He returns to Europe—Nelson also returns to England.

Internal Affairs of France.—While victory and diplomacy continued to elevate the glory of France, every thing in the interior kept pace with my fondest hopes. The state was becoming regenerated with the most wonderful rapidity. I labored with great ardor; apart from the incorrigibles of the faubourg St. Germain,* and a few visionary democrats, the entire nation applauded my labors, and every one manifested his admiration with enthusiasm. To avoid the accusation of self-sufficiency in praising my own works, I will quote the

* This is the quarter occupied by the old nobility.

expressions of a man who was my admirer as a visionary (*idéalogue*), and my enemy as a fanatic and as an historian.

"Glorious in war, glorious in peace, Napoleon eclipsed, in the dazzled eyes of the people, the most brilliant reputations in ancient or modern history; the remembrance of his exploits in Egypt and in Italy, electrified all minds and constituted the charm of every conversation. The antique style of his speeches and his proclamations carried his hearers back to the golden ages of Athens and of Rome, and revealed a great genius as well as a great soul.

"It is he who has rescued the republic from danger, and twice raised it to the highest pinnacle of glory and power. When he is absent, it languishes; when he returns, it revives. Have his enemies triumphed in his absence—the new Hercules strangles them on his return.

"His absence was the signal for war; his presence was that of victory and peace, not only with Austria, but also with Russia, England, Turkey, Portugal, Germany, and the Prince of Orange.

"He obtained, even from barbarians, a treaty favorable to France; Tunis and Algiers have become our friends; the French need no longer fear the cruelties of the ferocious African; their vessels plow the waters of the Mediterranean unmolested; the pirates of Lybia no longer insult the Republican flag. It is he alone who has stifled civil discords, restored the exiles to their country, and given to Pope Pius VI. the honors and peace of the tomb. It is he who, by his respect shown to Pius VII., has calmed the consciences and preserved the morals of the people.

"He has immortalized his age by the redaction of many important codes. Our finances owe to him their prosperity; the magistrates, the payment of their salaries; the army, the honor of its colors and the regularity of its support; travelers, the safety of the roads; merchants, the restoration of the channels of interior trade; seamen will some day owe to him the freedom of the seas.

"France everywhere resumes her former glory: palaces, decayed by time or mutilated by the fury of the mob, are repaired; new monuments rise up to attest our glory to future ages; the hand of art, everywhere in France, contributes to the beauty of nature; ruins, the deplorable signs of past discord, are rapidly disappearing; magnificent edifices are springing up under the empire of a magnanimous government. Such are the fruits of the peace which he has conquered and of the concord which he has restored.

"The Revolution is ended; the source of the evils and sorrows of the world is shut up."

These eulogies are merely a repetition of what was said in France. The orators at the tribune; the magistrates by their deputations; writers in their productions, could not find phrases sufficiently sonorous for sounding through Europe my great deeds, or for interpreting worthily the bursts of national gratitude. They intoxicated me with incense. However exaggerated the expressions of those who announced themselves as the echoes of public opinion, my conscience told me that in reality these eulogies were true, and that I merited them.

Nevertheless I felt that our system was not yet complete; it wanted permanence. Great as was my desire to give to the Revolution a solid and reasonable basis, I nevertheless saw that I should encounter great opposition in accomplishing this, for there was still antipathy between the old and new regimes. They formed two masses whose interests were directly opposed. All governments which subsisted by the ancient public law, thought themselves endangered by the principles of the Revolution, and these had no guaranty but in forcing the enemy to treat, or in destroying him if he refused to recognize it.

I was the man destined to decide this contest; I found

myself at the head of that great faction which wished to destroy the system upon which the world had been governed since the fall of the Romans. And I found myself opposed by the hatred of all those who were interested in preserving this Gothic rust; they acted unwisely, for I alone could restore order and unite the interests of the two parties. If these factions had listened to reason, and made voluntary concessions, in eight days we should have been agreed.

A character more yielding than mine would have sought to avoid the difficulty, by leaving a part of the question to the decision of time; but when I had looked into the bottom of the heart of the two factions, when I saw that they divided the whole world, as in the time of the Reformation, I deemed that the task would be long and difficult. I nevertheless determined to use every exertion to accomplish it. The question was more complicated than some have supposed. The question was not reduced to standing or falling with the Revolution; it was to reconcile it with its enemies without, and to calm those within, till time could effect a complete fusion of their interests with our own: this required two generations. I shall show hereafter, that these writers have confounded the relations it bore to France, and its relations toward foreign powers; they confound the epoch of the Empire, with the epoch of the Republic.*

At the epoch of 1803, of which I am now speaking, I had devoted two whole years to healing the wounds of France, to uniting opposite interests and opinions, and to calming contending passions. In this I had succeeded beyond all hopes. But I was not deceived respecting the actual state of affairs. The royalists considered it as opening the way for a counter-revolution, and their adversaries thought I was advancing too rapidly in this course which they feared.

* The author here alludes to, and mentions by name, the pretended "Manuscript from St. Helena," an anonymous work falsely attributed to Napoleon.

To create within the nation a single French interest, and to cause it to be sanctioned and respected by foreign powers, this was the evident object of my mission. I saw that to give this new France a durable basis, it was necessary to reconcile its internal institutions with the old dynasties, and to render it so powerful that they could not attack it with impunity. We required the majority of Europe, in order that the scale might now incline on our side. There were two ways of securing this majority: one by voluntary alliances, and the other by submissions effected by the ascendency of our power. In the impossibility of obtaining the first, I was under the necessity of adopting the second.

Difficulties with England.—I was directing all my attention to the accomplishment of these important results, when I became involved in new difficulties with England. The peace of Amiens seemed only to serve her as the means of reconnoitring my edifice, so that she might attack it with greater advantage. She never manifested a disposition to execute this treaty. Instead of surrendering Malta, as had been stipulated in the treaty, the possession of this island fortress was set forth by her writers as the key to the Mediterranean, and as the only means which England had of opposing, in that sea, the alliance of France and Spain: the cabinet of St. James then resolved to retain it. Instead of evacuating Egypt, as had been agreed, General Stuart continued to occupy Alexandria, and seemed determined to remain there. I sent Sebastiani to reëstablish our former relations in the Levant, and to secure the promised evacuation. The tocsin was sounded against this mission, because his report had the appearance of a military reconnoisance, and announced that I had numerous partizans in that country; this served the English government as a pretext for maintaining itself there.

Moreover I had reason to complain of the gross and injurious personal attacks which were daily permitted to appear in the English journals, and in those of the *émigrés*. England breathed more animosity against me than ever William had shown against Louis XIV.; moreover, the situation of the two powers had been reversed, for now the Pretender to the legitimate throne was in England, and she repaid us with double interest the injury which the Stuarts had sought, with the support of France, to do their sovereign. I had then a double reason to complain. A general, placed by victory at the head of the most powerful state in Europe, daily insulted by journals and pamphlets in which the hand of the English minister was but too manifest, had good cause to be exasperated. My situation and feelings were different from a prince born on the throne, and I could not fail to be indignant that instead of acknowledging the merit of my military enterprises and of my administration, they, with the most violent animosity, represented my victories as so many butcheries, my government as a despotism, myself as a usurper, my principles and heart as those of a Caligula. I complained of this: they opposed to me the English laws on the freedom of the press: I remarked that foreign refugees had no right to destroy the pacific relations of two powers under shelter of the abuse of the press, and I demanded that these disturbers of the general peace should, by application of the *alien bill*, be sent out of Europe.

Mission of Lord Whitworth.—England, who had refused this concession, resolved to make us submit to whatever suited her policy. Not satisfied with assisting to deprive us of St. Domingo, she determined to injure us still further by a ruinous commercial treaty: that of 1786 had been too unpopular in France to authorize its renewal. Undoubtedly the exportation of the territorial products of France might, in the estimation of certain ministers, compensate for the loss of her manufactures: but the loss of our colonies had rendered too necessary a good system of home industry, to allow the importation of such merchandises as France could herself produce. I rejected the treaty of commerce, and insisted upon the evacuation of Malta. The cabinet of London sent me, as envoy, Lord Whitworth, under pretext of concerting measures for preserving peace, but in reality for the purpose of inciting me to war, for he was furnished with no means of reconciling our differences.

Conference between Napoleon and Whitworth.—Some weeks after his arrival I had a long interview with him, during which I described to him, perhaps with too much frankness, my own situation and that of Europe. I declared to him, that it was base to make treaties one day, and to refuse to execute them the next; that nothing would induce me to renounce the evacuation of Malta; that I would sooner see the English encamped upon the heights of Montmartre, than to see them in possession of that island.

I complained of the English journals, and especially of the asylum and pay which England had given to Georges and his accomplices, instead of sending them to Canada as had been agreed upon. "Every breeze that blows from England," said I to him, "comes loaded with hatred and animosity; how do they expect that I should not take offense? With respect to Egypt, I have already given assurance that the mission of Sebastiani had no hostile object. I might have sent there twenty-five thousand men to assist the Porte in driving out the English, whose presence authorized me to do so; *but, whatever desire I might have had to establish a colony there, I have not done so, because it was not worth the while to trouble the peace of the world and make myself the aggressor, in order to conquer a country which must sooner or later fall into the hands of France, either by a dissolution of the Turkish empire or by an arrangement with the Porte.*" These were indiscreet remarks, which the adroit Whitworth did not fail to repeat, and of which England took advantage in order to justify her own conduct.

After showing him that I desired peace, I enumerated the reciprocal chances in a war: I frankly spoke of a descent and the dangers which it presented; but as there was at least one chance in a hundred, this would be sufficient for me to undertake it. I reminded him that I had four hundred and eighty thousand men in arms, ready at a moment's warning; that Europe no longer desired to ally itself with England, and to sacrifice itself for her interest; that, nevertheless, I desired peace. "I am the most powerful on land; you rule the seas: together, we can govern the world, but the least difference between us will involve the whole universe. If I had not, on every occasion, experienced the animosity of England, I should have done every thing to conciliate her; participation in indemnities; continental influence; treaty of commerce; I would have yielded every thing to a power which had shown me consideration and good will, while, on the contrary, I could yield nothing to implacable enemies."

Hostile Declaration of George III.—This long conference was far from adjusting our differences: the English would see in it only my desire to colonize Egypt, as authorizing them to retain the possession of Malta, and to prepare to take the initiative in the war. The King's speech to Parliament on the eighth of March, left no further doubt on this subject. The allegations contained in this declaration were unjust. Can *distant and supposititious* projects of one cabinet toward a province belonging to another, be a legitimate cause for a rupture with a third? England can not deny that under Walpole and George I., she had designs upon South America: would this vague desire of her minister to form an establishment in South America, have been a legitimate motive of rupture for France?

Napoleon's violent Language to the English Minister.—I could not dissemble my resentment to Whitworth, at his next visit to the Tuileries; I addressed to him, perhaps with too much vivacity, the following words: "We have already carried on a war for ten years, and you wish it for ten years longer; you force me into it!" Then turning toward the other ambassadors, I said to them: "The English desire war; if they compel me to draw the sword, I shall not be the first to return it to the scabbard. *If they will not respect treaties, they must be clothed in black.*" Thinking that perhaps I had gone too far, I again addressed Whitworth in these terms: "Why all these warlike preparations? against whom are these armaments? I have not a single ship-of-the-line in the ports of France; if you wish to fight, I shall fight; you may destroy France, but you will never intimidate her. You say that you desire peace; then execute your treaties. Woe to those who will not respect treaties; they shall answer for the consequences to all Europe." I here broke off the conference, lest my feelings should carry me too far.

English Ultimatum rejected.—Nevertheless, my ministers having offered to agree to any arrangement that might satisfy the English respecting Egypt, they feigned to give up Malta as their own property, but reserved to themselves the right of occupying this place for ten years! Moreover they demanded, 1st, that the island of Lampedosa should be ceded to England by the King of Naples; 2d, that my troops should evacuate Holland and Switzerland; 3d, that an indemnity in Italy should be secured to the King of Sardinia. On these conditions they would recognize the King of Etruria, and the Ligurian Republic. Firm in my resolution not to deviate from the conditions of the treaty of Amiens, I rejected these separate articles, and a new resort to arms became the consequence. I confess that this was exposing much for a little gain; but could I, without disgrace and without danger, admit these propositions, which perhaps, after all, were not sincere?*

Military Occupation of Naples.—I could not carry on a war without securing, in compensation for the colonies which I would lose, some maritime country which might enable us to sustain this contest. To anticipate the enemy in the occupation of the *presqu'île* of Tarentum, and to close the ports of the peninsula against the English commerce, I directed my troops to reënter the Kingdom of Naples. St. Cyr concluded a new convention to this effect, and occupied the Abruzzos.

Invasion of Hanover.—My troops, reënforced in Holland, crossed the Rhine, and, under Mortier, took possession of Hanover. The Hanoverian troops collected to the number of about fifteen thousand on the Lower Elbe, capitulated at Altenburg, and were disbanded on condition of returning peaceably to their own homes.

Effect of these Operations in Europe.—These movements were certainly to our advantage; but they gave offense to the other powers; Russia had some interest in the fate of Holland, and Austria was not pleased to see the Germanic soil violated by the invasion of Hanover. But as the cabinet of Vienna knew that we were at war with King George, it

* English writers have sought for every possible pretext to justify their government in refusing to execute the treaty of Amiens, and in again disturbing the peace of Europe. But even Alison now admits that France was not chargeable with renewing the war. He says: "In coolly reviewing the circumstances under which this contest was renewed, it is impossible to deny that the British government manifested a feverish anxiety to come to a rupture, and that so far as the two countries were concerned, they [the English] were the aggressors."

Napier says: "Up to the peace of Tilsit, the wars of France were *essentially defensive*; for the bloody contest that wasted the continent for so many years, was not a struggle for preëminence between ambitious powers—not a dispute for some accession of territory—nor for the political ascendancy of one or other nation—but a deadly conflict to determine *whether aristocracy or democracy should predominate—whether equality or privilege should henceforth be the principle of European governments.*"

Thiers, in his Consulate and Empire, has discussed at great length, and with great fairness, all the circumstances attending the rupture of the peace of Amiens.

could not object to reprisals upon his states; it therefore contented itself with exchanging some insignificant diplomatic notes. The peace of Luneville, although imposed on Austria, left her so powerful that she had no desire to risk the uncertain chances of a new war. Thugut had resigned the ministry to Cobentzel, a statesman of more moderation; and I could hope to maintain with this court our relations of amity. Prussia had no motive to violate her neutrality. Russia observed me, and interposed in favor of Holland, Naples, and the King of Sardinia. Italy was nearly in accord with my system.

New Relations with Spain.—Spain had some objections to take part in a new war which might injure her ports and her colonies; she thought to avoid the conditions of the treaty of St. Ildefonso, and preserve her neutrality. This subject was discussed from the sixth of June to the middle of October, 1803. I was not anxious, at the time, that the Spanish navy should unite with ours, and I was not unwilling that the commerce of Spain should prosper under shelter of her neutrality, for France would always receive a greater part of the profits. But, in order not to renounce the advantages which France might derive from the treaty, I substituted for the stipulated contingent an annual subsidy of sixty millions, which was agreed upon in the convention of Madrid, on the nineteenth day of October, between Beurnonville and Cevallos, the Minister of Foreign Affairs.

England provokes her to declare War.—England got an intimation of this treaty, for she soon assumed a threatening tone. In fact this state of things did not suit the British ministry; it required, according to the absolute neutrality of Spain, at least the admission of English commerce into her continental ports; if she were to be excluded from these, war would be preferable. The negotiation continued one year, and assumed a hostile character as soon as the ministry had learned, through Admiral Cochrane, that a squadron of ten or twelve French vessels from St. Domingo, which had taken refuge in Ferrol, were to be armed and repaired in that port, and that the Spaniards were preparing for hostilities.

The war party had, at London, many advocates. The decline of the Spanish marine dispensed with the fear of any serious injury from its hostility; it added little to the material forces of France, but, during the war, all the possessions of Spanish America would be at the mercy of English expeditions, or of English agents who would there foment the spirit of independence; the vessels and galleons would become the prey of their cruisers and their armed vessels. This interest was too evident not to lead to a rupture. The cabinet of London gave orders to its vessels to attack the Spanish, and several frigates returning from Mexico with from fifteen to twenty millions in piastres or ingots of gold, were attacked and captured by Admiral Moore, without any previous declaration of war. This was pronounced piracy; England sought to justify herself on the grounds that Spain was an ally of France, and furnished her assistance. Spain now formally declared war, which she had vainly hoped to avoid by preserving amicable relations with the English government.

Portugal purchases her Neutrality.—Portugal had also purchased her neutrality by an annual tribute of sixteen millions, stipulated by the treaty of December twenty-fifth, at Lisbon, between General Lannes and the Portuguese Minister. The rest of Europe were equally on good terms with us. To draw still closer the bonds of friendship with the United States of America, I ceded to them Louisiana for the sum of seventy millions. I preferred placing it in their hands to running the risk of its falling into those of the English, on account of its vicinity to the United States and Mexico, from which countries I also desired to exclude British commerce.

Great Success of the English in India.—Hardly had the war commenced, when England began to gather the fruits of her former conquests. She doubled her power in the East by the conquest of Hindostan. The death of Tippoo had rid her of a dangerous rival; but there was still a more powerful adversary, in the Mahratta race—the celebrated Schindiah. He had just regained the power over the Mohammedan caste of Schah-Alloun: he, in fact, held the sceptre of Mogol. So long as this empire existed, the English power would be doubtful. The capitulation of the French army in Egypt had, it is true, diminished this danger. No sooner was this known in India, than Wellesley was emboldened to attack the army of Schindiah. According to the custom of this Company, it now supported the interest of the Mussulmans against the Mahrattas, as it had formerly sustained the interests of the natives and of the Nizam against the Mussulman Tippoo. The troops which had been disciplined by Peyron on European principles, deserted the Mahratta prince, who was defeated by Lake and Wellington in the decisive battle of Assey. Delhi and Agra fell into the power of the English, who, masters of the rich empire of Mogol, at length extended their dominion over forty millions of Hindoos.

This event furnishes the best apology that can be given for my expedition to Egypt, the main object of which was to prevent this result; unfortunately this blow was irreparable, and, although under Louis XVI. it would have furnished a subject for desperate war with England, I had not the means of opposing it, so much were circumstances changed. Besides, these vexatious events were not known in Europe till the beginning of 1803, at the moment that England proclaimed the rupture of the peace of Amiens. General Decaen, whom I had sent to take possession of the Isle of France and the poor trading establishment of Pondicherry, could do no great thing in the midst of that colossal power; he was soon constrained to abandon this feeble post on the continent, and to limit himself to the defense of the Isle of France.

Chances of a Descent upon England.—The continent exhibiting as yet no symptoms of an immediate attack upon France, I profited by the occasion to menace England with invasion. Although difficult, this operation has always been regarded as possible ; the descent once made, the capture of London was almost certain. The capital once occupied, a powerful party would be created against the oligarchy. Perhaps we should have encountered some dangers ; but Hannibal, in crossing the Alps, or Cæsar, in landing in Epirus, in Africa, or in England—did they look back? London is but a few miles from Calais ; the English army, scattered along the coast, could not unite in time to cover the capital. Of course this expedition could not be attempted by a mere *corps-d'armée ;* but its success was pretty certain with one hundred and fifty thousand men presenting themselves before London within five days after landing. Flotillas were the only means by which these one hundred and fifty thousand men could be landed in a few hours, and possession be gained of all the shallow waters. It was under protection of a squadron collected in the Antilles, and coming from there with all sail to Boulogne, that this passage was to be effected. If this reunion of the squadron could not be accomplished one year, it might another year. Fifty vessels sailing from Toulon, Brest, Rochefort, L'Orient, Cadiz, would unite at Martinique. Their departure would make England tremble for the two Indies, and while the British fleets were in search of them at the Cape of Good Hope, and in the sea of the Antilles, those vessels would unite before Boulogne and secure the landing upon the English coast. Ten hours only would be required for landing one hundred and fifty thousand disciplined and victorious soldiers, upon a coast destitute of fortifications and undefended by a regular army. It has been thought that English patriotism would have caused a *levée-en-masse* for the defense of their country, and that the retreat of my army would have been impossible. This patriotism would have been an obstacle under any circumstances, but preceded by a declaration of democratic principles, we should have found partisans enough in England to effect a disunion, sufficient to paralyze the rest of the nation. If the system of propagandism was ever an instrument of success, it certainly would have been on this occasion. But experience alone could decide this question; it has never been tried.

A motive more powerful than the difficulty of its execution might have prevented me from attempting this enterprise; this was the equivocal situation of my relations with the continent, and especially with Russia. Austria, at the instigation of Russia or England, might renew the war the moment that I should set foot on the British Isles, and we might, by this doubtful expedition, lose the fruits of ten years of victory. It is certain that such an expedition would never be prudent, without the alliance of one of these powers, and this consideration contributed not a little to my marriage, some years afterwards.

Preparations for this Descent.—At all events, as the menace would cost nothing, since I had no other employment for my troops, I could garrison them on the coast as well as anywhere else. This simple demonstration would compel England to make defensive preparations at a ruinous expense. This would be so much gained. In 1803 and 1804, I covered with camps the coasts of Boulogne, Dunkirk, and Ostend; considerable squadrons were prepared at Brest, Rochefort, and Toulon; the shipyards of France were covered with prams, shallops, gunboats, and other craft; and innumerable hands were employed in preparing the ports of the channel for receiving these flotillas.

On the other side, England prepared for the contest. Pitt, far from being discouraged by the imminence of the danger, deemed it his duty to resume the reins of government under these difficult circumstances: he did not confine himself to his famous bill of defense (June 18th, 1804), but leaving the peaceful duties of the exchequer, he put on the military uniform, and dreamed only of machines of war, battalions, forts, batteries. The aged and venerable George III. left the royal mansion, and daily reviewed his troops; camps were formed on the downs of Dover, and in the counties of Kent and Sussex. The English army, which in 1792 had numbered only seventy thousand men, was successively increased to one hundred and fifty thousand, including the regular militia, but exclusive of the forces employed without the limits of the three kingdoms. The public danger had caused three hundred thousand volunteers (*fencibles*) to be organized in regiments. Independently of a naval force of four hundred and seventy vessels, a flotilla of eight hundred guns covered the coasts of England and Ireland. The two armies were in sight of each other; they were separated only by the narrow strait. The preparations cost England dear, but it must be confessed that they revived the military spirit of the inhabitants, and prepared them for fighting me on land.

Extraordinary Plots against Napoleon.—Notwithstanding these immense preparations for defense, the English ministers were apprehensive of the result of my menaces; to make a diversion, plots were organized against me. In order to have a greater chance of success, they put in motion a multitude of conspirators. But we were informed of them in twenty-four hours, so rapidly are such secrets carried. But as I wished only to punish those who should commit a state offense, I was obliged to wait till indisputable proofs could be collected against them. Pichegru was at the head of this machination: this man, who had more bravery than talents, wished to act the part of a Monk; it suited his character. These projects gave me little trouble, for I knew their extent, and that public opinion at that epoch was against them. Had the royalists succeeded in capturing and murdering me, they would have been no nearer their object. There is a time for all things. Factions, although still stirring, had lost their force ; the fear which they had of each other had attached all reasonable men to my cause. The royalist chiefs, wholly forgotten since the pacification of La Vendée, now sought to reappear on the political horizon. This was the natural consequence of the increase of my authority. I was rebuilding a monarchy ; this was intrenching on their grounds. They supposed that my monarchy was the same as theirs. Mine rested wholly on great achievements ; theirs on hereditary rights. Theirs was founded wholly on ancient usages ; mine had no connection with these ; it moved in unison with the spirit of the age ; theirs made useless efforts to check that spirit. The republicans were alarmed at the height to which circumstances raised me : they feared the use that I might make of this power. They trembled lest I might rebuild the old royalty by the aid of my army. The royalists believed this report, and took pleasure in representing me as a foolish imitator of the old monarchs. Others, more adroit, reported that I was restoring the institutions of the country merely to present France to the Bourbons, as soon as it could be prepared for an offering. Mediocre minds, who were incapable of appreciating me, gave faith to these rumors. This caused the increase of the royalist party, and injured me in the estimation of the people and of the army ; both began to doubt my attachment to their cause. This opinion was calculated to produce disunion. It was necessary to undeceive, at any cost, France, the royalists, and the rest of Europe, with respect to my intentions. To attack these designs in detail would have produced only an ill effect, because it would not have reached the root of the evil. Moreover this could not be done.

I soon learned that Moreau was connected with these conspirators. It was necessary to deal carefully with this man, for he had an immense popularity. It was important to gain him over to my side. His reputation was too great for us to live as good neighbors. The plan of the campaign of 1800, which he did not understand, or was unwilling to appreciate, had thrown between us the apple of discord and unvailed his pretensions. He deemed himself too important a character to give passive obedience to me. It was necessary to find some fair means of separating him from me: he chose to effect this by taking every opportunity of censuring the measures of my government, and by rejecting all my advances to attach him to my party.

It has been said that I was jealous of him: this was untrue; but he was very jealous of me. I esteemed him as a good soldier; he had as partisans all who were jealous of me, and they were numerous. These men would have made a hero of him had he perished; I wished him to be no more than he really was—a second-rate man. In this I was perfectly successful: his absence effected his ruin; his friends forgot him, and he was no longer thought of.

The Duke d'Enghein.—But an incident of much greater importance was connected with this famous *procès*. My exterior police had received positive information of a plot formed against me at London by Georges, Pichegru, and other royalist agents, and at the same time, at Stuttgard, by an English agent, named Drake. The relation between these projects was not fully proved. At the same epoch, the Duke d'Enghein appeared on the borders of the Rhine, and it was said, that Dumouriez had just arrived there. This created a great stir among Fouché's people; to them there seemed no doubt that this prince was the soul of the whole plot; if such were not the case, would a Bourbon prince show himself at the gates of Strasbourg, on neutral soil it is true, but where he must inevitably encounter great danger? Could it be otherwise than that his presence there, and that of Georges and Pichegru at Paris, was a concerted affair? By concentrating the Revolution in myself, I had rendered more easy the project of its overthrow. It seemed to them that, the First Consul being disposed of, they had only to present the white flag to effect a restoration. In this they were mistaken: nevertheless all the circumstances of this event tallied wonderfully with those which were urging me to determine definitely the opinion of France.

The desire of pleasing me united the chiefs of the secret police to unravel this plot. Some letters which had been seized contained sufficient information to determine me to seize this prince, convinced, by the reports which I had received, that we should find in his papers a thousand proofs of his projects.

It was important, on one side, to silence the clamors of the party who had wished the Revolution without anarchy, but who now feared a royalist reaction, and, on the other side, to check the royalist chiefs from inciting new troubles in France. I therefore resolved to strike a decisive blow, which was indispensable to fix the opinion of the two millions of Frenchmen who had adhered to and fought for the Revolution.

Orders were therefore dispatched to Strasbourg to send a small column, in the night, to Kehl, to surround the village of Ettenheim and seize the Duke d'Enghein, and all other foreigners found at Offenburg, and conduct them to Paris. My aid-de-camp, Caulaincourt, was the bearer of these orders, and was directed to justify their execution to the Grand Duke of Baden, upon whose territory these captures were to be made. Dumouriez was not there; they had been deceived in the names, the Count Thumeri was mistaken for him. In all other respects the orders were fortunately executed.

The police continued to give assurances of a grand plot, and the capture of several trunks of papers which would prove every thing. I designed to establish a high national court, forming it of a part of the senate, the chief magistrates, and the highest officers of the army, and to get from it a deliberate and solemn judgment. I gave orders to this effect. Colonel Préval of the cuirassiers, an officer of distinction, was called from Compiègne, to make a report of the affair in conformity with existing laws. As his father had once been under the Duke d'Enghein, colonel of the same regiment, he very properly declined the duty. In the mean time the police had examined the papers of the prince; they found no proof of the conspiracy. It was now necessary to renounce the idea of a solemn judgment by a high national court, for the acquittal of the prince would only increase the odium of violating the territory of the Empire. There were two courses still to pursue: the first and most reasonable one was to retain him under strict police till the general peace, on the charge of inciting troubles in Alsace; the second of giving him up to a military commission to be tried as an *émigré* who had taken up arms against France, and, should he be acquitted by the commission, to retain him till the close of the war. On the advice of the principal functionaries, I adopted this last course. It has been seen that in this affair I was led on by a kind of fatality; for if I had known that no trace of a conspiracy would have been found, of course I should have avoided violating the territory of Baden, an action that would appear against me whatever were the issue. The fatal reports of my secret police produced all the evil. If the trunks of papers, which were announced by the police, had been taken, and the guilt of the prince had been proved before a high national court, all would have been in accordance with the strictest justice toward the accused, and my first design.

It is well known that this military commission condemned the prince, on his own confession, for invading, in 1793, the territory of France, with an armed band. It is also well known that I was left ignorant of the appeal which he made to me, and also of the letter which he wrote to me, till after the execution of the sentence of the court, which, according to military usage, takes place during the session of the court. I was left ignorant of the afflicting details which accompanied this catastrophe; it is enough to be responsible for the principal event—his capture and trial. In this I was drawn on by the perfidious suggestions of my admirers, by false reports, and by the force of events. Considered as a *coup-d'état* this was calculated to strike terror among the partisans of the restoration of the ancient monarchy, to silence internal discords, and to give to three millions of Frenchmen, who had raised me to power, a pledge of an eternal rupture with the Bourbons.*

The trial of Moreau and the conspirators was conducted with more formality, and was prolonged for several months. Moreau was banished. The other criminals required a severer punishment. They were all old offenders, often engaged in conspiracy, and it was necessary, once for all, to purge France of these characters. In this we succeeded, for these plots ended here.

Pichegru was found strangled in his bed. Some did not fail to say that this was by my orders. I was totally a stranger to this event. It would be difficult to conceive why I should snatch this criminal from judgment. He was no

* This account of the execution of the Duke d'Enghein is free from the passions and prejudices which disfigure so many of the pretended histories of the affair. Alison is entirely carried away by his prejudices and his desire to fix the whole blame of this unfortunate affair upon Napoleon. His account resembles that of a feed lawyer endeavoring to make out his case, more than that of an historian seeking for truth. Any one must be convinced of this by comparing Alison's quotations from Savary with Savary's own account.

better than the others, and the tribunals were there to judge him. I have never in the whole course of my life done any thing without some object.*

Government necessary for France.—These events produced much discussion on the course which I ought to pursue at this decisive epoch. Each one made comments according to his own views: some wished me to destroy the hydra of the Revolution and prepare a bed of roses for the return of the Bourbons; others wished me to connect the interests of the Revolution with my own, as First Consul for life, which, in their opinion, would have secured the Republic and Liberty, and at the same time have given a suitable stability to the first magistracy.

Had this question concerned myself alone, I should have been well satisfied to remain at the head of the state, with the title I then held; but it was one which concerned the interests of France, and I loved France too well to form for her an elective government which would be more dangerous even than the recall of the Bourbons. An elective government gives place to eternal convulsions. These elections lead to civil wars, and open the way for foreign influence. It is fortunate if each new consul does not cause the loss of a province, a colony, and a portion of the national independence. If England had been elective after Cromwell, Louis XIV.

* Alison's account of the trial and death of Pichegru is also full of the grossest errors and misrepresentations. He says it was impossible that Pichegru committed suicide. "Death to so old a soldier and determined a character could have few terrors; and the experience of the Revolution has proved that its prospect had hardly ever led to self-destruction." Alison seems to have forgotten his own description of the reign of terror and of the horrors of the "Revolutionary army." "To such a degree did the torture of suspense prey upon the minds of the prisoners that they became not only reckless of life, but anxious for death." "If a knock was heard at the door, every one, in agonized suspense, expected his fate. Unable to endure such protracted misery, numbers committed suicide." "The love of life was almost extinguished in every heart." &c. &c. This, however, is only one of the numerous instances in which Alison contradicts himself.

and the Stuarts would have subjugated the country and divided it between them.

Many thousand volumes have been written on the maxims of government, and on the institutions most suitable to be adopted by states; but really there has been but very little new on this subject since the time of Xenophon. These controversies will probably continue to agitate the world for a long time, for these discussions are not carried on in good faith on the one side, nor by men of experience on the other. The impracticable theorists would risk every thing else for a chimerical hope of what they call enlarging the *liberties of the people*; a phrase which each one interprets to best suit his own interests or passions.

Some of these mad theorists have believed in the possibility of a government wholly of the people, or in a pure democracy. Others have preferred an aristocratic government, under the patrician form in republics, and under the form of nobility in monarchies. These have their Jacobins who, under the mask of defending public prerogatives against the throne, merely defend their own feudal privileges at the expense of the administrative power. Such were the Senate of Stockholm, the Polish Diets, and the French *Parlements*. A third party advocate absolute power. They either think this best for the direction of public affairs, or, like the ambitious priests, they advocate it as the best means of enlarging their own authority. Much may be deduced both from history and reason in favor of each of these forms.

Democracy exists only where the people choose their rulers directly from their own ranks, and where these chiefs return immediately to this rank, at the expiration of their office. This government has never existed but in name, or in small states, peculiarly situated; even at Rome it was merely temporary. The people, led on by ambitious demagogues, have always in a very short time fallen into the hands of the aristocracy. In Europe at this day, no great state exists with this form of government; even the little Swiss cantons can barely sustain themselves; past experience in Europe tends to prove the truth of Corneille's verses:

> "Mais quand le peuple est maitre on n'agit qu'en tumulte,
> La voix de la raison jamais ne se consulte;
> Les honneurs sont vendus aux ambitieux,
> L'autorité livrée aux plus séditieux," &c.

A republic has no means of escaping great dangers but in forming an absolute power, like that of the Committee of Public Safety; there is no man of sense who would not prefer a monarchy of limited authority but strongly organized, to such a power. Theorists refer to the United States as proof that these evils are not necessary to a Republican form of government. To this it may be replied that the weakness of the American government was such in 1814, that, with ten millions of inhabitants, it suffered the disgrace of having its capital captured and sacked by a single division of troops coming by sea! This fact would seem good proof of the want of internal strength in such a government. The United States, with a strong government, would ere this have become masters of the whole American Continent, or, at least, of all north of Panama.

But, be this as it may, no comparison can be formed between that country and France: their situations are essentially different. A nation which has for neighbors only weak tribes of Indians, or European provinces separated from their central governments by three thousand miles of ocean, has nothing to fear from its enemies: it will be the dominant power, whatever may be the elements of its government. But the United States, placed in the centre of Europe, could not have existed ten years after the peace of 1783. With a new and unprejudiced people, laborious, agricultural, free from *proletaires*, without a nobility, having no dangerous neighbors—with such a people a democratic *régime* may flourish. But this case is very essentially different from France at the period of which I am speaking. Spartans and Romans can not be immediately formed of an old monarchy.

An aristocracy has the advantage of a government more strong and concentrated, but it is always egotistical, exclusive, jealous. *A monarch ennobles plebeian merit, but an aristocrat treats it with contempt*; a patrician of Berne or of Venice is more vain and exclusive than a duke, or a peer, or a grandee of Spain. Besides, with an elective aristocracy a great state is exposed to almost certain ruin. How many civil wars have resulted in Germany from the elections of its emperors? How often has France, Russia, and Sweden, given kings to Poland under its elective system?

A hereditary monarchical government holds the reins of state with a firmer grasp, is most capable of effecting internal tranquillity, and of carrying out, with a stronger hand, a good system of external policy: it is, therefore, best suited to a great nation, placed in the centre of Europe.

The rise or the fall of empires is never the immediate result of internal disorders, or of institutions more or less popular: this comes from external relations. The Greek Empire, with its effeminate emperors and its scullion nobility, might still exist, if Mahomet II. had never come to Constantinople; the degenerate Romans might still govern Italy with their base princes and bad laws, if the Attilas and Genserics and Theodorics had never entered there; Poland might still enjoy its anarchy and its *liberum veto*, if its neighbors had never parceled out its territory among themselves. Exterior policy is, therefore, the most important consideration of all, in forming the government of a state.

From these considerations, I concluded that the government best suited for France, in 1804, was a strong hereditary government, of a single individual, administered with reference to the general interest of the nation, and not for the advantage of a privileged *coterie ;* this head of the nation to be assisted by consulting assemblies (*assemblées consultatives*), which should have all the power requisite for a good council, but not sufficient to enable them to arrest the car of state for the sake of Utopian theories or personal ambition. To this fundamental basis was to be added :

1st. A well-matured system of election, which would secure a proper system of representation in the chamber of communes, giving a suitable influence, in the making of laws, to the interests of property, industry, and the administration. It is absurd to suppose that any administration can proceed when it is deprived of all influence in the discussion of laws.

2d. The equality of all citizens in the eye of the law, and in their eligibility to the public offices.

3d. A nobility, or rather a notability, for life, founded on services rendered to the state, admitting no hereditary nobility but the peerage of the eldest sons of chiefs who, by illustrious victories or eminent statesmanship, have acquired claims to the national gratitude ; and even limiting this peerage to three generations, so as to keep the ranks open for new services, and to compel the sons of peers to earn their own importance.

4th. The independence of the tribunals (courts), and guarantees of individuals, except in cases of high treason.

5th. A good penal code for the press, and a tribunal of censure composed of just and worthy men, not subject to removal from office.

6th. A national religion entirely independent of any foreign priesthood.

Of course this system was imperfect, for all human systems are so ; but such a government I deemed best suited to the condition of France in 1804; calculated, at the same time, to promote the security and grandeur of the nation, and the public tranquillity, and to put the public administration beyond the reach of demagogues and declaimers, who think to guide the state by unmeaning phrases. Such is the great object which I ever afterward kept in view; such have been the motives of my conduct during all the periods and intestine commotions of my government.*

Establishment of the French Empire.—Guided by these maxims, I did not deem it possible to any longer preserve the republican form of government in France; indeed, the majority of the people had become thoroughly tired of it; what France now wished was greatness. This I had assured to her; there was no one else from whom she could hope the durability of her present grandeur. She desired me as her permanent ruler. Every thing was precarious under the consular system; nothing was in its proper place. There existed a Republic in name, a sovereignty in fact; a feeble national representation, a strong executive power; authorities submissive; an army preponderating.

Nothing goes well in a political system where names and things do not agree. The government soon loses its importance by the falsehood and deception it is obliged continually to use; it falls into that general contempt inspired by whatever is false; for whatever is false is weak. There is but one secret that can lead to success: it is to be strong, because there is in strength neither error nor deception; it is naked truth.

I was sensible of the weakness of my position, of the fragility of our political edifice. It was necessary to build

* This paragraph is much abridged in the translation; but all the prominent views, and nearly the language of the original, is retained. The opinions here given on government are rather those of European than of American statesmen. They are stated with great fairness and candor, and are well worthy of consideration.

something solid upon which to base the new interests which owed their origin to the Revolution. The establishment of the Empire was resolved on, and a *senatus-consultum* of the eighteenth of May, 1804, declared it hereditary in my family. Carnot was the only one of note who opposed this measure.*

I could not become king, for in France the title was odious; fixed ideas were attached to it. The nature of my power being new, it was requisite that my title should be new also. I was not the heir of the Bourbons, and had no claim to their crown, though I had found it trampled under foot; but this was no reason why I should not wear another. I took the title of Emperor, because it was greater and less definite.

Impossibility of restoring the Bourbons.—My enemies, of the two opposite factions, have never pardoned me for this step; even my own partisans were astonished at it. Some had gone so far as to say that I really thought, at one time, of restoring the Bourbons, and that the menaces of the champions of the eighteenth Brumaire alone deterred me from it.

These suppositions are not very complimentary to myself. I was too well acquainted with the world, and with men and things, not to know that if I had accepted the title of constable, or mayor of the palace, or any other which these princes had seen fit to offer me, in less than six months I should have been either an exile or a rebel. A new Charles Martel, could I flatter myself to reign under the name of a new Chilperic, and to carry my victorious eagles, united to the lilies, from the banks of the Elbe to those of the Tagus?

* Napoleon's brothers disliked Carnot, and represented him to the First Consul as being opposed to his administration. Carnot's course was calculated to strengthen the opinion that he had leagued with Napoleon's enemies. But the emperor afterward learned to appreciate the integrity of his character, and only honored him the more for the independent course he had pursued. Carnot became one of his firmest friends in 1815.

Such a *rôle* is possible only under a monarchy which is uncontested, when the nation is perfectly united, and an imbecile prince is the only obstacle between absolute power and a great captain. But after a frightful revolution, all of whose elements are still in fermentation—the idea is utterly absurd.

I did not doubt the favorable intentions of these princes, but I was also well aware of the false position in which I should be placed. The words of Count d'Artois, on the restoration, *That there was nothing changed in France, except that there was one Frenchman more*, were really sublime; but at the same time perfectly Utopian, like Sièyes' *balance of powers*, *perpetual peace*, &c. The princes would return with royalists of all conditions; they would have to treat for the interests of a hundred thousand noble families, who had asked of them, as in 1816, "*s'il n'y avait qu'une legitimité.*" The princes would have been at the head of a counter-revolution, and I at the head of those who espoused the principles of the Revolution itself. I should either have consolidated this work, or have ended my career on the scaffold; an alternative which I did not desire. The only means of arranging the affair, was to act the Monk of France, and afterward to take refuge in Italy, placing on my brows the crown of king of the Romans. At the epoch of the negotiations of Campo-Formio, I received an anonymous letter, exceedingly well written, advising me to such a course. I thought it came from Louis XVIII. But would I have been any more legitimately the king of Italy, than emperor of the French? Would Austria have agreed to the establishment of a new state in Italy which would have expelled her forever from Lombardy? Would France herself have sustained me in this? A contrary course of these two powers was very certain; and under these circumstances, what madman would have left the command of five hundred thousand victorious Frenchmen for that of thirty thousand Italians, incongruous, disorganized, rent by civil feuds, and destitute of any preparations for defense?

Effects of establishing the Empire.—But let us return to the empire. Never was there a revolution effected with so little difficulty as this, in substituting the empire for a republic, which had cost so much blood. The reason is obvious: the principles of the Revolution and of the Republic were retained; the name was the only thing changed; this is why the republicans did not oppose the empire. Moreover, a revolution in a state is not difficult where no one's interests are affected. The great Revolution being now terminated in a permanent dynasty, its principles became stable. The Republic had merely satisfied opinions; the Empire guaranteed both interests and opinions. These interests were those of an immense majority, inasmuch as the institutions of the empire guaranteed the equality of all. It was, in fact as well as in law, a democracy, but a democracy stripped of its objectionable features. Liberty was restrained, for without restraints it is of no force in times of great crises; liberty is attainable only by the enlightened classes of the nation, and even these seldom make a good use of it; but *equality* is proper and suitable for all classes. This is the reason that my power is still popular with the nation, even after all the reverses which have crushed France.

My authority did not rest, like the old monarchies, on the false scaffolding of castes and intermediary bodies; it was direct, and had no other support than itself; for in the empire there was nothing else recognized than the nation and its ruler. But in this nation all were equally eligible to the public functions. The origin of the individual constituted no obstacle to his elevation; the entire movement in the state was upward. This upward movement constituted my strength; but I was not the inventor of the system: it sprung from the ruins of the Bastile; it resulted from the civilization and general intelligence which time had effected in Europe. It will be difficult to destroy this system; it will maintain itself by the force of things because fact and power must be combined; force can never spring from forms. It no longer springs from the *noblesse*, since the *tiers-état* are allowed to carry arms and constitute the military strength of the state; it no longer springs from the clergy, for the world has now learned the abuses and danger of that order.

That government is most wise which looks for its support to that part of the nation which is the most vigorous, giving it only such limits as may be necessary to maintain it in a salutary direction: these were the principles upon which I rested the foundations of my new edifice.

The destruction of old prejudices and prepossessions in France had laid bare the true source of power; it was, therefore, necessary to rebuild the authority of government on a plan entirely new; it was necessary to free this authority from all old prejudices, to get rid of that blind devotion called faith. It was heir to no rights; it was therefore necessary to found it on fact (*fait*), that is, on force. I did not ascend the throne as an heir of ancient dynasties, to repose quietly on the prestiges of habitudes and illusions, but to make laws in unison with public opinion, and to render France formidable in order to maintain her independence.

State of Europe.—I was well aware that the recognition of this empire would meet with a powerful opposition abroad; Louis XVIII., who was then living at Warsaw, had given the signal to all the other sovereigns, by an energetic protest against what he called my usurpation. Moreover the political atmosphere of the continent was far from serene. The dispositions of Russia began to appear less favorable.

Difficulty with Russia.—The Emperor Alexander was young, and passionately fond of military glory; inspired from his infancy by the great actions of Catharine, and of Peter the Great, and seeking with avidity for an occasion to prove himself their worthy successor, he wished to run the same career as myself: whether he allied himself to my projects against England, or joined England against me, we were destined to meet in the field of glory. In either case, he could not fail to increase the greatness of his empire, and to place himself, in history, on a level with his illustrious ancestors. Previous to 1803 he had appeared well enough disposed in my favor. The cannonade of Copenhagen, reaching even to Cronstadt and St. Petersburg, had sounded the alarm against English pretensions. This was sufficient to incline this prince in my favor, and the good understanding with which, in 1803, we together arranged the important affair of indemnities in Germany, proves what were the dispositions of Russia toward me at that epoch. But, after that, events induced Alexander to take an opposite course.

He proposed, at the end of 1803, his mediation for peace with England. They demanded that first of all I should evacuate Holland, Italy, and Switzerland. To the last point, I made no objections, but seeing the uncertainty of any successful mediation, I could not consent to the other preliminary conditions; indeed, nothing more could have been required of me in signing a preliminary treaty. I proposed an armistice and a congress, leaving things exactly in *statu quo* till peace could be arranged. The cabinet of London would admit no mediation till I had first evacuated Hanover; and, as it was impossible to come to an agreement, it became necessary to renounce all attempts at treaty. My refusal produced a coldness between me and Russia; Marcoff left Paris, leaving only D'Oubril as chargé-d'affaires. The character and personal feelings of this ambassador conduced very much to my first difficulty with Russia; perhaps this difficulty must necessarily have occurred on some other occasion, as we were destined, sooner or later, to be opposed; but at this epoch I was wholly occupied with my projects on England, and it will some day be regretted that I was not allowed to complete them. As a judicious historian has said: "It is for the general interest of Europe that the maritime superiority should belong to some continental power, for this is the only means of preserving the rights of nations, and of bringing to bear the whole continental force for the maintenance of the freedom of the seas." So long as my genius and my activity were directed against the British Isles, and on the coast of the channel, there was no necessity for an interference. But unfortunately the passions of men are sometimes stronger than their ultimate interests. The emperor of Russia had to complain that I had not given the king of Sardinia the indemnity for Piedmont which I had promised by the treaty of October, 1801; he made it a point of honor to insist on this. His troops still occupied the Republic of the Seven Isles, with the intention, undoubtedly, of not surrendering them till after the execution of all that had been agreed upon between us respecting Italy. The neutrality of the north of Germany, violated by my occupation of Hanover, made him suspicious of my ulterior views. The violation of the territory of his father-in-law, the elector of Baden, in the seizure of the Duke d'Enghein, appeared to him an attack upon the honor of his family; all combined to irritate him. On the seventh of May he addressed energetic notes to the Diet of Ratisbon, against this violation of the territory of the Empire, for which he demanded reparation. The king of Sweden, Gustavus IV., brother-in-law of the Emperor Alexander, and also son-in-law of the elector of Baden, scattered fire and flames throughout all Europe. Desirous of playing some important part, and thinking himself a second Gustavus Adolphus, of whom he was only the ridiculous *homonym*, he persuaded himself that it was still the age when thirty thousand Swedes could hold the balance of power in Europe; he affected to domineer over all the governments that did not hasten to imitate his example.

Russia refuses to recognize the French Empire.—The senatus-consultum which conferred on me the imperial crown, tended to complicate this difficulty; just as much as this event was for the interests of France, to the same degree was it opposed to the interests of the ancient dynasties. To recognize my empire, was to give up the ancient principles of legitimacy and the *divine right* of kings. Nevertheless they might, on a mature consideration of the subject, also see something in favor of their system of legitimacy, by the substitution of a monarchy for the Revolution. If the Emperor Alexander, looking on it in this light, had maintained a good understanding with me, he would undoubtedly have consulted state interest, though at the sacrifice of the self-love of dynasty. But in the existing state of affairs, this step added a strong motive to those already existing for a rupture. In fact, D'Oubril remitted a note, on the twenty-eighth of August, 1804, which was a kind of manifesto, and demanded his passports. Nevertheless Russia did not immediately prepare for war. D'Oubril remained at Mayence till the end of October, with the intention, perhaps, of giving me an opportunity of avoiding a rupture, by complying with their demands with respect to Baden and Piedmont. Whether or not this was the real object, is unknown, as I did not put it to the test.

Austria recognizes the French Empire.—The cabinet of Vienna, less scrupulous, or more disposed for peace, made no difficulty in recognizing me as emperor. This event confirmed me in my projects, for Russia was too distant* to threaten any immediate danger; I therefore resolved not to yield to her demands.

Indecision of the Porte.—Prussia, Spain, and Denmark hastened to give notice of their recognition of a dignity which was calculated to give greater stability to our friendly relations. But what surprised me most, was the hesitation of the Porte in recognizing my empire. It was not that the Turks felt aggrieved at the fate of the Bourbons, for they knew too well how their own fallen princes were treated; but all the members of the Divan had not forgotten the old alliances which united the Ottoman Empire to France. They remembered how their wars in Hungary had assisted Francis I. against Charles V., and Louis XIV. against Leopold I.; and how much, in turn, these were indebted to the first for their powerful diversions against Germany. In the last war of 1789–1791, Louis XVI., embarrassed by internal difficulties, had left to the Anglo-Prussian Alliance the care of intervention for peace. This was the first blow at the credit of France; the disorders of the Revolution, the destruction of the state of Venice, the acquisition of the Ionian Isles, the public discourses of Monge for the resurrection of Greece, and especially the expedition to Egypt, had exasperated the Divan against republican France, and had produced the strange phenomenon of the standard of Mohammed waving by the side of the banners of Russia and England!

Feeling the necessity of a good understanding with the Porte, I had sent Marshal Brune there, in the quality of ambassador; he was at Constantinople when I assumed the imperial crown. The English took every means to prejudice the Turks against me, representing me as the author of the expedition to Egypt, and as having still further intentions on that country, bringing up, as proof of this, the mission of Sebastiani and my vague allusions made to Lord Whitworth. Russia, having resolved upon a rupture with me, warmly seconded the representations of England. Brune was unable to destroy these prepossessions, and returned to France without having obtained my formal recognition, and also without any positive refusal; he left Ruffin at Constantinople, and I hastened to confirm his appointment, in order to leave the way open for a reconciliation.

The Pope at Paris.—In the mean time, Pope Pius VII. had given his consent to come to Paris, in order to agree upon such points as had been left undecided by the concordat. I wished to profit by this visit for my coronation and consecration. I hoped by the solemnity given to this august ceremony by the holy father, to remove from the eyes of the vulgar, every thing that might appear improper in my ascension to the throne. The venerable pontiff, grateful for the peace which I had given to the Church, and hoping to obtain the restoration of the provinces which had been detached from his states, did not hesitate, notwithstanding his great age, to cross the Alps, to act the part of Stephen III. in 754, by placing the crown of the sons of Meroveus on the head of Pepin, the father of Charlemagne, chief, like me, of a new dynasty. It was the only example of this kind which the vicar of Jesus Christ has ever given to Christian kings.*

* The following is Napoleon's letter to the Pope inviting him to the coronation. It is urgent, but perfectly dignified.

"*Most Holy Father*:—

"The happy effect produced upon the morality and the character of my people by the reëstablishment of religion, induces me to beg your holiness to give me a new proof of your interest in my destiny and in that of this great nation, in one of the most important conjunctures presented by the annals of the world. I beg you to come and give, to the highest degree, a religious character to the anointing and coronation of the first Emperor of the French. That ceremony will acquire a new lustre from being performed by your holiness in person. It will bring down upon yourself and our people the blessings of God, whose decrees rule the destiny alike of empires and of families.

"Your holiness is aware of the affectionate sentiments I have long borne toward you, and can thus judge of the pleasure that this occurrence will afford me of testifying them anew.

"And hereupon we pray God that he may preserve you, most Holy Father, for many years, to rule and govern our mother, the holy Church.

"Your dutiful son,

"NAPOLEON."

This coronation was delayed till the expression of the national will on the senatus-consultum could be formally received. The result of this imposing *plebiscitum* was presented to me, on the first of December, by a deputation of the Senate. Out of four millions of active citizens, more than three millions and a half had voted in favor of my being raised to the imperial throne; Henry IV. had not reigned in France by a public will so unanimous. I was the next day consecrated by the Pope in the church of Notre-Dame. After the sacerdotal benediction, not wishing to hold the crown as the gift of the Pope, I placed it on my head with my own hand. A deputation from each corps of the army assisted at this imposing ceremony, already made brilliant by the presence of the great constituted bodies of the state—ministers, ambassadors, senators, legislators, and prefects. Never had Paris witnessed, even under Louis XIV., any thing to eclipse the pomp of this great day; fine weather was the only thing wanting.

Political Declaration of the Legislative Body.—I now felt it necessary to exhibit pacific sentiments. At the opening of the legislative body, December 25th, I solemnly declared that I had no desire to add to the territory of the empire; that I would maintain its integrity; that I had no wish to augment my influence, but that I was determined to sustain what I had already acquired. My minister of foreign affairs declared to the chamber that England would eventually discover her error; that she would see the uselessness of her efforts against us; that she would lose in a war without any object; in fine, that her cabinet would return to different sentiments toward us, when it should be found that France would not concede to her the right of breaking treaties whenever she pleased, and that we would never consent to peace on any other conditions than those of the treaty of Amiens.

Napoleon offers Peace to the King of England.—A few

days afterward I resolved to write directly to George III. in order to propose peace, and to prove that another coalition would only tend to increase the continental influence of France. Not only did the mental alienation of this prince preclude the possibility of an answer, but the ministry declared these direct appeals to the sentiments of the king as opposed to the fundamental maxims of the English government. Lord Mulgrave, therefore, addressed an insignificant reply to Talleyrand. It was necessary, he said, before replying to these overtures, to consult with the continental powers on the means of stipulating engagements capable of providing for the security of Europe, and to ward off the threatening dangers. We shall soon see what were the *means* proposed by England to the emperor of Russia, in a note dictated by Pitt, at the very time that I wrote my letter.

Organization of the Grand Army.—Having terminated the fêtes of the coronation, I directed my attention to more serious preparations for a descent upon England. My army had been encamped for two years on the shores of the channel, wholly occupied in military exercises: never was there any thing finer or more martial. I had employed this leisure in perfecting its organization; experience had shown the necessity of adopting a system more strong than the isolated divisions which had been employed during the Revolution. I therefore organized *corps-d'armée*, of three divisions each, commanded by marshals. This number was sufficient to sustain the first shock against one entire army. I could then consider each one of these corps as a wing, and could reënforce a part of my line with facility, by carrying there one or two of these corps: moreover this concentration simplified the transmission of orders and the movement of the forces.

I formed powerful reserves of cavalry, and gave one light brigade to each corps of infantry; I gave cuirasses and elegant uniforms to my heavy cavalry, which before had been more like mere gensd'armes of police. An officer proposed, at this epoch, to form lancers, but he was ridiculed by the others, because our hussars had always been able to overcome the Austrian hulans; but I afterward had reason to regret that more attention was not given to this project. Lancers had not been properly appreciated, because they had been usually employed at outposts, or fighting as individuals. But, in charges in closed lines, lancers are equally formidable against infantry which they can more easily reach, and cavalry armed with sabres, which can not stand against them.

Nevertheless, in this organization I committed one great fault in disorganizing the staff-corps. In Italy many of my adjutants-general had done little else than grumble; this had prejudiced me against their comrades. I gave the death-blow to this body, which ought to have been the soul of the army. In order to induce the best captains in the staff to go into the line, I suppressed the grade of *chef-de-bataillon* of staff, thus depriving the captains of all chance of promotion to the grade of colonel. I afterward restored the grade; but the evil had already been done: the best subalterns had left. The higher grades of the staff were not affected. I then attached but little importance to the subalterns of the staff, supposing that my own movements would increase in proportion to the increase of my forces, and that they would be mere couriers, for conveying my orders. This might have been well enough if I could have been everywhere at the same moment; but in thus destroying this nursery for the staff, I disorganized the means of supplying my place on any part of the theatre of war where I myself could not be present. After-reflections convinced me that this circumstance contributed not a little to our reverses. Berthier, who was of the ancient school of staff, instead of defending a corps of which he was the natural chief, thought to make favor with me by subjecting it to every possible humiliation.

I gave the command of the several *corps-d'armée* to men tried in many battles. On ascending the throne, I had appointed sixteen marshals, selected from generals who had already been commanders-in-chief of armies: all were not at first assigned to my army.

Bernadotte had the first corps; he was a man of shrewdness, and a brilliant exterior: the plans of operation drawn up by him while minister of war, prove that he was better qualified for a lieutenant than for a general-in-chief.

Marmont, formerly my aid-de-camp and general-of-artillery, commanded the second corps, although he had not yet been made marshal. I have since had too much reason to complain of the conduct of this officer to be an impartial judge: I leave that task to posterity.

Davoust was placed at the head of the third corps. This man had received a good education, had a well-regulated mind, and very correct ideas of war. His rude manners, and a character at the same time distrustful and harsh, have created him many enemies, and, in the grave circumstances in which he was placed, party spirit has acted against him with great injustice. Severe, but just, toward his subordinates, he could maintain better order and discipline than any one else among his soldiers; no one of my marshals required more of his subordinates, and no one made them serve with more exactitude.

The fourth corps was given to Soult. This general, of a masculine frame, and a mind capacious, laborious, active, indefatigable, had given proof in Switzerland, and at Genoa, of superior talents; he was reproached with being too ambitious.

Lannes had the fifth corps. Covered with glory and wounds, this brave man was wanting only in a knowledge of the principles of the art of war; but he supplied this deficiency with an admirable judgment, and on the field of battle he yielded to no one of his colleagues.

Ney commanded the sixth corps. He is too well known throughout Europe to make it necessary to say much respecting his character. If, drawn on by a fatal destiny, in the difficult circumstances in which he was placed, he was not the *chevalier sans reproche*, he was incontestably, the *chevalier sans peur*. Lannes was perhaps as brilliant as he, in bold attacks; but the strength of mind which Ney displayed in the great disaster of 1812, where he successively commanded all the corps of the army, assigns to him the first rank among the brave men of modern times. Like many of his colleagues, he did not understand war on the map, but on the field nothing equaled his boldness, his *coup-d'œil*, and his *aplomb*.

The seventh corps, under the orders of Augereau, was formed later at Brest. Its chief had carried off the palm at Castiglione; an imposing personal appearance and soldier-like manners had made his fortune; but if he acquired a little *éclat* at the battle of Arcola, he never afterward justified his reputation.

Murat was placed at the head of the reserves of cavalry. His position as my brother-in-law and sovereign duke of Berg (which he afterward became) placed him among my lieutenants destined to command several corps. This cavalry officer, who, from his fine appearance, his courage and activity, had the honor of being my aid-de-camp, and my relative, never equaled the colossal reputation which I have given to him. He had natural sprightliness, brilliant courage, and great activity; but he has shown that while such a star may appear bright in the second, it becomes eclipsed in the first rank.

A man of very different stamp was placed at the head of the army of Italy. His victory at Zurich had entitled him to the command of a separate army. Massena had received from nature every thing that can make an excellent warrior;

endowed with great character, tried courage, and a *coup-d'œil* which inspired him with resolution the most prompt and the most happy, he can not be denied a distinguished place among modern captains. Nevertheless it must be confessed that he shone more in the fight than in the council.

Brune, Mortier, and Bessières, were also of the number of the elect. The first had his peculiar merit; he was, however, all things considered, a tribune general, rather than a redoubtable military man. The second, less brilliant, was more solid; his calmness and *sang-froid*, become proverbial among the soldiers, availed him more than success; he was one of those who was capable, under my direction, of commanding a corps. Bessières had served with me in the army of Italy as commandant of my mounted guards. He had a known valor, a spirit of order; he was methodic, but excessively timid in council.

Lefebvre, duke of Dantzic, was a true grenadier. Child of nature, he owed every thing to his natural *esprit*, to his great bravery, and to his simple and naïve character. He knew how to make himself beloved by the soldier, and to lead him to his proper position; this was all his merit.

Jourdan had been commander-in-chief of a great army. Victorious at Fleurus, under the most decisive circumstances, he owed to fortune a great part of his reputation. A good administrator, laborious, a man of order, instruction, and integrity, he would have made a good chief-of-staff of a great army under a general who well directed it.

Moncey, Perignon, and Serrurier, not having afterward fought under me as emperor, it is not necessary to describe them here; the two former had commanded in chief in the Pyrenees, and their operations in 1794 and 1795 gave indications of talent. Placed in the rank of senators, they no longer figured at the head of the troops, except at the crisis when the enemy was under the walls of Paris.

Macdonald and Lecourbe, having commanded armies, had claims to the baton of marshal; but the first had manœuvred so badly at the Trebia, that I deemed it best to postpone his promotion. Lecourbe had also permitted himself to be beaten in 1799, at Phillipsbourg; nevertheless he had shown so great an aptitude for mountain war in Switzerland, and afterward taken so important a part in the victories of Moreau in 1800, that he had deserved it more than some others. But he had made some malevolent remarks against me at the time of Moreau's trial, and I was not yet in a position to employ my enemies.

It is seen by this portrait of my generals, that, with the exception of Massena, Soult, and perhaps Davoust, there were none to whom I could intrust the command of a separate army. (The viceroy, Saint Cyr, Suchet, and Oudinot, were promoted only at a later period.) I thought, however, that these three were more than necessary at that period, when I myself could direct the *ensemble* of the grand operations, and had more need of valiant lieutenants than of able colleagues.

Notwithstanding the little defects which have been noticed, the military constitution of the empire was the best in Europe; for the other powers had not yet made the same progress as they did afterward, by imitating and in some things surpassing us.

The Army prepares to embark.—The first corps occupied Hanover; the second was at the camp of Ziest in Holland; the third, fourth, fifth, and sixth, from Ambleteuse to Montreuil; the seventh at Brest. One hundred and twenty thousand infantry, twelve thousand cavalry, eight thousand dragoons (to be mounted in England), four thousand artillerists, four hundred and fifty field-pieces, seven thousand horses, were ready to embark, and actually did embark several times; two thousand two hundred bateaux, shallops, and pinnaces, armed with more than five thousand cannon, divided into as many little squadrons as there were sections in the army, were prepared for the transport of the troops, at the moment that our fleets should either clear the channel, or at least call away for a time the enemy's forces.

All the *matériel* for this expedition was on board, and the immense extent of these preparations is sufficient proof that, if I was not deterred by the difficulty of this enterprise, I at least did not fail to appreciate the duties it imposed. Our *embarquement* consisted of fourteen millions of cartridges, ninety thousand cannon charges, thirty-two thousand extra muskets, one million five hundred thousand rations of biscuit, one million three hundred thousand flints, thirty thousand tools and utensils for engineers, eleven thousand saddles and sets of harness, four hundred and fifty cannon, seven thousand four hundred horses, in stable-boats; and one hundred and sixty thousand men of different arms. The perfect order which reigned in this immense flotilla, the frequent exercises by which I habituated the troops to embark and debark in less than an hour, at an appointed signal, the care with which each man was instructed in his particular duty—in a word, every thing had been provided that could secure success to this grand operation.

Napoleon's Project compared to that of Cæsar.—It is unnecessary to stop here to refute the parallel which some have wished to draw between the expedition of Cæsar and my project of descent; an absurd parallel, since there was nothing common in the two cases, except the starting-place; but the place of debarkation resulted from geographical positions, and depended in no way on the combinations of the general. Cæsar, conqueror of the Gauls, attacked with Roman legions the barbarous and divided people of Britain; he had a fleet superior to the miserable barks of the Britons, both in number, in strength, and in skill. He was certain of arriving at port, and certain of his means of retreat; more still, he went to certain victory. I, on the contrary, was to attack the most industrious and the proudest nation on the globe; a nation that ruled the seas with one hundred and forty heavy ships of war, armed with fifteen thousand cannon; a nation presenting a population of fifteen millions of inhabitants; a nation that in a little time could oppose to me, even deducting Ireland, at least two hundred thousand men, unwarlike and inexperienced, it is true, but animated by a love of country. The expedition of Cæsar was child's play; mine, the enterprise of the Titans; this is the only comparison that can be made. It is true that I was not, like Cæsar, going to subjugate and occupy proud Albion, but to ruin her shipyards, her arsenals, her manufactures, then to return to France and present myself to Europe in the attitude of a conqueror, which would enable me to dictate terms of peace.

However great my fears respecting the course of Russia, I confess that I was deceived respecting the pacific attitude of Austria, especially after her formal recognition of the French empire. If she had persisted, like Russia, in a system of neutrality which was so profitable to her, there was nothing to oppose to the execution of my project. But even should Austria determine upon hostilities, I deemed that she would require considerable time for preparation, and would wait for the arrival of the Russians. But three weeks was time enough for me to effect my descent, enter London, ruin the shipyards, and destroy the arsenals of Portsmouth and Plymouth. If I should succeed, would not this success be sufficient to prevent a continental war? Even under the most unfavorable supposition, could I not levy a double conscription to supply the place of the absent troops, and place my army in condition to make head against the enemy on the Rhine and on the Adige? The rapidity with which I hoped to strike the important blow, and to return to France, was the principal circumstance upon which I based my hopes of success; I overlooked neither the rashness nor the difficulty of the enterprise; my genius consisted in embracing rapidly, and with the same *coup-d'œil*, both the obstacles and the means of surmounting them.

Concerted Movements of the French Fleets.—Encouraged by so many motives, I gave orders to the navy department to prelude my descent by the union of our maritime forces. To do this successfully, it was necessary to appoint a distant rendezvous for our different squadrons of Toulon, Cadiz, Rochefort, and Brest. I resolved to direct them to Martinique, whence they would return to raise the blockade of the fleet of the Ferrol, and to advance together to the channel, to favor our expedition. Our measures were very skillfully arranged for this object; for they not only tended to secure the junction of the seven or eight squadrons now dispersed at Toulon, Cadiz, Ferrol, Rochefort, and Brest, but still more to give the alarm respecting the English establishments in the two Indies, and thus to entice away the greater part of the English naval forces, at the very moment when we were to appear on their coast. We were to profit by this departure of the British fleets, to throw troops into the colonies. General Lauriston was to recapture Surinam and the Dutch establishments on the American continent, where it was important to prevent the English from getting a footing; Reille was to get possession of St. Helena, in order to intercept the navigation to India, and favor our cruisers against the commerce of the East India Company; he was then to endeavor to throw a French garrison into the Cape of Good Hope. Other detachments were to sweep the waters of the Antilles, and recapture St. Lucia, Tobago, St. Pierre, etc., places which had already fallen into the power of the enemy.

The Fleet at Rochefort.—Admiral Missiessy sailed from

Rochefort, the fourth of January, with five vessels and some battalions of troops; but encountering a storm a few days afterward, he had to contend with the elements for thirteen days; he reached the Antilles, but not without damage. The beginning of February he landed at Martinique some succors of men and munitions, and then made General Lagrange attack Dominique, which he entirely reduced except Fort Rupert; he dismounted several batteries of the Roseau, and not wishing to spend time in a siege, he reëmbarked, after treating in the same way the Isles of St. Christopher, Nevis, and Montserrat. He received orders to return to Europe, inasmuch as the squadron of Toulon had been forced, by the storm, to return to that port. Nevertheless, he went *en route* to raise, for a moment, the blockade of the city of Santo-Domingo, the last post of our troops in that island, and where General Ferraud defended himself with a bravery worthy of a better fate. Missiessy had not executed my orders as I wished, and I replaced him in the command of the squadron of Rochefort by Rear-admiral Lallement, who received orders to put to sea.

The Toulon Squadron.—Admiral Villeneuve had not contended against the storm with the same constancy as Missiessy. He sailed from Toulon on the eighteenth of January, with eighteen vessels and frigates, and encountered the storm in which he had one vessel dismantled and three frigates forced to take refuge in Corsica, which inspired him with the fatal resolution to return to port. He refitted, and again set sail on the thirtieth of March, at the very time that the Rochefort squadron was on its return voyage; a circumstance, as will be seen, fatal to my plan. Arriving before Carthegena, he wished the Spanish squadron of seven vessels, which was there, to join him; but the Spanish authorities replied that this squadron had a different destination. He then sailed to Cadiz, where he found only five English ships, which hastened to retire. Villeneuve here was reënforced by a small number of vessels, and then set sail with fourteen ships and six frigates for the Antilles, and anchored at Martinique on the fifteenth of May. He was there joined by four other Spanish ships, which had sailed from Cadiz immediately after his passage, under the orders of the brave Admiral Gravina.

The Brest Squadron.—Admiral Gantheaume, who was to have left Brest for the same destination with twenty ships, was blockaded by Admiral Cornwallis with superior forces, and did not profit by the effects of the storm to secure a sortie from port. It now became necessary, for greater security, to direct Villeneuve to return and effect a junction near Brest, and to raise the blockade of that port: orders to this effect were dispatched by Admiral Magon, who sailed from Rochefort with two ships.

Nelson sails for Egypt.—Nelson, hearing of the departure of the Toulon squadron, was persuaded that it was destined for Egypt. The concentration of the corps of Saint Cyr, at Tarentum, at the extremity of the *presqu'île* of Naples, and the troops embarked on board the squadron, rendered this conjecture more probable than any other. Nelson each time directed his course to the mouths of the Nile. He was not a little surprised to learn that Villeneuve had raised the blockade of Cadiz, and continued his course in the ocean.

Villeneuve at the Antilles.—Although he had destroyed but ten ships in a cruise of two years, the English admiral made sail for Lisbon, as soon as the wind permitted him to pass the straits, and certain, from what he heard there, that the French had sailed for the West Indies, he resolved to follow on the eleventh of May, the very time that Villeneuve was at anchor at Martinique. But this officer knew not how to profit either by the start he had of the enemy, nor by the troops I had given him: he did nothing but attack Diamond-Rock, where the English had established a depôt for their cruisers in the Antilles. This rock, however important as a secondary post, was not sufficient to attract the entire attention of the admiral and his forces; as there was no place for landing troops, its capture was difficult. Colonel Boyer, who commanded the troops charged with this enterprise, creeping along from grotto to grotto, and from rock to rock, and drawing after him his tirailleurs with ropes, at last succeeded in capturing this little Gibraltar and one hundred and fifty prisoners. This perilous and difficult escalade is one of the finest feats in this maritime war.

He returns to Europe.—After having uselessly waited three weeks for the Brest fleet, Villeneuve decided to attack the English islands, and for this purpose drew reënforcements of troops from Guadaloupe and Martinique; he then received the order, by Rear-admiral Magon, June sixth, to return to Europe and unite with the squadrons of Ferrol and Rochefort to raise the blockade of Brest, where Gantheaume, with twenty-one vessels, had received orders to take position in the roadstead preparatory to taking part in the battle, if any should occur. Hearing at the same time of Nelson's arrival at Barbadoes, Villeneuve set sail on the tenth of August, without even taking time to land the troops which I had directed him to leave at Martinique, to push forward with success the war in the Antilles.

Nelson also returns to England.—Nelson, having learned his departure, and supposing that he would attack Trinidad, sailed to the assistance of that island. Finding himself deceived in this, he sailed to Antigua; he some days after learned that Villeneuve had returned to Europe, and set sail himself for Cadiz, giving warning to the several stations and to the admiralty; then seeking in vain for further news of our squadron, he returned with two vessels to England, sending the other nine to reënforce the fleet of Cornwallis before Brest, satisfied soon afterward that the union of all our forces at the same place had been our only object.

CHAPTER VIII.

THE WAR OF 1805, OR THE CAMPAIGN OF AUSTERLITZ.

Origin of a new Coalition against France—Pitt's Project to reduce her to the Limits of 1792—He negotiates with Russia—Napoleon assumes the Iron Crown of Italy—Alliance between Russia and England—Hesitation of Austria—Napoleon in Italy—His Fortifications and Camps of Manœuvre there—His Coronation at Milan—Return of the French Fleets to Europe—Villeneuve at Ferrol and Cadiz—Consequences of his multiplied Faults—Austria accedes to the new Coalition—Mission of Nowosiltzof—First Project of the Allies—Their Definitive Plan—Their Efforts to induce Germany to join the Coalition—The Austrians enter Bavaria—The French march from the Coast of the Channel to the Danube—Organization of the Grand Army—Passage of the Rhine—Direction of the French Masses on Donawerth—Mack awaits them on the Danube—Napoleon turns his Right and falls upon his Rear—His Confusion—Napoleon Manœuvres to cut him off from Bohemia—Murat's Faults—Mack attempts to Escape—Combat of Haslach—Napoleon returns to the Danube—Operations of the Austrians—They burn the Bridge of Elchingen—Ney's Operations—Battle of Elchingen—Investment of Ulm—Ney's Attack—Murat pursues Werneck—Mack summoned to Surrender Ulm—Conditional Capitulation—Defeat of Werneck—He Surrenders—Surrender of Mack—Fate of the Wreck of Mack's Army—Russia threatens to join the Coalition—Napoleon directs his Forces on the Inn—Passage of the Inn, The Salza, and the Traun—Remarks on Napoleon's March on Vienna—The Emperor Alexander at Berlin—Massena's Operations in Italy—His Instructions—Passage of the Adige, and Battle of Caldiero—Retreat of the Archduke Charles—Napoleon at Lintz—Propositions for an Armistice—Operations of Murat and Davoust—Kutusof passes the Danube at Krems—Affair of Dirnstein—Napoleon approaches Vienna—State of that City—Murat Captures the Bridge on the Danube—Critical Situation of Kutusof—Unskillfulness of Murat—Combat of Hollabrun—Kutusof effects his Junction—Napoleon at Schoenbrun—General Plan of Campaign—The French Army at Brunn—Operations in the Tyrol—New Attempts at Negotiation—Movements of the Allies—Napoleon's Disposition for their Reception—The Allies' Plan of Battle—Napoleon's Grand Attack on their Centre—Soult's Success—Check of the Enemy's Left—Success at the Centre and French Left—Napoleon and Soult attack the Enemy's Left—He is cut off from Olmutz and thrown on Hungary—Interview between Napoleon and the Emperor Francis—Remarks on the Battle of Austerlitz—Napoleon returns to Vienna—Treats with Prussia—Also with Austria—Operations in Hanover—The Dynasty of Naples ceases to Reign—Napoleon's Orders to Villeneuve—Nelson returns before Cadiz—Mutiny of the two Fleets—Battle of Trafalgar.

New Coalition.—The departure of such considerable naval forces from our ports, and the presence of one hundred and sixty thousand brave men opposite and within twenty leagues of her harbors, were well calculated to inspire England with real alarm; she felt it necessary to get rid of this threatening danger at all hazards. No sooner was Pitt replaced at the head of the ministry, than this indefatigable enemy of France sought, in every court in Europe, allies to oppose us. The vail which covers the origin of this third coalition against France has as yet been but partly raised: Russia appears to have given the impulse; some attribute it to the cabinet of London; be that as it may, both could not be long in coming to an understanding, after the Russian ambassador had left Paris, without gaining satisfaction on the several points of his complaint, and after the Swedish ambassador had followed his example.

The cabinet of St. James worked with all its power to excite these hostile feelings; Prince Czartorinski, the Russian minister of foreign affairs, having given the English ministry to understand the dispositions of the Emperor Alexander to oppose, by force of arms, any ulterior encroachments on my part, Pitt seized with avidity this overture, and a negotiation was entered upon immediately to bring about a formidable coalition, the only means of warding off the storm which was ready to break on England. It has been said that these communications of Czartorinski were a manœuvre concerted beforehand by men whose attachment to England was no secret. It was not enough for our implacable enemy to impose limits to the French power; he wished even to contest those which had been sanctioned by treaties, and to force us back within the limits of 1792. Without that, how could Austria be promised an aggrandisement sufficient to induce her to go to war? Without that, how could Prussia be persuaded to abandon her neutrality?

Pitt's Project.—The famous note of the sixteenth of January, which proposed to Europe the partition of our spoils, is a curious document, and one that fully justified any measure on my part to put France in a condition to resist such projects. Pitt proposed that Lombardy be given to Austria, that the king of Sardinia should not only recover Piedmont, Savoy, and Nice, but that the Republic of Genoa should be given to him, in order to strengthen him against France. Prussia was to obtain Belgium, so as to separate us from Holland, and to cut that country off from French influence. The small states on the left bank of the Rhine which had been ceded to us, both at Campo-Formio and Luneville, were to be given to Prussia, Austria, or to such other German princes as would take part in this league.

It was natural enough that the great powers should arm to prevent my ulterior aggrandisement; and in the same degree was it unjust and impolitic to wish to reduce us to the limits of 1792. This would have been well enough if the other states had returned to the limits which they had occupied at that epoch. But since that period, had not Russia, Austria, and Prussia divided Poland between them? Had not England acquired half of India? France, on the contrary—had she not lost her family alliance with Spain, Austria, Sardinia, and Naples? Her allies in India—had they not become British provinces? The ruin of St. Domingo—had it not destroyed our supremacy in the Antilles! In fine, had not our relative condition become inferior, by one half, to that of 1792? *To descend, while all her enemies were ascending in the scale of nations, ought not to be the fate of a great state, victorious for the last ten years! To attempt to subject me to such an ignominy, was to place me under the necessity of dying, arms in hand, or of subjugating Europe.* The fear of my ascendency and of my enterprising genius may explain the adhesion of the continental powers to this project of the cabinet of London; but the fear of seeing myself incessantly exposed to the same danger, ought also to explain the course which I pursued, to render myself the dominant power in Europe in order to escape this danger. Thus a reciprocal fear, carried to excess, often becomes the cause of the most violent political contests, and urges men beyond the bounds of reason, especially after revolutions.

Negotiation with Russia.—However unfavorably disposed the Russian cabinet might be toward me, it nevertheless could not fail to regard the project of Pitt as extravagant; but a new incident removed all these scruples. I had felt that Italy could not exist under a republican form by the side of my empire; it would have been preposterous. But I could not yield the reins to another, since Europe had conceded them to me, and especially as this peninsula was requisite to my maritime projects.

Assumption of the Iron Crown of Italy.—The Italian deputation which had come to assist at my coronation was constituted in a *consultum of state* under the presidency of Melzi, and after some weeks' debate, it presented me, on the seventeenth of March, a constitutional act, forming the Italian Republic into a hereditary kingdom, and offered to me the crown. To satisfy Europe, at least for the time, I at first proposed it to my brother Joseph, hoping by this apparent separation to diminish the unfavorable impression which so great an increase of my power might produce. But

Joseph showed some scruples about accepting a tributary throne, and presumed to dictate to me the abolition of treaties which subjected Italy to an annual contribution of thirty millions of francs, or the support of thirty thousand French troops necessary for its protection. I easily consoled myself for these scruples, which were incompatible with my projects, and got over them, by placing on my own head the iron crown of the Lombard kings which had once been worn by Charlemagne, but which for centuries had been buried among the relics of the palace of Monza To reply in advance to the reclamations of my enemies, I promised, nevertheless, to place this crown on the head of an adopted son, and to separate it from France, as soon as England should surrender Malta, and Russia evacuate the Republic of the Seven Isles; which would permit me also to evacuate the kingdom of Naples, and give to Lombardy a kind of independence. In fact, whether I was president for life or king, was of little importance to Europe; the essential thing was to have the crown of Italy separated from that of France, either during my life or at least at my death. This was all that Austria wanted; moreover, she preferred having on her frontier a kingdom, rather than a democratic republic.

I repaired to the Senate, on the eighteenth of March, to announce this important change. This offered an opportunity of exposing to Europe my political views, which I did in the following terms:

"The genius of evil will seek in vain for pretexts for involving the continent in war. Whatever has been united to our empire by the constitutional laws of the state will remain so. *No new power will be incorporated in it;* but the laws of the Batavian Republic, the act of mediation of the nineteen Swiss cantons, and this first statute of the kingdom of Italy, will be constantly under the protection of our crown; and we will never suffer any attack to be made upon them.

Under all circumstances, and on all occasions, we will show the same moderation, and we hope that our people will have no longer need of displaying that courage and that energy which they have always shown in the defense of their legitimate rights."

Alliance between England and Russia.—What I regarded as moderation, did not appear as such to the rest of Europe. The Emperor Alexander, on receiving this news, negotiated with England on Pitt's project of the sixteenth of January. Deciding upon war, he signed, April 11th, a treaty of offensive and defensive alliance with the cabinet of London. Nevertheless, he wisely entered into no stipulations respecting Belgium and the Rhenish Provinces, confining the question to the evacuation of Naples and Holland, the restitution of Piedmont to the king of Sardinia, and the independence of Switzerland. He engaged to send one hundred and fifteen thousand men immediately into the field, and, in order to provide for their support without embarrassing his finances, England stipulated a subsidy of fifty millions. By a subsequent article, the promised forces were increased to one hundred and eighty thousand combatants. Although these first steps were taken with the utmost secrecy, I could not be deceived respecting the hostile dispositions of Russia; but as Austria had made no declaration, how could I anticipate hostilities from a country from which I was separated by great powers and an interval of five hundred leagues impossible to pass?

Hesitation of Austria.—Possibly I might have warded off the storm, if I had consented to purchase the neutrality of Austria, by leaving the Italian Republic independent; but, I repeat, this would have been preposterous in the present organization of Europe, and after it had chosen a monarchical form of government, it was necessary either to assume the crown myself, or to see it on the head of a foreign prince; it was not to dispose of it in this way that we had conquered it. Besides, who could guarantee that my moderation would not be regarded at Vienna as a proof of weakness? This cabinet had exhibited too much malevolence for me to trust it; and I deemed that I had done enough in engaging for its conditional separation, by the solemn act of which I have just spoken.

In truth, most of the ancient dynasties were frightened at seeing me on a throne. Notwithstanding the polite assurances which had passed between us, they considered me still as a dangerous adversary; for I reigned only in virtue of a system which struck at the root of all the authority which time had built up for them. I was the offspring of the Revolution, and its representative. The Empire troubled them as much as the Republic; for they feared it even more, because it was more vigorous. With moderation and time I might have tranquillized them; but the unfortunate necessity under which I was placed of closing Naples, Holland, and Hanover against the English, created the alarm against me. It was in vain that I protested that these were merely defensive measures; they refused to believe me, and the great powers persuaded themselves that it was policy to attack me as soon as possible, and before I could consolidate my power. Austria, nevertheless, hesitated for some time, either because she feared the issue of this contest, or wished to avoid the first blows, or desired time for preparation. Persuaded that there was no need for precipitation, but that on the contrary, it was best to await for the most opportune moment, the cabinet of Vienna was inclined to make demonstrations, and to obtain a delay by means of negotiations; besides, it did not fully agree with England respecting the organization to be given to the continent.

Napoleon goes to Italy.—At the moment when my squadrons made sail toward Martinique, to secure there a more easy and advantageous junction than they could in European waters, I resolved to repair to Italy in order to be crowned at Milan, as I had been at Paris. This journey accomplished several objects equally important. The first was to augment the feeling of security of the English and to completely deceive them respecting my project; the second, to impose on Austria by my presence on her frontier; the third, to excite the public spirit of the Italians by appearing among them with a pomp unknown there, and well calculated to incite in them a love of glory and of country. In going to Lyons, I made a detour in order to visit Brienne, the cradle of my French education; I felt for it the gratitude it deserved. This place was yet to be the scene of one of my bloodiest reverses. Lyons received me with more enthusiasm than ever; the luxury with which I had surrounded my court, was a pledge of the further prosperity of her manufactures; interest and glory were combined in the acclamations of the brave Lyonnais.

Fortifications and Camps of Manœuvre.—In passing Alexandria I directed immense works which, in a few years, would render that place the most formidable in Europe, and the key of Italy. Twenty millions of money were to be applied to this important project. Situated in the southern basin of the Po, at an equal distance from Turin, Genoa, Milan, Placentia, and Parma, Alexandria was destined to become the refuge of a grand army in case of reverse, and an offensive base for all our operations in Northern Italy. Perhaps Pavia or Cremona had been better situated for operations against Austria, and for commanding the line of the Po; but in a political sense, Alexandria better suited my views. Sixteen regiments of infantry assembled in a *camp de manœuvre* near Marengo, to form a simulacrum of the battle we had just gained, reminded Austria of our superiority over her armies. Another camp of seventeen regiments, assembled for the same object at Castiglione, gave the cabinet of Vienna to understand that I was ready to measure arms with her as soon as she pleased.

Coronation of Napoleon at Milan.—My coronation took place at Milan, on the twenty-sixth of May, with all the solemnity worthy of the magnificent cathedral in which the ceremony was performed. Never, even in the days of Charlemagne, was such pomp seen by the Italians. After the consecration of the archbishop, Cardinal Caprara, I took the iron crown of the Lombard kings and placed it on my head. Milan was enthusiastic almost to intoxication, and Lombardy partook of the same feelings still more frankly, as the clergy had there praised me to the clouds as the restorer of the altars. The Pope, who traveled two days with me, had scattered his benedictions upon the people subject to my power, and had thus added to the *éclat* of my laurels in the eyes of the multitude. Fame, with her hundred voices, can never fully describe to posterity my activity during this journey, in organizing the new Italian monarchy, in dispatching orders to the expeditionary army at Boulogne; in giving instructions for my squadrons crossing the ocean; in regulating the internal affairs of France; in directing negotiations with Europe; and in maturing the project for the reunion of Genoa to my empire. One of the most eloquent writers of the present century, who only wants more decision in his opinions to equal the greatest historians of antiquity, has traced out an interesting picture of these operations, which posterity will place by the side of the finest compositions of Livy.*

In leaving Milan I placed the reins of the government of Italy in the hands of Eugene,† with the title of Viceroy;

* The author here alluded to is Mathieu Dumas.

† Eugene Beauharnais, Viceroy of Italy, Prince of Eichstedt, Duke of Leuchtenberg, &c., was born at Paris, September 3, 1781. He was the son of Vis-

this young prince was, in every respect, worthy of my confidence; he became the most faithful of my friends, and one of my ablest lieutenants. A short time afterward the sovereignty of Lucca was given to my sister Eliza Bacchiochi.* I repaired to Genoa, of which I took possession in great state and with a pomp which made the Genoese forget for a time the change which was to result in their position by the act of annexation of the fourth of June. When I deemed the moment had arrived for the approach of the fleet of Admiral

count Alexander Beauharnais and Josephine. He entered the army at the age of twelve, and served under his father and afterward under Hoche. He was next sent to Saint Germain-en-Haye, and passed several years in this school. He then accompanied Napoleon in Italy and into Egypt. He was made chef-de-bataillon at nineteen, colonel at twenty-one, general-of brigade at twenty-three, and viceroy of Italy at twenty-five. He early proved himself one of Napoleon's ablest generals. At twenty-eight he commanded the army of Italy, and at thirty-one gained great glory in the Russian campaign at the head of the fourth *corps-d'armée.* After the departure of Napoleon and Murat, he was left commander-in-chief of all the forces. He died at Munich, February 21, 1824. His son, the Duke Augustus, succeeded him. His eldest daughter, Josephine, is now queen of Sweden. His second daughter, Hortensia Eugenia, married the prince of Hohenzollern-Hechingen in 1826. His third daughter, Amelia Eugenia, married the emperor of Brazil in 1829

"Prince Eugene, under a simple exterior, concealed a noble character and great talents. Honor, integrity, humanity, and love of order and justice, were the principal traits of his character. Wise in the council, undaunted in the field, and moderate in the exercise of power, he never appeared greater than in the midst of reverses, as the events of 1813 and 1814 prove. He was inaccessible to the spirit of party, benevolent and beneficent, and more devoted to the good of others than his own.—*Encyclopædia Americana, Biographie Universelle.*

* Bacchiochi (Marie-Anne-Eliza Bonaparte), sister of Napoleon, was born in Corsica in 1777. She married Captain Bacchiochi in 1797, in compliance with the wishes of her mother, but in opposition to those of Napoleon. Her husband was a man of little ability, and acted a very subordinate part in the great events in which he lived. She was a woman of great talents, and her administration as princess of Lucca and Piombino, and as grand duchess of Tuscany, is marked by many important improvements. She patronized the arts, and was always the generous friend of distinguished talent. Boufflers, Laharpe, Chateaubriand, and Fontanes, were among those who sought her society, and on whom she conferred particular obligations. Her life was distinguished for charity and benevolence, as well as for taste in poetry and the fine arts, and great ability in the administration of affairs. She died in August, 1820, at Trieste.—*Encyclopædia Americana, Biographie Universelle.*

Villeneuve to the channel, I left Turin in the midst of a parade, and repaired, in the utmost secresy, in three days to Paris, and then to Boulogne, where all was ready for embarcation.

Return of the French Fleets to Europe.—While I was thus laying at Milan, Turin, Alexandria, Mantua, and Genoa, the foundations of the most vast designs, Admiral Villeneuve was returning to Europe in compliance with his orders. This return, for which the English were not at all prepared, was calculated to trouble them: they had only ten ships, under Admiral Calder, before Ferrol, where there were eighteen French and Spanish ships. There were only five, under Admiral Sterling, before Rochefort, where we had six ships and as many fine frigates, which soon found an opportunity to get to sea under the orders of Admiral Lallement. Villeneuve, having more than fifteen days the start of the English dispatch boats, it seemed very easy to surprise Calder before Ferrol, to give him chase and rally the combined fleet of this port, to reach Rochefort, and advance to Brest with forty ships. But by an inconceivable fatality, the English dispatch boats, favored by the heavy winds, made the voyage with such rapidity as to arrive in time to give information to their stations; that of Rochefort was ordered to join Calder without delay; this prevented us from effecting the projected junction without a battle. In fact, Calder finding himself in command of fifteen ships and three frigates, met, on the twenty-second of July, off Cape Finisterre, Villeneuve, who had nineteen ships and eight frigates. Foggy weather prevented them from seeing each other very distinctly; both formed in line and fought, ship to ship (*bord à bord*), one of those battles in parallel order, where skill is of no avail. The Spanish ships, disabled, fell into the midst of the English, and were captured; in other respects this battle was marked by no important results.

Villeneuve enters Ferrol.—Villeneuve gave chase the very next day to the enemy's squadron, which effected its retreat and raised the blockade of Ferrol to go and join the fleet before Brest; but the stormy weather decided him, on his side, to enter the bay of Vigo, being unable, on account of the wind, to reach the port which he sought. He nevertheless reached there a few days later, and, after being joined by five French and ten Spanish ships, made sail with his thirty vessels for Vigo on the thirteenth, and thence to Cadiz, where he arrived the twenty-first of August, the very time that he was expected to appear before Brest, and that Gantheaume was manœuvring to favor him.

Admiral Collingwood had resumed the blockade of Cadiz, but he had only half of this force, and one would think that Villeneuve might, at least, have profited by this circumstance to surprise and beat him, by placing him between the fires of the coast and of our own fleet. He, however, did nothing, and limited himself to entering the port. He had become so confused by the heavy responsibility that weighed upon him, that he even forgot to leave at Vigo instructions for Admiral Lallement, who was seeking him with six fine French ships from Rochefort, and who, for this purpose, appeared at Vigo two days afterward. But ignorant of Villeneuve's course, this admiral was unable to join him, and cruised in the ocean between Ireland and the Bay of Biscay.

As soon as Cornwallis learned the junction of our fleets, he sent Calder with twenty ships to Cape Finisterre to either observe or fight them. Not finding them any longer at Ferrol, the English admiral pushed forward to Cadiz and formed a junction with Collingwood. This circumstance would have completely secured the execution of my project, if Villeneuve, in obedience to my instructions, had sailed toward Brest. He could then either have met Calder, or have passed him on the way; in the first case, having thirty-eight ships against twenty, he must have beaten him, which would have forced Cornwallis to raise the blockade of Gantheaume to assist him ; in the second case, Villeneuve, passing Calder, would have appeared before Brest and surprised Cornwallis, with forces inferior to ours by a half, which would have been the most probable and the most desirable.

Villeneuve's Faults.—Deviating, on the contrary, from my plan, Villeneuve, instead of appearing in triumph before Brest, shut himself up, with a fleet of thirty-three ships and an army of ten thousand men, in the extremity of the Spanish peninsula, away from all the interests of France. Thus failed, through the pusillanimity of a single man, and the fortuitous circumstance of the rapid passage of two dispatch boats, the most profoundly conceived of all my plans ; for I am quite certain that, notwithstanding his want of energy, Villeneuve would have fully executed his mission, if, instead of finding at Cape Finisterre the two squadrons of Calder and Sterling prepared to receive him, he had surprised before Ferrol the single one of Calder in position of rendezvous and unprepared for fighting. The direction of Villeneuve on Cadiz ruined all hopes of effecting the descent, for this campaign, since the English, now seeing our designs, would be prepared to oppose them. Moreover, the reports which I had just received from my ambassador at Vienna, informing me of the threatening preparations of Austria, induced me to direct upon the continent the blows which I had flattered myself would, if not overthrow the English government, at least prevent it from ruling the seas and dictating laws to the universe.

Austria accedes to the new Coalition.—In fact my journey to Italy had decided Austria, who had been actively negotiating with England and Russia for renewing a coalition. General Winzingerode, aid-de-camp of the Emperor Alexander, was its most active agent. We have said that the cabinet of Vienna inclined to try an armed mediation, before openly deciding upon a rupture. This is usually the language of those who wish to gain time; Austria showed us at Prague what she understood by *mediation!*

Mission of Nowosiltzof.—Nevertheless, either to please Francis II., or to himself attempt some pacific arrangements, the Emperor Alexander resolved to send M. de Nowosiltzof to Paris. This negotiator got as far as Berlin, when the news of the reunion of Genoa to France caused him to be recalled. This reunion had, in fact, removed all chance of an adjustment of differences; for this territory was really the only one which the allies could give to the king of Sardinia in place of Piedmont. Moreover, how could they hope to make me renounce the crown of Italy, when I had just united to my empire a country whose independence was proclaimed at Luneville? War was now inevitable.

Writers in the pay of England have sought to throw all the blame of this war on me, as though the project of taking from us Belgium and the provinces of the Rhine was not of itself a declaration of war. However, of all the acts of my policy, the most difficult of explanation is this reunion of the Republic of Genoa. The time was not opportune; I was about to leave Italy in all haste for Boulogne to prepare the embarkation of my army to be ready to take advantage of Villeneuve's coöperation in the channel, as soon as he should present himself. It was for my interest to spare hostilities with Austria, in order to paralyze the hostile intentions of Russia. After the cabinet of Vienna had recognized me as president of the Italian Republic, I had reason to hope that she would also recognize my title as king, which would in no respect change matters, if the crown was to be separated from France at my death. But the reunion of Genoa to France, by effecting the destruction of a republic which had been consecrated by treaties, was calculated to cause suspicion of intentions upon the rest of the Italian peninsula; and to provoke a general coalition, at the very moment that I was directing my efforts toward the Thames. The epoch of the tacit adhesion of Austria to the treaty of St. Petersburg of the eleventh of April, is not known: but by the middle of July she was combining a plan of operations for the contingency of her armed negotiation not accomplishing its object; she gave in her formal adhesion to it on the ninth of August, with the exception of certain changes which she had proposed for the reorganization of the continent.

First Plan of the Coalition.—The first plan of the coalition was to send four hundred thousand men to the field, viz.: two hundred and fifty thousand Austrians, one hundred and fifteen thousand Russians, and forty-five thousand Swedes, or other smaller states subsidiary to the English. Austria deemed these troops insufficient to act effectually in Italy and against the formidable barrier of the Rhine. She replied by a memoir, well drawn up, in which she estimated the military power of France at six hundred thousand men, and deemed it necessary to augment the active forces. *The difficulty being to cause the Russians to arrive before I would anticipate them, and fall upon the Austrians; they deemed it indispensable to act with the principal mass in Italy, and to remain on the defensive in Germany.* The proposition was correct, but the inference was absurd: it was precisely because the reunion of the Russian forces in Germany was the Gordian knot, that rendered it necessary to place the mass of the Austrian forces upon the line of operation where this junction was to be effected; a line which was, moreover, for me the shortest and the most important. The cabinet of Vienna was blinded by its own egotism; it went to war merely to reconquer Italy, and it came to the false conclusion that it must direct its efforts there. Austria also exaggerated the forces which I could bring to the field. She supposed that she would have to oppose the whole of our military forces, which was not possible, as we had so many coasts to guard; I could never oppose to her in the field over two hundred and fifty thousand men.

The cabinet of St. Petersburg sent General Winzingerode to Vienna to discuss and fix upon a definitive plan. He observed that from Brody to Braunau the Russians would have to march two hundred and eighty-four leagues, and from Boulogne to Braunau the grand army would have two hundred and seventy-four leagues. So that, deducting the time required for me to receive the news of the entrance of the Russians into the Austrian territory and to put my forces in motion across France, the Russians would have time enough to reach the Inn, and even the Iser before I could. Alexander promised to have his reserves in readiness, to a number even exceeding the specified contingent.

Final Plan of the Coalition.—It was at length agreed with Austria:

1st. That she should act in Italy with one hundred and thirty thousand infantry and thirteen thousand five hundred horse; in Tyrol with fifty thousand men and two thousand horse; in Germany with sixty-six thousand infantry and twenty-three thousand horse; in detached corps with twenty-eight thousand men and fifteen hundred horse; making a total of two hundred and seventy-four thousand infantry and forty thousand horse.

2d. That Russia should bring one hundred thousand men into Germany, one half of which should arrive by the twentieth of October; that she should dispatch a corps from Corfu to debark at Naples, there form a junction with the English and the Neapolitans, and march in concert on the Po. A third Anglo-Russian corps would descend upon Hanover and Pomerania, and form a junction with the Swedish army under the orders of King Gustavus IV.; finally, a fourth Russian army assembled on the Bug, at the gates of Warsaw, should threaten Prussia, either to keep her in check, or to force her into the coalition.

Germany and the Coalition.—Nevertheless the allied cabinets failed to change the firm will of Frederick William, who wished at any price to preserve his neutrality. The allies demanded a passage through the Polish portion of his states, and he replied by assembling on the Vistula forces sufficient to compel respect to his territory.

I did not, till some time afterward, know positively the intentions of the coalition, but as early as July I saw indications of its existence, by the collection of Austrian forces in Italy and the Russians on the Bug. These last would not have troubled me, if Austria had remained neutral in my contest with England. I directed Talleyrand to demand explanations; Cobentzel gave very poor ones. I then signified to the cabinet of Vienna that it must withdraw its troops from Italy, or I should regard these armaments as a declaration of war. In the mean time we were preparing on both sides for the combat.

Austria, appreciating the influence of Bavaria, used every effort to bring her into the alliance, but she did not succeed: the Elector Maximilian Joseph remembered too well the part played by his ancestors, and the recent pretensions of the cabinet of Vienna to aggrandize itself at his expense; he was, moreover, personally attached to France, and, being certain that I would arrive in time to succor him, this prince resolved to take part with us, if the imperial troops should invade his states. The elector of Wurtemberg inclined for the coalition, as also did the elector of Baden, their family relations with Russia rendering this course very natural, but their proximity to Strasbourg and Mayence caused them to fear lest they should be made victims; this circumstance gave weight to the efforts of my ministers to attract them to our ranks.

The Austrians enter Bavaria.—The Austrians opened the campaign more maladroitly than ever. They thought to take me by surprise. This was fatal to them. I was prepared to strike on the Thames, if the continent remained quiet, or on the Danube, if the continent provoked me to hostilities, and to renounce my grand enterprise against England. I set out from Paris for Boulogne, announcing to Cobentzel that I only desired a continental peace, and that, full of confidence in the pacific protestations of his master, I was going to give the finishing stroke to my preparations for the descent. I had directed frequent *simulacra* of embarkation, in order to habituate the troops to execute it in the shortest possible time; we had become able to put one hundred and fifty thousand men on board ready for sailing, in half an hour; the *matériel* had already been embarked for a long time; I now ordered these *simulacra* to be redoubled, and an embargo put upon all the ports. An advanced guard of Ney's corps sailed from Montreuil along the coast, to unite at the camp of Boulogne. Soult's entire corps had been embarked for two days; my equipages were also embarked. These measures deceived Cobentzel; he announced to Vienna that in eight days I would be at sea. The Austrians believed him, and immediately inundated Bavaria with eighty-four thousand men, without waiting for the Russians. They thought, by this measure, to force the elector to join their party, which would have reënforced them with twenty thousand men, and moreover enabled them to carry the theatre of war to the Rhine; but in reality this step was calculated to postpone their junction with the grand Russian army, and thus increase their difficulties. Their calculation failed in both respects: Maximilian Joseph, knowing the enemy's projects, prepared to leave Munich, and as soon as the Austrians passed the Inn, he retired to Wurtsbourg with his whole army and his court. The Austrians, nevertheless, continued their march, which had now become a mere extravagance without object. After traversing Bavaria, and crossing the Iser and the Lech, they established themselves on the Danube and the Iller. The Archduke Ferdinand had the nominal command, but he had orders to follow entirely the advice of Mack, whom all Germany believed a great general, although he had already given proof of incapacity in Flanders and in Naples. The Archduke John, with forty thousand men, occupied the Tyrol. Another army of one hundred thousand men, under the orders of the Archduke Charles, advanced on the Adige, ready to invade Italy.

March to the Danube.—The news of the hostile preparations of the cabinet of Vienna and its menacing movements in Bavaria and Italy, reached me almost at the same time as the news of the naval battle between Calder and Villeneuve, and the retreat of the latter on Vigo. Even had the English expedition been my only object, it was now necessary to renounce it. In twenty-four hours my army, ready in every thing, faced to the right, and commenced its march for Germany; an embargo was upon the mail, and our columns, by six days' forced marches, were passing through Lorraine, at the time that it was still thought at Paris they were only at their embarkation. But as I would not leave my immense flotilla exposed to the expeditions of the English, I organized a *corps-d'armée* at Boulogne, with the *bataillons-de-dépôt* of the grand army, and gave the command of it to Brune. Another corps, under Collaud, guarded Antwerp and Flushing; finally, four camps of reserve were established at Strasbourg, Mayence, Juliers, and Alexandria. Marshals Lefébvre and Kellerman organized at Mayence the conscripts destined to the corps of the grand army, and, while waiting to prepare them for the line, formed them into divisions of reserve and of garrison. Independently of these movable forces, it was necessary to secure our other ports from danger, and also to defend all the coasts of France and Holland, and to prepare secondary means in order that all our energy might be directed to the exterior. I caused the establishment of the important institution of national guards, reserving to myself the right of organizing them, and of determining the time and numbers to be called into service. This means might, in case of need, furnish us one hundred thousand men for the defense of the interior: this was much. A conscription of eighty thousand men was decreed as a timely provision for recruits and to keep the active corps up to the complement. Considerable steps were taken to organize, at Strasbourg, transports of artillery, with horses and drivers hired in Alsace, Switzerland, and Lorraine.

Thinking that the English and Russians might resume their project of descent on Holland, or that, at least, they might take possession of Hanover, and, using it as a base, attack the Bavarian Republic, I proposed to Prussia to occupy this electorate, which Bernadotte left to march against Austria; and uncertain what course she might pursue, I charged my brother Louis with the command in Belgium and Holland.

Massena, with fifty thousand men in Italy, had to oppose the double forces of the Archduke Charles. Saint-Cyr went to take possession of Naples and disband their army, before the English and Russians could anticipate him; but a treaty of neutrality having been signed, on the twenty-seventh of September, with the duke of Gallo, the minister of the king of Naples, for securing the states of his master from the English and the coalition, Saint-Cyr had then to evacuate the kingdom in all haste, and march to the Adige, in order to reënforce Massena.

Organization of the Grand Army.—I reserved myself for

the head of the grand army, to punish Mack for the temerity with which he exposed himself to my attacks. The following is the state of this army:

Bavarians; two divisions, Wrede and Deroi.

1st corps, Bernadotte; Drouet's and Rivaud's division of infantry; and Kellerman's (the younger) cavalry.

2d corps, Marmont; divisions of Boudet, Grouchy, and Dumonceau; Guerin's cavalry.

3d corps, Davoust; divisions of infantry of Bisson, Friant, and Gudin; Fauconnet's cavalry.

4th corps, Soult; divisions of infantry of Saint Hilaire, Vandamme, and Legrand; Margaron's cavalry.

5th corps, Lannes; divisions of Suchet, Gazan, and Oudinot, combined grenadiers.

6th corps, Ney; divisions of Dupont, Loison, and Malher; Colbert's cavalry, foot dragoons, commanded by Baraguey d'Hilliers.

7th corps, Augereau; divisions of Desjardins and Mathieu.

Reserve of cavalry, Murat; cuirassiers, divisions of Nansouty, and D'Haupoult; dragoons, divisions of Klein, Walter, Beaumont, and Bourcier; light cavalry, division of Triellard.

Guards, Mortier; eight battalions of foot-guards; Bessières, horse-guards, fourteen squadrons.

Suchet's division at first belonged to Soult's corps, and was afterward detached. A new corps was afterward formed for Mortier, and composed of the divisions of Dupont, Gazan, and Dumonceau.

Passage of the Rhine.—The several columns of this army flew to the Rhine with the greatest rapidity. The reserves of cavalry under the orders of Murat, sustained by the corps of Lannes, passed this river at Kehl, on the twenty-fifth of September. They thus threatened the debouches of the

Black Forest, deceived the enemy, and masked the manœuvres for turning his right. The twenty-sixth of September, the corps of Ney, Soult, and Davoust, also effected their passage; the first debouching opposite Carlsruhe, directed his march on Stuttgard. The elector of Wurtemberg refused to permit them to pass his head-quarters at Louisbourg, and the electoral troops, without orders, having closed to him the gates of Stuttgard, Ney advanced his artillery to force them. General Pfuhl thought it more prudent to open them, and was reprimanded by his master. Soult crossed the river at Spire, directing his course on Heilbronn; and Davoust at Manheim, directing himself on Necker-Els. Marmont passed at Mayence and marched on Wurtzbourg, where he found the corps of Bernadotte, coming from Hanover, united with the Bavarian army of about twenty-five thousand men.

While these preparatory movements were being executed, I took care to attach to myself the elector of Wurtemberg, who was a little exasperated at the manner in which Ney had forced his way into his capital. Soon after my arrival at Louisbourg, I concluded with this prince a treaty which secured me an auxiliary corps of eight thousand men. I had already, some three weeks since, made a similar treaty with the elector of Baden, for a corps of four thousand men That of Hesse-Darmstadt had promised the same number. These troops took no part in the war, but they served to guard my communications, which was much better than having them in the ranks of the enemy.

March on Donawerth.—The total force of my troops on the right bank of the Rhine, including the Bavarians, amounted to one hundred and eighty thousand. I resolved to profit by this superiority to destroy the enemy's army, by throwing myself on his rear, thus cutting off his communications with the Russians, who were approaching by Moravia. The corps of Ney, Soult, and Lannes, the cavalry of Murat, and my guards, were directed toward Donawerth and Dillingen; the corps of Davoust and Marmont marched to Neubourg; and Bernadotte and the Bavarians were directed on Ingolstadt. The two last crossed in their march the principality of Anspach, the possession of Prussia, who prided herself on her neutrality. This circumstance, to which I attached no importance, considering what had occurred in 1796 and 1800, was near embroiling us with Prussia. In 1796, it will be remembered, Jourdan, and the Archduke Charles passed over several parts of the territory made neutral by the Prussians; in 1800, Starray and Augereau fought also near Nuremberg, on the same territory.

Augereau, who was coming from Brest with the seventh corps, having a greater distance to march, was destined to cover our right on the side of the Grisons, and to guard the space between the Rhine and the Upper Danube.

Mack on the Danube.—If the Austrians had committed a grave fault in taking the initiative too soon, they were at least excusable from their hope to force Bavaria into their party; but when the departure of this court from Munich and its army for Wurtzbourg had destroyed this hope, it is difficult to understand why they continued their march to Ulm and stopped there. If they had any information of the rapidity with which my columns flew from Boulogne to the Rhine, they were unpardonable for having compromised the success of the campaign by engaging, in partial combat, forces whose union alone could secure success to the coalition; if they were ignorant of the march of my troops, the thing was still more absurd, for it was known to all France and Germany.

Napoleon turns the Right of the Austrians.—I lost no time in punishing Mack for this blunder. We were established on the Danube, just as we had been, in 1800, on the Po. The conduct of Mack assisted us wonderfully. This famous disciple of Lascy knew not how to take a decisive part. He flattered himself that he could cover the line of the Danube by carrying his right toward Rain under General Kienmayer, his centre to Gunzbourg, and his left under the cannon of Ulm. He thus found himself in battle facing the Rhine, at the very moment that we were debouching on its extremity, in order to assail him in rear. Kienmayer was too weak to prevent us from passing the Danube. On the sixth of October, Vandamme, sustained by the other divisions of Soult, got possession of the bridge of Donawerth; the next day, Murat, with his cavalry, passed to the right bank and pushed forward as far as Rain, after having forced the passage of the Lech. Kienmayer fell back upon Aicha. Davoust and Marmont debouched by Neubourg in the same direction. On the eighth Soult moved directly from Donawerth to Augsbourg. Ney ascended the left bank of the Danube from Dillingen to Gunzbourg; Murat, followed by Lannes, ascended the right bank of the river. Arrived at Wertingen, he found there a corps of twelve battalions which General Auffenberg brought from Innspruck, and which Mack had sent, too late, to succor Kienmayer. Our cavalry, assisted by the grenadiers of Oudinot, dispersed this corps and captured three thousand prisoners. On the other side, Kienmayer did not venture to give battle, but fell back on the Iser. On the ninth, Soult reached Augsbourg, and Marmont marched there also. Davoust moved by Aicha. Murat with his cavalry established himself at Zumarshausen. More than one hundred and twenty thousand men were thus poured like a torrent on the enemy's communications with Vienna.

Mack's Confusion.—Mack, blinded by his confusion, did not at all comprehend our manœuvres; he thought to withdraw himself from the difficulty by a change of front to the rear: he extended his right toward Memmingen, his centre between the Iller and Gunzbourg, and maintained his left under the cannon of Ulm, without any fixed project for warding off the chances which threatened him.* I made my dispositions accordingly. Bernadotte and Davoust received orders to march upon Munich, in order to follow Kienmayer, and to check the Russian army which was coming to his assistance, and had already passed Lintz. Soult moved by Landsberg to Memmingen in order to cut Mack off from the Tyrol. I myself moved on Ulm by the right bank of the Danube, with the cavalry of Murat and the corps of Lannes and Marmont.

Manœuvre to cut him off from Bohemia.—But it was not enough to cut Mack from his base on the Inn, and from the great road to Vienna by Munich; the object of this general being to effect his junction with the Russians, he could easily gain Bohemia, by filing from Ulm by the left of the Danube on Nordlingen and Manheim. This movement was the more to be feared as the enemy, by directing himself on our rear, would have taken all our parks, our depots, and trains; and by destroying the bridges of the Danube have run no risk from us. I had provided against this by reënforcing Ney with Gazan's division, Baraguey d'Hilliers' foot dragoons, and Bourcier's division of cavalry. He was directed to ascend the left bank of the Danube with forty thousand men, for the triple object of covering our communications, of cutting off those of the enemy, and of masking Ulm, the only debouch of the Austrians. However, not to entirely deprive myself of the coöperation of so considerable a force, I directed Ney to get possession of the bridges of the Danube, and to pass over his advanced guards who would cover them, and at the same time keep the marshal advised of events on

* Jomini says that, the Austrians having published nothing respecting the disasters of this campaign, it is impossible to know the object of Mack's operations and of his combinations.

our side, so that he could come and take part in the decisive battle, if it should take place within his reach. He had, on this occasion, a fine affair at Gunzbourg, where he succeeded in gaining possession of the bridge; he also occupied those of Elchingen and Leipheim. His right under Dupont was established at Albeck. The arrival of Murat at Burgau, contributed to secure his success, by taking in reverse the troops which were opposed to him.

Faults of Murat.—Although we were superior in number, these multiplied movements had somewhat scattered my army; and remembering the hot work at Marengo, I thought to avoid its repetition by giving to Murat the corps of Ney and Lannes, and the reserves of cavalry, in order to give more compactness to my detachments. This measure would also allow me to go in person to meet the Russians, if they should debouch on Munich before I could destroy Mack. I had reason to repent this choice: Murat did not comprehend the motives of my instructions to Ney; he thought that the enemy was concentrating in rear of the Iller, in order to base himself on the Tyrol, and ordered the marshal to entirely abandon the left bank of the Danube, so as to advance from Gunzbourg and Elchingen on the Roth, and thence on Ulm and Wiblingen. This was to completely expose the road to Bohemia and our own communications. Fortunately Ney took upon himself the responsibility of partly disobeying Murat's order; he directed the division of Loison to move from Elchingen to the Roth, and prepared to join him by Leipheim at Kissendorf; but he left Dupont and Baraguey d'Hilliers on the left bank of the Danube, notwithstanding the orders of the grand-duke of Berg. I was not informed of this particular till afterward; it gave me a high idea of Ney's military talent. I have since learned that the idea was due to one of his officers.

Mack's Attempts to extricate himself.—Mack, at length

recovered from the stupor into which our bold and rapid manœuvres had plunged him, felt that it was time to seek an issue. A council of war was assembled, and after stormy deliberations, it was decided, they say, that the Archduke Ferdinand should put himself at the head of a corps of the *élite* of twenty thousand men, to open for himself a passage by the route of Heidenheim and Nordlingen. Mack held Ulm with the rest of the forces, so as to favor this movement, flattering himself, undoubtedly, that he would afterward be able to throw himself into the Tyrol. If it be true that the Austrian generals adopted this plan of eccentric retreat, *à la* Bulow, this resolution was a suitable climax to all the folly they had already committed. It was only by throwing four thousand men into Ulm and concentrating all their other forces, that they could now hope to reach either Bohemia or the Tyrol, and not by dispersing their troops in all directions. To act thus was to ruin their army in detail.

Combat of Haslach.—Be that as it may, a corps of twenty-five thousand men left Ulm by the left bank, the same day that Ney, in consequence of Murat's foolish orders, had recalled the division of Loison from Elchingen to the Roth, and had himself left Gunzbourg with the division of Malher to join it; my generals thus seemed to open to the enemy an issue which they could no longer hope to force. As a further addition to these blunders, Baraguey d'Hilliers, charged with effecting a junction with Dupont near Albeck, neglected to do so. Dupont, reaching the village of Haslach alone, on the eleventh of October, with six battalions and three regiments of cavalry, exposed himself to the whole *corps-de-bataille* of Mack. Fortune repaired his faults. The Austrian general thought to extend his wings so as to envelope our little troop; his numerous cavalry moved too far to the left, while Dupont united his efforts on the centre at Jungingen. This village was taken and retaken six times. The

Ninth light, which at Marengo had won the name of *incomparable*, and the brave Thirty-second, the honor of the old army of Italy, immortalized themselves on this occasion. Thanks to so much valor, Dupont pierced the first line of the enemy, enveloped and captured an isolated column, maintained his position till night, retreated before day on Albeck, carrying away with him near three thousand prisoners. He, indeed, left on this bloody field of battle one third of his division, and the cavalry in his rear carried away nine pieces of cannon and his equipages; but he had triumphed with seven thousand men over twenty thousand, and had arrested the enemy's movement; he returned covered with glory and loaded with trophies. Baraguey d'Hilliers, who was to have assisted him, basely halted at Languenau, under the pretext that he would compromise his troops; a strange way of flying to the assistance of his colleague! The next day Ney, led into error by Murat, who always pretended that the battle was to be fought on the Iller, had recalled Dupont to Gunzbourg, in order not to compromise him alone on the left bank.

Napoleon repairs to the Danube.—I learned at Augsburg, on the twelfth, the movements which Murat had ordered Ney to make; I had at first intended to march with Davoust on Munich, where they feared the approach of the Russians and of the Archduke John; but I felt that without my presence on the Danube they would only commit blunders; I therefore proceeded in all haste to Pfaffenhofen, and directed my guard on Gunzbourg. Marmont marched on the Iller; Lannes was to guard Weissenhorn and Pfuhl; Soult fell back from Landsberg on Memmingen, to cut the road to the Tyrol. I received, on the morning of the thirteenth, an account of the unequal combat sustained by Dupont; there was no time to be lost; I hastened to Kissendorf, the head-quarters of Ney, to whom I had already sent orders by Berthier to resume his position at Elchingen, not understanding what motives had induced him to abandon it. This marshal had just left for Fallheim, to retake the bridge of Elchingen, where was heard a brisk cannonade.

The Austrians occupy Elchingen.—Mack, learning, on the twelfth, of Dupont's disappearance, caused the corps of Werneck to pursue him to Albeck. The corps of Laudon was to advance to Elchingen, in order to mask this debouch. The Austrian general knew not which way to turn; no sooner had he disposed of Dupont, than he learned that Soult had fallen on his extreme right at Memmingen, to invest the division of Spangen in that city, and drive the troops of Wolfskehl on Ochsenhausen. He sent General Jellachich from Ulm, on the thirteenth, to cover this route, and if possible to deliver Spangen. He was now too late; surrounded by twenty-five thousand men in a city inclosed by walls and an old parapet, destitute of provisions and munitions, Spangen surrendered, on the thirteenth, with about seven thousand Austrians. The idea of pushing Werneck on Heidenheim, while Jellachich moved toward Biberach, is proof enough of the character of the enemy with whom we were engaged.

They burn the Bridge of Elchingen.—The Austrian divisions of Laudon and Riesch, encamped on the heights of Elchingen, were to protect the march of Werneck and also, without doubt, that of the army which was to follow him. This was their advanced guard, which, at the moment of my arrival at Kissendorf, caused to be attacked, on the thirteenth of October, the bridge of Elchingen, where General Malher had only one regiment; the officer who commanded there caused one of the arches to be cut in order to protect himself against superior forces, and fell back on the right bank. Ney, seeing realized every thing that he had predicted to Murat, hastened to assemble the division of Malher on this point, and marched there himself with that of Loison. The Austrians, threatened in their turn by the approach of these forces, could do no better than burn the remainder of the bridge, which, however, they executed only in part.

Ney repairs the Faults already Committed.—Ney made every preparation to repair this bridge, so as to force a passage and return to the left bank, where he had been three days before. I, therefore, found on my arrival all the evil repaired, and my dispositions anticipated and perfectly executed: I had now only to combine the means of causing the rest of the army to conform to them. Lannes, who occupied Pfuhl and Kirchberg opposite Ulm, was to prepare to sustain Ney if necessary; Marmont received orders to relieve Lannes, and to put him in a commanding position on the Iller. Soult, as soon as he could force the surrender of the Austrians whom he had inclosed in Memmingen, directed himself toward Achstetten, in order to cut the road to Biberach. Dupont, receiving orders to move again from Brenz on Albeck, would favor Ney in the attack of Elchingen. Every thing was thus arranged for the entire investment of the enemy. Whatever course he might take, his loss was certain after the fourteenth of October.

Battle of Elchingen.—For several days the weather had been frightful; we were in mud up to our knees; the Danube had overflowed its banks; the bridge, partially burned, had been but partly repaired. On the morning of the fourteenth of October the weather cleared up a little: Ney passed, *en grand tenue,* at daybreak, with the voltigeurs of the Sixth light, and the grenadiers of the Thirty-ninth. The village of Elchingen rises in an amphitheatre on a small hill at some distance from the Danube; it is surrounded by gardens enclosed with walls which successively command each other; a vast convent crowns the summit. It is one of the most formidable posts that can be imagined. It was necessary to get possession of the first houses in order to protect the passage and the formation of the troops; afterward to drive the enemy from house to house, as our platoons debouched. Such an operation, executed in the face of fifteen thousand men and forty pieces of cannon, required all the intrepidity of Ney, who never exhibited a more brilliant courage.*

After several undecisive attacks, the Sixth light carried the convent by escalade, and the whole division established itself on the plateau, gaining the left of the enemy by the Chapel of St. Wolffgang. Here was fought a pitched battle; Ney saw that it was necessary to effect a change of front in order to save himself from being driven into the Danube, and to clear the passage; but in extending his right on the heights it was necessary to secure his left, the decisive point which the Austrians held by means of a wood, and whence they might recapture Elchingen. The intrepid Sixty-ninth regiment is directed to carry this wood, which is to become the safeguard of our new line. It rushes in with enthusiasm; terror precedes its steps, and death accompanies them; every resistance is overthrown. At the same time the cavalry of Colbert and Bourcier makes brilliant charges, sustained by the infantry of Loison; soon the division of Malher passes the bridge and enables Ney to follow up his success. The enemy is pierced and driven by Kesselbrun on Haslach in the direction of Ulm, with a loss of twenty cannon and three thousand prisoners: a detached corps only succeeds in gaining the road to Albeck, where every thing leads us to believe that the division of Laudon is intending to retire in order to follow Werneck. Ney, learning the presence of an enemy's corps on the right, deems it unsafe to pass the night near

* Jomini says that Ney had a warm altercation with Murat respecting the orders of the latter; "and as if to defy Murat in the exhibition of bravery, Ney on this occasion put himself in full uniform at the head of his column and directed each battalion himself; present wherever danger was to be found, he seemed to seek death; but death fled from him."

Haslach; and, for the better protection of the bridges, he returns to the heights of Albeck, where he establishes his head-quarters. While Ney is gathering his dearly bought laurels, General Dupont is fighting between Albeck and Languenau against the infantry of Werneck, who seems desirous of renewing the offensive.

Investment of Ulm.—On the morning of the fifteenth, the armies are still in presence of each other, but in such a position that the ruin of the enemy is inevitable. Mack, with his left now become his right, occupies the heights of Lahr and Mohringen before Ulm; Werneck extends to the north from Albeck toward Nerenstetten. The rain, which had ceased on the fourteenth, begins again worse than ever; notwithstanding the unfavorable weather our troops redouble their ardor. Ney directs the two divisions of Loison and Malher on Haslach; the cavalry of my guard sustains him. Dupont, who is still isolated, finds himself between Albeck and Languenau, opposed to superior forces. Lannes passes the bridge of Elchingen; and seeks to reëstablish that of Thalfingen, in order to second Ney: Marmont replaces him on the heights of Pfuhl and at the bridge of Kirchberg, on the Iller, Soult continues to approach Ulm from the south by the road to Biberach; finally, Murat with the cavalry also debouches from Elchingen on the heights of the left bank. It may be seen from these positions that the Austrians, turning their backs to the Rhine, have taken the place of my army, which in turn seems to have come from Vienna and to have taken the place of the Austrians. It was a repetition of Marengo, with still greater chances in our favor. The combat was not long; Mack, giving up all hope of holding out in advance of Ulm, retired within the place. His rear-guard was closely pressed, and everywhere the frightened enemy fled in disorder. Ulm, surrounded by a well bastioned enciente, and ditches full of water, is situated in the bottom of a valley commanded by the heights of Michelsberg and Tuilerie. Kray had established there, in 1800, a strong intrenched camp, the only system by which the place can be made susceptible of a long defense. Since then the exterior works had been destroyed: Mack had begun to rebuild them, but the work was only just commenced. Ney threw himself at the head of Malher's division on Michelsberg; the redoubt was carried; Loison followed up this advantage; Suchet carried the work on the height of the Tuilerie.

Ney's Attack on Ulm.—Being now master of Michelsberg, from which he commanded the city, and seeing some Austrians still on the outside, Ney pushed forward the Fiftieth regiment against the Stuttgard gate. His object was to terrify the enemy and then summon him to surrender, no disposition being made to sustain this attack. The brave Fiftieth, piqued at having had no part in the affair of Elchingen, attacked the enemy with great impetuosity, penetrated pell-mell with him to the gate; a battalion threw itself even into the intrenchments on the right. Suchet, seeing this attack, sent the Seventeenth light to sustain it, without knowing what was Ney's object. This regiment seconded the efforts of the Fiftieth at the gate; but the Austrians seeing from the top of the rampart that the effort was isolated, took courage, captured the first platoons which had entered, and closed the portcullis. Ney, satisfied with this demonstration, sent an officer to summon Ulm, and threatened Mack with a more serious attack.

Murat marches against Werneck.—During these audacious attempts, Dupont found himself pressed between Albeck and Languenau by Werneck. It is not known whether, being cut off from Ulm by the combat of Elchingen, he sought to effect a junction with Mack, or wished to get possession of Languenau to secure his retreat. I at first could hardly believe the report of Werneck's operations. Seeing the actual state of things, and that the enemy was decidedly cut in two, I ordered Murat to march by Albeck with three divisions of dragoons to second Dupont. I took every disposition to reënforce the posts of Gunzbourg and Donawerth by the foot dragoons, and I attached myself more particularly to the destruction of that half of the enemy's army which had taken refuge in Ulm, satisfied that the other could not escape our squadrons. The Archduke Ferdinand had entered there with Mack; but this prince, seeing the fate which would inevitably befall the wreck of his army, resolved to put himself at the head of his remaining cavalry and throw himself by Geislingen on Aalen, to rejoin the infantry of Werneck, and with him to gain Bohemia.*

Mack summoned to Surrender.—The next day, the sixteenth, I caused some shells to be thrown into Ulm; I then sent Colonel Segur to summon Mack to surrender, threatening him with the assault and destruction of his garrison. I offered him six days. Mack demanded eight; he pretended to be sustained by the Russians, whom he believed to be at Dachau; he boasted to the messenger that he was firmly resolved to eat up his three thousand horses rather than surrender; this was a confession that he was in want of provisions, and I had calculated that his invasion had been too rapid to allow him to collect large magazines. All that he had brought with him, or had levied in the country, was hardly sufficient for the fifteen days that he had laid idle on the Iller. Segur was sent to Ulm on the seventeenth; Berthier soon followed him, and after some parleys, Mack sent the Prince of Lichtenstein to my head-quarters to complete the arrangement. I had painted to him in the darkest colors

* Jomini says there is still an uncertainty respecting this resolution of the Archduke, and as the Austrians have published no account of the affair, he is obliged to trust to general rumors. Some say that the council of war was called just after the affair of Gunzbourg on the tenth; others that it was called on the night of the fourteenth and fifteenth, after the combat of Elchingen.

his desperate situation; I spoke to him of the horrors of an assault, reminding him that at Jaffa the obstinacy of a Scheik had forced me to destroy four thousand Turks; he returned fully convinced that they had no alternative but to capitulate.

Conditional Capitulation.—Certain that Munich was occupied by Bernadotte, Wrede, and Davoust; that the Archduke Ferdinand was pursued on Nordlingen by superior forces; and that the Russians could not yet think of passing the Inn; in a word, seeing that it was absolutely impossible for him to be succored, the Austrian marshal consented to give up the place on the twenty-fifth of October, if he were not succored before that time: in the mean while he surrendered one gate to Marshal Ney. I instantly detached the corps of Lannes on Aalen to second Murat in his pursuit of the Archduke.

Defeat of Werneck.—Hardly had twenty-four hours elapsed since this shameful transaction of Mack, before we received news of the signal advantage gained by my brother-in-law over the troops of the Archduke Ferdinand. Indefatigable in success, Murat first overtook the rear-guard of Werneck, at Languenau, on the sixteenth. To discover it, and, in concert with Dupont, to charge and overthrow it, was for him an affair of an instant. Two thousand prisoners fell into his power. He started again before day in pursuit of the principal corps on the road to Neresheim. Embarrassed by a convoy of five hundred carriages of artillery and equipages, Werneck could not fail to be overtaken by our soldiers, who flew on the wings of victory; forced to receive a disadvantageous engagement, he lost another thousand men. The archduke, despairing of escaping with his infantry, again separated from it with his cavalry, and took the road to Nuremberg.

He Surrenders.—Being assailed on the eighteenth, at

Trochtelfingen, near Nordlingen, cut off and surrounded on all sides, with his forces scattered and destitute of every thing, Werneck capitulated with about eight thousand men. The public opinion accused these old warriors, illustrious in many battle-fields, of having thus laid down their arms before forces about equal in number: the fact is, cavalry, inferior in numbers can not envelop good infantry, supplied with cannon. The great convoy which had filed to the left was taken the same day at Topfingen by a brigade of dragoons.

Surrender of Mack.—Informed of these successes the same evening, I saw the advantages I could draw from them. It was important for me to accelerate a *dénouement;* the corps which were investing Ulm were in want of every thing. We had made our rapid marches without any magazines; in truth, we passed over so vast an extent of surface, and through a country so very rich, that our troops had been in want of nothing while on the march; but in position, with concentrated masses, the case was very different. Moreover, I was impatient to march to the Inn, for fear that Bernadotte and Davoust would be alone exposed to the approach of the Russian army. I invited Mack to my head-quarters, and he was polite enough to come. I informed him of the capture of Werneck; I demonstrated to him that Bernadotte and Wrede had driven Kienmayer beyond the Inn, taking from him two thousand prisoners; that Soult, having passed the Danube above Ulm, had occupied in force all the roads to the Tyrol and the Voralberg; finally, I proposed to him to surrender me the place, without waiting a delay which had now become useless and without object. The poor man had so lost his senses that he fell into the snare. He forgot that he had just published a proclamation threatening the first man who dared to speak to him of capitulation, and that he had boasted that he would eat his last horse before he would surrender. Blinded by the captious proposition of leaving at Ulm the entire corps of Ney, estimated sufficient for the blockade, he thought to save his honor and his reputation by a ridiculous combination by which the lowest of his soldiers could not have been duped. He therefore consented to surrender Ulm the next day. Under the pretext of paralyzing Ney's corps at Ulm, Mack anticipated the period of his capitulation by six days, thus rendering disposable the corps of Soult, Marmont, and the guard, and also leaving me at liberty to direct my attention elsewhere; he seemed impatient to put the seal to his humiliation.

In consequence of this additional article, thirty thousand Austrians filed before me on the morning of the nineteenth, conducted by sixteen generals; they laid down their arms to be transported to France. Many of these soldiers, exasperated, threw away their arms on leaving the city, rather than surrender them in form, thus showing what indignation the blunders of their leaders had excited in the men. Forty colors, sixty cannon, three thousand cavalry horses, were additional trophies of this great event. Among the number of the generals who were taken prisoners, were Klenau, Giulay, Gottesheim, the two princes of Lichtenstein, whose valor and talents are attested on every page of our history.

I had already within the last ten years gained many brilliant successes; but never had I enjoyed a triumph like that, of an entire army defiling before me and laying down their arms, their colors, and their cannon. Placed on an eminence which commands the city and all the basin of the Danube, I could contemplate at my ease the spectacle which promised me such high destinies. Mack took position near me with his generals. While their columns were filing past, I consoled them on the vicissitudes of war; I deplored the blindness of the cabinet which had sent them to their destruction for the interest of England alone. Entirely devoted to my projects of making a descent on England, I asked nothing of

Austria; it was vessels, colonies, commerce that I wanted. What interest then could Austria have in shielding from my blows a power which caused all the troubles of the continent? So far it was well enough, but drawn on by my subject, I accompanied these remarks with some indirect threats against this imperial house: "Every empire," said I, "has its end, and the emperor may have reason to fear that the time of the house of Lorraine has already come." I had good reason to speak proudly after events so glorious which were entirely due to the skillfulness of my combinations; but this sentiment had no suitable place in my discourse. I wished to give the alarm at Vienna and to dictate peace. I have always been full of confidence in my superiority, but I was never blinded by pride. Nevertheless, this sortie made for a pardonable object, gave offense by its phraseology, and I felt that it might as well have been omitted.

Fate of the Wreck of Mack's Army.—Of Mack's entire army, the corps of Kienmayer, the Archduke Ferdinand, with three thousand horse, and the division of Jellachich, had alone been able to avoid destruction; this last division, having escaped from Ulm on the road to Fusen, and stopping to guard these defiles of the Tyrol, was also soon surrounded. The archdude, after having abandoned Werneck to his fate, followed at first the road to Nuremberg, then fell back on Altmuhl and Donawerth, to gain the road to Cham. He directed his rear-guard to take the road to Nuremberg in order to deceive Murat; he thus succeeded in effecting his escape, and reached Bohemia with two or three thousand horse.

Posterity, more enlightened than we are respecting the combinations of Mack and of the cabinet of Vienna, will assign to each the blame which properly belongs to them. It has been said that Mack had in his army a party more powerful than himself, and that he was opposed and disobeyed, and his army scattered in spite of himself. This is all very possible; but a general-in-chief should never consent to become the instrument of the destruction of his army; when placed between dishonor and glory, between the safety of the state and the loss of his army, he should be capable of taking a part worthy of himself. Mack, after being shut up within Ulm, might at least have attempted a sortie to follow Jellachich toward Fussen; it is always shameful to capitulate without an effort to escape.

An army of eighty thousand men was thus destroyed at a single blow without any great battle, and without its having cost me six thousand men. This commencement of the campaign was truly brilliant, but nothing could be decisive till we had beaten the Russians, who were approaching by forced marches to the assistance of their allies. Even before Mack had surrendered Ulm, I directed Soult to march for Landsberg and Munich; Lannes and Murat took the same direction immediately after the defeat of the Archduke Ferdinand.

Prussia threatens to join the Coalition. — Notwithstanding all our successes my position was becoming more complicated. The king of Prussia, who, on the eighth of September, had ordered out sixty battalions and as many squadrons to make demonstrations against the Russians on the Vistula, had just received the news of the violation of his territory of Anspach by our troops. The policy of the last ten years is instantly abandoned; a general cry for vengeance is raised in all his monarchy. The Prussian cabinet orders the formation of four corps at Hof, Heldesheim, Munster, and the reserve at Berlin. One division enters Hanover, now abandoned by the troops of Bernadotte, and reëstablishes there the government of the elector; at the same time notes are addressed to me demanding satisfaction for the violation of neutral territory. Nevertheless, the entire destruction of Mack's army, suspends for a moment this warlike order of Prussia. I rather expected this result; I felt certain of the success of my operations as soon as Mack had taken position near Ulm, and I thought, in authorizing the march of my troops, that I should have plenty of time and means to satisfy Frederick William, should my plan succeed.

Napoleon directs his Forces on the Inn.—To scatter the storm which was gathering about us, it was more urgent than ever to profit by the immense advantages which I had just gained, and the ascendency which they were calculated to give me over the first Russian army, which, by the disaster of Mack, was to be exposed in the same manner to our blows. In fact, Kutusof had just arrived with forty thousand men at Braunau on the Inn, where he formed a junction with the corps of Kienmayer which Bernadotte and Wrede had pursued and cut up in two combats. General Merfeldt had joined it with some reënforcements and taken the command. The first movement of the enemy was to advance on Haag; but the news of the capitulation of Ulm did not long leave them under the comfortable illusion of being able to resume the offensive. I had no sooner finished the directions for sending our prisoners to France, and for fortifying Augsburg sufficiently to secure it against an attack, with a good *tête-de-pont* on the Lech, than I left post haste, on the evening of the twenty-fourth, for Munich. After remaining here three days, I hastened to the Inn with the well-founded hope of treating Kutusof as I had done his predecessor. Of course I expected a greater resistance, but the disproportion of the means was such that I could not doubt the result. Soult and Marmont had also taken the road to the Inn. Lannes, whom the surrender of Werneck had rendered disposable, soon fell back on Bavaria, and Murat, although he had gone to Nuremberg in pursuit of the wrecks of Prince Ferdinand, threw himself with his usual activity by Newmark on Ratisbon, and arrived, almost as soon as I did, on the Inn.

Passage of the Inn, the Salza, and the Traun.—Augereau had passed the Rhine at Hunigen on the twenty-sixth of October ; I left to this marshal and Ney, in concert with the Bavarian division of General Deroi, the task of destroying the corps remaining in the Tyrol. Every thing being prepared for the passage of the Inn, we advanced, on the twenty-eighth of October, in three columns. Bernadotte, sustained by Marmont, passed at Wasserbourg, and directed himself on Saltzbourg, whose defense had been assigned to the corps of Merfeldt. Davoust found the Russians at the bridge of Muhldorf, which they had burned ; he restored it and reached the Salza at Burghausen ; but having no bridge for passing this river, he was obliged to stop and repair the one which had been destroyed ; this gave the allies two days' march the start of him. The reserve and Soult followed the same road. Lannes, at the left, marched from Landshut on Braunau. Everywhere the enemy, seeing the danger to which he would be exposed by a general engagement, retired before our columns, after exchanging a few rounds of cannon. He evacuated, without resistance, the place Braunau, whose bastioned enciente had not even been armed, so confident had the Austrians been of invading France, instead of seeing us at Vienna. Braunau was an excellent post for securing a base on the Inn, in concert with Saltzbourg which also was respectably fortified, although its works were commanded by the surrounding heights. We might then regard the Salza and the Inn as an excellent base of operations, since Bavaria, Ulm, Ingolstadt, and all the interval to the Rhine was within our possession and in our favor.

Having passed the Salza and the Inn, Murat took the lead of the pursuit with his cavalry ; on the twenty-ninth, he had an engagement at Ried with the rear-guard of Keinmayer ;

the thirty-first, a more serious affair took place at Lambach; we here found ourselves engaged, for the first time, with the Russian infantry; a corps of four thousand men wished to keep their possession on this side of the Traun, in order to give their equipages time to pass this defile. The division of Bisson assailed them; the Seventeenth of the line wished to revenge itself for the affair of Trebbia, and it did so with glory; it nevertheless found worthy adversaries; it was only after a severe fight, in which Bisson was wounded, that the enemy, while beginning the retreat, saw himself driven back with great loss.

Napoleon's March on Vienna.—I resolved to pursue my march on Vienna. Certain critics have blamed this; they think I should have rested on the Inn till I could collect new forces; they do not hesitate to pronounce my march on Austerlitz an extravagance. The principal reason given for this opinion is that a Prussian army was threatening to move on the Upper Danube. For the satisfaction of these critics, I will say that I always fully considered these movements. Time was requisite for an army to come from Berlin to Ulm, especially as this army had begun to move against the Russians on the Vistula, and, benumbed by ten years' peace, was incapable of immediately taking the field. The rule of war the most indisputable is, to strike an enemy who is unprepared. Kutusof had exposed himself to my blows, and it was necessary to punish him. By remaining on the Inn, I should have permitted the Archduke Charles, Ferdinand, Keinmayer, and Kutusof to unite in Upper Austria with the army of Alexander, and two hundred thousand men, well-provided with every thing, would then have been opposed to me; without including the Prussians, whom my position on the Inn would not have prevented from advancing to the Upper Danube. Might they not as well have advised me to return to Strasbourg? In fact, if I had remained at Passau, there was nothing to oppose the march of the duke of Brunswick by Nuremberg on Ulm. To prevent such an operation it was necessary either to retreat behind the Rhine, or to anticipate the enemy by attacking the Russians; the one course was disgraceful, the other glorious; there could be no hesitation. I judged more wisely than my critics in deciding that it was for my interest to fight successively those distant corps. I was superior in battles; I ought therefore to seek them. If I lost a battle, I might then fall back to the Danube or submit to the mediation of Prussia, whom I should then render arbiter of negotiations.

By occupying Vienna, I would intimidate Berlin; I would profit by the immense resources of Austria; I would destroy all concert between the Russian army and that of the Archduke Charles; I would become master of all the movements. It requires a very strong desire for aspersion to draw conclusions as false as those who have censured me for this project. If the Prussians marched into Swabia, the Archduke Charles into Upper Austria, and the Emperor Alexander on the Danube, to take position on the Inn was to select a point such that all these three masses might concert their operations and from some common object. Grant that this position had been advisable, if the motive had been to secure ourselves from being turned by the Prussians; but then we should have been turned on the Inn, as well as at Vienna, after the enemy had placed himself on the Upper Danube and on our communications with France. Besides, when I decided to march on Vienna, I did not yet know what part Prussia would take. She had talked very loud, but when one wishes to go to war, he makes less noise about it; moreover, I knew that Prussia really wished to obtain her object by threats. I intended to offer her reasonable satisfaction; but there was still time enough, for it was not till the middle of November that she appeared seriously disposed to join our enemies.

The Emperor Alexander repairs to Berlin.—The Emperor Alexander, informed of the sensation produced at the court of Berlin by the affair of Anspach, thought proper to repair in person to that city, certain of engaging, by his seducing manners, a prince who had resisted all the seductions of his diplomacy. A treaty was signed, on the third of November, between these two powers; but I did not know of this before the arrival of Count Giulay at my headquarters at the gates of Vienna.

We will return to my movements on this capital. I followed, with the mass of my forces, the right bank of the Danube. Two corps marched by the mountains, as much to cover the march as to turn the large rivers that intersect this route. We pressed the enemy so close that in spite of his excellent position on the Traun, he did not arrest our march for a single moment, but abandoned to us the city of Lintz with its fine bridge over the Danube. It was not difficult to see the advantages to be derived from this. I immediately resolved to send across a corps of twenty thousand men commanded by Marshal Mortier,* with orders to descend the left bank, so as to threaten the Russians with the loss of their communications with Moravia, and thus force them to surrender to us without opposition the strong positions which defended the approaches to Vienna. Should they persist in maintaining their position, this corps would get possession of their bridges, cut them entirely from Moravia, and thus complete their investment. To make sure of this operation, Captain Lostanges, of the navy, was directed to form a considerable flotilla of boats on the Danube, and descend this river at high-water.

Massena's Operations in Italy.—While my vast designs

* This corps, as has already been said, was composed of the division of Dupont, detached from Ney's corps, that of Gazan, from Lannes' corps, and the Batavian division of General Dumonceau, detached from the second corps.

were developing themselves with a success that even astonished myself, my army in Italy was no less fortunate, and had accomplished with the same precision the task which had devolved on it. The Austrians had committed three capital faults in their plan of campaign ; the first, in engaging offensively their weak point ; the second, in remaining inactive in Italy with their strong force ; the third, in employing an army in the Tyrol, where it remained, waiting its turn, a mere spectator of the defeat of the others. The Archduke Charles had above one hundred thousand men, without including the garrisons and the corps of the Tyrol. It is probable that this army was not prepared at the beginning of the campaign, otherwise it would be difficult to see why it did not cross the Adige the very day that Mack passed the Inn. Perhaps the archduke waited for the junction of Kutusof and Mack on the Lech ; but this would have been a no less false combination. *In war it is always necessary to act wherever you are better prepared and stronger than your enemy.* The archduke, by taking the initiative, had thrown Massena behind the Mincio and perhaps behind the Po. If this success had not saved Mack, even if it had increased the distance which this prince had been compelled to pass over to come to the assistance of the threatened monarchy, it would nevertheless have made a happy diversion by the beginning of October, and the archduke, informed by the Tyrol of the disaster of Ulm, might have fallen back on the Carinthia more at his ease, and without being pressed, as he actually was. But instead of taking the initiative, they gave this advantage to Massena. The armies were separated by the Adige, which, since the treaty of Luneville, had formed the boundary between the two empires ; the city of Verona was cut in two parts ; we occupied that on the right bank, and the Austrians the other half, with the strong castles. They had cut two arches of the bridge.

Instructions to Massena.—At the moment of the passage of the Rhine by my army, I thought that Mack would either be destroyed or driven back on the Inn, and that, sooner or later, the archduke would be forced to make a retrograde movement. To deprive him of the passage of the Adige, or at least to be better prepared ourselves for an attack, I had directed Massena to get possession of that part of Verona which belonged to Austria, to rebuild the bridges and establish himself at St. Michel, in a position closed in by the Adige and the mountains, where the numerical superiority of the enemy would be of little advantage to him; at least so that he would not venture to pass the Adige lower down; to do this would have been one of those audacious movements, which we were not accustomed to see on his side. Massena acquitted himself perfectly in the delicate task; he got possession of Verona and the bridges, on the seventeenth of October, and debouched conformably to my orders. The archduke, more occupied with his own security than with the conquest of Italy, had covered with intrenchments the celebrated position of Caldiero and Colognola, formed, as is known, by the spur of the Tyrol mountains, which blocks up the road to Vicenza, and slopes down insensibly to the Adige. These heights, bristling with vines, trees, rocks, and redoubts, seemed impregnable: Massena remained before them from the eighteenth to the twenty-ninth of October; and the archduke, seeing that the events in Swabia took away all hopes of success in Italy, thought it unnecessary to sacrifice his men in driving him beyond the Adige.

Passage of the Adige and Battle of Caldiero.—Massena, hearing, on the twenty-eighth, of the capitulation of Ulm, and the destruction of Mack's army, applied himself to the execution of my orders, which he accomplished with as much audacity as skill. Fearing that the archduke might gain a march or two of him by means of the formidable position which he held, Massena drove in his outposts on the twenty-ninth, and ventured to attack him there the next day. Convinced that all hopes against the centre would be useless, he thought to turn the left by throwing across the Adige the division of Verdier,* reënforced near Zevio, while, at the opposite extremity, Molitor† gained the mountains. Massena, with the divisions of Duhesme and Gardanne, attacked Caldiero; the division of Serras at the extreme left was guarding Rivoli and the space between Lake Garda and the Adige. To assail eighty thousand men in their intrenchments with forty thousand, was more than rash; nevertheless it was near proving successful. Verdier could not execute his passage; Molitor was forced back after heroic efforts Our soldiers, electrified by the news from Ulm, wished to show that they were in no ways inferior to the grand army. The centre fought with fury. The Austrians debouched offensively between their works with a strong mass of the *élite*. Massena attacked the head of the column with grape, and assailed it in flank; exposed to cruel losses, without being able to penetrate the ranks of our braves, it was forced to retreat, and very much cut up: the carnage ended only with the approach of night.

The next day Verdier was more successful in effecting his passage; but isolated in the midst of the enemy, he considered himself very fortunate in effecting a junction with Duhesme, but not without being vigorously assailed and ha-

* Jean Antoine Verdier was born at Toulouse in 1767, and entered the French army at the age of eighteen. He served with distinction in all of Napoleon's campaigns, and was noted for being wounded in nearly every battle He was promoted through the different grades to the rank of lieutenant-general, and in the campaigns of 1813 and 1814 commanded the Franco-Italian corps-d'armée under the Viceroy Eugene. He was always conspicuous for his bravery.

† Gabriel Jean Joseph Molitor was born at Huningen in 1770. He first entered the army as a volunteer, and was made captain in 1791. He rose to the grade of general at the age of twenty-nine. He served with distinction in most of Napoleon's campaigns, and rose to the rank of lieutenant-general. He won the baton of marshal in the campaign of 1813, in Spain.

rassed by the left of the Austrians. On the thirty-first there was a repetition of these bloody scenes—scenes glorious to both sides, but without any results proportioned to the devotion and the animosity of the combatants. Our troops slept, as it were, during these three days, at the foot of the enemy's ramparts. This affair had cost us more than six thousand men; the Austrians had lost at least as many, for at the centre their heavy column had cruelly suffered; two thousand prisoners had been taken.

Retreat of the Archduke.—The archduke had sent away his *impedimenta;* he began his march on the first of November, leaving Frimont to cover his retreat. To favor this operation they pushed forward the brigade of Heister from the heights of Colognola in the direction of the castles of Verona. As soon as Massena perceived the movement of retreat, he made dispositions to profit by the sacrifices he had made so as not to let the enemy escape. Frimont was cut to pieces and driven back behind the Brenta. The brigade of Heister, which had exceeded its instructions in advancing to the castle of Verona, was surrounded and taken prisoners to the number of four thousand men.

Whatever may be the numerical superiority of the army in retreat, the duties of the rear-guard are none the less difficult; for it is always singly exposed to all the efforts of the enemy; as the army seeks to accelerate its retreat, it is never disposed to delay its movements to come to the assistance of its engaged corps. The Brenta, the Piave, the Tagliamento, the Isonzo, facilitated the retreat of the archduke, who finally reached Laybach without having been very seriously cut up, but always hemmed in so close that he could not move with all the celerity demanded by the circumstances. The only serious trouble that he experienced was that the corps of his right, engaged in the mountains of Sette-Comuni and in the gorges of the Brenta, were for a moment cut off, and had to throw themselves by Belluno and Primolan to gain the valley of the Drave. A very lively combat of the rear-guard took place, on the twelfth of November, at the passage of the Tagliamento. The archduke halted there to decide whether he should march by Tarvis and Villach in order to join the Archduke John, and move with him on Saltzbourg; but the news of our impetuous march on Vienna had decided him to take the road to Laybach. The archduke had thrown into Venice a strong garrison, which, by its advantageous position, might give much trouble to Massena. The corps of St. Cyr coming from Naples to the Adige fortunately supplied him with the means of observing this place, and of continuing his march. The grand army pursued its march with an ardor which seemed to redouble with its fatigues, although the cold had now become pretty severe, and from Lambach the ground and the roads were covered with snow.

Napoleon at Lintz.—I stopped at Lintz two days, for several motives: the first to dispatch Mortier across the Danube with his corps; the second, to await the elector of Bavaria. We had moved with so much velocity that this respectable prince, a refugee, as it were, at Wurtzburg, had not been able to meet me on his return to Munich. He now came to congratulate me on the triumphs I had gained, and to which he had contributed his share, and at the same time to concert with me respecting future operations. I engaged him to unite some detachments for observing the western frontier of Bohemia, in concert with Baraguey d'Hilliers.* The division

* Louis Baraguey d'Hilliers was born at Paris in 1764. He was an officer at the breaking out of the Revolution, and served as brigadier-general under Custine and Menou, but afterward fell into disgrace. In 1796 he joined the army of Italy, and in 1797 was made a general-of-division. In 1804 and 1805 he commanded the cavalry of the reserve, and distinguished himself in the brilliant operations of the campaign of Ulm. He afterward served in Italy, Spain, and the campaign of 1812, in Russia, but died during the retreat.

of Deroy, charged with the reduction of Kufstein, was afterward to take possession of the Tyrol conjointly with Ney. A point more delicate claimed all my solicitude. The Russians, English, and Swedes had just landed in Hanover, and Prussia, instead of covering us on that side, was assuming a menacing attitude. We had in those countries merely the single garrison of Hameln, and it was to be feared that Holland might become the object of the coalition. I announced with great formality the organization of an army of the north, under my brother Louis, which was to be composed of six divisions, independently of the corps of Augereau, who would leave Swabia to march to the low countries by Mayence. I even circulated the report that I myself was going to Amsterdam, and had directed a palace to be prepared for my reception.

Propositions for an Armistice.—While at Lintz, I also received a message from the emperor of Austria; this prince, informed by Count Giulay of what had taken place at Ulm, and my conversation with Mack, and of the demoralization of his armies, and the disasters caused to the country by the war, sent this general to me to demand an armistice and to propose peace. The emperor himself came to Molk to accelerate negotiations. This step might be sincere, but I had reasons to doubt it. How could I grant a suspension of arms which would allow the allies to unite their three armies on the Danube, and give Prussia time to enter Bohemia or Bavaria? How could I trust to the sincerity of a pacific overture under such circumstances? To inspire me with a confidence so blind, there was only one means; that of giving by the armistice certain pledges, by agreeing immediately upon the preliminaries of peace, and by sending away the armies whose reunion might become threatening to me, if I did not profit by the advantages of my position to prevent it. I required that the Russians should return to Poland, that

Austria should disband the *levées-en-masse* in Hungary, and yield to me Venice and the Tyrol; otherwise I should be forced to continue my operations on Vienna. Great astonishment was manifested at these propositions, as though I had left my camp at Boulogne to fly with one hundred and fifty thousand men to the Inn and destroy a powerful Austrian army, and then return just as I had come, without gaining the slightest advantages. Certainly, if Austria had been willing to instantly quit the enemy's ranks and place herself among the number of my allies, and renew the treaty of 1756, with only such alterations as the change of circumstances required, I should have been unjust to strip her of her territory; I ought, under such circumstances, to have left her the Tyrol and Venice. But such was not the case; Austria left the enemy's ranks merely to gain time and to recruit herself, until a more opportune moment for recommencing the war. Perhaps I might have joined to the demand of these two provinces the proposition of afterward increasing the territory of Austria, if she had consented to the alliance. In fact these conditions, though not at all out of proportion to my success, appeared rather hard to the cabinet of Vienna, which was expecting the assistance of the grand Russian army, and of the armies of the Archduke Charles and John, without including the support which Prussia was promising to the coalition. Nevertheless, this negotiation did not retard our march for a single moment.

Operations of Murat and Davoust.—The enemy had abandoned to us the Ems; Murat, Lannes, and Soult pushed him lively on Amstetten. Here the Prince of Bagration*

* Prince Bagration was of Georgian origin, and first distinguished himself under Suwarrow, of whom (in the words of that marshal) he afterward became the right arm. He won great reputation in the campaigns of 1806 and 1807. In 1812 he commanded the second corps of the Russian army. He was wounded at the battle of Moskwa, where he was greatly distinguished, and died soon after from the effects of his wounds.

made an obstinate stand, on the sixth of November, in order to give Kutusof time to file past. A combat took place in the woods, corps to corps, between the Russian grenadiers and those of Oudinot. Our soldiers, more intelligent, more impetuous, more alert, and better armed, triumphed over the bitter obstinacy of their valiant adversaries; these, being forced to retreat, were overthrown by the hussars who cut off several hundred prisoners. On the seventh, Murat pushed them on as far as Molk, which place the emperor of Austria had but just left.

The valley of the Danube, closed in at the south by the mountains of the Tyrol and Styria, offers only one great road below Lintz; this road runs along the river at a greater or less distance from the stream. A lateral road runs by the foot of the mountains on Steyer and Waydhoffen; but here it turns to the left toward St. Polten and rejoins the great road so as to avoid the terrible chain of the Wilde-Alpen, a spur of which forms the Wiener-Wold, a woody chain which cuts the valley transversely between St. Polten and Vienna, extending quite to the Danube. The first of these cities is therefore situated this side of the Wiener-Wold, and at the mouth of the defiles; a sharp angle closed in by the river Trasen, offers to an army the best position for covering Vienna on this side. I had every reason to believe that the enemy would receive battle here, especially as the second Russian army could here effect a junction by Krems. In order to turn this position, I directed Davoust, Marmont, and Bernadotte on the road from Steyer; but on learning the difficulty of the route and the scarcity of provisions for an army in so wild a country, the latter returned to the valley of the Danube; Marmont received orders to descend from Steyer to Leoben, and Davoust to continue his march as far as Lilienfeld in order to descend on Vienna. This marshal ascended with great difficulty the rocky mountains which separate the St. Gaming from Maria-Zel, a real chamois country, which name it bears; his advanced guard fell unexpectedly upon the columns of Merfeldt, who had undoubtedly taken the road to Leoben for fear of falling near St. Polten into the midst of my army. To fall on this column, cut it in two, drive one part on Neuhaus, and capture three thousand prisoners, was for the braves of the first corps but the work of an hour. The wreck of Merfeldt regained Neustadt in the greatest confusion.

Kutusof passes the Danube.—The battle which I expected at St. Polten did not take place. Kutusof,* whose troops were cut up and reduced to thirty-five thousand men, thought, and most correctly too, that by passing the Danube at Krems, he would get rid of a hot pursuit which daily cost him some of his brave troops, and besides would shorten some four days the distance he had to march in order to reach Brunn. He, therefore, recrossed the river at Mautern, the ninth of November, on a fine wooden bridge of twenty-eight arches, the only one existing between Lintz and Vienna, and this he burnt after his passage. Murat finding no enemies before him, moved on with still greater ardor beyond St. Polten, and pushed on the tenth, to Burkersdorf, to within four leagues of Vienna. Soult, who had received no orders to pass St. Polten, allowed himself to be drawn on to Sigartz-Kirchen. I had remained at Molk with my guards. Bernadotte, returning from Steyer, had reached St. Polten.

Affair of Dierenstein.—Kutusof, having rid himself of us

* Kutusof, prince of Smolensk, was born at St. Petersburg, in 1745, and entered the Russian army in 1759. He distinguished himself in the wars against Poland and the Turks, and after the storming of Ismail, in 1789, was made lieutenant-general. He served in several campaigns against the French, and in August, 1812, after the resignation of Barclay de Tolly, was made general-in-chief of the Russian army. He displayed excellent judgment in his dispositions, but was inactive in his pursuit of the retreating enemy. He was opposed to prolonging the war, and died in 1813. Kutusof had a fine education, and was regarded as one of the most accomplished soldiers in the Russian army.

for a moment, went to fight Mortier, who, as will be remembered, was moving along the left bank of the river below Lintz. Here the chances were in favor of the Russian general, for he knew that he was going to attack with the mass of his forces an isolated corps whose rapid march had considerably separated its troops. Mortier, wholly occupied with cutting off the enemy when he should pass the Danube to take the road to Moravia, promptly debouched, on the eleventh of November, from the defiles of Diernstein, whose castle is made memorable by the detention of Richard Cœur-de-Lion; he had with him only the division of Gazan and a brigade of dragoons; the division of Dupont was following at an interval of a march, and the Dutch still farther in rear. After having passed Diernstein, Mortier encountered the advanced guard of Miloradowich, whom he drove quite to the gates of Stein; but this success, which produced him a few hundred prisoners, was almost fatal; for at this moment, the division of Doctorof, led on by General Schmidt, the ablest of the Austrian chiefs of staff, descended by the mountains behind Diernstein, and closed the gate of this terrible defile, at the same time that General Essen reënforced Miloradowich with his reserves and threw himself in front on the plateau of Loiben; nothing but a miracle could now save Mortier. He had gone to meet the division of Dupont, ordering it to accelerate its march; on returning to the division of Gazan, he found it completely hemmed in by the enemy, and had great difficulty in cutting his way, sword in hand, to rejoin it. Placed in the alternative of cutting a way out or of dying there, he decided to force an issue. But this was no easy matter; the road from Loiben to Diernstein passes between two high walls which occupy a part of a very deep defile formed by the mountains and the Danube; the battalions of Doctorof, collected in this gulf in very deep columns, offered no means of forcing his way through; it was exceedingly difficult to pass either to the right or to the left, on account of the mountains and the river. Major Henriod, at the head of the One Hundredth regiment, threw himself against the head of the enemy's column; they fought with the bayonet; two of our pieces charged with grape swept the whole length between the walls, and did the greater execution as the Russians had not been able to bring a single cannon with them, and now had no other arm than the bayonet. General Schmidt was killed by one of these discharges. Doctorof was not a man to allow himself to be easily taken; but the brigade which he has detached up the Danube to secure his own communications in this coupe-gorge, is soon attacked by the division of Dupont. Doctorof now finds himself between two fires, in the same situation in which he thought to place Mortier; he has but a few minutes to escape through the very ravine that he had followed in descending from the mountains; for if Dupont penetrates as far as the entrance to this ravine, it is all over with the Russian column, which has no artillery. It retreats in all haste; Mortier drives back his rear-guard with a facility that surprises him, and hardly has he passed Diernstein than, instead of the enemy, he encounters the column of Dupont. One can easily imagine the electric effect produced on our soldiers by the sight of their comrades and liberators. Those who have, in war, been placed in similar situations, can alone fully appreciate the scene. This junction enables Mortier to repel Essen and Miloradowich, who are pressing him in rear. After this warm work, being in want of provisions, munitions, and artillery, my lieutenant deems it prudent to repass the Danube at Spitz by means of our flotilla; considering himself fortunate in escaping with the loss of fifteen hundred men. The allies lost as many, and suffered still more sensibly in the death of General Schmidt, the friend and companion-in-arms of the Archduke Charles; he fell as a brave man in the attack of Loiben.

Napoleon enters Vienna.—This affair of Mortier in no respect changed the state of things. I had in some measure foreseen it; for on arriving at Molk, I arrested the march of Murat and Lannes, who, exceeding my instructions, rushed on toward Vienna more rapidly than I wished. I even made Soult retrograde from Sigartskirchen to Mautern; Bernadotte remained at Molk. But after I had learned at St. Polten, on the twelfth, the issue of this affair and Mortier's return to the right bank, I promptly took such measures as were then required. The advanced position of Murat on Vienna, and the certainty that none of the enemy's corps covered the approaches to that city, gave me hopes of effecting an abrupt entrance, of surprising the great bridges of the Danube, and of debouching by the road to Moravia, before Kutusof could reach there from Krems.

I was the more stimulated to this course by the return of Count Giulay to my head-quarters on the twelfth; instead of bringing me the adhesion of his sovereign to the conditions which I had offered, he came to announce that Prussia had finally decided, on the third of November, to make common cause with Russia and Austria. I well knew the tardiness and irresolution of this cabinet; I was prepared to strike an important blow, and to spread terror through Europe, by the capture of Vienna; this of itself would suffice to allay the storm. Moreover, the possession of this capital would force the Archduke Charles to march toward Hungary, and thus open my communications with Massena; I would then have no further trouble about our communications in Swabia, if they should be threatened by the Prussians. For the success of this bold design it required the concurrence of unusual circumstances; fortune exceeded my hopes. I removed my head-quarters to Burkersdorf, on the thirteenth; Murat and Lannes arrived before Vienna, conformably to my instructions.

State of that City.—Built in the superb basin formed by the Styrian Alps on the south, the Crapack mountains on the east, and on the west by Mount Bisamberg, the chain of Bohemia and the secondary mountains of Upper Austria, Vienna is perhaps, next to Constantinople and Naples, the most agreeably situated capital in Europe. Having long served as the barrier of Germany against the kings of Hungary and the Turks, it had always been a military post, and well fortified. Taken by the Hungarians in the middle of the thirteenth century, it had afterward resisted all its enemies; every one knows the famous siege it sustained in 1683 against the Turks, when, notwithstanding the bravery of its defenders under Count Stahremberg, it must have eventually fallen before the Vizier Kiuperli, if the Poles, under the great Sobieski, had not gone to its assistance, and entirely defeated the Ottoman army in a great battle under the very walls of the city. For this event, which saved Europe from the crescent, as Charles Martel had delivered it from the Moors on the plains of Tours, the Poles deserved no little gratitude on the part of Austria. The old enciente of Vienna was well bastioned, even on the side next the Danube; it contained about one hundred thousand inhabitants; but the city had outgrown these walls and the immense suburbs, covering a space of eight thousand toises, contained double the population of the old town. These exterior portions had been covered with intrenched lines as a security, probably, against the invasion of the Turks; but these lines, having only a slight relief and an insignificant ditch, were incapable of defense; the enciente of the place, however, required a regular attack; my whole army could have made no impression upon it without siege artillery. Vienna, with Prague, was the grand arsenal of the Austrian monarchy; and, with the exception of some of the English arsenals, was the largest in Europe. It contained two thousand pieces of brass cannon, six hundred of which were of siege calibre, one hundred thousand firearms, etc., etc.

Murat surprises the great Bridges of the Danube.—The corps of Merfeldt had crossed the city in order to reach the left bank of the Danube; his rear-guard held the bridge with every thing prepared for its destruction. If this rear-guard and the militia of Vienna had raised the drawbridges of the fortifications and armed the ramparts, we should have been under the necessity of passing the Danube somewhere else, and of renouncing these immense captures; moreover, this passage would have been no easy thing, and have required time and means which we did not have at hand. The Emperor Francis, in leaving Molk, had passed through Vienna on his way to Presbourg, and after having closed there the session of the Hungarian Diet, he departed for Brunn in order to join the Emperor Alexander, whose army was to concentrate at that place. The Austrian monarch had recommended the inhabitants of his goodly city to Count Wurbna, his grand chamberlain, whom he left there as governor; instead of inciting the inhabitants of Vienna to imitate their ancestors, this good courtier preached to them submission, and even threatened to punish any who by partial resistance should disturb the good order of the city. Moreover, the greater part of the nobility had taken refuge in Hungary. The tender solicitude of a prince for his capital and its inhabitants is certainly very commendable; but is this the highest of his duties? Were these pathetic homilies of M. Wurbna well-timed, when a resistance of ten days might have saved the monarchy?

With such dispositions we could encounter no very great obstacles, for the Regency, without even waiting for our summons, hastened to send Count Zinzendorf to meet me with proposals for the surrender of the city. Murat had already received orders to accelerate his march. At break of day on the morning of the thirteenth, at the approach of the dragoons of Sebastiani, the gates were opened; our astonished soldiers traversed this superb city: the grenadiers of Oudinot followed; the enemy hastened to the bridge; the staff made signs to the artillery officer who was stationed with a piece in the middle of the bridge, for defending its approach, and giving, at the proper time, the signal for its destruction. A report of the pacific mission of Count Giulay had been circulated; this officer and the prince of Auersberg believed that a parley had taken place and an armistice been signed; our soldiers approached them and surrounded the officer and his troop; our column was on the bridge. Prince d'Auersberg undecided, had now no other resource but flight, and our soldiers, still more astonished at the easy capture of this magnificent bridge of two hundred and fifty toises in length than in that of Vienna itself, rushed across it in pursuit of the enemy. Prince d'Auersberg was tried by a council of war, but his carelessness had caused an irreparable evil. Hearing at Burkersdorf of this strange event, I hastened, at midnight, to examine the bridge and determined what course I should now pursue; I bivouacked there for the night; I hastened the arrival of my troops; I threw Murat by Stockerau on the road to Znaim, and returned with my guard to establish my head-quarters in the beautiful palace of Schoenbrunn, the Versailles of Austria.

Critical Situation of Kutusof.—Kutusof, having left Krems on the thirteenth, in order to gain the great road to Moravia, heard the next day of the passage of the Danube, and the march of Murat. He thus found himself engaged between the two roads that lead from Vienna and Krems to Znaim, a situation the more difficult as I had ordered Mortier and Bernadotte to cross the Danube at Mautern by means of the flotilla, to harass his rear. The Russian general had but little hopes of reaching, before Murat, the direct road to Hollabrunn, and even if he did, Mortier might still force his march and arrive by Schrattenthal at Znaim as soon as the enemy. Kutusof decided with promptness ; he threw Bagration with a corps of the *élite* on Hollabrunn with orders to defend it to the last extremity, and he himself crossed directly on Schrattenthal. To maintain himself with nine thousand men against Murat and Lannes, two days' march in advance of the army, was a difficult task ; as a climax of embarrassment, general Nostitz, who covered the retreat of the Austrian corps on Znaim, summoned by Murat to separate himself from the Russians, under the pretext of an armistice, was so inconceivably simple as to open the road to our cavalry columns, which appeared suddenly and unexpectedly before Bagration ; they were soon supported by the grenadiers of Oudinot ; a most terrible combat ensued ; the Russians were forced to retreat on Schongraben.

Negotiation of Murat.—Murat, who was hurrying to reach Znaim before Kutusof, since on this might depend the fate of the war and the ruin of the Russian army, thought to neutralize Bagration as he had Auersberg and Nostitz ; he, therefore, sent him a messenger, but this time the ruse turned against himself. Kutusof was particularly distinguished for his great finesse : hearing of the arrival of a French messenger, he thought to save his army by sending General Winzingerode* to Murat to enter into negotiation and conclude

* Baron Winzingerode was born in 1769 in Wirtemberg. He first served in the Austrian army, but afterward joined the Russian army, and, being a great favorite of the emperor, he was rapidly promoted. He, however, was never greatly distinguished as a general. Being a bitter enemy of France, he had much influence in shaping the policy of the Russian government, and in negotiations with foreign powers, against Napoleon. In the campaign of 1812 he attempted to enter Moscow after this city had been occupied by the French, being still ignorant of such occupation. On seeing the mistake his command deserted him and fled, and he was surrounded and captured. He displayed a

an armistice. Winzingerode was aid-de-camp to the Emperor Alexander; he took upon himself to stipulate in the name of this prince. The Russian army was to retire into Poland by easy marches; the French, on this condition, were to suspend their march on Moravia; the respective armies were to remain in position till I should ratify the arrangement! Murat thus fell into the same snare which, within three days, he had twice set for the enemy; Kutusof could not save Bagration, who was in sight of our videttes, but he pushed forward his army by a forced march, while the courier flew to Schoenbrunn to obtain my approval. Better advised than my lieutenant, and certain that he had been deceived, I reprimanded him severely, and ordered him to attack instantly.

Combat at Hollabrunn or Schoengraben.—Soult's corps having joined Murat, the destruction of Bagration seemed inevitable; on the evening of the sixteenth, our columns rushed forward to the attack; Oudinot, Vandamme,* Murat's dragoons, vied with each other as to which should have the honor of being first on the field. The right of the Russians was turned and the centre pierced, in spite of the most honorable resistance; they fought hand to hand amid the smoking ruins of the village of Grund. The enemy's left was cut off; nevertheless, by means of the night and a surprise, they succeeded in effecting a passage through our columns, and escaped, leaving us, as a trophy, a village filled

white handkerchief and claimed to be the bearer of a flag of truce. For this attempted violation of the laws of war in regard to a flag of truce, he was placed under guard and sent to Metz for confinement, but was rescued while on the way. He died in 1818.

* Dominique Joseph Vandamme was born at Cassel in 1771. He entered the army when very young, and in 1793 was made a brigadier-general. He was made general-of-division in 1799. He was afterward promoted to the rank of lieutenant-general and made peer of France. He died in 1830. Vandamme was regarded as an excellent officer, and served with distinction in most of Napoleon's campaigns. In addition to his military promotion, he was highly honored by the emperor, and received important commands and employments.

with dead and a few hundred prisoners. One third of the corps of Bagration had fallen in this contest, which continued till eleven o'clock at night; but he had the glory of carrying off the remainder, safe and sound, from the midst of forty thousand men by whom he was in a measure surrounded.

Kutusof effects his Junction.—Having rejoined Murat, we arrived at Znaim on the seventeenth. Kutusof had already departed for Brunn, and no further obstacle preventing his junction, he effected it on the nineteenth at Wischau. Sebastiani pushed the enemy's rear-guard, and captured many stragglers.

Measures taken at Schoenbrunn.—I had passed two days at the palace of Schoenbrunn, but this delicious abode had not been a Capua for me; many imperious motives had retained me there, and never had I displayed more activity than during these two days. I was not merely waiting for definite information of Kutusof; I had yet to regulate the administration of Austria, and provide for the future wants of my army. A contribution of one hundred millions was levied for this purpose. Moreover, I caused Marmont to reconnoitre the road to Styria, to gain information of the armies of the Archduke Charles and of the Archduke John. I had also to provide for the security of Hungary, a powerful kingdom, whose Diet had just ordered great levies: I pushed Davoust on Presbourg to hold this country in check. Mortier, with the eighth corps, occupied Vienna. Bernadotte, passing the Danube at Mautern, marched on Bohemia with the first corps and the Bavarian division of Wrede; they advanced on Iglau to check the Archduke Ferdinand, who had again collected twelve or fifteen thousand men. This apparent dissemination of my forces will astonish tacticians who preach concentration of masses; it was, nevertheless, indispensable, and a proof of my familiarity with war. I knew that it would require ten or twelve days for Kutusof to join the Russian army and recover from the fatigues of so difficult a retreat. To show my corps-d'armée at Presbourg, at Iglau, and at Leoben, was to act at the same time on the morale of the Hungarian nation, on the Archduke Charles, who was coming from Italy, and on the Archduke Ferdinand, who was defending Bohemia; I could afterward recall my corps when it should be necessary to strike. The sublimity of the art consists in knowing how to divide, to pursue, to act on minds, to intimidate, to deceive the enemy, and to unite when necessary to fight! Never has any general pushed this art as far as I have. To be convinced of the rapidity and impetuosity of my system, it is enough to remember that on the eighteenth of October I was at Elchingen treating with Mack for the surrender of Ulm, and one month after I found myself at Brunn, having crossed the Inn, the Salza, the Traun, the Enns, and the Danube, having fought at Amstetten, at Mariazell, at Krems, at St. Polten, and at Hollabrunn.

My combinations perfectly fulfilled their object; not only did Davoust receive from the Hungarian deputies the assurance that this kingdom should not trouble the combinations of my army, if I would not overrun the territory beyond Presbourg; some even went so far as to propose to declare the independence of Hungary, if I would afford them protection.* Bernadotte explored the road to Iglau, and satisfied himself that the enemy was not in condition to trouble us on that side. Marmont made a useful diversion in favor of Massena, and facilitated his operations by occupying Bruck; I knew very well that he was not in sufficient force to contend with the archduke; this was not the object; my purpose was to

* For this proposition to take up arms for the independence of his country one of the most distinguished of the Hungarians was, after the peace, condemned by the Austrian government to twenty-one years' imprisonment.

show to this prince a strong head of column in the mountains of Styria, and to turn him from a direct march on Vienna to the longer but securer road to Hungary. I thus increased the interval which separated him from the Russian army; I very much retarded the epoch when they could act in concert; this was employing a detachment to a good purpose; finally, when the time should arrive, Marmont would again return to Vienna, uniting there with Mortier, and permit me to mass my forces between the Danube and Brunn, and to act as I might wish on the two armies, or to choose my line of retreat. In the mean time Davoust was to carry one of his divisions to Neustadt, in order to sustain the second corps if it should be obliged to fight in the gorges of Sommering.

Remarks on the Plan of Campaign.—I more and more appreciated the wisdom of my resolution to push on to Vienna and afterward to ascend into Moravia. This second movement was a consequence of the first; for, to be successful, it was necessary to increase the interval between the two allied armies, and to enlarge my base of retreat, by rendering it more easy on Passau. Prussia was not yet prepared to act immediately: 1st, because she was awaiting the troops with which she had formed the cordon of the Vistula; 2d, because she preferred to accomplish her objects by negotiation rather than to engage in the war. The cabinet of Berlin was very formal; and notwithstanding the Emperor Alexander's visit to the tomb of Frederick at Potsdam, King Frederick William had made only a conditional engagement. He wished to try once more to make an arrangement with me.

The French Army at Brunn.—On the twentieth, I removed my head-quarters to Brunn. On arriving at this city, I was utterly astonished to see that the Austrians had not even put the smallest garrison in the citadel, a well-fortified place, which could be taken only by a regular siege. I am willing to admit that too many fortifications enfeeble active armies, and cannot of themselves save an empire; but under the present circumstances the occupation of Brunn was too important not to have left there a garrison of two or three thousand men; they could not have been better employed. It is true that the place was not in a complete state of defense, for it was not expected that it would be so soon surrounded by our battalions. Nevertheless we could only have blockaded it, and it was strong enough to hold out a week, which was sufficient to accomplish its object. The corps of Lannes, Soult, and Murat cantoned between this city, Austerlitz, and Wischau. We here had some days' repose, the first which my troops had enjoyed since they left Boulogne. In three months we had flown from the coasts of England to the confines of Moravia, destroyed an army, and captured the capital of proud Austria. Our soldiers had found wine and provisions, but their shoes were in a horrible condition; they marched with their naked feet in the snow. This repose was demanded both to recruit my troops, and by the situation of the respective forces. We will profit by this moment of respite, to look back to what had been passing around me within the last month; for, drawn on by the rapidity and increasing interest of my march, I have deferred speaking of the operations of the secondary corps which I left in our rear.

Operations in the Tyrol.—While I advanced with so much impetuosity on Vienna, Ney and Augereau had obtained no less success in the Tyrol. It is known that this mountainous country, forming, as it were, a bastion which commands both Italy and Germany, has always been regarded by the Austrians as the key of those two countries. They thought that the mountains rendered them masters of the plain; and if this axiom be true in tactics, it was reserved for me to show its falsity in strategy. Five principal roads debouch from the Tyrol into Germany, cross the chain of the Alps, and are closed by the same number of forts at Fieldkirch, Reiti (Fussen), Scharnitz, Leiten, and Kufstein. The Archduke John here commanded, at first, forty-five or fifty thousand men. A part of these had been withdrawn to second Mack in Swabia, on the one side, and the Archduke Charles in Italy, on the other. Nevertheless he still had, including the militia, thirty-five thousand men. Ney, leaving Ulm, with only ten thousand, presents himself toward Scharnitz, on the fifth of November. A Bavarian division threatens Kufstein, or rather observes this fort and covers Bavaria; Augereau, who has just crossed the Rhine at Hunninguen, advanced by the Black Forest on Kempten, where he finds himself in presence of the division of Jellachich, who left Ulm the evening of the combat of Elchingen, and sought safety in the Voralberg. Ney, unaccustomed to count the number of his enemies, attacks the bastioned fort of Scharnitz, which closes the gorge; he is repulsed. One of his columns climbs the rocks, turns and carries the little fort of Leutasch, descends to Seefield in rear of Scharnitz, which is closed only on the side toward Germany, forces the garrison to seek safety in flight, captures five or six hundred prisoners, and then audaciously advances to Innspruck into the very centre of the enemy's corps.

The Archduke John concentrated his forces on the Brenner to cover the retreat of Jellachich and the Prince of Rohan, one of whom was at Meran and the other in the Voralberg; he ordered them to fall back in all haste on Botzen. They were too late. Jellachich, surrounded at Dornbiren by Augereau, was obliged to lay down his arms with five thousand men, and was taken back to Bohemia on condition of not serving again for a year. The Prince of Rohan, more fortunate, at first drove back the posts of Loison at Botzen, on the nineteenth of November; but after having passed this city he found the debouches on the Carinthia occupied by the

French troops; the Archduke John, fearing for his own rear, which the retreat of the Archduke Charles had left entirely exposed, thought best to abandon Brenner on the night of the fifteenth, in order to retreat by Villach and Klagenfurth on Cilly, where he effected a junction with his brother. Rohan, isolated in the midst of the Tyrol mountains, still hoped to effect his escape on the side toward Italy, by passing in rear of Massena and reaching Venice; he descended by the gorges of the Brenta on Bassano. St. Cyr, who was blockading Venice, attacked and defeated him at Castel-Franco. The Prince of Rohan, seeing no further resources, surrendered on the twenty-fourth of November with about five thousand men. Massena, who was at this time on the Isonzo, detached in haste his reserve of grenadiers to second St. Cyr in this operation; but every thing was decided before their arrival. After these events Augereau placed himself near Ulm to observe Prussia; Ney turned the Tyrol over to a Bavarian division and marched to Salzbourg.

New Attempts at Negotiations.—We will return to my army, which we kept cantoned, from the twenty-second to the twenty-eighth of November, between Wischau and Brunn, within two or three leagues of the Russian army, which was waiting under Olmutz, the arrival of its guards and reserves. I had profited by this interval to send, on the twenty-fifth, General Savary, to the Emperor Alexander, less to carry him new proposals of peace than to learn from him what conditions the allies would agree to. The Austrians sent me in return MM. Stadion* and Giulay to learn from me what

* Count Jean Philippe Stadion was born at Mayence in 1763. After receiving a most liberal education, he repaired to Vienna and obtained employment in the diplomatic corps under Prince Kauntz, who was then prime minister. From that time forward he took a prominent part in all the diplomatic discussions in Europe till the fall of Napoleon. In 1813, he was made minister of finance, which office he continued to hold till 1818, when he was sent as the representative of Austria to the congress of Aix-la-Chapelle. He then retired to private life, and died in 1824. His elder brother Count Frederic Stadion,

were my pretensions; they hoped that the adhesion of Prussia, the march of the Archduke Charles on Vienna, and the union which had finally been effected between the Russian and Austrian forces, would make me abate the conditions which I had proposed at Molk. Never, however, were we further from an agreement, for the allies demanded nothing less than the famous project of Pitt; they merely allowed me to infer that possibly they might deign to leave me Belgium, but that I must certainly evacuate all Germany and Italy; on the other hand I determined not only to keep what I had, but I also demanded of Austria, Venice for the kingdom of Italy, and the Tyrol for the Bavarians. Cannon alone could bring us to an agreement. I, however, proposed an armistice; the envoys of Austria having observed that it depended on the Emperor of Russia, and that they were not authorized to agree to it, I induced them to repair to Vienna, where they could continue the negotiation.

The next day, the twenty-eighth, Count Haugwitz, the Prussian minister, arrived at my head-quarters; he brought me the complaints of his master, which I had seen for a month in all the gazettes of Germany; he demanded satisfaction for the violation of his territory, and the entire evacuation of all the German soil. These conditions contained nothing objectionable, since they made no question of Italy and Holland; but the other allies would not agree to them.

We were engaged in this discussion when it was announced to me that the Russian army had just broken up its camp at Olmutz, and carried the post of Wischau, which covered my cantonments. I showed Haugwitz that it was necessary for me to leave him to provide for the security of my army,

born in 1761, also filled several diplomatic offices, and the two are often confounded. The latter represented Mayence and Wurtemberg at the Congress of Rastadt.

that very probably we should be engaged in a fight, and that our affairs could be better arranged at Vienna, with Talleyrand, than in my bivouacs; I persuaded him to go to this capital, assuring him that I was ready to do every thing calculated to lead to an adjustment of our difficulties. I prepared to give him a more categorical answer from the field of Austerlitz.

Movements of the Allies.—The Russian guards and reserves, under the orders of the Grand Duke Constantine, having arrived on the twenty-fifth, the enemy's army commenced operations on the twenty-seventh, and easily carried our advanced post of Wischau. We were not ready for them; for the difficulty of supplying so large an army in position had induced me to defer as long as possible the concentration of all my forces. Besides, it was important, as has already been said, to keep Bohemia and Hungary in check, and I had calculated that by means of Brunn I should always have three days for drawing to me the corps of Bernadotte and Davoust; I had made every preparation by directing them to echelon toward me so as to diminish the distance. I accordingly ordered Murat, Lannes, and Soult to break up their cantonments and assemble in the rear of Brunn; but so as to cover that place. Bernadotte received orders to leave the single Bavarian division at Iglau, and to join me by forced marches. Davoust was to move in all haste on Nicolsburg; Mortier was to give Vienna to the division of Dumonceau (of Marmont's corps), and also to direct himself on Brunn; Marmont himself had been instructed to leave Neustadt to approach Vienna. The forces which I had in hand on the twenty-ninth did not exceed fifty thousand men; the allies had eighty thousand, and it was, therefore, for their interest to push me closely in order to force me into battle. It is true, that by means of the good positions of the fortified place of Brunn and its environs, which the enemy had so generously surrendered to us, I should not have fallen back very far; nevertheless, it was for the interest of the enemy to seek either to cut me up or to force me to battle; in war every thing ought to be attempted that conforms to military principles; fortune does the rest.

I was not without anxiety respecting the course which the enemy might pursue; the reputed obstinacy of the Russians gave some apprehensions; they had fought at Hollabrunn as they had in the time of Frederick at Zorndorf; but the Emperor Alexander having no experience in war, distrusted both himself and his generals, most of whom had fought only against the Turks; he was now merely the auxiliary of the Austrians; these latter understood their own country better than he did, and he depended on them to guide him. Nothing could be more fortunate for me; at the head of their projectors was the same Weyrother, whom I had used so admirably at Roveredo, Bassano, and Rivoli, and over whom Moreau had gained so cheap a victory at Hohenlinden. The reports of Savary and the conversations of an aid-de-camp whom the emperor of Russia had just sent to me with him, had already given me the measure of his councillors; I saw that they were disposed to do many foolish things, if I would only afford them an opportunity.

After they had taken their first steps, they deceived themselves respecting the state of affairs. The retreat of my advanced guard induced them to believe that, instead of venturing to give battle, I only thought to escape by retreating on Vienna. Acting under this impression, instead of attacking us boldly, they amused themselves with extended movements by their left, and by throwing themselves into the cross-roads in order to cut off our retreat on Vienna. This was a gratuitous fault; for a little reflection should have convinced them that I would not retreat in the direction of the Archduke Charles, where I might find the bridges of the

Danube destroyed, while I had in my rear Bohemia, a fertile country, through which passes the most direct road to Bavaria. It is true they had some interest in manœuvring in the direction of Hungary to prepare a junction with the archduke; but it was too soon to do this; that prince was still in Carniola, and the Russian army was waiting the corps of Essen at Olmutz; it was therefore not the time to abandon this road to throw themselves inconsiderately on that of Goeding.

Napoleon's Dispositions for their Reception.— On the twenty-ninth the enemy made a short march of two leagues and a half from Wischau to the heights of Kutchreau. This march, though short, indicated a determination to direct themselves toward Auspitz; but with them the plan of the evening was never the plan of the following morning. Renouncing the project of manœuvring strategically in order to entirely gain our right, they again moved directly on us. But they still advanced timidly. On the thirtieth they bivouacked at Hogieditz. I spent the day in riding over the environs; I saw that I had only to support my right and anticipate the enemy's project by occupying in force the plateau of Pratzen from the Santon to Kresenowitz to check them in front. But this would only lead to a contest with equal chances; I wished something better than that. The inclination of the allies to gain my right was manifest; I thought I could strike a decisive blow by allowing them to extend their left, and therefore placed on the heights of Pratzen only a detachment of cavalry.

On the first of December the enemy, debouching from Austerlitz, took position opposite us at Pratzen, his left extending toward Aujest. Bernadotte arrived from Bohemia, and entered into line; Davoust reached the Abbey of Raigern with one of his divisions; that of Gudin bivouacked at Nicolsburg. The reports which reached me from all directions of the march of the enemy's columns confirmed me in my opinion. At nine o'clock in the evening, I passed along the whole length of my line, for the double purpose of judging the direction of the enemy's forces, and of animating my troops. I had just made them a proclamation, not only promising them victory, but even explaining to them the manœuvre by which I was to obtain it. This is undoubtedly the first time that a general ever confided to his whole army the combination by which he expected to secure a victory; I had no fear that the enemy would be informed of it; if he had been, he would not have put any faith in it. The news of my presence before the front of the corps-d'armée, passing from one to the other like electricity, reached the extremity of the line with the rapidity of lightning; by a spontaneous movement all the divisions of infantry, raising bundles of blazing straw on the ends of long poles, gave me an illumination whose imposing and novel appearance had in it something majestic. It was the first anniversary of my coronation!!

The aspect of these fires reminded me of the vine faggots with which Hannibal deceived the Romans, and the bivouacs of the camp of Liegnitz, which had saved the army of Frederick by deceiving Daun and Laudon. As I passed before each regiment, the cry of *Vive l'Empereur*, made and repeated far and near by each corps, carried to the enemy's camp proof of the enthusiasm which animated our soldiers. Never did any scene on the field of battle present a pomp so august and imposing; every soldier partook of the confidence with which these proofs of devotion inspired me.

The line, which it took me till midnight to pass, extended from Kobelnitz to the Santon. Soult's corps formed the right, placed between Sokelnitz and Puntowitz; he was opposite the enemy's centre. Bernadotte bivouacked behind Girskowitz; Murat at the left of this village, and Lannes in a position commanding the road to Brunn; my reserves were established in rear of Soult and Bernadotte. By placing my right under the orders of Soult, it was evident that on him would fall the greatest weight of the battle. But in order that his movement should produce the promised result, it was necessary to begin by removing the enemy's troops which debouched toward Blasowitz and by the road to Austerlitz; it was probable that the emperor's and the general head-quarters would be found there, and that it would be necessary to strike there first and then fall on their left by a change of front; this, moreover, was the way to cut off their left from the road to Olmutz. I therefore determined to second at first the movement of Bernadotte's corps on Blasowitz with my guards and the reserve of grenadiers, to turn back the enemy's right and then turn against the left, which would find itself so much the more compromised as it had advanced past Telnitz. My project had been determined on the night before, as I announced it to my soldiers; the essential point was to seize the right moment. I had passed the night in bivouac; the marshals were assembled about me to receive my final orders. I mounted my horse at four o'clock in the morning; the moon had gone down, and the night was cold and dark, though the weather was fair. It was important to know whether the enemy had made any movement during the night which might derange my plan. The reports of my guards confirmed the opinion that the movement had been from the enemy's right toward his left; his fires appeared to extend further in the direction of Aujest. At the break of day, a light fog slightly obscured the horizon, especially in the valleys; suddenly this fog disappeared, the sun begins to gild with his rays the tops of the hills, while the valleys are still enveloped in a vapory cloud. We see very distinctly the heights of Pratzen, recently covered with troops, and now abandoned by the enemy's left; it is evident that he has followed out his project of extending his line beyond Telnitz. I readily discover another mass marching from the centre toward the right in the direction of Holubitz. It is now perfectly certain that the enemy's centre, striped of its forces, is exposed to the blows which it may please me to strike. It was now eight o'clock in the morning; Soult's troops were concentrated in two lines of battalions in column of attack in the valley of Puntowitz. I asked this marshal how long it would take him to gain the heights of Pratzen; he promised to do it in less than twenty minutes.—We will wait then, I replied, . . . when the enemy is making a false movement we must be careful not to interrupt him. Soon the firing begins more lively in the direction of Sokelnitz and Telnitz; an aid-de-camp comes to announce that the enemy debouches in large forces. I was only waiting for this; I give the signal; Murat, Lannes, Bernadotte, Soult, ride at full gallop for their respective corps. I also mount and ride toward the centre; in passing before the troops I incite them anew, telling them: *The enemy has just imprudently exposed himself to your attacks; close the campaign by a clap of thunder!* Cries of *Vive l'Empereur*, attest that I am understood, and become the true signal for the attack; before describing this, we will notice what has occurred in the army of the allies.

Disposition made by the Allies for the Battle.—If we are to believe the disposition projected by Weyrother, their design was to act tactically on the same plan which they had first wished to execute by strategic manœuvres; that is, to act with their reënforced left so as to gain my right, cut me off from the road to Vienna, and throw me back beaten on Brunn. Although my fate was not connected with the road to Vienna, for, as has been said, I proposed that to Bohemia, nevertheless, it must be confessed that this plan offered to the allies some chances of success; but to give it success required something more than the action of this isolated left; it was essential to support it successively by the centre and the right, which should have been prolonged in the same direction. Weyrother, as he had done at Rivoli, manœuvred by both wings, or at least such appears to have been his project.

The left, under Buxhowden, composed of the advanced guard of Kienmayer and of the three Russian divisions of Doctorof, Langeron and Pribichefski, numbered thirty thousand men; it was to advance in three columns from the heights of Pratzen by Aujest on Telnitz and Sokelnitz, to cross the little stream which forms two lakes at the left, and fall back on Turas. The fourth column, under the orders of Kolowrath, with which the head-quarters moved, formed the centre; it was to advance by Pratzen toward Kobelnitz a little in the rear of the third; it was composed of twelve small Russian battalions under Miloradowich, and fifteen Austrian battalions newly levied. The fifth column, formed by eighty squadrons under Prince John of Lichtenstein, was to leave the centre, in rear of which he had passed the night, and to second the right by marching toward the road to Brunn. The sixth, on the extreme right, composed of the advanced guard of Bagration, numbering twelve battalions and forty squadrons, was destined to attack on the great road to Brunn the heights of the Santon and Bosenitz. The seventh, composed of the guards under the Grand Duke Constantine, formed the reserve of the right wing, on the road to Brunn.

It is evident that the enemy wished to turn my right, which he supposed to extend to Melnitz, while my army was collected in mass between Schlapanitz and the road to Brunn, ready for any event.

In accordance with this plan Buxhowden, already more advanced than the rest of the army, commenced this movement before the other columns; moreover the cavalry of Lichtenstein had moved from the centre to the right, so that the heights of Pratzen, the key of the whole field of battle, were left defenseless.

Napoleon's great Central Movement.—The moment I give the signal, all my columns move. Bernadotte crosses the defile of Girskowitz and advances on Blasowitz, sustained on the left by Murat; Lannes moves with equal rapidity on both sides of the Brunn road; my guards and the reserves follow some distance in rear of Bernadotte, ready to move on the centre, if the enemy carries his forces in that direction. Soult moves like lightning from Kobelnitz and Puntowitz, at the head of the divisions of St. Hilaire and Vandamme, sustained by the brigade of Levasseur. Two other brigades of Legrand's division are left as flankers to march and dispute the defiles of Telnitz and Sokelnitz against Buxhowden. As it is evident that he will force them, Marshal Davoust receives orders to move from Raygern with Friant's division and General Bourcier's division of dragoons, to check the heads of the Russian columns till we can engage them more seriously.

Soult's Success.—No sooner has Soult ascended the heights of Pratzen than he makes an unexpected attack on the column of Kolowrath (the fourth), which was marching to the centre in rear of the third, and which, deeming itself secured by the one which preceded it, was advancing in column of route by platoons. The Emperor Alexander, Kutusof, and his staff, are with it. Every thing that occurs unexpectedly at the head-quarters astonishes and disconcerts: Miloradowich, who is in front, hardly gets time to bring the battalions into combat as they are formed; he is overthrown, and the Austrians who follow him experience the same fate. The Emperor Alexander shows much coolness, and exposes himself in rallying his troops, but thanks to the ridiculous dispositions of Weyrother, there is not a single disposable division to serve as a reserve. The allied troops are driven toward Hostiradeck. Kamenski's brigade, which belongs to the third column, assailed on its right flank, succeeds in re-establishing their affairs for a moment; but this succor can not resist the combined efforts of St. Hilaire, Vandamme, and Lavasseur; the line of Kolowrath, threatened to be thrown into the marshy valley of Birnbaum, falls back on Waschau, as was prescribed by the disposition. The artillery of this column, stuck fast in the half-frozen mud, is abandoned to us, and the infantry, deprived of cannon and cavalry, can do nothing against the victorious Soult.

Check of the Enemy's Left.—At the same moment with this decisive blow, the two columns of the right of Buxhowden are crossing each other and becoming entangled about Sokelnitz, from which place they debouch notwithstanding the efforts of Legrand's division; Buxhowden himself also debouches from Telnitz, four battalions alone being insufficient to arrest him. Davoust now arrives from Raygern, and Friant's division drives back on Telnitz the enemy's advanced guard; as the contest is taking a more serious turn toward Sokelnitz, Davoust leaves only the dragoons of Bourcier before Telnitz and ascends the stream as far as Sokelnitz with the division of Friant. A combat of the warmest kind takes place at this point; Sokelnitz, taken and retaken, remains a moment in possession of the Russians. Langeron and Pribichefski even debouch against the heights of Marxdorf; our troops, disposed *en croisement*, charge several times on their flanks with success. This bloody contest being, however, only an accessory, it is enough to check the enemy without repelling him; indeed there would result no inconvenience even if he should advance still further.

Success of the Centre and French Left.—While things were taking such a favorable turn on our right, we were no less fortunate at the centre and left. The Grand Duke Constantine and the Russian generals here met precisely the same fortune as had already happened to the head-quarters and to the fourth column; they were to have been in reserve, but were the very first engaged. Bagration extended by the right toward Dwaroschena in order to turn and attack the position of the Santon. The cavalry of Lichtenstein, called from the centre to his assistance, was crossed in route by the other columns, so that the grand-duke and the guards arriving first near Krug, found themselves in the first line the moment when Bernadotte advanced on Blasowitz and Lannes on both sides the road to Brunn; the fight soon became hot. Having at last arrived after a long march, on the right of the grand-duke, the prince of Lichtenstein was beginning to form, when the hulans of the Russian guard, drawn on by their hot valor, threw themselves between the divisions of Bernadotte and Lannes in order to reach the light cavalry of Kellerman, who fell back before them. Victims of their own ardor, they were charged by the reserves of Murat, overthrown and driven under the fire of our two lines of infantry, where half of them were destroyed. In the mean time our progress in the direction of Pratzen had forced Kutusof to recall Lichtenstein to the assistance of his centre; and this prince, equally threatened on the right and left, knew not to whom to listen or where to render his first assistance; he hastened to send four regiments of cavalry, which arrived in time to witness Kolowrath's defeat. General Ouwarof was established with thirty squadrons between Bagration and the grand-duke; the remainder of the cavalry was placed on the left. On his side the grand-duke, seeing the French columns of infantry penetrate into Blasowitz and debouch from that place, determined to descend from the heights and meet them half way. This movement seemed to him necessary as well for his own security as to relieve the centre, for which they began to have fears.

While a furious combat of infantry takes place between the Russian guards and the division D'Erlon, the grand-duke's mounted guards (a regiment of cuirassiers) charge the right flank of this division, which is formed by the fourth regiment of the line detached from the division of Vandamme in order to cover the interval. The Russian cuirassiers fall upon this regiment, overthrow one battalion, but pay dearly with the lives of their braves for the honor of carrying off the battalion eagle. This hot contest, being isolated, was not dangerous; nevertheless as it was possible that the enemy might send other forces to sustain it, I determined to direct on this point Marshal Bessières with the cavalry of my guard. It being necessary to end the matter, I ordered him to charge. The Russian line, after the most honorable defense, was obliged to yield to the united efforts of Bernadotte and Bessières. The infantry of the guards, incapable of a longer resistance, fell back on Krezenowitz. The mounted guards, which arrived at this instant at Austerlitz, attempted in vain to reëstablish affairs; this regiment of the *élite* could do nothing more; being itself charged by my mounted grenadiers, which I advanced under the orders of Rapp, it was overthrown, and all the centre then took the road to Austerlitz. In the mean time Murat and Lannes had attacked with success the corps of Bagration and the cavalry of Ouwarof, which sustained it. Our cuirassiers had overthrown the left of this wing pressed by the divisions of Suchet and Caffarelli. Everywhere victory crowned our combinations.

Napoleon unites his Reserve with Soult.—Certain that Bernadotte, Lannes, and Murat would be more than sufficient to cope with the enemy on this side, I fell back to the right with my guards and the reserves of Oudinot, to aid Soult in destroying the left wing, which was now taken in reverse and compromised among the lakes. It was two o'clock when Soult, incited by our approach, united the divisions of St. Hilaire and Legrand to take Sokelnitz in reverse, while the troops of Davoust assailed it in front; Vandamme threw himself on Aujest; my guard and the grenadiers followed in rear, to reënforce, in case of need, these different attacks.

The division of Pribichefski, surrounded in Sokelnitz, lays down its arms; a few fugitives only escape to tell this disaster. Langeron, pushed in his turn, is not more fortunate, and only one half of his troops succeed in rejoining Buxhowden. The latter, who had spent five or six hours with the column of Doctorof in a useless skirmish near Telnitz, instead of falling back at ten o'clock on Sokelnitz, at last thought it time to provide for his own security; he put himself in march between two and three o'clock to return to Aujest and escape from the trap, by moving along the valley between the lakes and the heights. He was debouching from the village in column when Vandamme threw himself with impetuosity on his flank, penetrated into Aujest, and cut his column in two. Buxhowden, not being in condition to turn to the assistance of the others, continued his retreat with the two leading battalions to rejoin Kutusof; but Doctorof and Langeron, with the twenty-eight other battalions, found themselves inclosed in the gulf between the lakes, and the heights crowned by St. Hilaire, Vandamme, and my reserves. The head of the column on the side toward Aujest, escorting the artillery, attempted to escape across the canals formed for draining the lake; the bridge broke under the weight of the cannon. These brave men hoping to save their pieces, now sought to cross the extremity of the lake which was frozen over, but the ice, cut up by the fire of our batteries, broke under the weight of this mass, engulfing both men and cannon; more than two thousand were drowned. Doctorof had no other means of escape than to march along the shore of the lake to Telnitz under our fire, and to gain the dike which separates the lake of this name from that of Melnitz. He succeeded, but not without enormous losses, in gaining Satschann under the protection of Kienmayer's cavalry, which made the most praiseworthy efforts. They together took the road to Czeitsch by the mountains, hotly pursued by us. The few pieces of artillery which the enemy had saved from the centre and left were abandoned in this retreat, made by horrible roads, which the rain of the night before and the frost rendered almost impassable.

The Enemy, cut off from Olmutz, is thrown on Hungary. —The position of the enemy was exceedingly difficult; I had gained the road to Wischau, which his troops could no longer reach. He was therefore forced to take the road to Hungary; but Davoust, one of whose divisions had reached Nicolburg, could, by a flank march, advance to Goeding, while we were warmly pressing him in rear. The allied army weakened by the loss of twenty-five thousand killed, wounded, and prisoners, and one hundred and eighty pieces of cannon, besides a quantity of stragglers, was in the greatest disorder.

The Emperor of Austria asks an Interview.—The emperor of Austria was unwilling to trust the fate of the monarchy to a final battle which might lose all. He sent to me Prince John of Lichtenstein to ask an interview; it took place the next day in a bivouac, on the bank of a ditch. We had no difficulty in coming to an understanding; I had strong reasons for ending the matter; the Archduke Charles was approaching the Danube; Hungary, incited by his presence, might rise; the enemy's reserves were approaching from Olmutz, the Archduke Ferdinand was driving from Iglau the Bavarian division of Wrede; Prussia was threatening to debouch from Saxony into Franconia with one hundred thousand men. In truth, all these were but distant difficulties, while I had in hand trophies certain and immediate. I convinced the prince of Lichtenstein that, in consenting to an armistice, I was forgetful of the interests of the victorious soldier to prove my desire for peace. I also persuaded the emperor of Austria of this, showing him that it would have been better to have permitted me to pursue my project against England than to have troubled its execution. The armistice was concluded, by which the Russians were immediately to retire to Poland, and negotiations were to be resumed at Presbourg to treat for a definitive peace.

Remarks on the Battle of Austerlitz.—Never was there a more brilliant success, and, I venture to say, never was there one better deserved. Victory had been announced the evening before; it was certain after ten o'clock in the morning, for Soult was then master of Pratzen, and Bernadotte of Blasowitz. Undoubtedly it was facilitated by the blind obstinacy with which Buxhowden marched to meet him according to the plan, without allowing himself to be turned aside by the attacks on the centre. If, on hearing the thunder of the cannon in his rear, he had immediately directed his sixty battalions on Kobelnitz by the left of the rivulet, we should have been a little embarrassed; nevertheless, concentrated about Schlapanitz, we should have received battle with the advantage of concentrated forces over a divided enemy; victory would not in that case have been so brilliant: but I should nevertheless, in all probability, have gained the field of battle. It would, however, be absurd to attribute to Buxhowden a reverse which was due only to the faulty disposition projected by Weyrother—a disposition which left the army without a centre, and which placed the head-quarters in the first line, and in the interval where was the decisive point of the whole field. The allies had but two means of assailing me with any possibility of success; one was to successively sustain the attack of the left by the rest of the army, renouncing the road to Olmutz and basing themselves on Hungary, which could have been done without violating the rules of strategy, since the Archduke Charles was approaching in that direction; the other was, to close the left on the rest of the army in order to preserve the road to Olmutz in their rear. To effect this, Buxhowden should have debouched by Sokelnitz and Kobelnitz on Marxdorf, instead of extending so far toward Telnitz.

Such was the famous day of Austerlitz; of all the pitched battles which I have gained, I pride myself most on this, both on account of the enemy over which I triumphed, and on account of the perfect success of all my combinations; this success was as perfect as though I had commanded the two armies and the manœuvres had been previously agreed upon. Ulm, Marengo, Jena, Ratisbon, were victories as brilliant; but they were the result of strategic manœuvres and a series of combats. The most remarkable of my tactical battles are those of Austerlitz, Rivoli, and Dresden.

Napoleon Returns to Vienna.—After the armistice, I hastened my return to Vienna, to accelerate negotiations and to put in order the internal affairs of my army; I had also an answer to give M. de Haugwitz.

Augereau was still in Bavaria; Ney's corps, after leaving the Tyrol to a Bavarian division, had gone to Saltzbourg. Massena and Marmont were debouching on Vienna. The army which had conquered at Austerlitz also approached the capital; I was thus about to find myself fully prepared to strike heavy blows, if the coalition should take a fancy to continue the war. They still possessed powerful means, but they were scattered. The Archduke Charles was too far off to act effectively with an army demoralized by its long retreat, and by the defeat of the other forces of the monarchy. He would, moreover, be exposed at the same time to the whole of my victorious army, reënforced by Massena, Marmont, and Mortier; the Russians were for a certain time out of reach. The Prussians—we will not anticipate their disaster, but for a moment consider their negotiations which were interrupted by the events of Austerlitz.

Treaty of Vienna with the Prussians.—Haugwitz now felt that the time for menacing me was past; I proposed to him to overlook the violation of a territory which in 1796 and 1800 had been no better respected by either belligerent, offering him the electorate of Hanover in exchange for Anspach, Cleves, and the principality of Neufchâtel. Prussia would, by this arrangement, gain too much for her minister to hesitate; moreover, it was the most honorable way for her to replace the sword which she had drawn too late from its scabbard. Haugwitz accepted it unhesitatingly, happy to carry to his master the news of an aggrandisement instead of a formidable war; I also gained by it, since I avoided a war with a natural ally, and compromised Prussia with England.

Treaty of Presbourg with Austria.—This treaty, signed on the fifteenth of December, and that with Austria concluded at Presbourg the twenty-sixth, put an end to the third coalition against France. Austria paid pretty dearly for it; I demanded of her the Venetian states to reënforce my Italian Kingdom and my maritime system; she also yielded the Tyrol and the Innviertel to Bavaria. In order to attach to myself irrecoverably these brave allies, I erected Bavaria and Wurtemberg into kingdoms, and the Margraviate of Baden into a Grandduchy. The Pays de Salsbourg, ceded to the grand duke of Tuscany by the peace of Luneville, was accorded to Austria. The grand duke of Tuscany obtained Wurtembourg, which put him more in my dependence. In exchange for Wurtzbourg and the duchy of Berg, which the elector yielded to me, Bavaria received Anspach, in addition to the Innviertel of the Tyrol. I, at the same time proposed peace to the Russians; but Alexander refused it; this refusal was noble, for in accepting it he would have accepted the humiliation of his allies. In refusing, he exhibited firmness in reverses, and confidence in fortune; this refusal showed me that the fate of the world was dependent on us two. Nevertheless we could no longer carry on war, for we were separated by neutral countries. The Russians returned to their homes.

Operations in Hanover.—While I was directing the thunderbolts into the ranks of our enemies, they were amusing themselves with a ridiculous war in the North. To turn to account the knight errant humor of Gustavus IV., king of Sweden, and to induce him to direct his forces to the continent, Russia and England had given him the command of an army to which he added fifteen thousand Swedes. After uniting in Pomerania with Tolstoy's corps of about ten thousand men, he passed the Elbe near Lauenbourg and advanced into Hanover. At the same time the Hanoverian troops and some English battalions debouched under General Don near Stade, and Lord Cathcart with another English corps soon followed. These forces, which amounted to more than forty thousand men, after having swept Hanover where I had only the garrison of Hameln, were intended to operate against Holland. Although I had foreseen this danger, sending my brother Louis to this latter country with the *cadre* of what I called the army of the North, it required no less than the victory of Austerlitz to ward off the storm, for the still doubtful attitude of Prussia complicated matters. Happily the folly of Gustavus came to my assistance. Furious against his allies, who reproved his impolitic and threatening tone toward Prussia at the very moment that the Emperor Alexander was at Potsdam treating with this power, the king of Sweden returned to Pomerania, threw up the command of the army, and thus destroyed the entire operation. After a discussion of three weeks, Gustavus went to Lauenbourg; but there Tolstoy's corps was put at the disposition of the king of Prussia, who negotiated to take charge of the security of the north of Germany. This separation gave new displeasure to Gustavus, and Tolstoy went into Mecklenbourg, whence he departed to return to Russia, when peace with Prussia had rendered his presence in Hanover wholly useless. The English also reëmbarked, and Gustavus, to complete his romantic operations, sent his troops back into Pomerania, leaving only five hundred men to guard Lauenbourg.

The Dynasty of Naples ceases to reign.—The court of the Two Sicilies had given, by its inconceivable conduct, the measure of its hatred toward me. I had concluded, on the twenty-first of September, a convention of neutrality with the marquis of Gallo, the Neapolitan minister at Paris; this treaty which was to remove far from his country the scourge of war and to put at my disposition St. Cyr's corps of occupation—a treaty advantageous to both parties—was ratified by the king on the eighth of October. This transaction, which seemed well calculated to save the kingdom of Naples, put its government in a false position. Before it was signed, Queen Caroline had moved heaven and earth to interest England, Russia, and Austria in her fate; the plan of the allies had stipulated the landing of twelve thousand Russians and six thousand English, to unite with twenty-five thousand Neapolitans, in order to advance on the Po for the deliverance of Italy. These forces appeared about the middle of November at the roadstead of Naples. To receive them, in violation of the engagements recently entered into with me, was to expose himself to my just anger; to repel the allies after having solicited them, was no less disloyal. Ferdinand, as usual, hesitated, but the malignant feelings of the queen prevailed; not satisfied with receiving the allies, she did all in her power to induce Ferdinand to unite his army to their troops. A plan of operations was formed to carry these combined forces into Tuscany, and to take in reverse my army in Italy. Eugene, in order to oppose this new enemy, was obliged to collect what he could of the Franco-Italian troops and national guards of the kingdom, on the frontiers of the March of Ancona.

Thus drawn on by a blind hatred, the queen sacrificed her people, her family, her crown, for the single hope of injuring me. Every impartial man will agree that by this conduct she authorized, in advance, whatever I might please to decide respecting her fate. If I had been beaten, this unexpected hostility had given me great embarrassment in Italy; victorious, I was not vexed at having a good pretext for ending the matter by getting rid of this implacable enemy; and of thus procuring a crown for one of my brothers. The kingdom of Naples ought to enter frankly into the system of France and Spain, as it had done at the epoch of the family pact of the Bourbons. As the queen was the only obstacle to the adoption of this system, it was necessary that she should suffer the consequences of her course of conduct. The very next day after the treaty of Presbourg, December 27th, I hurled my decree of anathema on this inconsiderate court; *I declared that it had ceased to reign.* Massena had already received orders, immediately after the armistice, to increase St. Cyr's corps to thirty thousand men and to direct it on Rome; after the peace, I ordered him to reënforce this corps and to take the command himself. We will leave him to his easy triumph and direct our attention to the maritime war, whose operations had not been less decisive than on land, but in a sense directly the reverse.

Napoleon directs Admiral Villeneuve to return to Toulon.—It will be remembered that Villeneuve, leaving Ferrol at the head of thirty-three ships, had returned, contrary to my instructions, to Cadiz, instead of making sail for Brest, and that this circumstance, in connection with the continental war, had decided me to renounce the descent. Being very justly dissatisfied with the conduct of this admiral, I ordered him to be replaced by Rosily, and the combined fleet to immediately set sail for the Mediterranean, to raise the blockade of Carthagena, to capture the small English station before Naples, to land the ten thousand men it had on board to reënforce St. Cyr at Tarentum, and to thus enable him to conquer Naples. Villeneuve was afterward to return to Toulon, to take in supplies and refit, then to send his cruisers in all directions in the Mediterranean and the ocean. I especially directed that one be established at St. Helena in order to capture the return ships from India. Little did I then anticipate the misfortunes that awaited me on this rock ! ! I hoped by thus exciting the fears of England respecting Egypt, to force her to keep large squadrons in the Mediterranean. This system was well calculated to form good sailors, to paralyze the enemy's forces, and to injure his commerce ; it, moreover, was particularly suited to the supposition that continental affairs might, for many years, force me to renounce the project of a descent. A proof of its advantages is the success obtained by Admiral Lallemant. It will be remembered that this brave seaman, being unable to effect a junction with Villeneuve, had cruised between Ireland and the Bay of Biscay till the end of December, and had then entered Rochefort in triumph, with one captured ship-of-the-line, a great number of prizes, and twelve hundred prisoners —a success the more remarkable as it had been gained in the very waters of England, and on a sea crossed in every direction by the merchant vessels of that nation.

Nevertheless, it must be confessed that this system exposed our naval forces to partial combats ; perhaps it would have been preferable to leave our fleet at Cadiz, which is a favorable port for a sortie, and very difficult to blockade, as in a heavy sea, produced ordinarily by south-west winds, the blockading forces are exposed to all the fury of the waves on a dangerous coast. Thirty vessels in Cadiz would have cost the enemy dearly, and they would have been more free to act in all directions than when at Toulon. The excessive expense which they would have occasioned us in one of the dearest ports of Europe, and the objection to spending so much money in a foreign port, were the motives for directing the departure of the fleet. My orders being imperative, it was the duty of Villeneuve to leave; nevertheless, if he was blockaded by twenty-nine ships, it was optional with him either to leave or to remain at Cadiz; he chose the former course.

Nelson returns before Cadiz.—While by a too literal execution of this order, he was going to his own destruction, the English admiralty, informed of his return to Cadiz, had ordered Nelson to leave Portsmouth in all haste and take the command of all the British forces in these waters. He was not a man to delay, and he left instantly with two or three ships which he found ready. This great sailor joined on the seventeenth of October the fleet of Admiral Collingwood and took the command.

Meeting of the two Fleets.—Villeneuve set sail on the nineteenth, with thirty-three ships and nine frigates. It is probable that he thought he was opposed only by the twenty-one ships of Collingwood and Calder; it is said he had been informed the night before of Nelson's arrival, but that, following the advice of a merchant captain, he did not believe it. As I had blamed pretty strongly his want of activity at Martinique, and as he wished to wash out the recollection of his inaction at Aboukir, and his return to Cadiz, he undoubtedly thought he would be forever dishonored if he did not give chase with superior forces. Full of this idea, and knowing that the grand operations in the channel no longer depended on the course he might now pursue, he decided to fight. Every circumstance seemed to conspire against us; the same admiral who had feared to advance toward Brest to fight an inferior and divided enemy, now, by a misplaced and untimely energy, was about to engage with equal forces against the best sailor of the age; if he deemed himself authorized to deviate from my orders in an operation as delicate as that of a junction with the fleet of Brest, why would he not venture to interpret them, when acting in a single sortie without any essential object to be accomplished?

Battle of Trafalgar.—The fatal rencontre took place on the twenty-first of October, off Cape Trafalgar, a little south-west of Cadiz. Villeneuve might still have repaired his fault, if he had taken the proper measures to secure a victory; but reposing on his order to all his captains to come into action, and obstinately pursuing the old errors of forming in parallel order, he waited for his adversary to treat him as he had already treated the squadron of Brueys at Aboukir. When one violates his instructions, he ought at least to know how to manœuvre, and to conquer or die. Nelson,* more skillful than his adversary, took advantage of the north-west wind which was blowing at the time, formed in two columns, cut

* Horatio Nelson was born in Norfolk in 1758, and entered the navy at the age of twelve as a midshipman. In 1779 he was promoted to the rank of post-captain, and distinguished himself in the Gulf of Mexico, and afterward in the Mediterranean, losing an eye at the siege of Calvi. For the victory off Cape St. Vincent, in 1797, he was raised to the rank of rear-admiral. For the victory of Aboukir, he received the title of *Baron Nelson of the Nile*, with a pension of two thousand pounds. At the battle of Trafalgar he received a musket-shot in the back, and shortly after expired.

His career in the navy was characterized by energy, boldness, good judgment, and great bravery. As a man, his reputation was tarnished by his cruelty at Naples, and his disgraceful conduct with Lady Hamilton.

the centre with fourteen ships, separating it from the right, while thirteen others defeated the left by successively passing along the line; this was sufficient to secure certain success; our fleet was totally defeated; sixteen ships were lost, in one of which Villeneuve was taken prisoner; the others made sail for our ports; but four of these, under Dumanoir, surrendered to equal forces under Admiral Strachan near Rochefort. Nelson, more fortunate than I, fell dead in the arms of victory. Gravina died of his wounds; he was a man of genius and merited all our regrets. Villeneuve,* sent back to France on parole, fearing the results of a trial by a council of war, committed suicide at Rennes.

This battle, which was more fatal to us than that of the Hogue, and which perhaps decided the empire of the world, if that empire depended on England or France, cost the victors only sixteen hundred men killed and wounded; a remarkable example of the difference of war on sea and on land. The smallest combats of an advanced guard, between 1805 and 1815, cost more lives than this naval victory. In the battles of Eylau and Moskwa, thirty thousand men were sacrificed, without giving any other advantage than the possession of the field of battle, that is, a few acres of ground.

After this epoch our fleets were no longer able to show themselves at sea, and the remainder of my reign was spent

* Pierre Charles Jean Baptiste Sylvestre Villeneuve, was born at Valensoles in 1763, and entered the navy at the age of fifteen. His promotion was rapid. In 1793 he was made captain of a ship, in 1796, rear-admiral, and in 1804, vice-admiral. He was a brave man, and prior to the battle of Trafalgar, was regarded as one of the most promising officers in the French navy. After the defeat and on his return from England after his release as a prisoner of war, he reported to the minister of marine. The reply was said to be so mortifying to the unfortunate admiral that he committed suicide, his body being found the next morning in his room pierced with six wounds inflicted by his own hand. He died at the age of forty-one.

in making preparations for a new contest with the English Leopard. I received this news during our march on Vienna, and all my astonishing success at Ulm and Austerlitz was requisite to console me for this disaster, which forced me to adopt a system of policy entirely new.

CHAPTER IX.

THE WAR OF 1806, OR CAMPAIGN OF JENA.

Napoleon returns to France—Crisis of the Bank—Relations with England—Progress of the English Power in India—Disastrous Maritime Expedition of the French—Continental Means of opposing England—Difficulty of forming Alliances with the Great Powers—System of Federate States—Reasons for the successive Additions to the French Empire—Death of Pitt—Blockade of Ports by a mere British Order in Council—New Difficulties with Prussia—The Cabinet of Berlin perverts the Treaty of Vienna—Motives for this Step—Negotiations of Haugwitz—A New Treaty—Discussions with Austria, for Cattaro and Wurtzbourg—A Federation substituted in place of the German Empire—Napoleon crowns the different Members of his Family—Joseph, King of Naples—Louis, of Holland—Eugene, Heir to the Throne of Lombardy—Murat, Grand Duke of Berg—Military Operations in Naples—Siege of Gaeta—Diversion in Calabria—Confederation of the Rhine, with Napoleon as Protector—Francis abdicates the Crown of Germany, and is proclaimed Emperor of Austria—Sensations at Berlin—Prussia entitled to the Presidency of the Confederation—Interior State of the French Empire—Mechanism of Napoleon's Government—The Public Credit restored—Conscription regulated—Monuments—Internal Improvements—Military and Maritime Works—State of Prussia—Negotiations with England—Treaty signed, but not ratified, with Russia—Mission of Sebastiani to Constantinople—Attack of the English on Buenos-Ayres—Rupture of the Negotiations with England—Prussia abruptly decides on War—Her extraordinary Ultimatum—First Movements of the French Army—The Position and Plan of Operations of the Prussians—Napoleon's Plan of Operations—Faults of the Prussians—Their Generals—Views of the Duke of Brunswick—Napoleon cuts off their Communications—His decisive Manœuvre—Battle of Jena—Battle of Auerstadt—Extraordinary Results of these two Victories—Combat of Halle—March on Potsdam and Berlin—Visit to the Cabinet of the Great Frederick—Entrance into Berlin—Operations of Hohenlohe—Fall of Spandau—Dispositions against Hohenlohe—Combat and Capitulation of Prenzlow—Fall of Stettin—Blucher retires on Mecklenbourg—Capitulation of Custrin—Measures for taking possession of the Country between the Rhine and the Oder—Armistice with the Saxons—Blucher driven to Lubeck—Fall of Lubeck—Capitulation of Blucher—Taking of Magdebourg—Napoleon at Berlin—The celebrated Berlin Decree—British Orders in Council—Armistice with Prussia, not ratified—Napoleon advances to the Vistula—Immense Results of this Seven Weeks' War.

Napoleon returns to France.—As soon as this double peace with Austria and Prussia had reëstablished the repose of Europe, at least for a time, I hastened to return to France, where cares not less important required my presence. My return to Munich was a real triumph: ever since the wars of the brave Charles Theodore, the ally of Louis XIV., and since the project of Austria, in 1778, to get possession of their country, the good Bavarians had nourished an inveterate hatred against the ambition of the cabinet of Vienna; they received me with acclamations so sincere and touching that never did I experience sentiments more grateful. The nation, appreciating what it was to gain in power and consideration by the royal crown which I placed on the head of a prince cherished for his virtues, could well see how different were these benefits from the designs of Austria. Some old cannon, taken from the electoral troops in 1703, which we found in the arsenal of Vienna, sent by my direction to Munich with a goodly number of Austrian pieces, taken in expiation, were conducted back with all possible military pomp. A patriotic excitement seemed to electrify the Bavarians from one end of the kingdom to the other. The national colors were unfurled by all the citizens with an enthusiasm that reminded me of the first days of 1790.

I profited by these dispositions to strengthen our relations by a family alliance. Prince Eugene, the viceroy of Italy, married the Princess Amelia, eldest daughter of the king of Bavaria, and Berthier, whom I had just placed in the rank of sovereigns, by giving him the principality of Neufchatel, married a niece of the king. My sojourn at Munich was celebrated by grand fêtes: public joy was at its height. I did not expect so warm a reception at the court of Wurtemburg, whose elector, a prince of noble character, did not profess the same sentiments toward us. He had merely yielded to force in joining me, at the beginning of the campaign; but from his being the maternal uncle of the Emperor Alexander, and from the position of his states, I felt obliged to treat him in the same way as I had Bavaria: I hoped, by elevating him to a throne, to attach him to me irrevocably. I was not deceived in this calculation.

My return to Paris was a succession of uninterrupted triumphs; the spectacle of the bridge of Kehl was particularly imposing, from the immense concourse of people on both banks of the Rhine, drawn together to see my passage. Louis XIV. had once pretended that there were no more Pyrenees between him and Spain; with more truth might I now say that there was no longer the barrier of the Rhine between France and Germany. I had been preceded in the capital by the deputation of the senate, which had come even to Vienna to congratulate me on two victories unparalleled in the annals of France, and which washed out so gloriously the bloody defeat our navy had just sustained at Trafalgar. They were preparing for me at Paris a most brilliant reception; but I returned in the night in order to escape ceremonies which wearied me, but of which I could give a striking example when it suited my projects.*

* Napoleon had previously sent home the flags captured in this war. Thiers thus describes the reception of the colors sent to Paris by Napoleon:

"These colors passed through Paris on the fifteenth of January, 1806, and were borne triumphantly along the streets of the capital, to be placed under the roofs of the edifices which were to contain them. An immense concourse collected to witness this spectacle.

"The cool and unimpassioned Cambacères himself says, in his grave Memoirs, that the joy of the people resembled intoxication. And wherefore, indeed, should they rejoice if not on such occasions! Four hundred thousand Russians, Swedes, English, and Austrians, were marching from all points of the horizon against France, two hundred thousand Prussians promising to join them, and all at once, a hundred thousand French, starting from the coasts of the ocean, traversing in two months a great part of the European continent, taking the first army opposed to them without fighting, inflicting redoubled blows on the others, entering the astonished capital of the ancient Germanic empire, passing beyond Vienna and going to the frontier of Poland, to break in one great battle the bond of the coalition; sending back the vanquished Russians to their frozen plains, and chaining the disconcerted Prussians to their frontiers; the dread of

Crisis of the Bank.—New cares awaited me at the Tuileries. The first which I had to attend to resulted from an event entirely unexpected: at the moment when I was founding the power and glory of France on a basis apparently immovable, the state was near being overwhelmed by an unexpected bankruptcy. Barbé-Marbois had taken it into his head to improve the funds of the treasury by exchanging one hundred and forty millions for Spanish bonds on Vera Cruz, which could not be realized. He was forced to have recourse to the bank to meet the expenses of the government; the bank was in its turn embarrassed, and its notes, which had braved all the revolutionary storms, lost their credit to such a degree that a panic-stricken multitude besieged its doors to get them exchanged for specie. Never was there a financial crisis more singular or more inopportune. Arriving at the Tuileries at nine o'clock in the evening, I passed the night in examining the accounts of the treasury, and at eleven o'clock the following morning a council of finance was convoked to devise means to remedy the evil. I had at this time no secret treasure in the vaults of the Tuileries; some resources were requisite to meet our immediate wants; we happily succeeded in obtaining them; confidence was gradually restored, and all Paris recovered from the panic. This crisis proved to me that the credit of a state is not always equal to its wants, and made me sensible of the necessity of providing a special fund ready for future events.*

a war which might be expected to last long, terminated in three months; the peace of the continent suddenly restored, the peace of the seas justly hoped for; all the prospects of prosperity given back to France, delighted and placed at the head of the nations—for what should people rejoice, we repeat, if not for such miracles? And as at that time none could foresee the too speedy end of their greatness, or yet discern, in the too fertile genius that produced it, the too ardent genius also that was destined to compromise it, one sympathized in the public happiness without any mixture of sinister presentiments."

* Napoleon's manner of dealing with the *United Merchants* whose speculations had so embarrassed the public treasury is thus described by Thiers:

"Napoleon instantly summoned a council to the Tuileries, and desired to be

Relations with England.—To this crisis succeeded new political difficulties; the great events which had marked this campaign of 1805, both on land and sea, had entirely changed

furnished with a detailed report of the operations of the company, which were still obscure to him. He required the attendance of all the ministers, and also of M. Mollien, director of the sinking fund, whose management he approved, and whom he thought to possess in a much higher degree than M. de Marbois the dexterity necessary for the administration of funds on a great scale. He sent an authoritative order to Messieurs Desprez, Vanlerberghe, and Ouvrard, and to the clerk who was accused of having deceived the minister of the treasury, to come to the Tuileries.

"All the persons who attended were intimidated by the presence of the emperor, who did not conceal his resentment. M. de Marbois began reading a long report which he had drawn up relative to the subject under discussion. He had not read far before Napoleon, interrupting him, said, "I see how it is. It was with the funds of the treasury and those of the bank that the Company of *United Merchants* calculated on providing supplies for France and Spain. And, as Spain had nothing to give but promises and piastres, it is with the money of France that the wants of both countries have been supplied. Spain owed me a subsidy, and it is I who have furnished her with one. Now Messieurs Desprez, Vanlerberghe, and Ouvrard, must give up to me all they possess; Spain must pay me what she owes them, or I will shut up those gentlemen in Vincennes and send an army to Madrid.'

"Napoleon appeared cold and stern toward M. de Marbois—'I esteem your character,' said he, 'but you have been the dupe of men against whom I warned you to be upon your guard. You have given up to them all the effects in the portfolio, over the employment of which you ought to have been more watchful. I regret to find myself obliged to withdraw from you the administration of the treasury, for, after what has happened, I cannot leave it to you any longer.' Napoleon then ordered the members of the company, who had been summoned to the Tuileries to be introduced. Messieurs Vanlerberghe and Desprez, though the least reprehensible, melted into tears. M. Ouvrard, who had compromised the company by hazardous speculations, was perfectly calm. He endeavored to persuade Napoleon that he ought to permit him to wind up himself, the very complicated affairs in which he had involved his partners, and that he should bring over from Mexico, by way of Holland and England, considerable sums, and far superior to those which France had advanced.

"It is probable that he would have managed the winding up of these affairs much better than any other person; but Napoleon was too much incensed, and too impatient to get out of the hands of speculators, to trust to his promises. He left M. Ouvrard and his partners the alternative of a criminal prosecution or the immediate surrender of all they possessed, whether stores, paper securities, immovables, or pledges received from Spain. They submitted to this cruel sacrifice.

"This was sure to prove a ruinous liquidation for them, but they had rendered themselves liable to it by abusing the resources of the treasury."

the respective situation of the two rivals who were disputing the commerce and influence of the world. The battle of Trafalgar had given the sovereignty of the sea to the English; it was necessary to adopt some new system to counterbalance these deplorable effects. It is an old adage that, *he who is master of the sea, is also of the land.* However paradoxical this may seem, it will not be denied that it has in it some truth, when we reflect upon the importance acquired by some of the smallest states, by the great extension of their navy, and the rapid increase of the Roman power as soon as it got rid of the rivalry of Carthage. The discovery of America and the invention of the compass, doubled the importance of the navy, and the power which it successively gave to the Dutch, Spanish, and English, had daily given force to this prejudice. I fully appreciated the influence due to this empire of the seas; but I nevertheless thought, with reason, that the principal cause of this influence was due to the divisions of the continental powers, and that the adage would become false, if ever these powers should come to a proper understanding. Fully convinced that France could never reach the apogee of her prosperity and power if she remained inferior to England on the seas, I resolved to do every thing in my power to build up our navy and to find, in the results of the victories of Ulm and Austerlitz, the means of saving America, of delivering India, of freeing Europe from a yoke which would ruin its commerce.

Progress of the English in India.—The English power in India had increased three-fold since the time of my expedition to Egypt; the fall of Tippoo, and the successive defeats of Schindiah, and of the Rajah of Berar, at Delhi, at Lassavary, and at Assey by Lake and Wellesley, and the submission of the Rajah of Bhurtpoor, and of Holkar, had increased the subjects of the English company to forty millions, and their disciplined forces, including Sepoys and

Europeans, to two hundred thousand men! Here was a power threatening the subjugation of Asia. All Europe took up arms to prevent the union to France of some valleys of the Apennines; but no one troubled himself about the progress of the English power in the east and in the Gulf of Mexico!

To obtain my object, required time and peace; but an honorable peace: one that would not deprive France of the means of accomplishing her ends. This could hardly be hoped for, when we think of the violent hatred against me breathed by the English journals, whose inevitable result was to embitter my feelings of hostility. I had not, like Hannibal, sworn in my infancy eternal war against the enemies of my country, but I had to avenge myself for numerous personal attacks which had been instigated by the English government. I felt that their attacks were directed against my person as much as against France; that I had to prepare for a contest without end; in a word, that I must make my cause triumph or die; the future grandeur of France was not less interested in it than my own honor and my repose.

Maritime Expeditions of the French.—Not being able to contend with her either by great fleets or by means of a descent, I determined to strike England wherever I could reach her. Encouraged by the operations of Villeneuve in the Antilles, I ordered to sea one half of our fleet at Brest in two squadrons; the first, under Vuillaumez, was to go to the assistance of the Cape of Good Hope, and to throw in there a garrison of French troops; the second, under Leissegues, was to do the same at Santo-Domingo, where General Ferrand had alone sustained, for three years, all the efforts of the blacks and mulattoes. After doing this, these two squadrons were to cruise for prizes. The last reached its destination and landed the troops; but attacked by Admiral Duckworth in the roadstead where the ships were repairing, it was taken *en flagrant délit;* the superb ship Imperial, of one hundred and thirty guns, assailed by three hostile ships, was defeated; to prevent her being taken they ran her aground. The Diomède suffered the same fate; three others fell a prey to the English.

Vuillaumez, hearing, during his passage, that the Cape of Good Hope had fallen after eight days' attack into the power of Popham and Baird, who had landed there, made sail for Martinique: my brother Jerome served with him as *capitaine de vaisseau.* Soon afterward, chased by the three squadrons of Warren, Strachan, and Lewis, Admiral Vuillaumez detached the Vétéran, commanded by my brother to return to France to inform me of his position and the loss of the Cape. This ship made rich prizes off the Azores, but was overtaken by a part of the enemy's cruisers on the coast of Brittany, near L'Orient. Vuillaumez's squadron encountered a violent storm and was dispersed; the admiral reached Havana with his ship; three others were captured or burnt, and only one returned to our ports.

More fortunate in the Indian seas, Admiral Linois there captured rich prizes, and for a long time sustained the Isle-of-France. But in returning to Europe after the capture of the Cape of Good Hope, he fell, by night, into the midst of a squadron of the enemy and was taken, after a very brave defense, with the Marengo, which he commanded.

Means of opposing England on the Continent.—The unfortunate issue of these last naval operations confirmed me in the opinion that it was necessary to resort to more powerful means against England. It was necessary to find on the continent the means of striking her power and her commerce; in subjecting to my influence the coast-countries, I might some day have sailors and ships; and in the mean time by the possession of these coasts I would close all access to the monopoly of my enemies. The surest means of effecting this was by close alliances with the continental powers; but how could I hope to effect this, with any unanimity, against the commercial interests of some and the ambition of others? The latter, humiliated by our victories, sought only for vengeance; the former prospered only by their maritime relations and the benefits of their neutrality. This want of unanimity rendered necessary the alliance of at least one of the powers of the first rank. I had just acquired proof that we could not grapple with the British Colossus, without some continental counterpoise against the coalitions which the cabinet of St. James plotted against us, every time that it saw itself seriously threatened. It was only by this counterpoise that I could make auxiliaries of our continental forces, and direct a great part of the population and revenues of France to a maritime war.

Difficulty of forming Alliances.—The alliance of 1756 with Austria, had been formed by Louis XV. for this special object; and the family treaty with Spain, so creditable to M. Choiseul, and soon extended to the reigning houses of Naples and Sardinia, had perfected the federal system of France. The treaty with the cabinet of Madrid had been renewed; it was also essential to renew that with Austria. But could we attach to ourselves this power, beaten in a hundred combats and stripped by us of her preponderance in Germany and Italy? Had not the war of the Revolution established between these two ancient allies a rivalry, if not eternal, at least of long duration? Ought I to end this rivalry by stripping France of the fruits of her victories, in order to enrich a rancorous power whose interests might have been the same as those of Louis XV., but whose principles and views were now so much opposed to ours? Russia, on whom England could inflict much injury, feared also the more immediate ascendency with which I threatened Europe, and armed herself against me; I could not now seek her alliance, for we were at war. Prussia, enriched by her neutrality, hoped to see all the storms pass around her without being herself exposed to them; moreover, she alone would not have been sufficiently powerful to form the desired counterpoise. With her seven millions of inhabitants we could not oppose both Austria and Russia, without also employing all the resources of France; but this would not accomplish my object. Although this power as an ally was utterly insufficient to secure the continental equilibrium in a maritime contest with England, yet in my contest with the North, as will be shown hereafter, Prussia was the most desirable ally to render us arbiters of Europe. The situation of France in the two cases was entirely different, as also was the influence to be exerted by Prussia.

System of Federate States.—What course then remained for me to take? By surrounding France with many small states of the second order, united in a federation and interested by benefits received from us to fight for our cause, she would acquire a sufficient preponderance on the continent to render Austria and Russia less disposed to run risks of war; this would eventually enable me to direct all my power against England alone, and all my influence against her commerce.

Additions to the French Empire.—Such were the true causes of the successive additions to my empire, and of the kingdoms given to the members of my family. It was not increase of territory that I desired; but the elements of power to oppose the power of the English and of their allies. In proportion as the British squadrons destroyed our fleets, or captured some colony in the two Indies, in the same proportion did I declare the reunion of some province, to convince England that she would gain nothing by prolonging the war, and that each of her acquisitions would only tend to the increase of mine. This system was undoubtedly contrary to the principles of international law, as understood by publicists, which forbid conquests except where successions or marriages give legitimate claims; but it was not I who first set at nought these rules; Frederick the Great, and Catherine had, forty years before, shown how they regarded the matter; and many others had done the same before them. Moreover, the English claimed the right to do on the sea whatever Europe could not prevent. As the most abusive force was the only public law which they acknowledged, why was I not entitled to reprisals on the continent? If the sea belonged exclusively to the power that had the greatest number of ships, why should not the land belong to the power that possessed the greatest number of battalions, and knew best how to use them for the general interest of nations?

In accordance with the considerations here given, I resolved to profit by my great success in the campaign of 1805, to give a marked preponderance to my federate system! The kingdoms of Naples and of Holland, and the confederation of the Rhine were the result.

Death of Pitt.—At the moment that I was laying the foundation of these new systems in consequence of the treaty of Presbourg, I learned, on returning to Paris, the sudden death of the celebrated Pitt (January 23d). It has been said that the end of this great man was accelerated by the disappointment caused by the news of the battle of Austerlitz, which promised long prosperity to the empire which he had flattered himself would be overthrown. Be this as it may, the selection of his successor by the king proved that England required a change of system. Fox was placed at the head of the new administration. The choice of this orator, the well-known advocate of peace, was a good augury, although the position and individual opinion of a statesman is not always a sure criterion to judge of his conduct as a minister. Louis XII. once said that the king of France did not avenge the injuries of the duke of Orleans; a minister taken from the ranks of the opposition would be unworthy to hold the reins of government, if he could say that the opinions of the orator at the tribune should be those of the chief of the administration. Pitt had also figured on the benches of the opposition before taking the helm of affairs. Nevertheless the colleagues given to Fox (Erskine and Grey), were also reckoned among those who had constantly inclined toward peace.*

Blockade by a simple Order in Council.—However moderate might be the views of these new ministers, they were, nevertheless, English; and by their side sat Grenville, Windham, and Moira, whose sentiments were very different. One of their first measures was to declare, by an order in council of May 16th, the blockade of the ports of the channel from Antwerp to Havre. This new idea of blockading ports by a simple order in council was absurd; it was the more untimely as I then had no forces on this coast. I should have ordered immediate reprisals for this Algerine

* Charles James Fox was born in 1748, and was the second son of Lord Holland, so long the rival and opponent of the Earl of Chatham, father of William Pitt. It is a little singular that the second sons of these great parliamentary leaders should have inherited the talents, rivalry, and distinction of their fathers, while the elder sons, who inherited the titles and estates, were men of inferior ability. Fox was carefully educated and entered parliament in 1768, before he was of legal age. In 1770, he was made one of the lords of the admiralty, and the next year a commissioner of the treasury. His early parliamentary efforts gave little promise of his future career; but in the debates on the war with America, he displayed the highest talents both as a statesman and orator. From that time to his death, he acted both in parliament and in the ministry as one of the great party leaders.

William Pitt was born in 1759, eleven years after his great rival. He was carefully educated and entered parliament very young. At the age of twenty-three he was appointed chancellor of the exchequer, and at twenty-four was made prime minister. He continued from this time to his death one of the party leaders both in and out of parliament.

Pitt died on the twenty-third of January, 1806, and his rival Fox, on the fifteenth of the following September.

legislation, if new negotiations with the cabinet of St. James had not determined me to postpone my vengeance.*

New Difficulties with Prussia.—The state of the continent was not so pacific as was thought; indications of a new storm, though distant, were seen at all points of the horizon. I had already received at Munich the unexpected news that the king of Prussia was unwilling to ratify the treaty of Haugwitz, without exceptions which totally destroyed its character. It was true that, by an excess of excusable zeal, Haugwitz had acted contrary to his instructions, and perhaps had misinterpreted the orders of his master. The position of the king was very critical; he had just formed with England an agreement to protect her troops in Hanover, on condition that they would assist him if he should be attacked by France; this convention was even posterior to the treaty of Vienna, the latter having been signed on the fifteenth of December, and the former concluded at Berlin on the twenty-second. Haugwitz did not reach Berlin with his treaty till the twenty-fifth, three days after the convention. The Emperor Alexander proposed to the king to place at his disposal all the Russian army, as had been agreed upon at Potsdam. To throw himself into my alliance, in violation of engagements just made, was not worthy of the character of Frederick William; he, therefore, gave Haugwitz a cold reception; but state interest overcame his scruples; it was necessary to

* This British order in council was not only a violation of international law, as determined by the publicists of Europe, but was in direct contradiction to the definition of a blockade given by Great Britian in her treaties with foreign powers. In the convention of 1801 with Russia, it was stipulated that a blockaded port must have ships stationary or sufficiently near to constitute "*an evident danger in entering.*" The same definition is implied in treaties previously made between Great Britian and the Baltic powers, and with the United States; and in 1804, the board of admiralty instructed the naval commanders and judges of the vice-admiralty courts in the West Indies, not to consider a port as blockaded unless it was *actually invested.—Halleck's Int. Law*, ch. xxiii., § 7. *Wheaton's Elem. Int. Law*, pt. iv., ch. iii., § 28.

decide either to accept the treaty or to sustain alone all the weight of my anger.

The Cabinet of Berlin changes the Terms of the Treaty.—Influenced by his counsellors, the king took one of those intermediate courses which, instead of arranging matters, usually make them worse. He ratified the treaty on condition that he should temporarily occupy Hanover until peace; but that he would not yield his three provinces till England should sanction this acquisition. This was so unexpected that I had already ceded Anspach to Bavaria as an indemnity for the duchy of Wurtzbourg, which had been exchanged with the grand-duke of Tuscany for Salzbourg, the latter having been given to Austria. It would have been better to wait for the ratification at Berlin before disposing of the ceded provinces; but the evil had already been done, and there was no remedy. In giving to the king a rich electorate for small provinces detached at a great distance from his monarchy, I had given to him three times the population and revenues which he had given to me; he would be no longer in contact with our frontiers, and thus exposed to be drawn into any new war which we might have with Germany or Russia. This certainly was the most ample reparation which I could possibly offer him for the violation of his territory. Could I have done better had I punished Bernadotte for obeying my orders? Was it necessary that I myself should go to Berlin with a rope about my neck, as formerly the emperors of Germany went to make the amende-honorable to Rome? It seemed to me more simple for us to say, "We are natural allies; Hanover belongs to me by right of conquest; in yielding it to Prussia, I shall aggrandize her at the expense of my most bitter enemies, the provokers of all coalitions; the interest of the monarchy and of France were in this case the same, and it was better to accept such satisfaction than for Prussia to expose herself to my victorious army; at a time when Austria was incapable of rendering her assistance, and the Russians too distant to act in time."

Motives of this Step.—The moral reasons of Frederick William for refusing to accept the spoils of George III, with whom he was in the state of alliance rather than of war, were creditable to him. It was also evident that this acquisition could not be permanent, unless sanctioned by England at the declaration of peace. *Occupation is the result of conquest; but the possession is made legitimate only by treaties or by long and undisputed occupation.* The country which Frederick William was to receive for his three provinces, was certainly the most valuable; but then he might not be able to obtain an undisputed title, and might thus involve himself in permanent hostilities with England.

Negotiations of Haugwitz.—This disagreeable alternative resulted from the fault of Haugwitz, who, blinded by the apparent advantages of his treaty, had not given sufficient care to drawing it up. He should have stipulated that if the cession of Hanover became a positive obstacle to the conclusion of a general peace, and the welfare of Europe required its retrocession to England, an equivalent indemnity should be given to the king of Prussia. This clause having been neglected, the king might still have proposed it to me, and it is probable that I should have accepted it. If, on the contrary I had refused it, the king would have had the option between war with me and the uncertain chance of having it with the English. If he had adopted the first course, he ought instantly, but silently, to have sent a negotiator to St. Petersburg to recall the Russians into Silesia, and to have treated with the Austrians; if he adopted the second, he should have accepted the treaty as it was, observing to me that if this determination brought on war between Prussia and England, the cabinet of Berlin, decided to run all chances with me, would conclude an alliance offensive and defensive, which would secure to it a part of these chances if they should be favorable. But it was unable to decide, and of all parts it chose the one most objectionable to me and least advantageous to Prussia.

By a caprice still more incomprehensible, at the very moment when this cabinet was, by this conditional ratification, involving its position toward me, it entered Hanover with one part of its army, and reduced the remainder to the peace complement, thus disbanding half its forces. It thought to arrange every thing by sending Haugwitz to me at Paris, to plead a cause which could not be sustained either in appearance or in reality. If the refusal which he brought me had been accompanied by a declaration of war, I should have understood it; but to accept the odium of an invasion of Hanover, and, notwithstanding this, to put every thing in question with me, was a proceeding which the most acute would find it difficult to explain. This incident, taken in connection with the progress of the anti-French party at Berlin, and the credit enjoyed by Hardenberg, a well-known partisan of England, whose subject he was (being a Hanoverian), and a thousand other circumstances, convinced me that, notwithstanding the noble character of Frederick William, I ought hereafter to be on my guard with Prussia. Except the cabinet, every thing at Berlin took a hostile aspect; the army, ashamed, it said, of the silly part it was made to play, demanded war at all hazards; numerous groups of officers had insulted the hotel of the pacific minister who had preferred the aggrandizement of his country to an untimely war; lieutenants of hussars wished to decide upon the great interests of the state.*

* Christian Henry Charles, Count of Haugwitz, was born in Silesia in 1758. He early engaged in diplomatic affairs, and succeeded Hertzberg as Minister of Foreign Affairs and President of the Prussian cabinet. He was greatly distinguished as a diplomatist, but retired from public life after the battle of Jena,

A new Treaty.—Far from allowing myself to be imposed on by this new event, I saw instantly the use I might make of it in my present position and that of Europe, to strike a master blow; it was requisite that Prussia in fifteen days should enter into my system and under my direct influence, or fall before my attacks. It was evident that the treaty of Vienna, mutilated of ten lines which destroyed its character, was null and void; I declared to Haugwitz that his cabinet had destroyed itself, and that matters must be submitted to a new negotiation. I required the instant surrender of the provinces which Prussia had given me in exchange, as I had already ceded Anspach; I obliged her to renounce the cession of twenty thousand inhabitants which Bavaria was to make her; finally, I forced the cabinet of Berlin to close its ports to the English.

The same ministers, who had rejected the treaty of Haugwitz, negotiated between equal powers with reciprocal advantages, having no longer an army in hand, were too happy to treat even with these onerous conditions. I expected this result, for I had seen at a glance the position, into which these weak counsellors had precipitated the king; I, nevertheless, was surprised at their eagerness to commit this new act of condescension: I had constantly found Frederick

of which he was a witness. He died in 1828, after having been blind for some years.

Charles Augustus, Prince of Hardenberg, was born at Hanover, 1750. In 1778 he was made Privy Councillor, and 1790 Minister of State. In 1795, he signed the treaty between Prussia and the French Republic. From that period till Haugwitz retired from public life, these two statesmen were at the head of parties, the latter, of that which favored an alliance with France, and Hardenberg of that which opposed it. After the overthrow of Napoleon, he represented Prussia in the congress of Paris, and the congress of Vienna, in 1814 and 1815. He was created a prince, and made President of the Council of State. He was present in 1818, at the Congress of Aix-la-Chapelle; in 1819, at Carlsbad; in 1820, at Vienna, at Troppau and Verona. Although opposed to the liberal party in Prussia, and in his latter years, considered as "the active agent of the Holy Alliance," he nevertheless deserved much credit for the abolition of feudal privileges in Prussia. He died in 1822.

William pursuing a course of wise policy, although the treaty of Potsdam had abruptly followed the hostile demonstrations of the Prussians on the Vistula, still there were sufficient motives for it in a violation of their territory, thus giving it the appearance of a well-marked policy ; it even denoted a decision of character strong enough to promise a rupture instead of a *dénouement* so favorable to my views ; this victory of the pen in the treaty of Vienna had surpassed all my hopes. I had taken Europe without its cuirass, and the question now was to profit by this circumstance ; an occasion soon presented itself.

Cattaro and Wurtzbourg.—Hardly had the new treaty of February 15th been ratified at Berlin (eight days after), than new difficulties, resulting from two grave events, were likely to embroil me with Austria ; the cabinet of Vienna in ceding to me Venetian Dalmatia, had engaged to give me the important port of the mouths of the Cattaro ; it had merely withdrawn its own garrison from this place, and the Russians of the fifteenth division, stationed in the Seven-Isles, having thrown in there a detachment reënforced by Montenegrins, so that we could get possession of it only by a resort to force. I demanded that Austria should put me in possession of this port ; and, as I could not go by land from Venice to Dalmatia without passing by Trieste and Croatia, I claimed the right of passage which Austria had always given to the Venetians. An event of a different nature in Germany was near embroiling us ; the Austrians had sent their troops to take possession of Wurtzbourg which had been ceded to the grand duke of Tuscany, not to the cabinet of Vienna. This movement might have suited the ancient usages of the German Empire, but it did not at all agree with my projects on Germany. I ordered the march of the prisoners who were crossing Swabia to be suspended ; I incorporated in my army the battalions of depôt which formed the corps of reserve of Lefebvre and Kellerman* which increased it above the complement; I directed the prince of Neufchatel (Berthier), whom I had left in Bavaria, not to turn over Braunau to the Austrians, and to capture such of their battalions as should dare to enter Wurtzbourg after receiving notification to retire.

A Federation in place of the German Empire.—My course was decided; certain of the alliance of Prussia, I wished to throw myself at the head of two hundred and fifty thousand men on Austria, who was now without an army, or to profit by my attitude to force her to execute her treaties, and, at the same time, to renounce the German Empire.† The firmness of my attitude and the completion of all the corps of my army imposed on her so much the more as hers was in the greatest disorder, and she had vainly waited for the arrival of the prisoners of Mack's army to effect its reorganization. The weak condition of this power, and the declaration of war by Prussia against the English rendering me master of Germany, I determined to profit by circumstances which might never again occur so favorable, to secure my ascendency on the continent and to furnish me with the means of triumph in my maritime quarrel.

Napoleon crowns several Members of his Family.—I had already given the prelude of this system in placing my brothers on thrones which would at the same time increase the lustre of my family and place the neighboring states in a more direct dependency. The imperial throne was hereditary in my family; it also commenced a new dynasty which time must consecrate as it had legitimated all the others; for since the time of Charlemagne no crown had ever been

* The elder Kellerman, or duke of Valmy.

† Jomini says that Napoleon was perfectly right in requiring Austria to execute her treaty in relation to the Cattaro, but that he carried matters unnecessarily far in demanding her renunciation of the German Empire.

given with so much solemnity. I had received it by the voice of the people and the sanction of the church. My family, being called to reign, ought not to remain in the ranks of society; this would have been a contradiction. We were rich in conquests, and it was necessary to connect these conquered states intimately to the system of the empire, in order to incline the continental balance on our side. It is paradoxical to pretend that people are bound by any other ties than those of common interest. History is filled with proofs against such opinions; it abounds with examples of treaties made for the single interest of the governing families. This becomes a great misfortune where the general interests of the people are not those of their chiefs; but this is no new thing; how many princes and even republics have made treaties which were opposed to the general interest of the country? Undoubtedly the freedom of the seas at which I aimed was desired by all states, and more especially by those bordering on the seas; but the smaller states were unwilling to submit to be for a long period deprived of their commerce for the vague hope of obtaining this general maritime freedom. Under this point of view their momentary interests, as well as that of their reigning dynasties, were opposed to us, since we would not allow their connection with England. It was not in my power to change this situation of things, but I could do much by substituting for a hostile administration, a government interested in our success. This was the only means by which we could induce those people who were indifferent, to battle for our cause; this was the only way of making them endure, in spite of themselves, long sacrifices whose fruits were beyond the reach of their short-sighted judgment.

Joseph King of Naples.—I accomplished those objects by placing my family on the vacant thrones. The first which presented itself was that of Naples. This unhappy country required a master to save it from anarchy and civil war: my brother Joseph ascended this throne which Massena had just conquered.

Louis, King of Holland.—Holland had long since lost the energy necessary for a Republic; she was no longer capable of playing such a part; she had shown this at the time of the expedition of the duke of York. The grand-pensionary Schimmelpenninck, was expected to live but a short time; *and I could not leave to the caprices of an elective system the chances of an alliance with a people so necessary to my projects against England.* I had reason to suspect that the nation might recall the House of Orange, after what had passed in 1787. Holland therefore seemed to require a sovereign, and I gave to her my brother Louis.

Eugene made Heir to the Throne of Lombardy.—The iron crown of the Lombard kings was already on my head; it would have been imprudent to give it to another; the example would have been dangerous. Austria, the power most interested in the fate of Italy, had recognized me as king; but to calm her fears and the fears of the rest of Europe, I appointed Eugene Beauharnois viceroy, securing to him at my death the heritage of this crown.

Murat made Grand Duke of Berg.—I gave to Murat the grand-duchy of Berg. My sister Pauline Borghese had the Principality of Guastalla; Eliza Biacciochi was proclaimed princess of Lucca, of Piombino and of Massacarara; Berthier, as has already been mentioned, had the principality of Neufchatel, which had been ceded by Prussia.

Military Operations in Naples.—Carried away by the course of my recital, I have disposed of the crown of Naples without saying any thing of the events which put it in my power. It will be remembered that after the peace of Presbourg I had directed Massena to take revenge for the bad faith of this court in violating its treaties. This general crossed the Garigliano on the eighth of February, and marched in three columns on Gaeta, Capua and Itry. The Neapolitan troops disappeared in every direction, without making the slightest resistance. The court fled to Sicily, terrified at my proclamation of the twenty-seventh of December. Joseph entered Naples on the fifteenth of February. The deputies of the regency had already surrendered Capua; never was a conquest more easily made. It seemed as if some snare had been laid for us; so slight was the resistance made to our taking possession. The prince of Sicily had collected in Calabria a nucleus of a Neapolitan army of about eighteen or twenty thousand men under the prince of Rosenheim and Count Damas, flattering himself that the Calabrians would rise *en masse* to second him, as they had done under Cardinal Ruffo in 1799. General St. Cyr was charged with reducing Apulia and Abruzzo as far as Tarentum; Reynier was directed to overrun Calabria; Massena was employed in the defense of Naples and the siege of Gaeta. Reynier having completely routed the division of Damas at Campo-Tenesa, while Duhesme pushed on by the Basilicata against the division of Rosenheim, the Neapolitan army dispersed; the princes embarked at Reggio with only two thousand men. My brother received, while in Calabria, the decree giving him the crown of Naples. This news was received in the capital with every demonstration of joy; there appeared to be no regret at the change; they had become wearied with an odious administration; they hoped every thing from a better future. Nevertheless, the joy manifested by our partisans was troubled by the sudden appearance of Sidney Smith, who, having taken command of the English squadron, might possibly add a *bombardment* to the illuminations and public fêtes in celebration of this event! But as little inclined to burn a palace, which would have been useless to his cause, as he had been eager to burn our arsenal at Toulon, this admiral was content to frighten the Neapolitans, and then carry by a *coup de main* the island of Capri, notwithstanding the heroic defense of a company which occupied it.

Siege of Gaeta.—But the position of Joseph at Naples was not yet without its difficulties. Gaeta still prolonged its defense. This place, situated on a rock, connected to the land only by a hill of four hundred toises perfectly fortified in amphitheatre, offered only a single front of attack, and this was exceedingly difficult to be reduced. The prince of Hesse-Philipstadt, a Hessian officer, full of courage and energy, was in command. The garrison, daily supplied by sea, was disposed to assist him. The siege was commenced near the end of May under the direction of Generals Campredon and Vallongue; Dedon commanded the artillery.

Diversion in Calabria.—During the four months that Reynier had occupied Calabria, the court of Sicily had had time to foment an insurrection there. When every thing was ready, and the English thought they could, with advantage, fall upon a weak and isolated corps, General Stuart made a descent at the head of nine thousand Anglo-Sicilians, in the Gulf of St. Euphemia. Reynier, having hastily collected a division of six thousand men, marched to meet the enemy and attacked him, the fourth of July, on the heights between Maida and the sea; but he was vigorously repulsed and forced to retreat on Crotona. This check became the signal for a general revolt. The Calabrians, assembled at the tocsin, fell on our isolated detachments; everywhere our soldiers were either murdered or forced to cut their way sword in hand.

In the mean time Massena was pressing the siege of Gaeta. Vallongue, general of engineers, who had directed the preparatory works and established the grand breaching battery, was killed on the fourteenth of June by a musket-ball. The works of attack had been pushed forward till the twenty-eighth with a rare constancy, for the place had for the past two months fired incessantly upon our troops, without their returning a single shot. Finally, on that day (the twenty-eighth) the batteries which General Dedon had armed with fifty pieces of thirty-three pounders, and twenty-four mortars of the largest calibre, opened their fire, all at the same time, in presence of the king. The prince of Hesse returned it with great tenacity, but on the tenth day, he received a severe wound in the head which forced him to resign the command. A breach was opened near the citadel; a second, still more difficult, was made in the three-tier bastion which commanded the front. Massena had formed two thousand five hundred grenadiers for an assault when the place capitulated. The garrison, seven thousand strong, were permitted to go to Sicily. The place had fired in three months one hundred and seventeen thousand shot, and twenty thousand shells.

As soon as Massena, by the reduction of this important place, had removed all fear of a hostile descent, he left Naples to join Reynier, and, at the head of fifteen thousand men, to reduce Calabria. After having completely beaten the insurgents at Cocozza, he dispersed without difficulty, but not without some fighting, this swarm of barbarians who had been incited by their priests. General Stuart, unwilling to expose the honor of the British flag by trusting too much to their assistance or by advancing too far into the interior of the country, deemed it best not to risk a battle with superior forces, and reëmbarked for Messina on the fifth of September. The insurrection by a wise union of vigor, energy, and clemency, was gradually extinguished; and, by his parental administration, Joseph might now consider himself firmly seated on the throne of Ferdinand IV.

Confederation of the Rhine.—It now only remained for

me to regulate the affairs of Germany, more important than all the others for the execution of my grand federative project. The German Empire had received rude shocks by the Reformation, the thirty years' war, and the peace of Westphalia; by the wars of Charles Theodore against Leopold, and of Frederick the Great against Maria Theresa; and lastly by the campaign of 1799. If we add the scission introduced by the neutrality of the North, the manner in which Hanover had been treated by me, and Pomerania by her own sovereign, and lastly, the erection of Bavaria and Wurtemberg into monarchies, it will be seen that this political mummy, completely mutilated, would necessary fall at the slightest breath; it required but one more blow to finish its destruction. My army was still on the Danube; Soult was still in possession of Braunau. I caused to be signed, on the twelfth of July, a treaty by which Bavaria, Wurtemberg, Baden, Hesse-Darmstadt, and Nassau renounced all connection with the Roman Empire, in order to form a confederation of the Rhine, under the presidency of Baron D'Alberg, arch-chancellor, who took the title of *Prince Primate;* the statutes conferred on me the title of *Protector*.

Apart from these last two clauses and all that might concern me personally in this important transaction, it accorded perfectly with the new situation of Europe, and with the special interest of Germany. To be convinced of this it is only necessary to look back on the part which this country has played in Europe for the last two centuries; if the internal strength of Germany was nothing, her external influence was still less. Bandied about between the preeminence of Austria, the opposite influence of Prussia, the influence of France and Russia, its relations with England, formed through Hanover, and its connection with Sweden through Pomerania; Germany, like Italy, had become a mere geographical figure to be learned by school-boys; but as for a separate power and a separate nation, they no longer existed: such is the inevitable fate of all federate and elective states when surrounded by neighbors sufficiently strong and sufficiently adroit to control them. This state of things, which only required the application of the rule *to divide and conquer*, was well suited to the France of the eighteenth century, which was then weaker than Austria; but since the partition of Poland, victorious France was interested in reconstituting Germany, making it independent of Austria and Russia. To give a common centre to sixteen millions of Germans was for our interest as well as theirs; for being unable to maintain themselves without our assistance, their interests would for a long time be intimately connected with ours. On the other hand, they would constitute a separate *nation* having their own alliances and interests, independent of the house of Austria: in a word they would form a real Germany. The project was certainly excellent; but there was an error in its execution. I ought to have given to this federation a German chief, selected from one of the most powerful houses, and have satisfied myself with connecting it to France by treaties offensive and defensive, without assuming a title which wounded the German pride and added nothing to my power. As it was, this confederation did not suit my empire; I ought to have rendered it useful to France, to Germany, and to the rest of Europe.

Francis abdicates the Crown of Germany and is proclaimed Emperor of Austria.—This treaty was sent to Vienna to receive the sanction of Austria. I also sent it to Berthier and to the minister Otto at Munich, in order that they might exchange its ratification, or, in case of the refusal of Austria, that my army might instantly take position on the Inn. The cabinet of Vienna having received it at the same time with the news of the treaty signed by D'Oubril, deemed it unwise to risk a war, without an army and without allies, in defense of a title which had been utterly vain for the last century. It appeared preferable to abdicate a throne which had caused it more than one ruinous war without equivalent advantages; to renounce a pompous but not hereditary title, and to satisfy itself with that of hereditary emperor of Austria, Hungary, and Bohemia. Francis II. therefore abdicated, by his declaration of August 6th, the German crown which he had received in 1792, and commenced, under the name of Francis I., the series of emperors of Austria. This even surpassed my hopes; I almost expected to be obliged to seek this sanction at the gates of Vienna; undoubtedly the treaty signed by D'Oubril contributed very much to this result.

Sensation at Berlin.—This event, announced at Berlin immediately after the nomination of my brother Louis to the throne of Holland, and of my brother-in-law Murat to the grand-duchy of Berg, threatened Prussia with new collisions which she had hoped to escape. The counsellors of Frederick William could sound the abyss half opened beneath their feet: they now regretted that they had not either adhered frankly to the first treaty of Haugwitz, or to that of Potsdam with Russia; but the opportune moment being past, could they now fight alone? Was it for their interest to do so? There seems no doubt that the negative was the true answer to these questions. Prussia, it is true, played a second part in the German Confederation; it was important to preserve this, in order to augment her federative system and cover herself with neutral provinces; but her religion prevented her from taking the first part in the Roman Empire, and she could easily console herself for its fall, if she should succeed in forming a counter-confederation at the north, by allying to herself Saxony, the elector of Hesse, Pomerania, the dukes of Mecklenbourg, and the dukes of Brunswick—countries already subject to her influence, and which she might place still more directly under her protectorate. This would increase her in proportion to my aggrandizement, and preserve the relative position of the two provinces. Frederick William chose this course in preference to war; he negotiated this confederation, treating with its members rather as equals than as dependents, whereas I had vassals rather than allies, and acted by decrees rather than treaties.

Presidency of the Confederation of the Rhine.—It would perhaps have given my work a more solid basis if I had given the presidency of the Confederation of the Rhine to Prussia instead of a feeble prince whose heir, loaded with my favors, so ill recompensed me for them. The nation and court of Prussia, gained over by such a favor, would probably have become frankly attached to my destinies. I should then have had faithful allies from the Rhine to the Niemen; and, supported on such a base, I might have undertaken any thing. It may be said that this was uselessly destroying the power of Austria to erect another in its place equally formidable. Nothing is less true. Austria alone had twenty-four millions of subjects exclusive of the German empire; Prussia on the contrary had only ten millions, Hanover included; but the presidency of a federation of kings of hardly ten millions of subjects, would not have added to the strength of Prussia in the proportion of its own positive power. Moreover, Prussia would have been indebted for this grandeur to me, whereas Austria was indebted to me only for having opposed her; this would have made a great difference in the sentiments of the two powers. Prussia, raised to an empire at the expense of Austrian influence would have been an eternal rival to the court of Vienna: she would have been under our influence for the next century. If ever my policy had been interested in doing so, a word from me would at any time have been sufficient to make these provinces of the confederation the adversaries of their president.

Internal State of the French Empire.—But external policy did not occupy all my thoughts; it was necessary to consolidate my work by giving to France institutions suited to the new social order which she had adopted; as has been said by one well qualified to judge: "It was necessary to create my age for me, as I had been created for it. It was necessary to be a legislator, after having been a warrior. It was not possible to carry back the Revolution, for that would have been to again subject the strong to the weak, which was contrary to nature. It was necessary to accommodate to it an analogous system of legislation. This system will survive me, and I have left to Europe a heritage which it can not reject without falling into barbarism or anarchy.

"There was really in the state only a vast democracy, led by a dictatorship. This kind of government is well-suited for execution; but it is of a temporary nature, inasmuch as it could only last during the lifetime of the dictator. I was to render it perpetual by creating durable institutions and corporations and by placing them between the throne and the democracy. It was useless to attempt any thing with the old lever of habitudes and illusions; I was obliged to make every thing a reality. It was therefore necessary to found my legislation on the immediate interests of the majority, and to create my corporations with these interests, because interests are certainly the most real and tangible things in this world.

"I made laws whose effect was immense, but uniform. They had for their principle the maintenance of *equality*. This is so strongly stamped on these codes that they alone will be sufficient to preserve it."

I resolved at this epoch to establish an intermediate class. It was to be democratic, inasmuch as any one could enter it, and at any time; it was to be monarchical, inasmuch as it could not die, and would serve as a barrier against this same democracy; it was to be strictly national, inasmuch as it would include all who had rendered eminent services to the state. But public opinion was not yet prepared for the execution of this project, and I was obliged to defer it till a more suitable opportunity. In the mean time, the same message of March 30th, to the senate, announcing the distribution of states to my family, and of the interior *régime* imposed on France, also announced the establishment of twenty-one grand fiefs of the empire in Italy. Bernadotte was indebted to his relationship to my brother Joseph for the principality of Ponte-Corvo; Talleyrand had the duchy of Benevento. These titles, followed shortly after by those given to my generals and grand functionaries, by the several classes of the Legion of Honor, and the senatorship, gradually destroyed the ideas of equality and the leveling of ranks; but the *equality of rights*, which is the only reasonable one, was preserved.

Mechanism of Napoleon's Government.—After the disorders of the Revolution it was important to reëstablish order, for this is the test of its strength and durability. Administrators and judges are essential to a state, for on them alone depends the public order, that is, the execution of the laws. I associated them to the movement which animated the people and the army, and even to their own recompenses: I had instituted an order which would honor the administrators, for it had already received its character from the soldiers who had entered it; I made it common to all who should serve the state, because the first of virtues is devotion to country. Those who did not understand my motives have reproached me for this. They said that illustrious warriors, conquerors in a hundred battles, should not be decorated with the same cordon as an administrator who, at ease, in the bosom of repose, makes his fortune, even though he has managed the public finances with perfect probity. Far from disputing the necessity of having an order purely military, I afterward wished to reëstablish one, by instituting the *Trois-Toisons*. But the Legion of Honor had a double object, which I should not have accomplished if I had confined it to the military. It served to unite all classes of the nation, for in it none were subordinate or excluded. It formed around me an intermediate corps, a kind of notability composed of the *élite* of the nation, which would be attached to the imperial system by its vocation, its interests, and its opinions; in a word the cross of the Legion of Honor was to France what the Ring of the Knight was at Rome. This numerous body, although clothed with civil and military power, was popular with the people, inasmuch as it was drawn from their ranks. They had confidence in it, for its interests were connected with their own.

The empire was based on a strong organization. The army was formed in the school of war; it had learned to fight and to suffer. The civil functionaries were accustomed to strictly execute the laws, for I allowed nothing arbitrary or latitudinarian in their interpretations. They were formed with promptness and exactitude. I had given everywhere a uniform impression, for throughout the whole empire there was but a single command. Thus moved this great governmental machine within the limits which I had formed for it. I had at one time the grand idea of rendering all public employments irremovable, except for offenses tried before a tribunal and with a formal judgment. I saw in this a great moral advantage and a pledge of stability. A man who holds a public employment for life, thinks twice before he risks its loss. The state in this way secures more faithful men for its servants, and the public employés are no longer exposed to arbitrary dismissals; there is much less chance for intrigue and favoritism.

I put a stop to defalcations by centralizing, on a single point, the entire fiscal machine. Nothing in this department was left vague and undefined; all half responsibilities of the provinces were superseded, for experience had proved that this system only tended to enrich petty speculators at the expense of the treasury, the people, and the public welfare.

The Public Credit restored.—I had restored the public credit, by not using, and by establishing, certain sinking funds. To the abuse of loans which paralyzed France, there had succeeded a system of imposts which relieved her finances. Nevertheless it was possible for me to give a wider base to our *credit de bourse.* The fear of *abuse* had prevented me from making any farther *use* of loans, a valuable resource which should always be managed with great care. I proscribed stock-jobbing, by forbidding all action of the treasury on the public funds. We frequently had much more specie in deposit than was requisite to raise the value of these funds above par. But I always opposed any resort to such measures, and by these scruples deprived myself of great resources.

The Conscription regulated.—I perfected the system of conscription by a law rigorous, but grand, and the only one worthy of a people who cherish glory and liberty; for such a people should trust its defense to no one but itself. So true is this, that nothing else can be substituted for it, and it is still preserved by those who sought to render it odious.

Public Monuments.—I added several great monuments to those which France already possessed. The four most important are not yet completed, viz.: that of Mont-Cénis, the Triumphal Arch of the Simplon, at Milan, the Arc de l'Etoile, and the Temple of Madeline at Paris. They will serve as witnesses of my glory, and will tend to elevate the souls of our descendants; the people value these noble images of their history. The column of the Place Vendome will live as long as that of Trajan. My throne was brilliant not merely by the glory of arms. The French love grandeur, even in appearance. I decorated the palaces; I collected there a numerous court; I gave to it an austere character; no other would have been suitable. It has been said by some that my court was neither amusing nor amiable, and that the ladies detested me. It is true that they played but a pitiful part in comparison with that under Madame Dubarry, and that they were made subordinate to the grandeur of the state. Louis XV. would, perhaps, have suited them better, but with the exception of the dowagers of the Faubourg Saint-Germain, and those women who renounced all the duties of their sex to make themselves celebrated at any price,* I believe that the French ladies rendered me justice, at least prior to 1813. They amused themselves at my court in a manner more serious than at the Parc-au-Cerf and in the orgies of the Regency; nevertheless, they did amuse themselves.

Internal Improvements.—I did not limit all my cares to these monuments, symbols of power and glory; I directed equal attention to all commercial and industrial establish-

* This seems intended for Madame de Staël, and women of her character. Madame de Staël was the daughter of Necker, the Minister of Finance under Louis XVI. She was born in 1766, and married the Baron de Staël-Holstein in 1786. She afterward separated from her husband and lived with a young French officer named Rocca. Her marriage to this officer was not known till after her death. She at first manifested a great admiration for Napoleon and sought to gain him over to her views in regard to the independence of Switzerland, but failing in this, and other political projects, she formed for him a strong aversion. Napoleon disliked female politicians, and while he showed much attention to Necker, he avoided the society of his daughter. She did not fail to resent this by sarcastic remarks upon the emperor, which were repeated even in the salons of Paris. She died in 1817.

Her mind was of a masculine character, which was exhibited in all her writings. Although her style is irregular and has too much pretension, we find in all her works original and profound thought. She had a lively imagination which naturally led her to exaggeration, and often caused her to give a false coloring to facts. While her writings are valuable and interesting, her statements are not always reliable. Although she wrote much upon literary subjects, her taste evidently ran to politics, in which she was less successful. *Corinne* is the most brilliant and popular of all her works.

ments. Of course I did not forget those of a military character. Many new communications were opened to commerce; I connected Italy with France by four magnificent roads through the Alps. I here undertook works whose execution had before seemed impossible. The roads of the Simplon and Mont Cenis, and that of the Corniche, which runs from Nice by Genoa to Florence, are lasting monuments of my genius. I afterward learned in my exile that Austria and Sardinia have followed with giant steps the career which I opened to them; imitation is not difficult when we have living models before our eyes. We must nevertheless render justice to governments which can learn something; there are so many which never learn any thing!

I encouraged the progress of agriculture by promulgating laws for the protection of property, and by distributing equally the public burdens. The canals of St. Quentin, Burgundy, and of Alsace, have united the Seine and the Saône to the Rhine, and to the North Sea; the latter secured to us outlets for our agricultural produce into Holland and to the Weser, especially when the coast trade was interrupted; the former secured to us a communication with Belgium. All kinds of manufactures were encouraged both by premiums and by laws protecting them from foreign competition.

Military and Maritime Works.—My activity redoubled with my solicitude for whatever concerned our system of fortifications. The works ordered at Alexandria were calculated to secure us a permanent establishment beyond the Alps; some thought that it would have been better to have established a good fortified place at Pavia or Cremona; the question is too long to be discussed here. With the same hand that projected the works of Buderich to secure the Weser by both banks of the Rhine, and to complete the general system of defense of this superb barrier, I traced the plans for fortifying Cassel and Kehl, which had just been ceded to us by the grand dukes of Baden and Darmstadt. I employed a portion of the contributions of Austria to establish a *tête-de-pont* on the Lech; I at the same time constructed good temporary fortifications for the security of Dalmatia.

Antwerp, and Venice especially, were not forgotten. The description of the immense works ordered for these two forts would itself fill a volume. The country of the Morosini, the Alviani, and of the Dandolos, might, under my care, one day arise from its ruins, if not as the capitol, at least as the great *place-d'armes* and entrepôt of the Levant. The superb arsenal, the only heritage which Venice had preserved of her empire of the seas, was beginning to resume all its wonted activity; the vast forest of Illyria and of Macedonia would supply us with timber; Hungary with copper; commerce could procure us canvas and cordage; Dalmatia and Albania would supply us with good sailors. Who could say that Greece with her fifty isles would not one day furnish us a nursery of intrepid sailors?

At the same time that I rebuilt these great ports, I ordered the defenses of Brest, Cherbourg and Rochefort to be augmented. I was at the same moment carrying on the most important negotiations; the great works of engineering, of civil architecture, of arsenals, of canals; the internal administration and legislation of France. Not of France alone; all Europe seemed too small for my ardent imagination, and for my love of toil, which seemed to increase in proportion as difficulties multiplied. I ask no other panegyric on my reign than the publication of my correspondence with the chiefs of the army and of the several ministries, and of the projects submitted to my council.*

* The following extract from Alison, gives a more complete account of the interior condition of France about this time:

"Though completely despotic, the imperial government had one incalculable

But we will now turn our attention from my labors to elevate France as high as it was possible without a commercial marine, to the affairs of Germany, where the Confedera-

advantage: it was regular, conservative, and systematic. The taxes were heavy, but the government expenditure was immense, and enabled the people to pay them with facility; no forced loans or arbitrary confiscations swept off, as in the time of the republic, the accumulations of years by one fell exaction; no uncertainty as to enjoying the fruits of industry paralyzed in any branch of employment the hand of the laborer. Every thing was orderly and tranquil under the imperial sway; the emperor demanded indeed more than half their sons from his subjects of every degree, but a boundless career was opened to the conscripts; and visions of a marshal's baton or a general's staff danced before the eyes of many a youthful aspirant, who was destined to an early and unheeded grave in the field of battle, or amidst the horrors of the hospital. The stoppage of all external commerce, combined with the vast and constantly increasing expenditure of government, produced an extraordinary degree of vigor in domestic industry and internal communication; the roads, the canals which connected the provinces with each other, were covered with wagons or boats laden with the richest merchandise; the cultivators everywhere found an ample market for their produce, in the vast consumption of the armies; the manufacturing cities vied with each other in activity and enterprise; and even commercial wealth, reviving from its ashes under the firm rule of the emperor, exerted its energies on internal traffic, and turning inward, promoted internal circulation through the great arteries of the empire. Beet-root was largely cultivated as a substitute for the sugar-cane, and though the saccharine matter obtained from that useful vegetable was inferior in sweetness and richness to that which the West India islands yielded, yet it was superior in clearness and delicacy, and, as a native production, was justly admired. Lyons, Rouen, and the Flemish cities again resounded with the activity of the artisan; their ruined fabrics were restored, the empty warehouses replenished; and the vast internal consumption of the empire, deprived of all foreign competition, rapidly raised from the dust the prosperous manufactures of the monarchy, which the confiscation of the Revolution had to all appearance irrevocably destroyed.

"Much as this extraordinary flood of internal prosperity was owing to the rapid circulation of wealth, occasioned by the great expenditure, exceeding thirty millions sterling, which was drawn from the ordinary revenue of the empire, more still was to be ascribed to the enormous sums which were extracted from one half of Europe in the shape of subsidies, contributions, or the maintenance of the imperial armies, which were all expended, directly or indirectly, for the benefit of the French people. The immense sums, amounting to about twenty-four millions sterling, have been already mentioned, which were extracted from Prussia, and the countries between the Elbe and the Vistula, in two years subsequent to the irruption of the French armies into their territories in October, 1806. But exorbitant as this was, it constituted but a part of the great system of foreign plunder which formed so important an element in the general system of the imperial government. We have the authority of

tion of the Rhine seemed likely to again endanger the peace of Europe.

Affairs of Prussia.—Frederick William received with grief

the able and impartial biographer of Napoleon for the assertion, "that since their departure from the heights of Boulogne two hundred thousand French soldiers had been constantly fed, clothed, paid, and lodged, at the expense of foreign states; above four hundred millions of contributions (£16,000,000) had, in addition, been levied in money or goods, from the countries occupied by the imperial troops; the treasury had received part of this sum, and the remainder, expended on the services of the army, had reduced by one half the amount required from the French exchequer for its support. A few years before, Louisiana had been sold by the First Consul to America, to obtain a supply for the pressing wants of the treasury; on his return from the campaign of Austerlitz, the emperor found the treasury exhausted, and the bank on the eve of insolvency; but the campaign of the next two years gave him a year's revenue in advance in the coffers of the state, besides a large reserved treasure in the vaults of the Tuileries. When such extraordinary supplies were obtained by foreign plunder for the French treasury, it is not surprising that a very great degree of prosperity should have pervaded all the departments, and in an especial manner made itself felt at the metropolis; and, in truth, all the great and splendid works thenceforward undertaken by the emperor, and which have shed such an imperishable lustre round his name, were carried on by funds wrung, directly or indirectly, from the suffering inhabitants of his subject territories.

"And these works, undertaken under the imperial government, were really such as to justify the enthusiastic admiration of a people even less passionately devoted than the French to public splendor. They were thus noticed in the report of the Minister of the Interior, in August, 1807, when Napoleon met the chambers after his return from Tilsit; and after making every allowance for the exaggerated style of such state papers, much remains to attract the admiration of succeeding ages, and demonstrate the great objects to which, in domestic administration, the ambition of the emperor was directed. 'Thirteen thousand leagues of public roads have been kept in order or repaired; the two greatest works undertaken for centuries, the roads of Mont Cenis and of the Simplon, have, after six years of labor, been completed. The road from Spain to Italy is in progress; the Apennines are the theatre of a series of works which will unite Piedmont to the shores of the Mediterranean, and complete the union of Liguria to France; eighteen rivers have seen their navigation improved or prolonged beyond hitherto impassable barriers by means of locks, dykes, or towing-paths; four bridges have been erected during the last campaign; ten others are in full progress; ten canals, almost all commenced during the present reign, are in full activity. Nor do the maritime harbors offer fewer prodigies. Antwerp, so recently insignificant, has become the centre of our great maritime preparations; for the first time that part of the Scheldt sees vessels of seventy-four and eighty guns floating on its bosom; fourteen ships of the line are on the stocks within its walls; many are finished, and have descended to Flushing; that harbor has seen its docks deepened, its entrance

the news of the overthrow of the German Empire, upon which I had not consulted him. Even those of his counsellors who had pardoned Haugwitz for the acquisition of Hanover, could see in this new movement only a manifest attempt on the interests of Prussia. They contended that as it was my interest to extend my influence in Germany, so was it the interest of Prussia that Germany should remain an independ-

improved, and it is already capable of containing a squadron; at Dunkirk and Calais, piers have been constructed; at Cherbourg two vast breakwaters erected; at Rochefort and Marseilles equally important maritime improvements are in progress.

"'The existence of our cotton manufactures being secured, investigations are in progress for the discovery of places suited to the culture of that important article; the improvement of the linen fabrics has been the object of constant solicitude; veterinary schools have been established, and already fill the army and the fields with skilled practitioners; a code is preparing for the regulation of commerce; the school of arts and mechanics at Compiègne flourishes, and has been transferred to Chalons; others on a similar plan are in the course of formation; Italy opens an extensive mart for our industry; the war, changed into a contest for commercial independence, has become the greatest stimulant to French industry; every one of our conquests, while it is a market closed to England, is a new encouragement afforded to French enterprise. Nor has the capital of this great empire been neglected; it is the emperor's wish that that illustrious city, become the first in the universe, should befit by its splendor so glorious a destiny. At one extremity of Paris a bridge has been completed, to which victory has given the name of Austerlitz; at another, a second is commencing, to which Jena will afford a still more glorious appellation; the Louvre advances to its completion, marking, in its matured progress through centuries, the successive ages of Francis I., of Henry IV., of Louis XIV., restored to life by the voice of Napoleon; fountains without number flow night and day in all parts of the city, testifying, even to the humblest classes, the care which the emperor bestows on their most trifling accommodations. Two triumphal arches are already erected, or founded, one in the centre of the palace inhabited by the Genius of Victory; the other at the extremity of the most beautiful avenue of the finest city in the world. The tomb of Dessaix has been erected on the summit of the Alps, whose rugged precipices are not less startled at the monument of our perfection in the arts, than they were at the passage of the artillery drawn by the arms of valor. The fine arts in France are occupied almost entirely in tracing on marble or canvas the glorious exploits of our armies, while the mind of the emperor, ever meditating fresh triumphs, has selected, for his antagonist the Demon of Ignorance; and, by the establishment of twelve colleges for the study of law, and gratuitous schools for the teaching of medicine in all the principal cities of the empire, has laid the foundation of the extension of general knowledge in the most essential subjects of public instruction.'"

ent power between her and my great empire. Nevertheless, the peace party once more carried the day; Frederick recognized the league of the Rhine, and endeavored to establish that of the North. He did not succeed in this as easily as he anticipated; England and Russia opposed it, because it included Hamburg and the Hanseatic towns, and I, because it included Saxony, for I had intended this country for the Confederation of the Rhine: its geographical position made it the key of the Elbe; it would be an ally equally precious against Prussia or against Austria; moreover, the House of Saxony had been from time immemorial the friend of France, and its alliance with the Prussians since 1792, had not yet effaced the enmity that had sprung from the seven years' war. It served my purpose to insinuate to Saxony that she ought to remain firm, and to Prussia that she must not employ threats or force, if her alliance should meet with opposition. In addition to the dissatisfaction which these obstacles gave to Prussia, the English, on the closing of the ports, had captured three hundred Prussian vessels; the ports were blockaded by Anglo-Swedish squadrons; the commercial class was in consternation, the military vociferated more and more; statesmen deplored the loss of Germany. If the government had attempted to stifle all the germs of discontent, it would have needed the revolutionary tribunal of Fauquier Tinville. Frederick William opposed to this torrent a firm and unshaken will; he could do nothing more. A single spark in this mine was sufficient to cause its explosion: this spark was soon furnished by my negotiation with England.

Negotiations with England.—While laboring to enlarge the basis of my power, I did not lose the hope of consolidating so many glorious works by a maritime peace, without which my edifice could have no durable basis. The first overtures were the result of a fortuitous event, which was a good augury. One of those monsters who spring from civil wars; one of those wretches who think that the spirit of party or of sect justifies any crime; in a word, a French favorite, ventured to propose to Fox to assassinate me, and for this purpose to purchase a house on the avenue of St. Cloud where I passed daily in a carriage. Fox, more generous than the instigators of Georges Cadoudal, expelled this man from the kingdom, and notified me of his infamous proposition. The resulting correspondence led to reciprocal explanations. There was much difficulty at first respecting the form of negotiating, England wishing to treat in concert with Russia; but it seemed to me improper to introduce a third power with whom I had no particular difficulties to settle, especially as that power might throw its whole weight in the negotiation against me; I therefore declined the proposition; an intermediate course was agreed upon, by the Emperor Alexander's consenting to send, on his part, a negotiator to Paris. He sent me D'Qubril under pretext of an exchange of prisoners.

In the mean time, Fox had demanded the release of Lord Yarmouth, who had been detained at Verdun in consequence of reprisals for French vessels seized before the war, and whose cargoes (not military) had been detained. In passing through Paris on his return to London, Talleyrand manifested to him the desire which we all had for peace; he told him among other things that we demanded nothing of the English, and that they could hope nothing of real interest from a war. Lord Yarmouth returned with instructions, and conferences were opened. It seemed that an arrangement would be made; the English themselves proposed the state of *uti-possidetis*, and appeared satisfied with keeping Malta and the Cape of Good-Hope;* they exhibited a disposition to

* This place was taken from the Dutch by Admiral Popham and General Baird, on the 8th of January.

give up the rest of the captured colonies. Unfortunately, Fox was taken sick; Lord Spencer took the portfolio, and under pretext that Yarmouth had indiscreetly divulged the contents of his instructions, they added Count Lauderdale to the legation. The negotiation immediately began to retrograde. It was pretended by the English that in the first conferences the state of respective possession had been admitted, with the exception of Hanover, which was to be restored to England. If the question had been settled in this way I should have left every thing to the English; Malta, the Cape, Surinam, Demarara, Berbice, Tobago, and moreover, have restored Hanover, without obtaining any thing in return! I declared these conditions incompatible with my honor; and as I had just placed my brother on the throne of Holland, I could not begin his reign by stripping the Dutch of all their colonies. The case of Joseph was similar; I might as well recall him from the throne of Naples, as to deprive him of Sicily, the gem and the granary of that kingdom.

I confess that I did not sufficiently appreciate what England would have to sacrifice in recognizing the basis of *uti-possidetis* of both France and her allies. I at length yielded the question of the colonies and of Hanover; but in exchange I insisted on Sicily. Perhaps I committed a grave error. I might have taken the English at their word of *uti-possidetis* except Hanover; and have immediately sent a skillful negotiator to Berlin to propose to the king to second me in the desirable work of peace, by accepting a compensation. It would have been sufficient that England promised not to interfere in the arrangement of this continental affair, provided her electorate were restored. But Lord Lauderdale would certainly have found some pretext for withdrawing the proposition when he found it accepted with so much haste on my part; indeed, he found sufficient excuse for contestations in the interpretation to be given to the basis of *uti-possidetis.* There was reason to believe that an attempt might be made to confine it to the French empire, properly so called, excluding all the states dependent on France. In fact, the English negotiator, in a moment of indiscretion, when discussing the affair of Sicily, said that so far from yielding this country, he had orders to demand the restoration of Naples to Ferdinand IV.*

Treaty with Russia.—In the mean time M. D'Oubril had arrived at Paris to treat in the name of Russia ; as we had no colonies for mutual cession, it was not difficult for us to agree ; I demanded the restitution of Cattaro, which belonged to me, the integrity of the Ottoman Empire, and the independence of the Seven-Isles ; I promised the evacuation of Germany. A secret article authorized the exchange of Sicily for the Balearic Isles. The treaty was signed July 20th.

The Emperor Alexander strongly reproved the conduct of his negotiator ; D'Oubril was disgraced ; the council of the empire declared that he had exceeded his powers, and the emperor refused his ratification, without alleging any other motives. This refusal wounded me, for it disappointed my hopes. My journals made loud complaints. These are instruments used for producing momentary effects. It would be absurd to judge of my sentiments from the paragraphs of the gazettes ; it is not in newspapers that history is written.

If I had formed vast projects for the grandeur of France and of my empire, I was not so simple as to expect that these projects could be executed without exciting the enmity of my neighbors, who were interested in opposing the part which I wished to play. We have accused each other of

* Mr. Alison attempts to give to these negotiations a character and coloring essentially false. The published correspondence is very far from supporting his assertions, which seem to spring from his own prejudice, rather than a just appreciation of the facts of history.

ambition and exaggerated pretensions: this was a matter of course; but now, as the interest of the moment is past, it is well to render unto Cæsar the things that are Cæsar's. I doubt not, the emperor of Russia in my position would have acted as I did; had I been in his place I should unhesitatingly have opposed the projects of the French empire on Germany. It was, perhaps, the establishment of the Confederation of the Rhine that caused the cabinet of St. Petersburg to refuse its sanction on the twenty-fourth of August. This pact had been formed on the twelfth of July; but it had not been published when D'Oubril signed his treaty on the twentieth. It was not till the first of August that a notification of it was given at Ratisbon.

The emperor Alexander judged correctly that, although we had no provinces for retrocession, he nevertheless could not remain indifferent to the fate of states with which he was intimately connected. *If the first duty of a state is its own security, the second is the security of neighboring powers whose existence is necessary for its own preservation.* This rule is true, whatever may be the opinion of old writers on international law. The emperor of Russia had, like me, guaranteed the acts of the deputation of the empire in 1803; he had been the guaranteeing power for the integrity of this empire since the treaty of Teschen in 1779; it could therefore hardly be expected that he would ratify a treaty concluded after the destruction of this empire, and therefore giving to that act his implied sanction. Moreover, on the twentieth of June, I had placed my brother Louis on the throne of Holland, and the Russian policy might see in this something opposed to its future interests. It would be impossible to deny that the cabinet of St. Petersburg was interested in the independence of these northern traders who had so many relations with its ports, especially if the commerce of neutrals should ever again be respected. Besides,

Russia had no particular interest in making peace, as war could not reach her.

It has been said that D'Oubril declared that he signed the treaty of peace to save Austria who was threatened with danger. I had ordered Berthier on the sixteenth of July, to march my army on the Inn, if Austria should refuse to ratify the Confederation of the Rhine. It appears that this order, secret as it was, came to the knowledge of the Russian negotiator; but what is not less remarkable, the treaty which he signed, reaching Vienna at the same time as the act of confederation, contributed not a little to produce the abdication of the emperor of Germany; it therefore had for me all the advantages of a real peace—an effect directly the opposite, undoubtedly, to what was anticipated. The motive of D'Oubril, as has been alleged in his justification, was wholly new; it certainly was a singular method of delivering Austria, from immediate danger, by binding the Russians for a certain time so as to prevent them from marching to her assistance. There is a mystery connected with this which time alone can clear up.

Mission of Sebastiani to Constantinople.—Before the conclusion of this treaty and before knowing what decision might be taken at Vienna and at St. Petersburg relative to the Confederation of the Rhine; and under the apprehension of a new general conflagration on the continent, I had seen the advantage of opposing to Russia a powerful diversion on the Dniester. The thing did not seem easy; for it will be remembered that our relations with the Porte were near being compromised at the event of my coronation, and that Marshal Brune had returned from Constantinople without being able to obtain an open recognition of me as emperor. The corruption of the Divan, the recollection of our expedition into Egypt, and English influence, had raised up obstacles which time alone could remove. Nevertheless, the campaign of Austerlitz had very much increased our credit with the Porte, and given a high idea of what they might undertake with our support. Selim III. loved France; he was more enchanted with our success, if possible, than the French themselves, and resolved to send me an ambassador to congratulate me on my ascension to the throne.

Anxious to learn what advantage could be drawn from this disposition, I sent as envoy to Constantinople General Sebastiani, an adroit, skillful, enterprising man, whose agreeable manners perfectly fitted him for a negotiator, and who, in the quality of a military officer, might be doubly useful in this mission, if Turkey should eventually be drawn into the war. I nevertheless, recommended to him great prudence, and gave him instructions respecting his negotiation. These instructions wholly pacific, directed him, however, to use his address to obtain the dismissal of the hospodars of Wallachia and Moldavia, who were mere agents of Russia. I considered this not only the first step toward the restoration of our influence at Constantinople, but one well calculated to lead to war. I had no reason to repent it, for Sebastiani perfectly accomplished this part of his mission, and the treaty of D'Oubril having been rejected, it procured me the desired diversion more happily and completely than I had anticipated. The clause of the treaty which guaranteed the integrity of the Ottoman Empire contributed, without doubt, to give him more credit than his predecessors, and he deserved it.

The occupation by Marmont's corps of the little Republic of Ragusa, a tributary to the Porte, was directed at this epoch; it was necessary for the occupation of Venetian-Dalmatia and the mouths of the Cattaro, and to secure us from the attacks of the Greek population of Montenegro, incited by the Russian division of Corfu to take up arms against us; Marmont received orders to cause it to be occupied by the division of Lauriston. This step was represented by our enemies as a new act of hostility against the Porte; but it affected that power too indirectly, and was of too little importance, to be weighed against the advantages to be derived from an alliance with me.

Attack of the English on Buenos-Ayres.—During these negotiations the maritime war was still going on; but the English, who had no rivals on the ocean after the battle of Trafalgar, made no very important enterprises this year. That of Admiral Popham against South America, without the orders of the ministry, was not carried on by means sufficient to produce any results. After the reduction of the Cape, Popham, having first received some reënforcements at St. Helena, landed Beresford at Buenos-Ayres. This key of the River La Plata surrendered without resistance, on the twenty-seventh of July, and the English captured some rich prizes; but two Frenchmen, in the service of Spain, organized the inhabitants, and in concert with some royal troops which had retired into the environs assailed the English in the city and forced them, after a rude combat, to capitulate on the twelfth of August. Popham, two months afterward, attempted to take revenge by attacking Monte-Video, but was repulsed.

Rupture of the Negotiations with England.—The news of these events had not yet reached Europe when the negotiations with England were broken off. As soon as Lauderdale ascertained that Russia had refused to ratify the treaty, he demanded his passports, certain of having me embroiled with Prussia respecting Hanover, and perhaps with Spain for the Balearic Isles. The discussion on some of the accessories was continued till the end of September. Fox died on the thirteenth. Had he lived, it probably would not have changed the face of affairs, for I was placed, by the Confederation of the Rhine, on grounds where I could no longer hope to treat without making more concessions than had at first been demanded.

Notwithstanding all the fine hopes to which it had given rise, never, probably, was there a negotiation more fallacious and more incomprehensible than this. Any one will be convinced of this by examining with a little attention what had preceded it, and what followed.

The grand project of Pitt which had set Europe on fire in 1805, looked, according to the diplomatic notes themselves, at nothing less than the reduction of France to the limits of 1792. This was nearly the same as that proposed to me at Chatillon in 1814, when the enemy was at the gates of Paris. The battles of Ulm and Austerlitz had undoubtedly defeated this grand project, and changed the state of affairs on the continent; but on the other hand the battle of Trafalgar had placed England in a position relatively as advantageous as before. How then can we believe that the state of *uti-possidetis* could possibly enter into the head of an English minister, only one year after this famous project which in twenty lines disclosed the entire policy of the cabinet of St. James for twenty years? A government at the head of which figured Grenville and Windham, which in 1805 had refused to allow me the limits of the treaties of Amiens and Luneville—did that government propose, in good faith, to recognize the annexation of Piedmont and Genoa to France? Did it consent that Holland and Naples should become, though not an internal part of my empire, yet subject to it like grand feudatories, whose sovereigns were not only members of my family, but also high dignitaries of the French Empire, and in that quality subject to its jurisdiction? Finally, did they recognize the crown of Italy on my head, they who had wished to discuss the smallest changes made in 1800 in this peninsula? No, they never intended this in good faith!

If any one has the least doubt on this subject, let him

recollect the treaty of Bartenstein, signed April, 1807, between Russia and Prussia, and participated in by England. I had then in my power the entire monarchy of Frederick; I was in an attitude more formidable still than in 1806, and yet Russia and Prussia, allies of England, agreed never to lay down their arms till Germany should be delivered from my forces and my influence, and the crown of Italy placed on some other head. It is true that Fox thought neither as the minister of 1805, nor as those of 1807, for at this last epoch it was Canning who directed the department of foreign affairs; but Fox could not make a peace against the wishes of the whole English nation: he treated neither for himself only, nor by himself alone.

Notwithstanding these views and motives of England, the truth of which can not be contested, I frankly confess that I managed my part of this negotiation unskillfully; even at the risk of giving but the half of Naples to Joseph, and of restoring the whole of it to Ferdinand, I ought, if possible, to have procured from Russia and England the recognition of my empire and of the establishments bestowed on my other brothers. I acted ill toward Prussia, by pronouncing several times on the fate of Hanover without even consulting her. Accustomed to success, I had no fears of a war with her; and, to tell the truth, the Confederation of the Rhine appeared to me so important and the moment so opportune, that I was determined to brave the efforts of all Europe rather than renounce it. The English would perhaps have declined all question relative to the recognition of our establishments in Italy, as they had already done at the peace of Amiens; but, I repeat it, this would have been a more just cause for continuing the war than the demand made for Sicily.

Prussia abruptly decides on War.—Although the propositions relative to Hanover had no results, they nevertheless produced at Berlin an explosion like powder. The queen,

Prince Louis of Prussia, the duke of Brunswick, and Baron Hardenberg, had been, since the treaty of Potsdam, at the head of the war-party. They now had no difficulty in influencing the king, who had been able to calm public opinion only by the advantages of the acquisition of Hanover in exchange for all the vexations which he had suffered.

They profited by these appearances of felony to incite all minds against me, without inquiring whether I would really demand back Hanover, and if, even supposing that I did, I would not have given Prussia ample compensation. They pretended to see in me only an ally of bad faith, who took back with one hand what he had bestowed with the other; a violator of territory, who arbitrarily disposed of what did not belong to him. They went even so far as to publish that I had bribed D'Oubril, and that, to induce his master to make peace, and to recognize me as emperor, I had proposed to him the partition of Prussia, giving Warsaw to the Grand-duke Constantine!

It was not necessary to resort to such absurd stories to completely turn heads which for a whole year had been in ebullition. Suddenly the Prussians recollect that they are the depositories of the glory of the great Frederick: the government which had restrained these impulses now sets the example. The king can see in this apparent loss of Hanover only the real loss of his monarchy, of the last pledge of his security, of the personal honor of the king himself. It only remained for him to fall gloriously, or become disgraced as a coward. The general cry, *To Arms!* is heard from Potsdam to Königsberg; war is decided on without even waiting for the coöperation of Russia. An alliance is negotiated with her, but they were unwilling to wait for her troops, as a war of honor allows of no delay!

Her extraordinary Ultimatum.—This long torpor is followed by romantic rage. General Knobelsdorf, who has replaced Lucchesini as ambassador at Paris, remits me an extraordinary ultimatum, wanting in the proper respect due to a great power. They summoned me: 1st, *to evacuate Germany, commencing on the day when the king could receive my answer and continuing without interruption*; 2d, *to detach Wesel from my empire*; 3d, *to send my answer before the eighth of October to the head-quarters of the king!*

Assuredly Scipio before Carthage would not have held more imperious language to the conquered! Any one would have thought that this was the day after the battle of Rosbach!

The cabinet of Berlin acted the more foolishly toward me in this matter, inasmuch as its interest was to gain time. If it had demanded, in suitable terms, the evacuation of Germany within a reasonably stipulated period, it would have acted rightly, and thrown on me all the odium of the aggression. In attacking me when I was engaged with the Russians, and Austrians, the Prussians could have done me much injury; but to thus, unreasonably and alone, declare war against me, was so extraordinary that I could not, for some time, believe it. Nothing, however, was more true, and it became necessary to prepare for the campaign.

First Movements of the French Army.—I knew that the Russian army, cantoned on the Niemen, would be an inevitable auxiliary; but this required time, and I might reach Berlin before it could; moreover, I hoped that Sebastiani would succeed in inciting Turkey to war; for a treaty signed between England and Russia had given to the latter Moldavia and Wallachia, as the price of the efforts which she would make against France. But I was not a man to wait for the uncertain coöperation of Selim III. before falling on my adversaries, who were now fully exposed to my attacks; I ordered the assembling of my army, and departed for Mayence. The sixth of October I arrived at Bamberg. My army was one hundred and eighty thousand strong. The main body, composed of the five corps of Bernadotte, Davoust, Soult, Ney, Lannes, and the cavalry of the grand-duke of Berg, assembled at Cobourg, and at Bamberg; my guard, under Lefebvre, took the road to Bamberg; Augereau left Frankfort to threaten the road to Cassel and then to incline to the right; Mortier assembled the eighth corps on the confines of Westphalia; my brother Louis, with fifteen thousand Gallo-Batavians, took the direction of Wesel; Marmont remained in Illyria with the second corps, charged with covering Ragusa, occupying the Cattaro, &c.

Position and Plan of the Prussians.—The Prussians had advanced into Saxony and induced the elector to unite his troops with theirs. The elector of Hesse-Cassel prepared to do the same. They posted themselves on the northern side of the forest of Thuringia. The corps of Ruchel of twenty thousand men formed the right at Eisenach. The principal army, of fifty thousand men, commanded by the king, and under him by the duke of Brunswick, took position in the environs of Erfurth. The army of the left, commanded by the Prince of Hohenlohe, of about fifty thousand Saxo-Prussians, was concentrated on Blankenhayn; a corps of this army was detached under the orders of Tauenzien, in order to cover the extreme left at Schleitz.

Napoleon's Plan of Operations.—There were only three plans by which we could operate against Prussia: the 1st, by my left, debouching from Mayence and Wesel on Westphalia; but this would have been absurd; the 2d, to act in mass at the centre by the road to Eisenach on Cassel or Leipsic; the 3d, to throw myself in mass by my right, to turn the enemy's left and cut off the Prussians from Berlin by Hof and Gera, as I had cut off Mack from Vienna, by Donawerth, and Melas, by Marengo. It was evident that this last was not only the best, but the only feasible plan.

Faults of the Prussians.—To avoid the catastrophe there remained to the Prussians only two courses: that of falling, by the middle of September, on my cantonments which were scattered through Franconia, or of awaiting me defensively, with their forces concentrated on the upper Saale, supporting their left on the frontiers of Austria. I might have beaten them in front; but then they would have had a secure retreat on Dresden and Silesia. They could have united with the Russians on the Oder, and thus have saved their monarchy. On the contrary, they pushed forward their right to Eisenach, set down their centre under Erfurth, and permitted their isolated left to remain in the environs of Schleitz. This was precisely what I desired.

Their Generals.—The king, in putting himself at the head of his army, had exhumed, as it were, the old generals of the seven years' war to serve him as guides; the duke of Brunswick and Mollendorf were to lead the army to victory. The former, a vanguard general under his father, the great Ferdinand, had never, since that period, fought except at Kaiserslautern against Hoche, where he had bravely defended his camp. A good administrator, valiant in combat, but timid in council, he had learned nothing during the past fifteen years, although these years had been rich in lessons for every military man capable of profiting by them. Mollendorf, not less brave, was equally unskillful; age had paralyzed within him those qualities which had formerly given him so great a reputation; but age had not given him genius; genius is never the fruit of age or of experience. The Prince Hohenlohe and Massenbach, his right arm, had just enough mind and knowledge to select the false in war. In a word, there was not, in all that brilliant circle of the counsellors of Potsdam, a single individual who sufficiently comprehended my system of war to judge of the three simple hypotheses which I have mentioned, and to conclude that it was by Cobourg and Hof that I would turn my army, if they ventured to cross the Saale. They ran to their own destruction with a presumption that can hardly be described.

Plunged in a lethargic sleep for the last ten years, they were so certain of driving us back to Mayence, that they made no preparations for putting in a state of defense the fortifications of their first line, not even those situated within a few marches of our cantonments; while I was piling up bastion upon bastion at Kehl, Cassel, and Wesel, they did not plant a single palisade at Magdebourg, nor put in battery a single cannon at Spandau!

On the other hand, their army was fine, well armed, and admirably disciplined; the artillery was excellent, the cavalry had not yet forgotten Siedlitz and his immortal lessons; the staff was well instructed, but instructed in details, to the neglect of principles; so that, in fact, this army, so superb in appearance, was a body without a soul.

Views of the Duke of Brunswick.—The duke of Brunswick, in pushing forward his army to Eisenach, hoped to hurry along the Elector of Hesse who had already assembled a contingent of twenty thousand men to reënforce the army. His project was afterward to cross the debouches of Franconia on three points so as to fall on my line of the Main, where he imagined I would remain on the defensive. This was judging very singularly of my character, my position, and my former practice. How was it possible for him to suppose that a captain, who had thrown himself, with the rapidity of the eagle, before the united forces of Austria and Russia, would go to sleep in rear of the Main, when opposing the isolated forces of a power of the second rank, especially when there were such strong motives for acting vigorously before the arrival of the Russians, and before the Austrians could be aroused to action?

At the news of my first movements on Cobourg, the

duke recovered from an illusion which proved all his simplicity of character; he renounced the offensive, and resolved to concentrate his army near Weymar in order to await us in front. This concentration was wise, but it should have been made on the left of Hof, instead of drawing this left wing to the *corps-de-bataille*, and thus opening the road which led directly to my object.

Napoleon seizes the Enemy's Communications.—My plan was very soon decided on when I arrived at Bamberg and learned what had taken place about Erfuth. An ordinary general in my place would have been satisfied with defeating the enemy; I carried my views still further, and resolved to effect their total destruction. I arranged my plan to cut off their army from the heart of the Prussian monarchy, to turn them by the left, and establish myself between them and the Elbe. It was true that in acting thus on their communications, I should somewhat expose my own; but this could be done without danger since we were superior in numbers, and by inclining from Gera to the west, I could cover the roads of Hof, Nordhalbein, and Cobourg, which in case of reverse would carry me to Franconia.

My army penetrated Saxony on three routes; at the right, Soult, Ney, and a Bavarian division marched from Bareith by Hof on Plauen; at the centre, the grand-duke of Berg, Bernadotte and Davoust, marched from Bamberg by Cronach on Saalbourg; at the left, Lannes and Augereau, setting out from Schweinfurt, took their direction by Cobourg and Groffenthal on Saalfeld. The first engagement took place on the eighth of October. A Prussian detatchment which attempted to defend the Saale at Saalbourg was driven away by the grand-duke of Berg; the next day my column of the centre, pursuing its way, found at Schleitz the corps Tauenzein. Bernadotte attacked it, gaining a decided victory. My left also began with success. On the tenth, Lannes attacked, at Saalfeld, the advanced guard of the army of Hohenlohe, commanded by Prince Louis of Prussia. The enemy was beaten and lost a thousand men and thirty cannon. Prince Louis, a young man of great promise, not wishing to survive the shame of a defeat, preferred being slain: he had lived as a valiant knight, and he died like a hero. After having been my admirer, this prince became my sworn enemy, because he deemed me dangerous to Prussia; his patriotism carried him astray, and notwithstanding what he did against me, I am happy to do him justice.

I had expected greater resistance. The recollection of Frederick, of Seidlitz, of Leuthen, of Prague, had given me the highest opinion of this army, and I had remarked to one of my officers at Mayence, that this campaign would not be like that of Ulm; *that we should have earth to move in this war.* These first victories undeceived me; they were a good augury for the campaign. I then felt that I could cheaply dispose of the Prussian army, which did not exhibit sufficient consistency to sustain the weight of a great reverse.

Decisive Manœuvre.—By these first movements we had succeeded in turning the enemy's left by anticipating him on the twelfth at Gera; it was now my object to cut him off entirely. For this purpose my left served as the pivot for a grand change of front of the whole army. The thirteenth, we occupied the following positions: Davoust, Bernadotte, and Murat, with his light cavalry only, moved on Naumbourg, where we captured considerable magazines intended for the Prussian army; Soult was in march from Gera on Jena; Ney at Roda; Lannes at Jena; Augereau at Kahla; a Bavarian division flanked my right by establishing itself at Plauen.

Before leaving Gera on the twelfth, I wrote a letter to Frederick William to offer him peace. I intrusted this letter to an officer of staff, Montesquiou, with directions to take it to the king. This step was ill-judged; Montesquiou, if we are to believe Prince Hohenlohe, was arrested on the night of the thirteenth, by the outposts, traveling alone and without the usual precautions of a flag of truce; the prince took him for a spy, and retained him near himself, sending the letter to the king, who did not receive it till the battle. It must be confessed that it was now rather too late, and difficult to avoid war. I nevertheless had two chances in writing this letter; either the king would make peace by subscribing to all my conditions, or he would persist in the resolution taken on leaving Berlin, to conquer or die. In either case it might serve to keep him in suspense on the night of the thirteenth, and the morning of the fourteenth, so that he might not have time to decide on making a forced march by night to avoid being taken in reverse. This was a justifiable *ruse-de-guerre*. I appeared the friend of peace while advancing to my object. This letter was not the worst manœuvre of the campaign; if the king had received it as I had supposed, it would not have prevented him, whether he accepted peace or not, from marching with all his army on Freybourg. It then depended on him to save himself militarily and politically. The date of this letter written at Gera was sufficient to tell him to hasten his retreat and escape from the embarrassment by answering it.

Battle of Jena.—The enemy, concentrated in the environs of Weimar, had no apprehension of my manœuvres till after their success; but at last, seeing that we were already masters of the road from that city to Leipsic, and of the magazines of Naumbourg, he resolved to retreat in order to reach the Elbe before us. On the evening of the thirteenth, the king and the duke of Brunswick, with the principal army, moved toward Sulza. The prince of Hohenlohe, charged with covering this march, remained near Cappellendorf on the height of Jena; he was supported by the corps of Ruchel, which fell back to Weimar. I took care not to give the enemy time to escape. Already in possession of his communications, I resolved to secure his ruin, by giving him battle. Although the defile of Jena, through which we had to debouch, was difficult, it was not an obstacle to us who had crossed the St. Bernard and passed the rock of Bard; Lannes, in pursuing the advanced guard of Tauenzien toward Jena, had had the audacity to climb the mountain of Landgrafenberg, and to place himself on the summit opposite the Prussian army, which I myself discovered encamped on three lines. I did not know that it was divided; I believed that it would fight in one body according to the system of Frederick. I hurried the march of my guard, and made it climb, at ten o'clock in the evening, a very steep path to the plateau of Closewitz, which it was important for us to occupy as a kind of *tête-de-pont*, to enable us to ascend the mountain and debouch from this chasm; Soult followed near by; he arrived during the night on my right, and Augereau on my left; Ney bivouacked at Roda.

Supposing the entire army of the king to be collected on this point, and that his left extended in the direction of Apolda, I ordered Bernadotte to march to Dornbourg, and Davoust to move from Naumbourg by the left of the Saale on Apolda, in order to fall on the extremity of the enemy's line and take him in reverse. Murat joined me at Jena with his light cavalry. These dispositions were good for the position I supposed the enemy to occupy; but if I had foreseen that the king of Prussia would attempt to pierce by Naumbourg, and that Bernadotte had already reached there, I should not have exposed Davoust alone to sustain the shock of the mass of the enemy's forces, and have sent Bernadotte away to Dornbourg, where he was equally useless to me and to Davoust.

On the fourteenth, at break of day, the combat began.

The night had been cold ; a thick fog obscured the horizon ; we could hardly see two steps before us : this was a double good fortune to us, since the enemy could not discover whether we were yet in readiness on the plateau. I mounted my horse at eight o'clock, and, riding in front of Suchet's division, I exhorted his battalions in these words : "Soldiers ! This proud Prussian army is turned, like that of Mack at Ulm ; it will now fight only to find means to retreat ; the corps which shall allow it to escape, will be dishonored !" The advanced guard of Prince Hohenlohe was driven back by Lannes, from the defiles of which it still held the head ; we possessed Lutzerode and Closewitz. At the noise of this combat, Hohenlohe raised his camp of Cappellendorf and advanced to meet us on Vierzehnheiligen. For two hours I satisfied myself with this feeble success, merely keeping up the combat till the arrival of my cavalry and the three corps which I was expecting. Ney, by a deplorable excess of zeal, dissatisfied at being in reserve in rear of Augereau, attacked alone, with three thousand men of the *élite*, the whole Prussian line of Vierzehnheiligen ; he suffered for an hour the whole fire of the enemy, and forced me to sustain him by Lannes. This premature attack vexed me the more as I still supposed that we were dealing with the entire army of the king, concentrated on this point. At length, the columns of Soult and Augereau having at last debouched, as also the main body of Ney's corps, I renewed the attack : the duke of Dalmatia threw himself on the left of Hohenlohe, Ney and Lannes on the centre toward Vierzehnheiligen, and Augereau on Isorstedt.

The victory was not for a moment doubtful ; the whole Prussian line was completely routed. Ruchel, arriving from Weimar with the reserve, out of breath, had not sufficient *coup-d'œil* to perceive that affairs were in too bad a state for him to repair them with his twenty thousand men.

Instead of limiting himself to covering the retreat of Prince Hohenlohe, he had the imprudence to engage himself against the main body of my army, and being unable to take us in flank, he met us in front. His troops were defeated and he himself severely wounded. His defeat only added to the enemy's losses. The flying foe was closely pursued and thrown beyond the Ilm, which they passed below Weimar. This city was occupied by our troops the very night of the battle, though situated six leagues from where it had commenced.

Battle of Auerstedt.—While we were gaining the victory of Jena, Davoust obtained at Auerstedt a no less signal success against the army of the king. The latter had put himself in march the night before to gain Naumbourg and Freybourg. The division of Schmettau, which led the march, advanced to Gerstedt, and his reconnoitring parties, pushed into the defile of Kosen, made prisoners of a similar reconnoitring party sent out by Davoust. The duke of Brunswick, being informed of the presence of this marshal's corps at Naumbourg, persisted in the opinion that it was merely a detachment of partisans; instead of pushing forward Schmettau to Kosen the same night, he left him in position and caused to bivouac the two other divisions and the reserve between Eberstedt and Ranstet; the head-quarters were at Auerstedt. It may be inferred how little the king expected the fate that awaited his army, when it is known that the queen even remained there, with an inconceivable security; he had great difficulty in inducing her to return to Weimar.

In the mean time the duke of Brunswick, informed of the existence of a corps of our troops at Naumbourg, and knowing that there was a road from the plateau of Kosen directly to Freybourg on the Unstrutt, hoped to reach that city without being obliged to fight his way through our troops. He ordered, for the next day, Schmettau's division to establish itself on the heights of Kosen, and to protect the march of the four other divisions which would defile in its rear. This was very well for his escape, if Davoust had remained immovable at Naumbourg; but even supposing the king's army had thus effected its escape, what must have become of Hohenlohe's corps of fifty thousand men, thus deserted in the midst of our army? If they had wished to steal away, ought not Hohenlohe to have been directed to march in the night on Sulza with his infantry in order to effect a junction there with the king and to render the operation more certain? This was the only means by which the army could be saved from impending ruin. The division of Tauenzein and all the cavalry of Hohenlohe should have remained in the camp of Cappellendorf to mask the march, and even if the ten battalions should be compromised alone, they ought still, at daylight, to have taken the road to Erfuth, or even have followed the king by that of Eckartsberg. It is evident, however, that the duke of Brunswick understood much better how to get an army into difficulty, than to devise the means of extricating it.

The king's army moved at break of day; the fog, of which we have already spoken, retarded its march. Nevertheless, the division of Schmettau, arriving near Hassenhausen, encountered the division of Gudin which Davoust had sent during the night to secure his debouch from the defile of Kosen. An hour more, and it would have been too late; our troops, crowded into the defile, would have never been able to effect a debouch, but would have been roughly handled. Davoust, having reconnoitred the ground the night before, and having received my orders at two o'clock in the morning, proposed to Bernadotte to march with him by Kosen on Apolda, and even offered him the command of the two corps. The order of the prince of Neufchatel to Davoust, was to the effect that if the first corps had already joined him they should march together; but this phrase had not been repeated to Bernadotte. The latter insisted on the literal wording of *his* order, to march on Dornbourg. All that his colleague could say to convince him was useless; he in fact took the road by Cambourg. This obstinacy, which it is difficult to explain, was very near compromising the corps of Davoust and preventing the success of the battle, as we shall soon see.

The king of Prussia had repaired in person to the division of Schmettau, and, impatient at the fog which prevented him from seeing what was going on around him, he directed Blucher to advance with two thousand five hundred horse and charge the troops which had debouched on the plateau. Gudin had just arrived with his column near Hassenhausen; our light cavalry opposed itself to the superior cavalry of Blucher and was forced back; but the brigade of Gauthier now had time to form its squares; the king ordered them to be charged; but the artillery placed on the road, and sustained by the infantry, rendered vain all the efforts of Blucher and his squadrons.

This unexpected resistance frightened the duke of Brunswick; he wished to put his army in battle array and wait the clearing up of the fog. The old general, Mollendorf, pretended that we had there only a flying corps, and that it ought to be driven back into the ravine of Kosen. The king being of the same opinion, ordered the divisions of Wartensleben and the prince of Orange to cross the ravine of Auerstedt. It was a great fault that, after having resolved to take the initiative, they did not cause this defile to be passed during the night; the Prussian army would have then reached, in good order, our columns while in march. Wartensleben, who debouched on the first, formed on the right and attacked the left of Gudin. At the same time Blucher, having advanced on Puncherau, found himself in rear of our right flank, and charged it with as much vivacity as the fog, which had begun to clear up, would permit. The moment was decisive. Davoust, placing his squares checkerwise, assisted by Gudin and the heroic firmness of his infantry, repelled several successive charges. Blucher had his horse killed under him; his squadrons, finding in all directions a barrier of iron and a murderous fire which strewed the ground with their brave men, took in disorder the road to Eckartsberg. The arrival of Friant's division on the right secured our success on this point. But Gudin was soon assailed on the left by the troops of Wartensleben; Schmettau, who had already lost half his men, was sustained on the two flanks by the prince of Orange.

It was now nine o'clock; the duke of Brunswick resolved on a general attack on our left; he put himself at the head of the division of Wartensleben. The immovable Gudin held firm against this new effort, notwithstanding the great disparity of numbers. The attack was not very vigorous, though courageously made; the Prussians sought too much to preserve their lines and distances as though they were on parade. Our soldiers, squatting behind the hedges, the little ditches, the willows and the gardens which surrounded Hassenhausen, poured into them a murderous fire of musketry. Several battalions fell back, and the duke of Brunswick in endeavoring to rally them, was mortally wounded; Schmettau experienced the same fate; Wartensleben had his horse killed under him. Deprived of its chiefs, the Prussian line hesitated and halted, but did not fall back. Gudin was likely to be defeated, when the division of Morand appeared on the plateau, and directed itself to our left. This powerful reënforcement of fresh troops, ardent for the fight, was decisive. The Prussians, having been driven out of Hassenhausen and unable to make a stand in rear of that place, the king resolved to make another charge of cavalry like that of

Blucher in the morning. Prince William executed with courage several charges against the troops of Morand, arranged in squares by battalion and disposed checkerwise. The devotion of this prince, carried to obstinacy, failed against the formidable front presented by our brave infantry; arrested in his progress by the close array of our bayonets, and exposed to a murderous musketry and the grape of our batteries, the prince, himself being wounded, was unable to check the disorder of his squadrons; a part fled on New Sulza and a part on Auerstedt.

Friant, on his side, penetrated as far as Tauchwitz, turned the left of Prince Henry and the extremity of the enemy's line. No sooner was Morand clear of the enemy's cavalry than he threw himself on Rehausen. The king was found in the hottest of the strife; one horse had already been killed under him; showing great courage and *sang-froid*, he himself directed a part of his reserve against our left; but beaten in flank by the artillery and infantry with which Davoust had crowned the Sonenberg, it was impossible for him to restore the combat and prevent Morand from carrying Rehausen. Disorder and confusion was beginning to appear in the Prussian infantry.

Davoust judged that this was the moment to strike the decisive blow: the heights of Eckartsberg commanded the enemy's left; the possession of this gave us at the same time the tactical and strategic point of the field of battle, since it secured the direct road to Freybourg and closed the enemy's only line of retreat. Gudin's division marched there by Tauchwitz and Gernstedt; that of Friant, by Lisdorf. Nothing could resist the impetuosity of their attack. The aged Mollendorf, being wounded by a ball, gave the command to Kalkreuth; but as the last remaining portion of his reserve had been unable to check the attack on Eckartsberg, there was now not the slightest hope of restoring the combat, his troops passed in disorder the deep ravine of Auerstedt.

The king, ignorant of Prince Hohenlohe's defeat, ordered the retreat on Weimar; the ruin of his army would have been complete if Bernadotte had executed even one half of what there was for him to do. Leaving Naumbourg at three o'clock in the morning and arriving at Cambourg toward six o'clock, he could still debouch from that place on Sulza, attack the king, and completely cut off his retreat; he preferred to continue his march on Dornbourg, where the ravine of the Saale is much more difficult, so that he did not reach the environs of Apolda till night. Nevertheless, his unexpected appearance on these heights, which at a distance flanked the road to Weimar, and the rencounter of the stragglers of Hohenlohe's corps, completed the despair of the Prussian troops who fled in all directions. The king received in the midst of this catastrophe the letter which I had sent him on the twelfth from Gera, by M. Montesquiou to avoid the war. A glimmer of hope seemed for a moment to animate his torn heart; he sent me Count Denhof, his aid-de-camp, to propose an armistice; but I could not now stop in my victorious career; the war, begun with a thunderbolt, would place Prussia at my feet, and I could treat only at Berlin.

Such was the issue of the celebrated battle of Auerstedt. Frederick William could say with Francis I.: *All is lost save honor.* Although beaten by a corps inferior, by one half, he could attribute it only to the inexperience of his troops and of his generals. Three hundred and twenty-four officers slain or wounded, ten thousand men *hors-de-combat*, the duke of Brunswick, Marshal Mollendorf, Prince William, Generals Schmettau and Wartensleben wounded or slain, proved that if they manœuvred badly, they nevertheless fought heroically. The division of Gudin had alone three thousand five hundred men and one hundred and thirty officers *hors-de-combat*, an enormous loss, being one half the force present. No better proof can be given of the intrepid countenance which it opposed to the successive efforts of the enemy; Davoust and all his other soldiers rivaled them in glory; they won indisputable claims to the admiration of posterity. No battle in all the wars of the Revolution offers a contest so disproportionate, with a success so brilliant. I could hardly believe the reports, which I regarded as very exaggerated, but which the Prussian accounts proved to be moderate. Davoust had purchased this victory with the blood of seven thousand brave men; but happily a good number of them were only slightly wounded, and more than half returned to the ranks.*

* Alison, in giving an account of this battle, with his usual disregard of facts, and readiness to accuse Napoleon of falsehood and meanness, says, "Napoleon's official account of this battle of Jena, in the fourth bulletin of the campaign [it was the fifth bulletin] is characterized by that extraordinary intermixture of truth and falsehood, and increasing jealousy of any general who appeared to interfere with his reputation, which, in one who could so well afford to be generous in that particular, is a meanness in an especial manner reprehensible." After pointing out his meanness, jealousy, and neglect of Davoust, he quotes the bulletin itself as proof of these charges, thus: "On our right the corps of Marshal Davoust performed 'prodigies.' Not only did he keep in check, *but maintained a running fight for three leagues, etc., etc.*" Now what will the reader think of Mr. Alison's veracity when he finds that not only are his charges in this case utterly untrue, but that he has falsified the language of Napoleon in order to give plausibility to his malignant accusations? The sentence which he translates, "but maintained a running fight for three leagues, etc.," is in the original, "*mais mena battant pendant plus de trois lieues,*" etc. Instead of treating Davoust with neglect, he mentioned him with unqualified praise in his short and hasty bulletin, placing his name before all the other marshals, made him duke of Auerstedt for his heroic conduct on that occasion, and to honor him still more, designated him as the first to enter the Prussian capital—thus showing to the whole army his right to the precedence. Moreover, a few days afterward, in reviewing his troops on the road to Frankfort, he called Davoust and his officers around him and addressed them in terms of the highest respect and admiration. Davoust, deeply affected by the approbation and generosity of the emperor, replied, "Sire, the soldiers of the third corps will always be to you what the Tenth Legion was to Cæsar." Both he and his corps showed in many a hard-fought field how much they were gratified with the manner which Napoleon had taken to prove his "falsehood," "unceasing jealousy," and "reprehensible meanness," and we doubt that there was a man in the whole army who would not have been delighted at similar proofs of *neglect*.

Extraordinary Results of these Victories.—The night following this double battle was not less fatal to the Prussians than the battle itself. The army of the king, taking, in disorder, the road to Weimar, met near Buttelstedt the fugitives of the army of Hohenlohe, and the confusion was then at its height. Prince Hohenlohe had reached Wipach almost alone. Nothing had been provided for the retreat. To make no provisions for the case of a retreat is one of the greatest faults which a general can commit; even where one can gain battles as I did, this neglect is hardly pardonable. Undoubtedly he ought not to render these dispositions public, but he ought to prepare a rallying point for a corps which may be momentarily cut off.

The two chiefs were *hors-de-combat*, the third in flight; there was no one to remedy the evil. The different corps crowded upon each other, mingled together, and then dispersed; never was there so deplorable a scene, except the night after the battle of Waterloo. Some took the road to Erfuth; others to Colleda, the main body reached Sommerda, but in horrible confusion. Blucher, coming from Colleda to Weissensée with six thousand horse, found himself anticipated there by Klein's division of dragoons; but he saved himself by declaring that an armistice had been concluded. Kalkreuth, hotly pressed at Greusen by Soult's corps, tried to use the same stratagem, but he was attacked and defeated; he gained Sondershausen in a deplorable state. Hohenlohe there rejoined the remains of his forces. Mollendorf, who had taken refuge at Erfuth with six thousand men and eight thousand wounded, was there surrounded by Murat and Ney. The governor of this place, susceptible of a good defense, capitulated the next day, and even surrendered the two citadels which commanded it.

The operations of a single day had decided the fate of the Prussian monarchy; we already had in our hands sixty colors, two hundred pieces of field artillery, and twenty-five thousand prisoners. But to give the enemy no time to reorganize his forces, it was necessary that we should not give him a moment's rest; I took my measures accordingly.

Although the duke of Brunswick had manifested the design of concentrating his forces, he had either not done so, or had begun to do it so unskillfully that his army had been taken *en flagrant délit*. While one half of his army had fallen at Jena and another had fought in retreat on Freybourg and Naumbourg, two other corps under the duke of Weimar and General Winning were marching on the other side of the forest of Thuringia and to Eisenach; a fourth corps of fourteen thousand men formed a reserve under the duke of Wurtembourg, at Halle. The thunderbolt which had just struck the Prussian army, thus situated, would have consequences the more grave as there was no chief, and the king himself had not a moment to lose if he hoped to regain the capital and the Oder; each of his corps had to save itself as well as it could. Here Bulow could have found a fine model of eccentric retreat! Hohenlohe and Kalkreuth saved themselves by Hartz on Magdebourg. The first was there to take the command in chief, rally all he could find, and march on the Oder toward Stettin; but he was forced to describe the arc by Magdebourg, and as we held the cord of this arc, we could have anticipated him at any point, had it not been for the difficulty of passing the Elbe. While Murat, Soult, and Ney, followed him on Nordhausen where his rear-guard was cut to pieces, I took, with Bernadotte, Lannes, Davoust, Augereau, and my guard, the road to Dessau, in order to pass the Elbe at that place, to direct myself on Berlin, to cut off the enemy from the Oder, and at the same time to seize on the enemy's capital and communications. The result of these marches, well combined, and rapid as lightning, ought to find favor even with the detractors of my glory; but how can we expect that blind men should appreciate my system of war, when even the duke of Brunswick could not understand it?

Combat of Halle.—Bernadotte encountered, at Halle, on the seventeenth of October, the corps of reserve under the Duke Eugene of Wurtemberg. This prince had just received indirect news of the battle of Jena, with circumstances so terrible that he could not believe it. He was waiting for two thousand men of his corps who were on the march from Magdebourg on the left bank of the Saale by Sandersleben; whether he was surprised, or whether he could not venture to cut the bridge on the Saale before the junction of this detachment, he was so abruptly driven back by Dupont's division that he had not time to complete his dispositions to gain Magdebourg as he had intended. To assail the battalions left at the bridge of the Saale, to enter pell-mell with them, was, for our troops, the work of but fifteen minutes; the main body of the Prussian corps, encamped in rear of the city, committed the foolish act of attempting its recapture; a very warm combat ensued. Dupont debouched by the Leipsic gate, sustained by Rivaud and the cavalry of Tilly, which attacked the enemy in the direction of Neumark, and gained possession of the road to Magdebourg. The enemy could not long hold out against the superiority of Bernadotte, who, to complete the victory, endeavored to cut off the road to Dessau; the duke exerted himself to save this last communication; he succeeded in doing so, and put himself in retreat, closely pursued by the columns of Dupont and Rivaud. He passed the Elbe at Dessau, and, after having imperfectly burned the bridge, reached Magdebourg, weakened by the loss of thirty pieces of cannon and five thousand men. The regiment, which was approaching by the left of the Saale, completely surrounded in the defile of Krollwitz by Drouet and the cavalry of Tilly, were made prisoners.

This contest of twelve thousand Prussians against the

superior forces of Bernadotte was favored by the excellence of the post, but the result did no great honor to its defenders. The duke would have done much better by sending to the absent regiment an order to save itself at Magdebourg as best it could; he could then have destroyed the bridges of the Saale, and retaken, untouched, the road to Dessau and Wittenberg. This would have retarded our march for two or three days, and have saved the corps of Hohenlohe and Blucher, and the place of Stettin.

March on Potsdam and Berlin.—At the same time Davoust, who had entered Leipsic on the eighteenth, took the direction to Wittenberg, and my head-quarters followed to the same place. Considerable captures of English merchandise were made in this rich city. Lannes marched to Dessau; Bernadotte descended the Saale as far as Bernbourg and Achersleben, and received orders to throw a bridge across near Zerbst, so as to cut off the corps which he had just beaten, but which had already taken refuge under Magdebourg. Lannes caused the bridges of Dessau to be restored, and Davoust, followed by Augereau, entered Wittenberg, on the twenty-third, without resistance. A feeble Prussian detachment found there had the *mal addresse* to set fire to the bridge without burning it. We immediately directed our march on Potsdam, and entered this place on the twenty-fourth.

Visit to the Cabinet of Frederick the Great.—It would be difficult to describe my feelings in ascending the steps of the palace of Frederick, and in visiting, at Sans-Souci, the places immortalized by the great king. For seven years he had resisted the attacks of half of Europe; in fifteen days his monarchy had fallen before my eagles: thus move the affairs of nations, according to circumstances and the men who preside over their destinies. I found in his cabinet his music-desk, and another on which was the Art of War by Puiségur.

The book was open at the chapter entitled *du port de l'épée:* it was here, undoubtedly, that Frederick had been reading. My surprise was extreme at finding here the gorget, the sword, the belt, and the grand-cordon of his orders, which he had worn in the seven years' war. Such trophies were worth a hundred flags, and to forget them is proof of the disorder and stupor which reigned throughout Prussia on hearing of the disaster which had befallen their army. I sent them to Paris to be deposited in the Hotel des Invalides; many of these old soldiers were cotemporaries of the disgraceful defeat of Rosbach; I was proud to send them these proofs of the signal vengeance I had taken for that defeat.*

* The following is Thiers' description of Napoleon's visit to Potsdam and Sans-Souci.

"Having waited to allow his *corps-d'armée* to get the start of him a little, Napoleon set out on the twenty-fourth of October, and passed through Kropstadt on his way to Potsdam. Performing the journey on horseback, he was caught in a violent storm, though the weather had continued very fine ever since the opening of the campaign. It was not his custom to stop for such a reason. However, he was offered shelter in a house situated amid woods, and belonging to an officer of the hunting establishment of the court of Saxony. He accepted the offer. Some females, who seemed from their language and dress to be of elevated rank, received, around a great fire, this group of French officers, whom, from fear as much as out of politeness, they treated with much civility. They seemed not to be aware who was the principal of these officers, around whom the others respectfully ranged themselves, when one of them, still young, seized with a strong emotion, exclaimed, 'That is the Emperor!' 'How came you to know me?' asked Napoleon, dryly. 'Sire,' she answered, 'I was with your majesty in Egypt.' 'And what were you doing in Egypt?' 'I was the wife of an officer, who has since died in your service. I have solicited a pension for myself and my son, but I was a foreigner, and could not obtain it; and I am come to live with the mistress of this house, who has kindly received me, and intrusted me with the education of her children.' The countenance of Napoleon, who was displeased at being recognized, stern at first, all at once assumed a soft expression; 'Madam,' said he, 'you shall have a pension; and as for your son, I charge myself with his education.'

"The same evening he took care to affix his signature to both these resolutions, and said, smiling, 'I never yet met with an adventure in a forest, in consequence of a storm; here is one, however, and a most agreeable one.'

"He arrived in the evening of the twenty-fifth of October, at Potsdam. He immediately went to visit the retreat of the great captain, the great king, who called himself 'the philosopher of Sans-Souci,' and with some reason, who

On the twenty-fifth of October, Davoust entered Berlin, where we found a superb arsenal and immense stores of provisions. Our march had been so impetuous that the capital had not received a single courier from the army, and was in nearly the same state as when the king departed. They had carried off the archives, but they had left all the instruments of war. The same day the fortress of Spandau, which they had been so imprudent as to leave unarmed, surrendered to Marshal Lannes. They found eighty pieces of cannon in the arsenal and one thousand two hundred men as the garrison. I marched at the head of my guards to Charlottenbourg to sustain Lannes; I remained there the twenty-seventh, in order to direct measures for the pursuit of the corps of Hohenlohe.

Napoleon enters Berlin.—I made my entrance into Berlin on the twenty-eighth; I had already made a triumphal entrance into Milan, Cairo, and Vienna; but nowhere had I been received with so much *empressement* as by these Prus-

seemed to wield sword and sceptre with a jeering indifference as if in mockery of all the courts of Europe, one might venture to add, of his own people, if he had not taken so much pains to govern them well. Napoleon went through the great and little palace of Potsdam, desired to be shown Frederick's works, crowded with Voltaire's notes, sought to discover in his library on what books he was accustomed to feast his great mind, and then went to the church of Potsdam, to inspect the modest tomb where rests the founder of Prussia. At Potsdam were kept the sword of Frederick, his belt, his order of the Black Eagle. Napoleon seized them, exclaiming, 'What a capital present for the Invalides, especially for those who have formed part of the army of Hanover! They will be delighted, no doubt, when they see in our possession the sword of him who beat them at Rosbach.' Napoleon, in seizing these precious relics with so much respect, most assuredly offered no affront either to Frederick or the Prussian nation. But how extraordinary, how worthy of meditation is that mysterious concatenation which binds, blends, separates, or brings together, the things of this world; Frederick and Napoleon met here in a very strange manner. That philosopher king, who, unknown to himself, had been from his elevated throne one of the promoters of the French Revolution, now lying in his coffin, received a visit from the general of that Revolution, become emperor and conqueror of Berlin and Potsdam! The victor at Rosbach received a visit from the victor at Jena! What a sight! Unfortunately, these reverses of fortune were not the last."

sians who had so much declaimed against me without taking the trouble to examine the causes of these complaints. They received me rather as a liberator than as a conqueror. In truth the bourgeoise class, so numerous and respectable in the German states, regarded me as the defender of the principles which had triumphed in the Revolution; jealous of the pretensions of the nobility, this class had taken no part in those petty and absurd stories that had provoked the war.*

* Thiers, speaking of Napoleon's sojourn at Berlin, says: "There was in Berlin Prince Ferdinand, brother of the great Frederick and father of Prince Louis, as well as the princess his wife. There were also the widow of Prince Henry and two sisters of the king's, one lying-in, the other ill. Napoleon went to visit all these members of the royal family, with all the signs of profound respect, and touched them by testimonials coming from so high a personage, for there was not then a sovereign whose attention had so great a value as his. In the situation to which he had attained, he knew how to calculate his slightest tokens of kindness or severity. Exercising at this moment the right belonging to all generals in time of war, that of intercepting correspondence, to discover the movements of the enemy, he seized a letter from the Prince de Hatzfeld, in which he appeared to inform Prince Hohenlohe of the position of the French army around Berlin. The Prince de Hatzfeld, as head of the municipal government established in Berlin, had promised upon oath not to attempt any thing against the French army, and to attend solely to the quiet, safety, and welfare of the capital. It was an engagement of loyalty toward the conqueror, who suffered an authority which he could have abolished to subsist for the benefit of the conquered country. The fault, however, was very excusable, since it proceeded from the most honorable of sentiments, patriotism. Napoleon, who was apprehensive that other burgomasters would imitate this example, and that, in this case, all his movements would be revealed from hour to hour to the enemy, resolved to intimidate the Prussian authorities by an act of signal severity, and was not sorry that this act of severity should fall upon one of the principal members of the nobility, accused of having been a warm partisan of war, but accused falsely, for the Prince de Hatzfeld was of the number of the Prussian nobles, who had moderation because they had understanding. Napoleon sent for Prince Berthier, and ordered Marshal Davoust, on whose severity he could reckon, to form a military commission, which should apply to the conduct of the Prince de Hatzfeld the laws of war against *espionage*. Prince Berthier, on learning the resolution adopted by Napoleon, endeavored in vain to dissuade him from it. Generals Rapp, Caulaincourt, and Savary, not presuming to hazard remonstrances which seemed misplaced from any other lips than those of the major-general's, were alarmed. Not knowing to what means to resort, they hid the prince in the very palace, upon pretext of having him arrested, and then informed the Princess de Hatzfeld, an interesting person, and who was then pregnant, of the danger which threatened

Operations of Hohenlohe.—The campaigns of Jena and of Ulm will some day serve as models to teach generals the art of concentrating their forces at the proper time, and then

her husband. She hastened to the palace. It was high time; for the commission, having assembled, was applying for the evidence. Napoleon, returning from a ride in Berlin, had just alighted from his horse, the guard beating the march; and, as he crossed the threshold of the palace, the Princess de Hatzfeld, conducted by Duroc, appeared all in tears before him. Thus taken by surprise, he could not refuse to receive her; he granted her an audience in his cabinet. She was seized with terror. Napoleon, touched by her distress, desired her to approach, and handed her the intercepted letter to read. 'Well, madam,' said he, 'do you recognize the handwriting of your husband?' The princess, trembling, knew not what to reply. Presently, however, taking care to cheer her, Napoleon added, 'throw that paper into the fire, and the military commission will have no evidence to convict upon.'

"This act of clemency, which Napoleon could not refuse after he had seen the Princess de Hatzfeld, was, nevertheless, a sacrifice for him, because it was part of his design to intimidate the German nobility, particularly the magistrates of the towns, who revealed to the enemy the secrets of his operations. He learned subsequently to know the Prince de Hatzfeld, appreciated his character and his understanding, and was glad that he had not given him up to military justice. Happy the governments that have discreet friends, who contrive to delay their severities! It is not necessary that this delay should be long, before they have ceased to purpose acts upon which, at first, they were most resolutely bent."

Alison's account of this affair is discolored by prejudice, and full of errors. He says that Napoleon ordered Prince Hatzfeld "to be seized and *executed* before six o'clock that evening." On the contrary Napoleon ordered him to be *tried* by a military commission for violating the laws of war. Again, Alison says: "If the prince had been shot, it would have been, like the death of the Duke d'Enghien and the bookseller Palm—*an act of deliberate murder.*" In his desire to abuse Napoleon, he entirely ignores the laws of war. The offense of which the prince was accused, was, by the laws of war, capital, and, if found guilty by the commission, the sentence of death followed.

It is said that Prince Hatzfeld, as the head of the magistracy, had taken the usual oath to the conquering power. But it makes little difference whether he had or not taken such oath. The obligation is implied by his submission. He could have fled with his government, or have resisted with arms in hand. In the latter case he would have been treated as a prisoner of war. To submit to the conqueror and accept his liberty, he was bound by the laws of war to communicate, during the military occupation, no information to the expelled government. By attempting to send such information to Prince Hohenlohe, he was guilty of military treachery, or what the continental writers denominate *military treason.*

Alison's attempt to justify the conduct of Hatzfeld by comparing it with the French ministers to Russia and Rome, is simply ridiculous. International law

to divide them after the blow has been struck. The destruction of the Prussian army was so extraordinary that to explain it I shall be obliged to enter into details.

While I was marching on Berlin, Murat, Soult, and Ney had pursued the *débris* of the Prussian army on Magdebourg. The king, correctly judging their desperate condition, took the road to the Oder, and left the command-in-chief to Prince Hohenlohe, with the care of reorganizing the army under the cannon of this important place. The thing was impossible without his being besieged there; for Soult had followed with so much impetuosity that the rear-guard had scarcely entered the camp under Magdebourg when Legrand's division threw itself on the enemy, driving every thing within the place, where there reigned the greatest confusion.

Prince Hohenlohe here learned the issue of the combat of Halle, and my march on Dessau and Wittenberg; he nevertheless hoped that the destruction of the bridges of the Elbe would give him time to reach Stettin before us. It has already been seen that those bridges had fallen untouched into our power. He had now to choose between three plans: first, to remain and reorganize a force of fifty thousand men under the protection of Magdebourg, keeping the field as much as he could on the two banks of the Elbe, and waiting the effect of the arrival of the Russians on the Oder; even shutting himself up in the place, if he could do no better. For this plan there would have been necessary an abundance of

gives to diplomatic agents the right to collect and transmit such information. And for that very reason, diplomatic agents of an enemy are seldom permitted to exercise their functions in territories occupied by the opposing belligerent. But the case of a private citizen or a civil authority is very different. By being permitted to exercise their civil functions or to pursue their ordinary occupations, they incur the obligation to give neither aid nor comfort to the enemy of the occupying forces, although that enemy is their own legitimate government. Their allegiance to that government is, for the time, suspended, and they owe a temporary and limited allegiance to the conqueror.

This principle is well established, and the rules of law applicable to such cases are too well known to be misunderstood.

provisions and munitions; but he had neither. The second, was to throw himself on Soult and open a road to Hanover so as to unite with the division of General Lecocq, and fight in Westphalia as long as he could. The third, was to lose not a minute in gaining Stettin; he chose the last, and, under the circumstances, the resolution was a very natural one.

Hohenlohe hoped to leave Magdebourg with sixty-eight battalions and one hundred and fifty-nine squadrons, including those which the prince of Wurtemberg had saved from Halle and destined to cover his march; the disorder was so great that Kalkreuth, instead of *echelonning* his numerous cavalry on the left bank, had sent them to canton on the right bank of the Elbe near Sandau, and instead of leaving twenty-six feeble battalions to guard Magdebourg, fifty-two entire squadrons, through mistake, remained in the place.

There are two roads leading from Magdebourg to the Oder; the best and most direct is that by Brandenbourg and Berlin; the other is to the north by Rothenau, Ruppin, Zehdenich, Prenzlow, and Stettin. The prince could not take the first without encountering our columns which were debouching from Wittemberg on Potsdam; by taking the second he would approach his cavalry which was marching from Sandau on Neustadt, and would prolong the time when we could reach him. He could, in fact, take no other course; but he ought to have provided the best measures to execute this movement, and to have marched as compactly and rapidly as possible. The road to Stettin, which he followed meets at Zehdenich with that of Oranienbourg which I had taken; he should have allowed neither delay nor rest till he had reached this city with the main body of his forces, or at least with his numerous squadrons. It was the more probable that he would arrive there before our troops, as Murat had followed in rear by Hartz, and had just caused Magdebourg to be surrendered by General Belliard. How was it possible for the French troops, scattered as they were between Halberstadt and Magdebourg, having to cross the Elbe, to arrive at Zehdenich before the prince of Hohenlohe? This, however, actually occurred, Murat having reached Zehdenich by rapid marches, before the columns of Lannes, who led my march.

The prince of Hohenlohe, leaving Magdebourg the twenty-third of October, marched in three columns on Rothenau at the head of twenty-eight battalions and thirty squadrons; the main body of the cavalry passed the Elbe lower down, and rejoined the rest of the army near Neustadt. Blucher took command of the corps of the duke of Wurtemberg, destined for the rear-guard. Hohenlohe had, therefore, on the twenty-fifth, at his disposition, fifty battalions and one hundred and sixty squadrons; but instead of marching in a single compact mass and bivouacking on the road, making the inhabitants and the Prussian authorities furnish him with provisions, he took it into his head to distribute his troops in cantonments in the villages, thus fatiguing them by useless marches to and from the cantonments, and producing disorder and want of discipline by an absurd dispersion. The system was the more objectionable as they were likely to be forced to cut their way sword in hand, and were not in a situation to make the slow marches required by magazines. In addition to all these faults, instead of placing his numerous cavalry on his right to flank him in the direction that we were approaching, he threw it on the extreme left at Witstock, while the infantry marched on Neu-Rupin, and a feeble advance-guard under Schimelpeninck on Zehdenich. This city, situated, as we have said, at the debouch of the road which I had taken, was therefore the decisive point which it was necessary to reach before us; and as the advanced guard arrived there, it is certain that the rest of the corps might very well have reached it, if the dispositions had been better made.

Fall of Spandau.—The fall of Spandau, which took place the same day (the twenty-fifth), acquired so much the greater importance by the approach of Hohenlohe's corps. Bernadotte, who was informed of his march on Brandebourg, soon gave me advice of it, and advanced in the direction of Fehrbelin and Cremmen.

Dispositions to destroy Hohenlohe.—The grand-duke of Berg, having nothing further to do in the environs of Magdebourg after the enemy had reached this fortress, received orders to turn rapidly toward Baldi or Dessau to pass the Elbe there; he marched with so much celerity that he arrived at Spandau at the moment of its surrender, and immediately directed himself by Oranienbourg on Zehdenich. Lannes, who was to follow him, only reached Oranienbourg on the twenty-sixth. I kept Augereau and Davoust in the environs of Berlin, to be prepared in case the enemy should escape the other corps and attempt to fall on our rear. The first guarded the important bridge of Neubruck on the Havel; the second was to throw his light cavalry as far as Oderberg.

The prince of Hohenlohe, on the twenty-sixth, learning the presence of our troops at Oranienbourg, took the tardy resolution to force his march, moving his infantry by Gransée on Zehdenich, and the next day Prenzlow, so as to gain the defile of Lacknitz near Stettin, on the twenty-eighth, where he would be safe. The cavalry took the same direction by Witstock and Woldeck. On his arrival at Gransée, Hohenlohe received the unexpected news that General Schimelpeninck had been beaten at Zehdenich by the cavalry of the grand-duke of Berg, and had saved himself in disorder on Prenzlow. It was ridiculous to lose his direct communication in consequence of a skirmish of cavalry, when ten thousand Prussian horse were marching to Witstock without any object. Nevertheless Hohenlohe, renouncing all hope of opening a passage, resolved to gain Boitzenbourg-pres-Prenzlow, by making a detour by Furstenberg and Lychen where he waited Blucher and a part of the column of cavalry which he had ordered to join him in place of Schimelpeninck's troops. This idea was absurd, for as our troops held the direct and shortest road to Templin, the enemy must expect to meet them in column with the chance of being sustained the more easily by the corps d'armée which arrived first at Berlin (Lannes and Davoust). Hohenlohe reached Lychen on the twenty-seventh, and in vain waited there for Blucher, who had been informed too late of this forced march, and had not yet passed Templin; not being joined by the expected cavalry, and as he had no time to lose, he continued his march on Boitzenbourg.

Murat was not a man to allow himself to be easily passed. Informed, in his march from Templin on Prenzlow, of the direction taken by the Prussians, he moved with the divisions of Grouchy, Beaumont, and Lassalle on Wichmansdorf, where he attacked the gens-d'armes of the guard which flanked the march. To assail, turn, and overthrow this superb regiment of cuirassiers on the shores of the lake, was the work of a moment. Some of the officers of this corps had insulted the French ambassador, in order the more surely to involve the king in the war; they expiated this conduct by the disgrace of being forced to capitulate in the open field, which cavalry should never do.

Hohenlohe, frightened at this news, formed his infantry and hesitated whether to enter Boitzenbourg or take the cross road between Prenzlow and Passewalk; this last course was certainly the most prudent; but on the report of a patrol, he decided to enter Boitzenbourg for the night, and, the next day, to take the road to Prenzlow, where he would find provisions and forage for his troops.

Combat and Capitulation of Prenzlow.—On the twenty-eighth, the corps advanced on Shonermarck and Gustrow; it entered Prenzlow without any great obstacle; but the grand-duke of Berg, arriving by the road to Templin, and not being able to occupy a city with his cavalry, he caused it to be turned by a detachment of dragoons, while he advanced with two divisions on the small stream of Golmitz, fell impetuously on the rear of the Prussian column, pursued it even to the faubourg, cut to pieces and captured the regiment of the king, cut off the rear-guard of Prince Augustus, and forced him, after a good defense, to surrender with his battalion.

The Prussian infantry had passed Prenzlow and taken, for some unknown reason, the road to Passewalk instead of that to Stettin. Murat summoned the prince of Hohenlohe to surrender, and Lannes, who had arrived there himself, although his corps was still distant, also summoned the enemy in order to deceive him. Convinced that he had no more hopes of gaining Locknitz, which he supposed to be in possession of our infantry, attacked in front by a division of cavalry and in rear by two others, the prince laid down his arms with seventeen battalions and nineteen squadrons, amounting to not less than twelve thousand men.

Fall of Stettin.—The grand-duke of Berg seemed almost omnipresent; no sooner had we obtained this brilliant success than Lasalle's division of light cavalry advanced on Stettin, whose imbecile governor surrendered to our hussars, with a garrison of five thousand men. Murat immediately directed himself on Passewalk, where the great column of Hohenlohe's cavalry had taken refuge on learning the disaster of its chief. Six regiments of cuirassiers and a brigade of infantry, fatigued, it is true, by forced marches, surrendered without the slightest resistance. A single brigade, cut off from Prenzlow the night before, presented itself at Stettin; the governor refused to open his gates, on the twenty-eighth, to his own troops, but the next day he opened them at the first summons of our advance-guard. This brigade reached Anclam, where General Becker's division attacked it and forced it to surrender.

Blucher retires on Mecklenbourg.—Of all this army, which a few days ago was so brilliant, there remained only Blucher and the old corps of the duke of Weimar, commanded by General Winning, who, after having given the slip to Soult, had passed the Elbe near Sandau and gained Mecklenbourg. Blucher, informed of the defeat of Hohenlohe, immediately inclined toward Neustrelitz, where he joined this corps, which now formed a little army of twenty-one thousand men. Before following his ulterior movements, we will return to my army.

Capitulation of Custrin.—Davoust, after remaining some days in advance of Berlin, took the road to Frankfort-on-the-Oder, and to Custrin. This place, which is situated on an island in the Oder, and which Major Heyden had heroically defended in the seven years' war, surrendered to our light troops, separated as they were from the place by the double channel of the river! Before we could take possession of the work, it was necessary that the garrison should furnish us with boats! Master of this important bulwark, and having no more enemies before him, Davoust took the road to Posen. Augereau occupied Frankfort; my guards remained at Berlin; Ney continued the blockade of Magdebourg.

Napoleon's Measures for securing his Conquests.—While my eagles crossed, with rapid flight, the space between the Rhine and the Oder, and conquered in three weeks the whole country between the two rivers, I neglected no means to consolidate my power and secure these possessions. Already Mortier, with the two feeble divisions of the eighth corps, had occupied the principality of Fulda. The prince of Orange, to whom it had fallen at the peace of Luneville, as an indemnity for the Stadtholderate, had just been fighting in the ranks of my enemies. I punished him for this, by seizing his states. Mortier afterward advanced on Cassel, in concert with the king of Holland.

The Elector, a vassal, in some measure, of Prussia, and one of my most bitter enemies, had left for England, carrying with him a considerable treasure, the fruit of the subsidies which his house had constantly received from England since the coalition of 1703, against Louis XIV. The twenty thousand men which he had organized to fight me laid down their arms and were disbanded by inferior forces. The king of Holland afterward advanced on Hanover with the Gallo-Batavian army, and after some slight skirmishes he invested the Prussian division of Lecocq in Hameln and Nieubourg, took possession, almost without opposition, of the whole electorate, the duchy of Brunswick, and the Hanseatic cities of Bremen and Hamburg. The Bavarian and Wurtemberg contingents, after having taken possession of Bareith, and covering the right wing of the grand army in its decisive march, directed themselves by Plauen on Dresden, and advanced toward the Oder in concert with Davoust; they formed the ninth corps. The contingents of the other petty princes furnished garrisons on our rear; that of Hesse-Darmstadt at Spandau and Stettin, and Nassau at Berlin.

Armistice with the Saxons.—I also thought to attach to myself the Saxons; before the war I had already issued a proclamation, showing them that the projects of Prussia were tending to nothing less than their reduction to the condition of a Prussian province. I signed an armistice with the Saxon general who had been taken prisoner at Jena; the remainder of the contingent left the Prussian army at Balbi on the Elbe, and the elector immediately opened negotiations with us.

Blucher pursued to Lubeck.—Informed of the junction

of Blucher with the corps of General Winning, I directed Bernadotte to follow this little army, while Murat cut it off from Stralsund and Rostock, and Soult prevented it from regaining the Lower Elbe. Pursued in this way, it was difficult for him to escape. After a combat of the rear-guard at Nossentin against Dupont, and quite a brilliant cavalry engagement near Criwitz, Blucher directed himself on Schwerin. It appeared that he first wished to take the road to Gustrow, undoubtedly for the purpose of embarking at Rostock, or of reaching Stralsund; but Murat having already arrived at Demnin, he inclined to the left toward Mecklenbourg, with the intention of throwing himself on the Lower Elbe and fighting his way into Hanover. Anticipated on all sides, he fell back on Gadebush-sur-Lubeck, where he arrived the fifth of November. Bernadotte marched there by Schonberg, and Soult by Ratsbourg: they were sustained by the cavalry of Murat. Arriving by the north, Bernadotte learned that the remainder of the Swedish detachment which had so presumptuously occupied the Pays-de-Lauenbourg, had just embarked on the Trave at Lubeck. The course of this river is sinuous; the navigation to Travemund is difficult and slow; a brigade of Dupont's division, sent half way to Schlutup, captured a battalion of the guards and the remains of a rich convoy.

Fall of Lubeck.—Our columns, reaching Lubeck on the sixth, at break of day, immediately began the attack. Bernadotte assailed with Drouet's division the Mecklenbourg gate and the adjacent bastion; the place was only a simple enciente, much out of repair, but capable of resisting a *coup-de-main*; it was unarmed; the Prussians had hastily placed on the ramparts their field-pieces. It is said that two Prussian battalions imprudently placed in advance of the gate and overthrown by the brigade of Frère, were the cause of our columns entering pell-mell with the enemy. The braves of the Twenty-seventh light, and the Ninety-fourth of the line, fell upon the enemy, carried the palisaded tambour of the gate and the nearest batteries, and, sustained by the rest of the corps, penetrated into the streets.

Blucher had just retired to his quarters when our soldiers penetrated the town and pursued after him; he had barely time to mount his horse; his staff was captured. The columns of Soult encountered greater obstacles in carrying the Hanover gate, and they had just succeeded in effecting an entrance, when they met Rivaud's division. Blucher succeeded in effecting an issue by the Holstein gate with four or five thousand infantry, and joined his cavalry, which was cantoned on the left bank of the Trave; the rest, to the number of about eight thousand, were killed or taken prisoners. A bloody contest was carried on from street to street and from house to house, in the public establishments. A soldiery influenced by cruel scenes is not easily restrained, and the inhabitants of this flourishing city had naturally to suffer all the horrors of a city taken by assault; but Soult and Bernadotte at last succeeded in restoring order.

Capitulation of Blucher.—The refuge which Blucher had sought behind the Trave could only save him for a single day, for the neutrality of Denmark left him no issue; he was forced to lay down his arms the next day with his remaining ten thousand men.

Fall of Magdebourg.—The destruction of the Prussian armies was not the only result of the battle of Jena; the Prussians were so discouraged that they surrendered the most formidable bulwarks of the monarchy. To those already cited, we must add Magdebourg, which important place, with a garrison of eighteen or twenty thousand men and six hundred pieces of cannon, was surrendered by the aged Kliest, after a few hours' bombardment, to Ney whose force did not exceed the garrison of the place! Hameln and Nieuburg also surrendered at the first summons of a Gallo-Batavian division under the orders of Savary.

Napoleon at Berlin.—While my lieutenants were pursuing in all directions the remains of the Prussian army, I had remained at Berlin, my presence being unnecessary in these various pursuits. I had to provide an administration for the great states which we had conquered, to urge forward measures necessary for our security, to review the corps which had just come to replace our losses and increase our force; in a word, to provide the means of profiting by so much success.

The celebrated Berlin Decree.—It was also at Berlin that I issued my formidable degree of reprisals against the British Order in Council, which declared the ports of the channel blockaded. In reality this paper blockade was rather insignificant, for England had not ships enough to carry it into effect; but it was the form and the principle which was in violation of the law of nations.

Maritime law in the full extent given to it by England, authorized the right of visit to ascertain that the vessel was really of the nation whose flag it bore, and that it carried nothing contraband, that is, naval stores. It also interdicted the entrance to ports blockaded strictly enough to render it dangerous to enter, and the vessels warned not to enter, should they attempt to do so by ruse, were subject to be seized. In order therefore to effect a real blockade, it was necessary to have a sufficient number of vessels of war before each military or merchant port included in the blockade.

The Order in Council, declaring all the coast of France from the Seine to Antwerp in a state of blockade, arrogated the right of seizing all vessels sailing for these ports, whether they were really invested or not. It thus gave to a ministerial decree an artificial force more powerful than all the

British squadrons together; for, admitting this principle for a hundred leagues of coast in 1806, England might very well extend it by a second decree to all the coast of France and her allies, and thus annihilate the commerce of Europe; which, in fact, she did not fail to do. A great nation, possessing, with its allies, more than two thousand leagues of coast, a hundred ships of the line, colonies, and inhabitants with any blood in their veins, could not tolerate such legislation without disgracing itself. I was indignant at it, and my victorious position authorizing me to act, I in my turn thundered forth a decree which excelled that of the English ministry.

British Orders in Council.—The cabinet of London did not long remain my debtor: an order of January 7th, 1807, declared good prize any neutral vessel trading from one port of France to another, or to a port of her allies! Rome and Carthage never exhibited such animosity; their quarrels never extended beyond their own political power and that of the allies who were successively drawn into the whirlpool of their contest; they never attacked the prosperity of all that breathed on the two hemispheres!*

* This and other British Orders in Council issued in regard to blockades, the preëmption of neutral goods, and trade with French colonies, were most disastrous to neutral commerce, and especially to that of the United States. Notwithstanding the specious arguments by which English statesmen and English judges attempted, at the time, to justify these measures, very few can now be found who will defend them. The publicists of the continent and America have almost unanimously condemned them, and even British writers, while defending them on the ground of political and military necessity, virtually admit that they were contrary to the established principles of international jurisprudence. But these violations of law and justice on the part of Great Britian did not justify the retaliatory decrees of Napoleon. Both were equally violations of the rights of neutrals.

The following are Thiers' remarks on Napoleon's Berlin decree, and the British Orders in Council.

"England herself had just authorized all sorts of excesses against her commerce by taking an extraordinary measure, and one of the most ontrageous that can be imagined against the most generally admitted right of nations, and which is called a *paper blockade*. As we have already explained several times,

Armistice with Prussia not Ratified.—While I was fulminating my decrees against the new maritime rights claimed by Great Britian, my armies had completed the destruction

it is a principle with most of the maritime nations that every neutral, that is to say every flag, not a party in a war between two powers, has a right to sail from the ports of one to the ports of the other, to carry any merchandise whatever, even that of the enemy, excepting contraband of war, which consist in arms, munitions of war, and provisions cured for the use of the armies. This liberty ceases only in the case of a seaport blockaded by a naval force, so that the blockade be efficacious. In this case, the blockade being notified, the faculty of entering the blockaded place is suspended for neutrals. But if, in the restrictions imposed upon the freedom of navigation, we do not stop at this certain limit of the presence of an effective force, there is no reason why we should not lay an interdict upon whole tracts of coast, upon pretext of blockade. England had already sought to overstep the limits of the real blockade, by alleging that, with a few sail, insufficient in number to close the approaches to a sea-port, she had a right to declare the blockade. But at last she had admitted the necessity of a force of some sort against the blockaded port. Now she did not stop at this limit, already so vague, and, at the time of her momentary rupture with Prussia, occasioned by the occupation of Hanover, she had ventured to forbid all commerce to neutrals on the coasts of France and Germany, from Brest to the mouth of the Elbe. This was the abuse of strength carried to the utmost excess, and thenceforward a mere British decree was sufficient to lay under interdict all the parts of the globe which England was pleased to deprive of commerce.

"This incredible violation of the right of nations furnished Napoleon with a just pretext for authorizing the most rigorous measures in regard to English commerce. He devised a formidable decree, which, however excessive it might appear, was but a just reprisal of the violences of England, and which had moreover the advantage of completely answering the views which he had recently conceived. This decree, dated Berlin, the twenty-first of November, applicable not only to France, but to the countries occupied by her armies or in alliance with her, that is to say, to France, Holland, Spain, Italy, and all Germany, declared the British Islands in a *state of blockade*. The consequences of the state of blockade were the following:

"All commerce with England was absolutely prohibited;

"All goods, the produce of English manufactures, or of English colonies, were to be confiscated, not only on the coast, but in the interior, in the houses of the merchants by whom they should be harbored;

"All letters coming from or going to England, addressed to an Englishman, or written in English, were to be stopped at the post-offices and destroyed;

"Every Englishman whatsoever, seized in France or in the countries under subjection to her arms, was to be declared a prisoner of war;

"Every vessel having only touched at the English colonies or at any of the ports of the three kingdoms, was forbidden to enter French ports or ports under subjection to France, and, in case of false declarations being made on this subject, she became a lawful prize;

of the Prussian forces between the Rhine and the Oder. Murat, Davoust, and Lannes, had already passed the latter river to enter Prussian Poland. Winter was approaching; it was necessary to consolidate our astonishing successes. There were two means of doing this: the one, to complete the destruction of Prussia and divide the country among my allies; the other, to pardon her and attach her to my car by benefits which she could not fail to value after her defeat, and then join with her in effecting the reëstablishment of Poland.

The king of Prussia, having reached the Oder, sent to me the marquis of Lucchesini to treat for an armistice or for a

"Half of the produce of the confiscation was destined to indemnify French and allied merchants who had suffered by the spoliations of England;

"Lastly, the English who fell into our power were to serve for the exchange of the French or their allies who were taken prisoners.

"Such were these measures, assuredly inexcusable if England had not taken pains to justify them beforehand by her own excesses. Napoleon was fully sensible of their severity; but, in order to induce England to relinquish her tyranny at sea, he had recourse to a like tyranny upon land. He wished most especially to intimidate the agents of the English commerce, and principally the merchants of the Hanseatic towns, who, laughing at the orders issued respecting the Elbe and the Weser, distributed the prohibited goods throughout all parts of the continent. The threat of confiscation, a threat soon followed up, would make them tremble, and, if not close the outlets opened clandestinely to British commerce, at least render them very narrow.

"Napoleon, saying to himself that all the commercial nations were interested in the resistance which he was opposing to the unjust pretensions of England, concluded that they would submit to the inconveniences of a struggle which had become necessary; he thought that, these inconveniences falling particularly upon the speculators of Hamburg, Bremen, Leipzig, Amsterdam, and on smugglers by profession, it was not worth while to limit his means of reprisal, out of regard for such interests.

"The effect of this decree on the opinion of Europe was immense. Some regarded it as a revolting excess of despotism, others as a stroke of profound policy, all as an extraordinary act, proportioned to the conflict of giants maintained by England and France against each other, the one daring to seize the dominion of the sea, hitherto the common route of nations, and to interdict all commerce to her enemies, the other aiming at the entire occupation of the continent by force of arms, to reply to the closing of the sea by the closing of the land. Unheard-of spectacle, without example in the past and probably in the future, exhibited at this moment by the unchained passions of the two greatest nations of the earth."

peace; he was accompanied by General Zastrow, whose noble and respectable character was the best guarantee of the sincere intentions of the king. Duroc treated with them at Charlottenbourg. It was difficult to come to an understanding when they were every moment receiving news of the surrender of some new corps, or the fall of some new place. The negotiators saw that, by showing a desire for an alliance, they softened the rigorous terms of the treaty. One is always disposed to do more for an enemy who becomes your ally, than for an adversary who signs a pure and simple peace, and may immediately return to the ranks of your enemies.

I consented to an armistice which left to Prussia, Magdebourg and all her states between the Elbe and the Niemen; she lost Hanover, and all her states in Franconia, Saxony, and Westphalia. If an alliance should actually be formed, I might indemnify her for these losses.

But Magdebourg with twenty thousand men capitulated the same day that Duroc signed the convention of Charlottenbourg; could I surrender this main bulwark of the monarchy for a simple armistice, subject still to the acceptance of a prince who was at Königsberg in the midst of the Russian columns which he had called to his assistance? It was necessary to make a new treaty; I left for Posen and could sign it only in that city; I could not rely much on its ratification, for the king of Prussia, after the conduct which his cabinet had induced him to pursue in the affair of Haugwitz, would have lost in the eyes of his contemporaries and of posterity, if he had again abandoned the Russians, eighty thousand of whom were already on the Vistula and crossing his states.

Napoleon advances to the Vistula.—In the mean time, my army, having found no enemy between the Oder and the Vistula, had advanced on Warsaw and Thorn. I had only to observe Stralsund and the Swedes in my rear, and to reduce the six fortresses of Silesia. I assigned the first to Mortier till I could relieve him by a new corps of observation on the Elbe. The reduction of Silesia was assigned to my brother Jerome ; he had as yet no establishment ; before providing him with one, I wished to give him an opportunity to distinguish himself. He had at first embarked in the Brest squadron, but, as he did not like the sea service, I appointed him to my army ; Vandamme was his guide ; he commanded twenty-five thousand Bavarians and Wurtembergers, forming the ninth corps. To reduce Glogau, Breslau, Brieg, Neisse, Schweidnitz, and Glatz, whose garrisons formed a force as numerous as his own, was no easy matter, although his opponent, the prince of Anhalt-Pless, was a man of neither head nor heart. Glogau fell without resistance, but the other places were better commanded and made much better defense.

Immense Results of this Seven Weeks' War.—Thus terminated the war of seven weeks—very different from that of seven years. Never was there a victory with such results. In this short time my power had extended from the banks of the Rhine to those of the Vistula ; a hundred thousand prisoners, four thousand pieces of cannon, six great fortresses and many smaller ones—such were the trophies of a skillful manœuvre, of the impetuous valor of my army, and of the inexperience of my adversaries. Whatever may be the opinion of the eloquent author of the "*Précis des événements militaires,*" these successes were merely the result of a skillful application of the principles of war by us, and a total neglect of them by our enemies. To deny the existence and influence of these principles, is to deny the light of the sun. My genius consisted only in applying these principles almost constantly, and in giving to this application its greatest possible extent. In this I exerted all the superiority of my judgment, the grandeur of my character, and the extent of my views. This is what distinguishes the great warrior from the mediocre general. But far from me be the thought of ever putting in doubt the existence of military principles, and their influence on the fate of armies?

CHAPTER X.

THE WAR OF 1807, OR THE CAMPAIGNS OF EYLAU AND FRIEDLAND.

Condition of the Enemy's Forces—Poland—Napoleon's Measure for securing his Rear—The King of Prussia rejects the Armistice—The Russian Army—Invasion of Moldavia—Position of the two Armies—Napoleon takes the Offensive—Combat of Pultusk—Napoleon prepares for Winter Quarters—Measures for securing his Position—Continuation of the War between Russia and Turkey—Benningsen takes Command of the Russian Army—Affairs of Silesia—Benningsen attacks Napoleon's Left—Movements of the Latter—His Project accidentally Discovered by the Russians—Soult fights at Bergfried—Combat of Landsberg—Combat of Liebstadt—Battle of Eylau—The French Army resumes its Winter Quarters—Combat of Ostrolenka—Embarrassment of Napoleon's Position—Menaces of Spain—Austria offers her Intervention for Peace—The English threaten Constantinople—Passage of the Dardanelles—Sebastiani rouses the Turks to defend themselves—Retreat of the English—Napoleon's Firmness—Negotiations at the Camp of Finkenstein—Negotiations with England broken off by Perceval—Treaty of Triple-Alliance at Bartenstein—Operations in Pomerania—Negotiations with Sweden—Army of Observation on the Elbe—English Expedition into Egypt—Sieges in Silesia—Siege and fall of Dantzic—Resumption of Hostilities—Danger and escape of Ney—Napoleon Marches to his Assistance—Favorable Changes of Napoleon's Position—Battle of Heilsberg—Operations of Benningsen—Battle of Friedland—The Russians recross the Niemen—They propose Peace—Interview of the Emperors at Tilsit—The Peace Signed—Prussia—Conditions of the Treaty of Tilsit—Revolution at Constantinople—Projects on Turkey—Special Stipulations at Tilsit.

Condition of the Enemy's Forces.—The king of Prussia had retired to Königsberg. Of all his army, there remained hardly twenty thousand men fit for service; but one hundred thousand Russians, coming to his assistance, were already advancing on the Vistula. I marched to meet them; on entering Poland, a new theatre was presented for our arms; here was the old land of anarchy, and of liberty crushed by foreign domination; the Poles only waited my coming to throw off the German yoke.

Poland.—Not to recognize the advantages to be derived from Poland would have evinced ignorance of the eighteenth century; but in order that this country should serve as a barrier against Russia, and a counterpoise to Austria, required a complete reëstablishment of the Polish nation. This could only be brought about by a long and successful war: my ministers were not agreed on the policy of attempting this project; Talleyrand, old and worn out (*usé*), sighed for his hotel in Paris, and was vexed at the idea of a winter's journey to Poland: he opposed it. Maret approved the attempts, for he could see in it immense advantages, and some chances of success.

The promises of Dombrowski and Zayonscheck were encouraging. A formal deputation of Great Poland, presided over by Count de Zadinski, had nearly decided me by promising a prompt levy called the *Polish insurrection*, a kind of reserve in which each gentleman mounts his horse and leads to the field a certain number of his peasants. My orders had already been prepared, when a memoir drawn up by an officer attached to my person, changed my resolution. It represented, in strong colors, the advantages to be derived from an alliance with Prussia, by generously pardoning her, and by aggrandizing her with Polish territory, which it would be possible to cede and still preserve to the Poles their nationality; thus obtaining the counterpoise, so essential to my policy, without exposing me to an interminable war with Prussia, Russia, and Austria. This memoir particularly pointed out the fact that the reëstablishment of Poland would form an eternal bond of union between these three powers; that a rupture with Austria at this time might bring on our rear one hundred and fifty thousand men, which would render our position on the Vistula embarrassing, unless we could support ourselves on Prussia. By completely amalgamating the Polish nation with an industrious and intelligent people, would be of great advantage to the former.

I confess that these arguments nearly persuaded me to adopt this course; an armistice was already negotiated; but the inconceivable capitulations of Erfurth, Stettin, Prenzlow, Magdebourg and Lubeck, diminished my desire for an alliance with an army so demoralized. The conditions of the armistice were effected by these capitulations, and as I expected that the arrival of the Russians would cause them to be rejected, I resolved to try the Poles, notwithstanding the rigors of the season. In fact it was preferable to go to Warsaw to fight the Russian army in the midst of a population ready to join us, than to await it in the midst of the humiliated Prussians, who upon any reverse of my army would have gone over to the enemy.

Kosciusko, who for several years had been residing at Paris, was sent for; but he was unwilling to attempt any partial revolution. He demanded the formal and complete restoration of his country; but this I could not engage to do, as Austria was in possession of a third of the former kingdom of Poland. It would have closed the door against a reconciliation with Russia, and at the same time have involved us with Austria. I, therefore contented myself with sending Dombrowski and Zayonscheck to Posen, to assure them of the interest that I would take in their country if they would assist me, and that I would soon follow them. I left Berlin on the twenty-fourth of November, and arrived at Posen on the twenty-eighth. I was received with an enthusiasm which surprised me, and which seemed a happy omen. They gave me fêtes which would have done honor to the most brilliant salons of Paris. I remained in this city a fortnight; the time was not lost, for I could still reach Warsaw as soon as my troops.

Notwithstanding the enthusiasm produced at Posen and

Warsaw, the Poles had not entirely fulfilled my expectations. They are a passionate people, chivalric and light; they act from impulse, not from judgment. Their enthusiasm is great, but irregular and short lived. Those who followed my standards exhibited admirable fidelity and valor; I here pay them the tribute of my gratitude; but as a nation, Poland should have done more. This was not the fault of the Poles; it was the inevitable result of circumstances. If Poland had had a more powerful and a more numerous *tiers-état*, she might have made a *levée-en-masse* for us. Perhaps by giving the Poles a plan, a system, and a *point-d'appui* more stable than the House of Saxony, they might, in time, have been able to maintain themselves. It was never a part of my character to do things by halves; I, however, pursued such a course with Poland; the results were not favorable. This course was forced upon me by my political relations; I could not act differently.*

* Some of the liberal writers on this campaign, have blamed Napoleon for not adopting more decisive measures for the restoration of Poland. There is no doubt that such measures would have been immensely popular in France; but it was thought by many that they would have been unsuccessful, on account of the unstable character of the Poles, and the powerful opposition of Russia, Prussia, and Austria. In speaking of this project, Alison says: It would have been alike grateful to every lover of freedom, and important as forming a barrier against Muscovite aggrandisement in Europe. But was it possible to construct such an empire, to form such a barrier, out of the disjointed elements of Polish anarchy? This is the point for consideration; and if it was not, then the French emperor would have thrown away all the advantages of victory, if, for a visionary and impracticable scheme of this description, he had incurred the lasting and indelible animosity of the partitioning powers. With the aid of two hundred thousand brave men, indeed, which Poland could with ease send into the field, he might, for a season, have withstood the united armies of Russia, Austria, and Prussia; but could he rely on their tumultuary assemblies sustaining the steady and durable efforts requisite for permanent success? What made Poland originally fall a victim to the coalesced powers, once little more than provinces of its mighty dominion? "The insane ambition," as John Sobieski said, "of a plebeian noblesse;" the jealousy of six hundred thousand electors, incapable alike of governing themselves or of permitting the steady national government of others. Was this fatal element of discord eradicated from the Polish heart? Is it yet eradicated?

Measures for securing the Rear of the French Army.—I profited by my sojourn at Posen to sign a treaty of peace with the elector of Saxony, and to strengthen, by this old ally of France, the system of the Confederation of the Rhine. A first contingent of eight thousand men took up their march to join me on the Vistula. I also completed the necessary measures for securing our rear.

On leaving Berlin and Meseritz, I had given Mortier directions for the disposition of his eighth corps. Since the troops of my brother Louis, under the orders of Savary, had reduced Hameln and Nieubourg, and completed the conquest of Hanover, their presence was no longer required there, and they returned to Holland to protect that country against the English. Mortier, after leaving Hesse, entered Mecklenburg, and was required to guard the coast of the North Sea and the Baltic, from Hamburg and the mouth of the Weser to Stettin, so as to observe the Swedes and the English.

A vast system was indispensable for securing our power in the immense countries which we had just invaded with the impetuosity of a mad torrent, and where strong resistance might still be encountered. Already some troubles had manifested themselves in Hesse where the partisans of the Elector profited by the absence of the eighth corps and the inevitable burdens of war, to stir up insurrection. I immediately gave

Was it possible, by reëstablishing Poland in 1807. to have done any thing but, as Talleyrand well expressed it, "organized anarchy?" These are the considerations which then presented and still present an invincible obstacle to a measure, in other points of view recommended by so many considerations of justice and expedience. It is evident that the passions of the people, their insane desire for democratic equality, were so powerful. that if reëstablished in its full original extent, it would speedily have again fallen under the dominion of its former conquerors; the same causes which formerly proved fatal to its independence would, without doubt, again have had the same effect."

Thiers discusses this subject at very considerable length, and with his usual accuracy and eloquence. His remarks are too extensive for quotation, and a mere extract would not do full justice to his well considered views upon the course of Napoleon toward Poland at this period of her history.

orders for suppressing these movements. Movable columns sent from Mayence by Kellerman, from Munster by Loison, and from Magdebourg by General Michaud, completely restored order.

Kellerman organized at Mayence, into provisional regiments, the conscripts destined for the several *corps-d'armée.* This mode of centralizing the surveillance, and awaiting small detachments, which are always dangerous, gave to this multitude of isolated recruits the consistence and force of a respectable army. Four of these regiments had already reached Berlin, where they relieved the contingents of Baden, of Wurtzburg, and the Northern Legion, formed of Hessian and Prussian volunteers. These advanced between the Oder and the Vistula to cover our communications and observe Colberg. A division of cuirassiers, drawn from Italy and concentrated at Leipsic under D'Espagne, moved toward Posen and Thorn. The grenadier division of Oudinot, reorganized at Berlin, marched toward Warsaw. Four other provisional regiments were formed at Mayence; and my army became thus secured in its recruits and in its communications. No one ever understood so thoroughly as I did the mechanism of this organization on the rear of an army, and of these successive levies, which served at the same time as means for periodically recruiting our regiments, and as reserves for guarding our line of operations.

The King of Prussia rejects the Armistice.—When the king received at Königsberg the armistice signed at Charlottenburg by MM. Lucchesini and Zastrow, he was the more indisposed to approve it, as he had, on the twentieth of October, signed at Grodno a convention with Russia, and the first Russian contingent had just entered the Prussian territory, under the orders of Benningsen. He therefore refused to ratify it, and the continuation of the war was the only course left for us both. We therefore were again to fight the Russians; and it was now the question whether it was best to await their coming, or to meet them on the way. The season was bad, but it was no better for them than for us. If I allowed them to advance, I deprived myself of the support and resources of Poland; they might induce Austria to join in the war, for she hesitated only because the Russians were too far distant to come to her assistance: they might incite the Prussian nation, which, recovering from the shock of a first disaster, felt the necessity of doing every thing to reëstablish itself.

The Russian Army.—The Emperor Alexander had shown great activity in repairing the losses of the campaign of Austerlitz; not only were all his regiments filled to the complement, but his army was augmented by thirty squadrons, and fifty-one battalions of new formation. If his entire army had been directed against me, it would have been difficult for me to sustain the contest with my army, scattered from Hanover to Warsaw. Happily I was soon relieved on this point by the news that General Michelsen had entered Moldavia at the head of eighty thousand men.

The Russian army was at this time divided into eighteen divisions, each, except the guards, composed of six regiments of infantry or chasseurs, ten squadrons of light cavalry, one company of pioneers, two batteries of position, and three batteries of light and one of horse artillery; making for each division eighteen battalions, twenty squadrons, and the enormous quantity of seventy-two pieces of cannon; the artillery was fine and well-served; the cavalry, so mediocre under Suwarrow, had vastly improved since then. This army was distributed as follows:

1st. The division of guards and grenadiers, under the Grand-duke Constantine, numbered thirty-three battalions, thirty-five squadrons, and eighty-four pieces.

2d. The army destined to act in Prussia, including the

first eight divisions under Osterman, Sacken, Prince Galitzin, Touczkof, Barclay de Tolly, Doctorof, and Essen, and also the fourteenth division, at first under Prince Gortschakof, and afterward under Count Kamenski; these together, amounted to one hundred and forty-seven battalions, one hundred and seventy squadrons, and five hundred and four pieces.

3d. The army in Moldavia under Michelsen, including the ninth, tenth, eleventh, twelfth, and thirteenth divisions, under Prince Wolkonsky, Muller, Zacomelsky, Miloradowich, Meindorf, and the duke of Richelieu. They together, counted ninety battalions, one hundred squadrons, and three hundred and six pieces.

4th. The intermediate corps under Count Apraxin, including the sixteenth, seventeenth, and eighteenth divisions, under General Rtisclief, Prince Labanof, and Prince Gortschakof, numbering fifty-four battalions, thirty squadrons, and one hundred and forty-four pieces.

The total of these forces was three hundred and twenty-four battalions, three hundred and thirty-five squadrons, and one thousand and thirty-eight pieces of cannon. But this did not include the corps of Georgia, of Finland, and the garrison-battalions, which formed an army entirely distinct.

Invasion of Moldavia.—To understand the motives of this invasion, which appeared to be an error, it is necessary to recur to preceding events. Russia, certain of war between us and Prussia, thought to appear in it merely as an auxiliary, as she had done in 1805, for Austria; she thus flattered herself that she could extend the limits of her empire to the Danube, and that England had too much need of her alliance not to second her in her project. For this purpose it was necessary to have a legitimate pretext for a war against the Turks.

The influence of Sebastiani furnished one sufficiently plausible. The first care of my ambassador was to follow out my instructions in procuring the dismissal of the Hospodars of Moldavia, Ypsilanti, and Morusi, elected under the protection of Russia, and consecrated by the treaty of Yassi. Russia had a right to complain of this, and she did so warmly; the threats of Count Italinski, supported by those of the English ambassador, who spoke of nothing less than the bombardment of Constantinople by a powerful squadron, caused the restoration of the Hospodars.

The Emperor Alexander, however, did not wait for this ratification, but immediately ordered Michelson to invade the principalities, and to seize upon the Turkish places on the Danube. This general passed the Dniester on the third of November, and advanced without obstacle to the frontiers of Servia. We were reciprocally pleased with this event; Russia, because she thought to profit by it, and I, because it produced a powerful diversion in my favor. Moreover, the rapid fall of the Prussian monarchy, changing the face of affairs, placed all the advantages of this aggression on my side. This invasion had been planned and ordered before the news of the disasters of Prussia was received at St. Petersburg. Otherwise the Emperor Alexander would have been too prudent to undertake, at the same time, the double task of opposing us, and of attacking the Turks.

Position of the two Armies.—When he received the first information of the march of the French on Berlin, he detached the corps of Benningsen and of Buxhowden to the assistance of the Prussians. Forty thousand Russians under the former arrived on the Vistula a few days before us, but fell back on Pultusk to await the second army which was approaching by forced marches. We therefore passed the river without obstacle. Davoust and Murat, who had entered Warsaw on the thirtieth of September, were not a little surprised at the sudden desertion of the post of Praga, and immediately sent over troops in boats to take possession of it (December 2d). Lannes sustained them, and my right wing established itself on the Bug; the left was not less fortunate. Ney, who was in possession of Thorn, debouched from this place, sustained by the cavalry of Bessières and followed by the corps of Bernadotte. At the centre, Soult and Augereau prepared, with great difficulty, the means of crossing the Vistula between Modlin and Wyssogrod. Leaving Posen, on the sixteenth of December, I arrived at Warsaw on the eighteenth. I urged forward the passage of these two corps; Augereau, not being able to throw a bridge across the river, passed his troops over in boats near Zakroczin between the twentieth and twenty-second. Soult, not being able to succeed at Wyssogrod, fortunately found means of effecting a passage at Plonsk.

The Emperor Alexander had given the command of his army to Marshal Kamenski, an octogenarian, who, in the wars of the Empress Catherine, had shown energy and vigor; but these qualities had been destroyed by age. Nevertheless, on uniting his forces, he signalized his arrival at the army by an advance movement. He carried his head-quarters to Nasielsk and cantoned the four divisions of his first army between the Ukra, the Bug, and the Narew. The second army was cantoned between Golymin and Makow, having one of his divisions on the left of the Narew. A Prussian corps, commanded by General Lestocq, encamped near the banks of the Drementz, on the road to Thorn; he connected himself with the right of the Russians, who reënforced him with some troops.

Napoleon takes the Offensive.—Not wishing to be inclosed by the enemy on the Vistula, and feeling the importance of giving ourselves a wider sphere in advance of Warsaw and Thorn, I, at the same moment took the offensive.

Ney, Bernadotte, and a part of the cavalry which had passed the river at Thorn, directed their march on Soldau and Biezun, manœuvring by their right to isolate the Prussian corps and cut it off from the Russian army. Lestocq, learning that Bessières had nothing but cavalry at Biezun, attempted to enter there; but our brave squadrons threw themselves on his infantry, drove them back into the marshes, and captured several hundred prisoners. On the twenty-third of December, at two o'clock in the morning, I repaired to the bridge of the Bug; Davoust having already crossed this river, threw a bridge over the Ukra, and manœuvred by his left to put himself in communication with Augereau, who was acting on Novemiasto, and Soult, who was moving on Plonsk. Lannes, on our extreme right, took the road to Sierock and Pultusk. Our concentric movement succeeded admirably; Augereau forced the passage of the Ukra at Kursumb after a combat in which the fourteenth of the line sustained the reputation it had won at Rivoli; he then advanced on Novemiasto. I moved with Davoust on Nasielsk, from which place we drove the division of Ostermann, notwithstanding the most strenuous resistance. Benningsen concentrated his troops on Stregoczyn. On all sides, the enemy's generals put themselves in retreat. I resolved to turn them by their right, with the intention of cutting off their line of retreat to Rozan. For this purpose I directed Soult by Chiconow on Makow; Ney, resting on the right, followed him as a second line. Augereau and the main body of Davoust's corps were also to move on Makow, passing by Golymin. One of the divisions of Davoust, which marched from Nasielsk on Putulsk, and the corps of Lannes, ascending the Narew from Sierock on the same city, were destined to attack in front the enemy's army which had taken that direction.

Old Kamenski, perceiving all the extent of the danger

with which he was threatened, ordered a general retreat by Ostrolenka on Lomza. The winter was late; we had had continual rains; the low grounds bordering the Narew were vast marshes; movements were difficult. The Russian general, whose faculties had become enfeebled by age, feared that his retreat might be delayed by his materials, and ordered his artillery to be abandoned if such should be the case; he himself took the road to Lomza. The order for such a sacrifice, which should be thought of only when absolutely necessary for the salvation of an army, excited against him the generals of his command. Not thinking the danger so imminent, they hesitated to obey him. Benningsen, who commanded the first army, assembled his forces at Putulsk; Buxhowden, commandant-in-chief of the second army, collected his at Makow; a considerable corps, composed of detachments of the two armies, took post at Golymin.

Combat of Pultusk.—On the twenty-sixth, the corps of Lannes, reënforced by the division of Gudin, attacked the army of Benningsen at Pultusk. The combat was very warm; we gained some advantage over the advanced guard, but when we came to attack the principal position, the shock became more severe; the Russians, profiting by the superiority of their artillery, repulsed the efforts of my lieutenant. I, however, did not attach much importance to this combat; for the decisive blows were to be struck at the left; Lannes, making it a point of honor to succeed, thought otherwise, and uselessly sacrificed many men. The same day I attacked Golymin with Davoust and Augereau, sustained by the cavalry of Murat. The Russians held their ground well; their first line, taken in flank by Augereau, yielded to us its position; they nevertheless maintained themselves at Golymin till night; this was more vexatious for us, than the unsuccessful attack on Pultusk, although the retreat of Buxhowden during the night was not made in very good order, and a part of his cannon was abandoned to us in the mud.

But I did not yet despair of the success of my plan. I counted on Soult, who ought, by this time, to be before Makow and established on the rear of the Russian corps which had fought at Pultusk and at Golymin. Ney and Bessières were to sustain him by gaining Chicanow, and advancing, as a second line, in the same direction. I was deceived in this expectation; the weather was horrible, and the roads almost impassable; in a word, the whole country was deluged, and we were in the mud up to our necks. This circumstance saved the Russian army by delaying the movements of my left. Soult could not reach Makow, and the roads on Rozan remained open to the enemy; he profited by it to escape on Ostrolenka. It is said that this retreat was made against the advice of Benningsen; this general, too much occupied with what was passing under his own eyes, had entirely lost sight of the *ensemble* of the operations. In repulsing the attack of a corps inferior in numbers to his own, he thought he had conquered us, and demanded permission to profit by this pretended victory and resume the offensive; it was unfortunate for us that he was not allowed to do so; the treaty of Tilsit would, in that case, have taken place six months sooner. Ney, on his side, having received orders to rest on Chicanow, had pushed forward to Soldan in pursuit of Lestocq, whom he drove from this city. The Prussian general, seeing that he was opposed only by an advance-guard, marched back in the evening and reëntered the city; a terrible combat followed; at length the valor of the sixty-ninth regiment overcame all the efforts of the enemy and repulsed him with a loss of a thousand men. In this contest the Russians exhibited a courage to which we were not accustomed, and my Egyptians immortalized themselves.

The French go into Winter Quarters.—As the Russians had escaped us, I had no desire to run after them, for the purpose of beginning a new campaign at a time of year so unfavorable to grand operations. The mud rendered transportation impossible; my battalions were hardly able to move, and the loss of ten thousand wounded in these secondary affairs, caused me to think more seriously of the results of my enterprise. I had imagined that the remembrance of Austerlitz had broken the *morale* of my adversaries; their firmness surprised me, and they employed such a quantity of cannon that I deemed it necessary to restore the equilibrium by augmenting my artillery. It was therefore important, in every view of the subject, to give repose to my troops, who were much in need of it. I cantoned them between the Omulef, the Narew, and the Ukra; my head-quarters and my guards returned to Warsaw.

Measures for securing his Position.—To give a good base to this new theatre of operations, I directed the repairs of the fortifications of Thorn and of the camp of Praga, so celebrated in the war of 1794. *Têtes-de-pont* were also planned at Modlin on the Vistula, and at Sierock on the Bug. Finally it was necessary to neutralize the advantages which the position of Dantzic gave to the enemy. The first Polish militia, levied by Dombrowski, joined to the contingent of Baden, and a French division, formed the tenth corps of at first ten or twelve thousand; it was afterward increased to fifteen thousand, and eventually to a much higher number. With this corps General Lefebvre was to observe the places of Dantzic and Colberg; the Hessian contingent, under General Rouyère blockaded Graudentz. Great magazines were established at Thorn and Sierock; considerable preparations were made for hospitals; first at Posen and at Warsaw, then in all the small cities which afforded resources. Thirty thousand tents, captured in the

Prussian arsenals, served as the first furniture for these establishments.

War between Russia and Turkey.—After my return to Warsaw, I received, on the thirtieth of October, a courier from Constantinople, announcing to me the declaration of war between the Porte and the Russians: Czerni-George, with the Servians, had gained possession of the important fortress of Belgrade, and Michelson advanced on Bucharest to act in concert with him. The news of the disaster of the Prussians, now decided the government to withdraw a reënforcement of thirty-six battalions and forty squadrons from this army of Turkey. These troops directed themselves in haste on the Bug. It was important for me to profit by this diversion, especially in influencing the cabinet of Vienna to take no part with Russia. I wrote to this effect to Sebastiani, and the following orders were addressed to Marmont in Dalmatia:

"A courier, which left Constantinople on the second of December, arrived at Warsaw on the thirtieth; the Porte had formally declared war against the Russians; and the Russian ambassador left with all his suite on the twenty-ninth of November. At Constantinople there is great enthusiasm for this war; twenty regiments of janizaries have left Constantinople; it is said that twenty thousand more have left Asia for Europe. Near sixty thousand men are already collected at Hirssow. Passwan-Oglu has twenty thousand at Widdin. The courier assures us that in Turkey there is the best of feeling. My intention is that you send to Constantinople five officers of engineers and as many of artillery. Write to the pashas of Bosnia and of Scutari, in order that they may send you firmans, certifying the arrival of these officers. Send staff officers to the pashas of Bosnia and Bulgaria, and assist them as much as possible in counsels, provisions and munitions. Possibly the Porte may ask for a corps of troops, and this corps can have but one object, that of securing the Danube. I am not much averse to your sending twenty-five thousand men on Widdin, as you will enter into the system of the grand army, forming its extreme right; twenty-five thousand French, sustaining sixty thousand Turks, would oblige the Russians not only to leave thirty thousand men on the Danube, as they have done, but to send double that number; which will make a very formidable diversion to my operations; but all that is still only hypothetical. What you can do immediately, general, is to send twenty or thirty officers, if requested by the pachas; but send no troops, except it may be some detachments at five or six leagues from the frontiers, so as to favor any expedition that may be made. You can count on the Turks as real allies, and you are authorized to furnish them what you can in cartridges, cannon, powder, &c., if they ask you for them.

"A Persian ambassador, and one from Constantinople, have presented themselves at Warsaw, and by the time you receive this letter they will be at Vienna. These two great empires are at heart attached to France, because France alone can sustain them against the ambitious enterprise of their enemies. In this important circumstance the English hesitate and appear to desire peace with the Porte; the latter power has employed for this purpose the threat of transporting forty thousand men to the gates of Ispahan, and our relations are such with Persia that we can march to the Indus. *What was formerly chimerical, ceases to be so at this moment, when I frequently receive letters from the sultans;* not emphatic and deceitful letters, but those which manifest great fear of the power of the Russians, and great confidence in the protection of the French Empire. Send some French officers to General Sebastiani at Constantinople, to correspond with him. The distance of Dalmatia from Warsaw is so great that you must take much responsibility on yourself. I have ordered General Sebastiani to send to Widdin an officer of his embassy, to serve as an intermediate correspondent with Constantinople; but this need not prevent you from sending one from your side to that city.

"French officers should be sent to travel through the different provinces of Turkey. They will make manifest the good-will which I bear the Grand Seignor; this will stir up their pride, and at the same time obtain valuable information, which you will transmit to me. In brief, general, I am the sincere friend of Turkey, and desire only to benefit her; conduct yourself accordingly. I regard the declaration of war between Turkey and Russia as the most fortunate event that could occur in our present situation. I notice that, in these conjunctures of such great interest, you do not give sufficient attention to the affairs of the pachas of Bucharest, Bosnia, and Scutari, with whom you ought frequently to correspond."

Benningsen takes Command of the Russian Army.—These events in Moldavia increased my desire to give a little repose to my troops, for in the interval, the diversions made by the Turks, if they were well-directed, would increase the chances of our success on the return of a favorable season. The Russians, on their side, cantoned in the environs of Lomza. The aged Kamenski had given up the command; he was replaced by Benningsen* whom, on his own report, they considered victorious, because he had repulsed an isolated attack.

* Baron Levin Augustus Benningsen was born in Hanover, 1745. He early entered the Russian service, and was distinguished in the war against Poland. In 1806 he was appointed to the command of the Russian army and fought the battles of Eylau and Friedland. After the peace of Tilsit he retired to his estates, but in 1813 he commanded the Russian army, called the *army of Poland*, entered Saxony, took part in the battle of Leipsic, and blockaded Hamburg. He afterward retired to his native country and died in 1826. He was the author of a book on light cavalry, published in 1794.

Affairs in Silesia.—Our affairs flourished still better in Silesia, a province doubly important on account of its numerous fortresses and its position with respect to Austria. The place of Glogau, attacked by the Wurtemberg troops under the orders of Vandamme, surrendered at the simple appearance of a siege equipage formed of Prussian pieces from the arsenal of Custrin. Breslau made more resistance. This great city, in a commanding position on the Oder, with a population of sixty thousand, presented an enciente almost equal to that of Strasburg. The works were out of repair, of slight relief, and mostly unrevetted. Nevertheless, it was a bastioned enciente, defended by six thousand men and inclosing sixty thousand inhabitants. General Thiele at first made a firm resistance; twice the prince of Anhalt-Pless advanced at the head of some Prussian battalions of five or six thousand peasants of Upper Silesia to relieve him. The wise dispositions of Vandamme and the valor of our troops triumphed over every obstacle. The wet ditches being frozen over, Vandamme threatened to make an assault. The place capitulated on the seventh of January, and the garrison became prisoners of war; we here captured three hundred pieces of cannon. Brieg and Schweidnitz suffered the same fate. The latter place, which had been the object of several campaigns under the great king, fell in silence, after a few days' siege, and without its even being known or thought of in Europe. The news of these conquests consoled me for the mud of Pultusk. I had reason to hope that they would act powerfully on the cabinet of Vienna, by depriving the Austrians of all hope of support in Silesia.

Benningsen attacks Napoleon's Left.—The principal armies did not enjoy the anticipated repose in their winter-quarters; seeking to extend the sphere of my supplies, and to close against the enemy the access to Dantzic, I had pushed the corps of Bernadotte on Elbing. Ney was to cover the interval between us by establishing himself at Mlava; but the want of provisions, and his impetuous activity, induced him to push on to Heilsberg. Benningsen having reorganized his army, and seeing himself on the point of being reënforced by two divisions of the corps of reserve, began operations in the middle of January. Some say that, having received orders to do every thing in his power to cover Königsberg, the last hold of the Prussian monarchy and the last asylum of its king, Benningsen was induced by the movements of Ney to march by his right, so as to close the road to this capital; others think that the hazardous movement of the sixth corps made him conceive the hope of cutting it off. Be the reasons what they may, he resolved to attack this corps; and although he thus engaged his army in a direction strategically false, it must be confessed that, by means of the gap left by Ney, the enterprise might have been fatal to us, if it had been executed more skillfully, and with more vigor.

Having left General Essen with one division on the Narew, where he was soon joined by the two others from the corps of Moldavia, Benningsen moved with his seven remaining divisions by Bischoffstein and Heilsberg on Gutstadt; independently of these divisions, the three light brigades of Generals Barclay, Baggavout, and Markof, formed a corps of advanced guard under the orders of Prince Bagration. The Prussian corps of Lestocq followed this movement by marching by Schippenbeil and Barteinstein on Preuss-Holland. It had been all over with Ney, if the Russian army had marched from Johannisburg on Neidenburg; but, instead of following on the rear of his corps scattered over a space of twenty-five leagues in columns by regiments, it made a long detour to reach his head and throw him back on his line of retreat; this fault enabled him to concentrate his forces in the excellent position of Gilgenbourg. Bernadotte, receiving timely warning of the enemy's approach, united his corps at Mohrungen. He was attacked there, on the twenty-fifth of January, by the Russian vanguard, which he drove back on Liebstadt. But this vanguard being sustained by the main body of the Russian army, Bernadotte was obliged to put himself in retreat on Strasbourg. Benningsen followed him by Osterode toward Loban.

These events forced me to recommence the campaign in mid-winter; the cold was excessive; the Vistula and the Narew were covered with enormous masses of ice, which, at any moment, might carry away our bridges; the ground was covered with snow; our magazines were not abundant, and even if they had been in great plenty, there were no means of transporting them. I was desirous of waiting for a favorable season, and feared that, if there should come on a thaw, we might have a repetition of the scenes of Pultusk: I did not wish to risk a Pultowa. Nevertheless, I soon saw the possibility of turning these things to great advantage, by seizing the occasion, which had once escaped us, of cutting off and annihilating the Russian army.

Napoleon's Movements.—I directed Bernadotte to continue to draw the enemy toward the Vistula. He was to have for his support the little *corps-d'armée* which Marshal Lefebvre had just collected at Thorn. All the other corps received orders to break up their cantonments. On the thirty-first of January, that of Lannes united at Brock; Davoust at Mesynitz; Soult and the cavalry at Willenberg, and Augereau at Niedenbourg; finally that of Ney approached Willenberg, where I established my head-quarters. The corps of Lannes remained on the Narew, to cover my rear and to hold in check the troops which the Russians had left on this river. With my four other corps and the cavalry, I resolved to march on Benningsen's rear, hoping to subject him to the fate of the Prussians at Jena. We began our march on the first of February; on the third we reached Allenstein with the cavalry and the columns of Soult, Augereau, and Ney; Davoust arrived at Wartenberg.

His Project discovered.—Every thing seemed to conduce to the success of my projects. Benningsen had fallen blindly into the snare; his attention was fixed on Bernadotte, whom he pursued with vigor. He was running headlong to his own destruction. An accident, very unfortunate for us, enlightened him as to the danger of his position, and snatched from me the fruit of one of my finest combinations. An aid-de-camp dispatched by Berthier to Bernadotte, permitted himself to be taken by the Cossacks. His papers, which he had not the address to destroy, informed the Russians of our projects, and the dangers with which they were threatened. They hastened to regain, by forced marches, their communications. To this misfortune we must add that Bernadotte did not receive my order and he did nothing as I had directed.

Soult fights at Bergfried.—On the third we found the Russians in battle array at Jonkowo; their left rested on the Elbe. The Prussians had concentrated at Osterode. I, nevertheless, did not despair of still being able to turn their left. I established the mass of my forces opposite the enemy's army at Jonkowo, and I directed my right, under the orders of Soult, by the right of the Alle on the bridge of Bergfried, situated beyond their flank. If Soult had been able to debouch at Bergfried on the rear of the Russians, the day would have been decisive; but they defended the bridge with so much obstinacy that we could not get possession of it before night. Benningsen profited by the obscurity to retire to Wolfsdorf.

Combat of Landsberg.—Vexed at seeing the enemy escape us again, I hoped to push him lively. He continued his retreat by Frauendorf and Landsberg on Preuss-Eylau. His rear-guard was much cut up on the fourth and fifth, and still more seriously at Hoff and Landsberg on the sixth. It maintained itself, it is true, with much vigor, against the grand-duke of Berg, who persisted in making the brigades pass, one after the other, through the defile of a marshy stream. The cuirassiers finally overthrew all before them, sabred two battalions, and took fifteen hundred prisoners.

Combat of Liebstadt.—The Prussians were isolated by this precipitate retreat of the Russians. Lestocq at first wished to open his way to Deppen; but his advance-guard was met, on the fifth, at Waltersdorf, by Ney's corps, which had already passed the Passarge at Deppen. It fought bravely, the cavalry of La Roche-Aymon especially gained great glory; but being overpowered by our forces, it was completely defeated, and lost sixteen cannon and many prisoners. The main body of the corps escaped destruction only by a forced march; it crossed the Passarge at Spanden and arrived, on the seventh, at Hussehnen between Preuss-Eylau and Zinter.

Battle of Eylau.—The Russians took position in rear of Preuss-Eylau. Their rear-guard, which was established in front of the city, was displaced on the seventh, after a bloody combat—worthy prelude of the next day's butchery; this affair was creditable to Generals Markof and Barclay, who commanded this rear-guard, and to the infantry of Soult which attacked it. The little elevation near Tenkniten was dearly won by the eighteenth of the line; we were left masters after vigorous efforts. The shock was not less terrible in Eylau. Barclay de Tolly, sustained by the divisions of Prince Galitzin, returned there twice in the dark, and yielded, the third time, only to the vigorous efforts of Legrand's division. We were in possession, after eight o'clock in the evening. Murat established himself opposite the enemy and reported to me that he was fighting them in retreat. The loss of Eylau rendered this supposition plausible. I believed the report, and, overcome with fatigue, went to sleep. I had been marching or working twenty hours a day since I left Warsaw. I, however, awoke before daylight, and visited my troops, when a terrible cannonade thundered on Eylau. Led into error by the reports of Murat, I had slept, as it were, under the very fire of the Russian batteries. The army had marched for eight days without magazines, through snow and ice; the troops of Soult had carried Eylau at night at the point of the bayonet, and the total pillage of the city, thus taken, could scarcely be avoided. Half of the regiments were dispersed through the houses; their waking was terrible.

I had expected a general affair the next day; I thought, however, that it would take place at a greater distance, for the evacuation of the city, covering the front of the field of battle of the enemy, was well calculated to support this opinion, and gave the greater probability to Murat's report. The Russians, having decided on giving battle, felt the importance of retaking Eylau while it was still covered only by Soult's corps, which was reduced to eighteen thousand men. Davoust, who had at first taken the direction to Domnau, was to approach my centre. Ney had received orders to march to Kreutzburg. I hastened the arrival of Augereau to the support of Soult, and placed my guard in the churchyard. Davoust received orders to incline to the left, so as to come into line; Ney was directed to return to the right; Bernadotte was still two marches distant, in consequence of the capture of the officer who was charged with his orders. This event proved the necessity of a cipher, the use of which I afterward adopted.

The Russian army had its right at Schloditten and its left at Klein-Saussgarten. It was about eighty thousand strong. Benningsen had effected some changes in its organization; he had combined the cavalry attached to the divisions so as to carry it to the wings, and the reserve; the infantry was formed on two lines of battalions alternately deployed, and in column of attack. The reserve, composed of the fourth and seventh divisions, was formed in two deep columns in rear of the centre, having at its left twenty-eight squadrons under Prince Galitzin. All the horse artillery (about sixty pieces) was united to supply the reserve with this arm. The artillery of the division, which amounted to, at least, one hundred and fifty twelves, and two hundred and fifty sixes and howitzers, was distributed along the front of the two lines.

Eylau is situated in a slightly undulating plain, bounded on three sides by ground still more uneven, and by hills and intervening lakes. The cold had been so great as to freeze over these lakes, and the armies could safely manœuvre on the ice that covered their surface; and as they were covered with snow, the cavalry charged across without at first perceiving them. Our position commanded that of the enemy; on the left only had he the advantage of the heights of Saussgarten, which he kept but for a moment, for they were too far from the *corps-de-bataille.*

With the exception of artillery, our forces were about equal; but as it appeared difficult for Ney to arrive soon enough to take part, and as Davoust could not arrive before the middle of the day, the enemy was better prepared for the action than ourselves. I, nevertheless, expected a victory, for I counted on the discouragement of an army hotly pursued for four days. But the Russian soldier is remarkable in reverses; the day after a defeat he shows the same countenance as the day after a victory. They fought like madmen. My own troops, to do them justice, performed miracles. Soult alone sustained the first effort of the enemy; and it required the brave soldiers of Austerlitz to resist such a shock.

The numerical superiority of the enemy in cannon was nearly fatal to us; I saw that the time had gone by when we could go forth to conquer a country with only forty pieces, as I did at Marengo. Soult had suffered considerably when the seventh corps debouched to form our centre, and to attack that of the enemy. Murat's cavalry, reënforced by the division of St. Hilaire, from Soult's corps, rested on the right so as to facilitate the arrival of Davoust. The snow fell so rapidly that the air was perfectly obscured; we could not see two steps before us.

While Touczkof was opposing Legrand's division in front of Eylau, General Doctorof advanced the two heavy columns of the reserve to oppose Augereau; the division of Essen manœuvred to take him in flank. Unfortunately this *corps-d'armée* directed its attack, without knowing it, between the reserve of the Russian cavalry and that of their infantry; it was perceived only when the squadrons were found pell-mell with the first division. They attempted to form squares, but it was too late; moreover the firearms had become so wet as to render them useless; and the troops of Augereau, assailed on all sides and exposed to the fire of forty pieces in battery, became the victims of a sad error. The division of Desjardins was half destroyed; and that of Heudelet fared no better; Desjardins was killed, and Heudelet severely wounded; Augereau was also wounded.

To relieve him a little, I ordered Murat to charge, with all the reserve of cavalry, on the enemy's centre. The division of Essen is pierced, and our mass of cavalry penetrates even to the third line of the Russians, which rests against the wood. The enemy's infantry, more disposed to be cut to pieces than to yield, close their ranks as our squadrons force their way through them; charged in turn by fresh troops, our cavalry is forced to retire after having lost Generals Hautpoult, Dahlmann, and many other distinguished chiefs. My aid-de-camp, Corbineau, is carried away by a shot. The retreat has become as difficult as the advance; for the Russians have reformed and faced to the rear, and it is necessary to open a new passage sword in hand. In the mean time one of the Russian columns, which had repelled Augereau, pursues the remains of this corps along the west street of Eylau, and pierces even to the foot of the churchyard, where I am standing with a battery of the guard, having at some distance six battalions of the old guard forming my last resource. I order my escort of one hundred men to charge the front of this column to arrest its impetuosity, and to give me time to make my dispositions. A battalion of my grenadiers advances and charges the first battalion of the Russian column, and stops it short; Murat on his side detaches the brigade of Bruyère, which takes it in flank. In an instant, this column is overthrown and sabred. It was a feeble equivalent for the disaster of Augereau. This corps experienced such great losses that it was obliged to dissolve after the battle.

While these things were passing about Eylau, and at the centre, St. Hilaire and a part of Murat's cavalry was fighting with even chances against the enemy's left, formed of the divisions of Sacken and Osterman, and sustained in reserve by that of Kamenski.

Affairs were threatening to take an unfavorable turn. I was waiting in fretful impatience for Davoust to debouch on our right, as he had been ordered; this alone could restore the victory. At last, about one o'clock, he appeared on the heights driving before him the detached brigades of Bagawouth and Barclay. General Benningsen, learning that his left flank was turned and falling back in all directions, reënforced it with the division of Kamenski; this was not enough; Davoust, seconded by the dragoons of Milhaud and the attacks of St. Hilaire, drove before him Osterman, Kamenski, and Bagawouth; the whole Russian left was driven back to Kutschiten. Benningsen was obliged to send successively all his disposable force to sustain this wing. So many forces collected on this point finally arrested the progress of Davoust. As a climax of contrariety, the Prussian corps of Lestocq, having escaped from Ney, arrived on the field of battle unpursued, it passed the Russian lines in rear, and assisted to restore their affairs on the left. Davoust, who had already occupied the village of Kustchiten in rear of the enemy's left, was now forced to fall back, and considered himself fortunate in holding the heights of Anklapen, for he had more than half the enemy's army on his hands.

Ney, who had allowed the Russians to escape, pursued only by a detachment, learned by accident that we were fighting at Eylau; he had neither heard the cannon nor received my orders. He promptly determined to move on Schmoditten so as to connect himself with my left. But it was too late to give a decisive turn to the battle, for night was already approaching, though the combat was partially continued till eight o'clock; nevertheless, the arrival of Ney in rear of the right flank of the Russians became a decisive circumstance, for it determined them to retreat during the night. To execute this retrograde movement with great security, they caused Ney to be attacked by the division of Sacken, which had suffered the least during the day. Ney sustained himself near Schmoditten, but the attack deceived him, and made him doubt the issue of the battle. He took position at some distance from the road to Königsberg, and the Russians filed off all the morning, as it were, under the very fire of his cannon.

The losses on both sides were enormous: ten thousand dead bodies covered the field of battle, and thirty thousand wounded lay in the barns and gardens of the neighboring villages. Nevertheless, nothing had been definitely decided. My army was so weakened that I was hesitating whether I should not fall back and accelerate my junction with Bernadotte and Lefebvre, when the news of Ney's arrival decided me to remain; and the retreat of Benningsen saved me the disagreeable apprehension of giving him the field of battle. He retired on Königsberg and covered himself with the Pregel; Murat followed him the next day to within two leagues of that city. This retreat of Benningsen offered me an opportunity for striking a terrible blow on the Russian army, which threw itself, with so much imprudence, into a *cul-de-sac*, with no other issue than the sea and the strand. If Bernadotte and Lefebvre had been within reach, I should have marched on Tapiau, and placed the enemy in a frightful situation; but the rest of my army, with the exception of Ney's corps, had suffered so much that I deemed it more prudent to give it repose and wait the reduction of Dantzic, before resuming the offensive. Bernadotte entered into line two days after, and also the cuirassiers of Nansouty. The corps of Lefebvre, directed on Osterode, might already be considered as a reserve. Independent of these reënforcements, I still expected the ten thousand grenadiers which Oudinot was marching from Warsaw on Pultusk and Willemberg.

Such was the cruel battle of Eylau, so interesting in the extraordinary circumstances that accompanied it, and so little decisive in its results. At eleven o'clock, Soult had suffered much, and Augereau's corps was comparatively destroyed. All had been lost but for the stand which I made for three hours at the cemetery of Eylau, at the head of my guard, my cavalry, and my artillery, which I directed myself. The army will not refuse to bear me witness that I was not the least moved by the critical position in which we were placed until the arrival of Davoust. I could have wished to see by my side, on this occasion, those of my detractors who have accused me of wanting courage and presence of mind.*

* In speaking of the results of the battle of Eylau, Alison evidently seeks to

The French go into Winter Quarters.—The enemy had forced me to leave my winter quarters. I had no desire to make a winter campaign. I was waiting for reënforcements,

exaggerate the French loss and to diminish that of the Russians. His statements are exceedingly erroneous, and are not sustained by reliable authorities. He estimates the Russian loss at twenty-five thousand, and that of the French at thirty thousand. Thiers estimates the Russian loss at seven thousand killed, twenty thousand wounded, and three or four thousand prisoners; and that of the French at three thousand killed and seven thousand wounded.

The following is his note explaining these estimates:

"It is seldom that one can state the losses sustained in a battle with such accuracy as one is enabled to do for the battle of Eylau. I undertook a careful examination, in order to arrive at precision, and here follows the truth, at least as nearly as it is possible to attain it in such a matter. The inspector of the hospitals certified the same evening, at Eylau, the existence of four thousand five hundred wounded, and next day, after going his rounds in the adjacent villages, he increased the total amount to seven thousand and ninety-four. His report has been preserved. The reports of the different corps make the number of men more or less severely wounded amount to not fewer than thirteen or fourteen thousand. This difference is explained by the manner in which the authors of those reports understood the word wounded. The chiefs of corps include even the slightest contusions, each of them naturally striving to make the most of the sufferings of his men. But half the men set down as wounded never thought of applying for any attendance, and this is proved by the report of the director of the hospitals. A month afterward a curious controversy was kept up by letter between Napoleon and M. Daru, who could not find more than six thousand wounded in the hospitals of the Vistula. This appeared disputable to Napoleon, who conceived that there must be more, especially if there were included in this number the wounded of the battle of Eylau and those of the actions which preceded it, after the breaking up of the cantonments. However, after minute examination, there were never found more than six thousand and some hundred, and fewer than six thousand for Eylau itself, which, taking account of the deaths that supervened, agree exactly with the statement of seven thousand and ninety-four furnished by the director of the hospitals. We think, therefore, that we are near the truth in computing the losses of the battle of Eylau at three thousand killed and seven thousand wounded. Napoleon, speaking in the bulletin of two thousand killed, and five or six thousand wounded, had, as we may see, not warped the truth much in comparison with what the Russians had done. One may even assert that, in the evening after the battle, he was founded in supposing that there were not more.

As for the losses of the Russians, I have adopted their own amounts and those which were certified by the French. We found seven thousand dead, and in the surrounding places five thousand wounded. They must have carried away a much greater number. Both, a German, says that they carried to Königsberg fourteen thousand nine hundred wounded, who almost all died

and especially for a supply of artillery and munitions. I, therefore, returned to my cantonments. The Passarge covered our left; the centre was on the Alle, from Guttstadt to Allenstein, and the right by the Omulef. I established my head-quarters at Osterode, and afterward at the chateau of Finkenstein. Bernadotte, on the left, occupied Holland and Braunsberg; Soult encamped at Wormdit, Leibstadt, and Mohrungen; Ney, was in advance on the Alle, at Guttstadt, and Allenstein; Davoust on the right at Hohenstein and Gilgenbourg. The cavalry was distributed among these corps, the better to cover the cantonments. Lefebvre returned to the investment of Dantzic.

Combat of Ostrolenka.—At the moment when I was establishing myself in rear of the Alle, the divisions which the enemy had left on the Narew, reënforced by that of Moldavia, attacked my right. Lannes was sick; Savary commanded his corps; fortunately for him Oudinot, who was in march to join me by Willenberg, had orders to sustain him, in case of need, and arrived at the required point. A Russian division was moving along the right bank of the river; Savary, seconded by Suchet, met and drove it back. At the same time two other divisions attacked Ostrolenka by the left bank. The enemy penetrated momentarily into the city; our troops drove him out, and debouched to give him combat; the affair turned to our advantage. The Russians retired with the loss of seven cannon and one thousand five hundred men, among whom was young Suwarof. This was the last event of this winter's campaign.

Difficulties of Napoleon's Position.—I wished to profit by the inaction rendered necessary by the unfavorable season,

from the cold. He admits, moreover, that they had seven thousand killed, and left five thousand wounded on the field of battle. Add three or four thousand prisoners, and you arrive at a total loss of thirty thousand men, which can scarcely be disputed. General Benningsen, always very inaccurate, admitted in his statement a loss of twenty thousand men."

to reduce the places which I had left in rear, and thus to strengthen me in my position. I had consumed almost all my artillery munitions; they were brought by post from Magdebourg and Custrin; it required time to replenish them. The superiority of the enemy's artillery had induced me to send to France for all the disposable companies of artillerists, and I had given them Prussian pieces, in order to use the ammunition which we had found in the Prussian arsenals. I oven directed French pieces to be cast to the Prussian calibres, for the same purpose. I also expected more than fifty thousand men from my depots, and from my allies of the Confederation of the Rhine. This epoch of repose, in the middle of old Prussia and Poland, is one of the most remarkable of my life; it was not the least critical, nor the least glorious.

The visit of Baron Vincent and General Neuperg, envoys of Austria to Warsaw, to speak of mediation, gave me real apprehensions lest she might send one hundred and fifty thousand of these mediators on the Elbe, which would have rendered my position very embarrassing. I saw my danger, and more than once regretted having allowed myself to be drawn into these distant and inhospitable countries, and having rejected the advice of those who wished to turn me from it. The cabinet of Vienna had, at this epoch, a more certain and honorable occasion to reëstablish its preponderance than that which it chose in 1813. But it knew not how to profit by the occasion, and my firm attitude saved me.

Menaces of Spain.—Even Spain, on whom I had reckoned with so much certainty, now added to the dangers to which I was exposed. At the very moment when I was hurling my thunderbolts against the Prussian army at Jena, Spain was threatening a rupture with me. The cabinet of Madrid, which had to complain of my selling Louisiana to the Americans, and proposing to exchange the Balearic Isles with

Sicily, was the less favorably disposed toward us as the battle of Trafalgar had destroyed all hopes of advantage from our alliance. The Prince of Peace had been severely reproached by the Spanish merchants, who had suffered from the closing of the seas and the loss of their commerce with America; he now hoped, by a change of policy, to regain his popularity.

This minister,* ignorant, as are most favorites at court, very much exaggerated the power of Prussia; because Spain had remained the same as at the time of Louis XV., he thought the relative power of Prussia and France must be the same as at the time of Frederick. Threatened by the English party, frightened by the non-ratification of the treaty signed by D'Oubril, and the coalition of Prussia, Sweden, Russia, and England against me, and undoubtedly persuaded that Austria would soon join them, he thought he could, with impunity, break all the ties which he had formed with France and thus restore to the Spanish nation the desired maritime commerce. The thing would have been natural enough if he had sought to obtain this neutrality by negotiation; but he thought it more simple to profit by my embarrassments

* Don Manuel Godoy was born at Badajos, in 1764, of a noble but poor family. He entered the body-guard of Charles IV., and soon became noted in the salons of Madrid for his fine person and great talent for music, especially his skill on the guitar accompanied by his own voice. He owed to this talent his introduction to the queen, of whom he ever after continued a favorite. His advancement was now most rapid, first in the army, and afterward in the council of state, to which he was transferred. He was soon made prime minister, and received the title of duke of Alcudia. After the treaty of Bâle, in 1795, he was made Prince of Peace, and loaded with wealth and honors. The queen compelled him, against his wishes, to marry one of the royal family, the Infanta Maria-Theresa, daughter of Don Louis, the brother of the king. After the exile of Charles IV., Godoy accompanied the royal family to Rome, where he took up his permanent residence.

He was a man of light character, and of very little education, but had great cunning as a politician. For fifteen years he governed Spain as absolute master, and continued to enjoy the friendship of the king and queen to the end of their lives.

to hurl against me a proclamation or manifesto, which, without designating me by name, was only too evidently directed against me. Eight days after, he learned the catastrophe of Jena, my entrance into Berlin, and the destruction of the monarchy which he had deemed capable of crushing me; he hastened to change the Spanish minister at the court of Prussia, in order to endeavor to allay my resentment.

Proffered Intervention of Austria.—To complete my embarrassment, it was only necessary for Austria to declare herself; she had certainly more motives for doing so than the cabinet of Madrid; for the latter had with me a community of interest in destroying the maritime supremacy of the English, and in saving America, which they had coveted for a century. The cabinet of Vienna, on the contrary, had reasons to endeavor to profit by this occasion in order to regain, at a single blow, both Italy and their power in Germany. This, of course, they desired to do, but, divided in opinions, and checked by the Archduke Charles, who was opposed to a war, they wished to gain, by negotiation, time to arm, and then to propose a forced mediation. In the mean time Austria offered her intervention, and what she called her good offices for the reëstablishment of peace! I was not blind enough to become the dupe of either Stadion or Godoy; but in these delicate circumstances it was necessary to dissemble my resentment toward the favorite of Charles IV., and to manœuvre, with firmness and address, with the councillors of Francis I.

The English menace Constantinople.—This course was the more wise on my part, as the threatening attitude of the English before Constantinople might increase the difficulties of our position, by bringing about peace between the Turks and the Russians. The news of Michelson's invasion of Moldavia, reaching the Divan at the same time as that of my victories in Prussia, had added to the importance of Sebastiani's position at Constantinople; he had acquired great influence there, and he justified the confidence reposed in him, by the use he made of this influence. The invasion of the Principalities, far from being imputed to the credit given to my minister by the Porte, appeared to be a full justification of the advantages of our alliance.

In the mean time England sought to realize the threat made by her ambassador of bombarding Constantinople; the squadron of Duckforth, which had blockaded Ferrol, received orders to enter the Mediterranean, with troops embarked at Gibraltar; it cruised in the Archipelago near Tenedos. The cabinet of London thought itself certain of the effect which the approach of this squadron would produce on a government which had trembled at the simple threat of its being sent; the English did not hesitate to demand of the Divan:

1st. The dismissal of Sebastiani;

2d. The alliance of Turkey with Russia and England;

3d. The cession of Moldavia and Wallachia to the Russians;

4th. The provisional surrender of the Dardanelles and of the Turkish fleet to the English.

I have been accused of being, in my policy, harsh and imperious; but, assuredly, I have never proposed to a power which I wished to make my ally to dishonor itself by surrendering to me her fortresses; this is the most I ever demanded of my conquered enemies; if I took those of Charles IV. by surprise, I saved him the humiliation of basely abandoning them to me.

Passage of the Dardanelles.—Such conditions were rejected by the ministers of Selim. Arbuthnot embarked clandestinely on board an English frigate, and rejoined the English squadron at Tenedos, from which place he continued to negotiate. The Turks, always indolent and presumptuous, lost this precious time without making the least preparation for augmenting the defense of the Dardanelles. Confident of the efficiency of their enormous mortars, which threw stone projectiles of some seven or eight hundred pounds to a considerable distance, but whose immense weight prevented them from being easily moved and pointed, they neglected all the advice given to them by French officers. Duckforth at length took advantage of a fête day when the Turkish artillerists were absent from their duties, and, with a very favorable wind, penetrated unexpectedly, on the nineteenth of February, into the channel, passed through it without any serious accident, after exchanging a few broadsides, burnt a ship and four frigates off the point of Nigara, and presented himself before superb Byzantium, and threatened to bombard the seraglio and the rich capital of the Ottomans. The panic was general, and if Duckforth had profited by it to instantly begin the attack, or obtain a compliance with the required conditions, he would have dictated law to the Porte, for there were not ten pieces in battery ready for service.

Conduct of Sebastiani.—The weak ministers of Selim decided unanimously to dismiss Sebastiani and to submit to the requisitions of England; the people responded by cries of indignation and rage. In these difficult circumstances, my ambassador showed great decision of character. Selim sent, at nine o'clock at night, one of the great dignitaries of the Empire to carry to him the resolution of the Divan, to show to him how great were the regrets of the Porte, and to assure him that the cries of the multitude directed against his person proved the danger to which he would be exposed by prolonging his sojourn at Constantinople; the reply of Sebastiani was noble. Rejecting the care which they wished to take of his person, he declared that he would not leave unless Selim should force him to do so, and that he would wait a resolution worthy of a great Prince: "Tell your powerful monarch," said he, "that he ought not to descend from the lofty rank in which he has been placed by his glorious ancestors, by basely surrendering, to a few English ships, a capital of eight hundred thousand inhabitants, who have arms, munitions, provisions, and who can batter these ships to atoms." Selim worthily appreciating this answer, was electrified by it; he determined to defend himself, and called Sebastiani before the Divan, which had been convoked in the night. The ministers partook of the generous sentiments of Selim, and were further encouraged by the exasperation which became more and more manifest in the capital, at the news of what was going on. This exasperation was no longer against Sebastiani, but against the English.

Constantinople had great resources for defense, especially in her superb marine arsenal; but time was wanting. Every thing was placed at the disposal of Sebastiani, who was seconded by the engineer and artillery officers who had been sent by my orders from Dalmatia. A superb tent was erected for him in the garden of the seraglio, where he could, at the same time, direct the works of the defense and also the negotiations, so as to deceive Duckforth, in order to gain some days by promises. The Marquis d'Almenara, the Spanish minister, seconded Sebastiani with all his power, and enjoyed with him the public confidence.

Every thing immediately took a new aspect; to the cold apathy and gravity of the Mussulman succeeded an electric fire which communicated itself even to the old men and children; all strove for the honor of assisting in the defense of the capital; some made gabions and fascines; others constructed batteries and armed them with cannon; in four days nearly three hundred pieces were mounted on the side most exposed to immediate danger; the tower of Leander was armed with cannon of heavy calibre, and furnished with furnaces for heating shot. A hundred gunboats, and the broadsides of the squadron, defended the channel between Pera and the Seraglio, where were situated the marine establishments of the Empire. The sultan himself assisted in the work. At the end of eight days, which time had been gained by negotiation, five hundred pieces were directed against the enemy's fleet, and two hundred Mussulmans, with their fire-vessels were ready to sacrifice themselves. Arbuthnot was sick, and he left to Duckforth the care of terminating a negotiation, in which the Turks exhibited a more lofty bearing in proportion as their preparations advanced. At the same time Ismail Pacha, former vizier, was sent to the Dardanelles, where he applied the same activity in arming and fortifying the castles.

Retreat of the English.—Duckforth, seeing himself on the point of being invested in the Sea of Marmora, finally decided to retreat. On the second of March the wind changed to the east and he took advantage of it to escape through the Dardanelles, saluted, as he progressed, by the artillery of the forts, which, a little better served this time, greatly damaged two of his best ships and sunk two corvettes. In this rash enterprise the English lost two hundred killed and five hundred wounded, and it would have cost them their entire fleet, if they had been opposed by enemies more enterprising and experienced. Sebastiani exhibited, on this occasion, as much skill as energy, and his conduct was worth to us a victory. If the English enterprise had succeeded, there would have been an immediate peace between the Porte and Russia, and the entire army of Michelsen would have marched against us. Twenty-five thousand men had already started for the Bug.*

* The following account of the passage of the Dardanelles by the British fleet is copied from the chapter on "Sea-coast Defenses," in "Halleck's Military Art and Science."

"The channel of the Dardanelles is about twelve leagues long, three miles wide at its entrance, and about three quarters of a mile at its narrowest point.

Nevertheless, the loss of the English had not been so great as to prevent their attempting to renew the enterprise with greater means; and the apprehension of this might tend to

Its principal defenses are the outer and inner castles of Europe and Asia, and the castles of Sestos and Abydos. Constantinople stands about one hundred miles from its entrance into the sea of Marmora, and at nearly the opposite extremity of this sea. The defenses of the channel had been allowed to go to decay; but few guns were mounted, and the forts were but partially garrisoned. In Constantinople not a gun was mounted, and no preparations for defense were made; indeed, previous to the approach of the fleet, the Turks had not determined whether to side with the English or the French, and even then the French embassador had the greatest difficulty in persuading them to resist the demands of Duckforth.

"The British fleet consisted of six sail of the line, two frigates, two sloops, and several bomb-vessels, carrying eight hundred and eighteen guns (besides those in the bomb-ships). Admiral Duckforth sailed through the Dardanelles on the nineteenth of February, 1807, with little or no opposition. This being a Turkish festival day, the soldiers of the scanty garrison were enjoying the festivities of the occasion, and none were left to serve the few guns of the forts which had been prepared for defense. But while the admiral was waiting on the Sea of Marmora for the result of negotiations, or for a favorable wind to make the attack upon Constantinople, the fortifications of this city were put in order, and the Turks actively employed, under French engineers and artillery officers, in repairing the defenses of the straits. Campbell, in his Naval History, says: 'Admiral Duckforth now fully perceived the critical situation in which he was placed. He might, indeed, succeed should the weather become favorable, in bombarding Constantinople; *but unless the bombardment should prove completely successful in forcing the Turks to pacific terms, the injury he might do to the city would not compensate for the damage which his fleet must necessarily sustain. With this damaged and crippled fleet, he must repass the Dardanelles, now rendered infinitely stronger than they were when he came through them.*'

"Under these circumstances the admiral determined to retreat; and on the third of April escaped through the Dardanelles, steering midway of the channel, with a favorable and strong current. 'This escape, however,' says Baines, 'was only from destruction, but by no means from serious loss and injury. * * * In what instance in the whole course of our naval warfare, have ships received equal damage in so short a time as in this extraordinary enterprise?' In detailing the extent of this damage, we will take the ships in the order they descended. The first had her wheel carried away, and her hull much damaged, but escaped with the loss of only three men. A stone shot penetrated the second, between the poop and quarter-deck, badly injuring the mizzen-mast, carried away the wheel, and did other serious damage, killing and wounding twenty men. Two shot struck the third, carrying away her shrouds and injuring her masts; loss in killed and wounded, thirty. The fourth had her mainmast destroyed, with a loss of sixteen. The fifth had a large shot, six feet eight inches in circumference, enter her lower deck; loss fifty-five. The

facilitate the renewal of peace between Russia and Turkey, should the former, in order to concentrate her forces against us, renounce the Principalities. To encourage Selim, I re-

sixth, not injured. The seventh, a good deal damaged, with a loss of seventeen. The eighth had no loss. The ninth was so much injured that, 'had there been a necessity for hauling the wind on the opposite tack, she must have gone down;' her loss was eight. The tenth lost twelve. The eleventh was much injured, with a loss of eight—making a total loss in repassing the Dardanelles, of one hundred and sixty-seven; and in the whole expedition two hundred and eighty-one, exclusive of two hundred and fifty men who perished in the burning of the Ajax.

"Such was the effect produced on the British fleet, sailing with a favorable wind and strong current past the half-armed and half-manned forts of the Dardanelles. Duckforth himself says, 'that had he remained before Constantinople much longer—till the forts had been completely put in order—no return would have been open to him, and the unavoidable sacrifice of the squadron must have been the consequence.' Scarcely had the fleet cleared the straits, before it (the fleet) was reënforced with eight sail of the line; but, even with this vast increase of strength, the English did not venture to renew the contest. They had effected a most fortunate escape. General Jomini says, 'that if the defense had been conducted by a more enterprising and experienced people, the expedition would have cost the English their whole squadron.'

"Great as was the damage done to the fleet, the forts themselves were uninjured. The English say their own fire did no execution, the shot in all probability not even striking their objects—'the rapid change of position, occasioned by a fair wind and current, preventing the certainty of aim' The state of the batteries when the fleet first passed, is thus described in James's Naval History: 'Some of them were dilapidated, and others but partially mounted and poorly manned.' And Alison says: 'they had been allowed to fall into disrepair. The castles of Europe and Asia, indeed, stood in frowning majesty, to assert the dominion of the Crescent at the narrowest part of the passage, but their ramparts were antiquated, their guns in part dismounted, and such as remained, though of enormous calibre, little calculated to answer the rapidity and precision of an English broadside.'

"Much has been said because the fortifications of the Dardanelles did not hermetically seal that channel (an object they were never expected to accomplish, even had they been well-armed and well-served); but it is forgotten, or entirely overlooked, that twelve *Turkish line-of-battle ships, two of them three-deckers, with nine frigates, were with their sails bent and in apparent readiness, filled with troops, and lying within the line of fortifications; and yet this naval force effected little or nothing against the invaders.* It is scarcely ever mentioned, being regarded of little consequence as a means of defense; and yet the number of its guns and the expense of its construction and support, could hardly have fallen short of the incomplete and half-armed forts, some of which were as ancient as the reign of Amurath."

This passage proves the importance of guns of large calibre, throwing heavy

solved to offer him all the assistance in my power. The Viceroy of Italy received orders to send Colonels Haxo of the engineers, and Foy of the artillery, distinguished officers, capable of securing the Dardanelles in a short time from the enemy's attacks. I also wrote the following letter to Marmont, who occupied Ragusa.

"The order of the emperor, general, is that you immediately send to Constantinople all your remaining officers of engineers and artillery, and a complete corps of six hundred sappers, *ouvriers** and artillerists; furnish this troop with good arms and equipments; send with these six hundred men pay for three months, or even more if you have the money; the *ouvriers* should take with them such utensils as are not likely to be found at Constantinople, and the officers of artillery and engineers should supply themselves as well as they can with such books as, under the circumstances, will be most likely to be useful.

"You will inform the Porte that, if it wishes other troops, you will supply them, on its direct requisition. Indeed, the emperor authorizes you to send as many as five thousand men, without further orders; but, for this purpose, you must have the requisition of General Sebastiani, and a formal *firman* of the Porte to the Pacha into whose territory you send these forces. Do not hesitate to send your artillery and engineer officers to Constantinople, for you will be supplied with officers of these corps from the kingdom of Italy, and these, in their turn, will be replaced by others whom I shall send from France. If you are in funds, send two hundred thousand francs, in gold, to General Sebastiani, for the troops, it being the intention of the emperor that they shall, in no manner,

projectiles, as a means of coast defense. Great advances have been made in this respect within the last few years.

* Literally workmen. The term in the French army corresponds very nearly to our artificers; but they have a separate military organization.

become a charge to the Ottoman Empire; if you are not in funds, notify me, in order that I may take measures accordingly."

Bold Front of Napoleon.—Notwithstanding the diversion expected from this war, the mud of Pultusk, and the carnage of Eylau were not of a nature to inspire me with much confidence; but I lost not a minute in preparation, for I knew the *value of time*, which my enemies never could appreciate. I thought that the least sign of weakness might lose all, and I acted as if perfectly certain of success. Satisfied with the poor explanation of the Spanish minister, I demanded, as a pledge of his sincerity, the contingent stipulated by the treaty of San Ildefonso; he sent fifteen or sixteen thousand men, under the Marquis of Romana, who crossed France during the winter. I first intended to employ them in Italy, but afterward determined to send them to protect the north of Germany from the attacks of the English. Although it was not prudent to remove forces from Italy, the object mostly coveted by Austria, I nevertheless withdrew the divisions of Boudet and Molitor, and an Italian division, which were directed on Saxony, to form, with the Bavarians and Spaniards, an army of observation on the Elbe. I determined not to evacuate Naples, persuaded that if I touched the smallest link in this vast chain, it would soon be broken. St. Cyr remained at Naples with my brother Joseph, and Marmont continued to carry on his operations in Dalmatia against the Montenegrins and the fifteenth Russian division. I even called Massena from Italy to the grand army, to prove to Austria that I did not regard the idea of a rupture on her part as within the range of possibilities.

Negotiations at the Camp of Finkenstein.—My camp at Finkenstein was a complete diplomatic arena; indirect negotiations were there renewed with Russia and England. I addressed a letter to the king of Prussia, offering him the most favorable conditions, if he should be disposed to treat with me. I hoped to detach him from the coalition, which would have enabled me to treat more advantageously with the others. These overtures, communicated to Russia and England, led to some conferences. The Emperor Alexander had expected to enter this war merely as an auxiliary, and to take advantage of it to acquire the Turkish principalities. On the contrary, he saw himself exposed alone to the whole weight of my forces, while Austria took no part, and England kept continually promising powerful diversions, but never made any. Undoubtedly the interests of Russia were connected with those of Prussia; but was it necessary to compromise the safety of the empire for a new ally whom Europe, though still more interested, had abandoned? I had some hopes of bringing him to peace. He was not opposed to treating, but he wished advantages on the Danube and the integrity of Prussia, things very difficult to reconcile with my present position. He, moreover, proposed a congress at Copenhagen of all the powers.

In the mean time I had received a Persian envoy, whose master, hearing of our victories, deemed it for his interest to form an alliance with us. Maret was charged with negotiating with him, and he succeeded in concluding a treaty offensive and defensive on the most advantageous terms. I sent, on my part, to the court of Teheran, General Gardanne with intelligent and well instructed officers of the different arms. We also negotiated with the Porte, who had charged Waleb Essendi to propose to me a closer alliance, on condition of not forming a separate treaty. I declined such a clause. My situation was too complicated to impose on myself such terms. Although the Ottoman Empire was still in the hands of Selim III., it was too vacillating an ally to subject my negotiations to the caprices of the Divan. I promised to take every possible interest in this empire which was my natural ally, but I could do nothing more.

With respect to the negotiations with England and Russia, the conditions were such that I could not accept them. On the one side they required that I should abandon the Turks, who, thanks to Sebastiani, had just exhibited so much energy against the English squadrons and our common enemies; on the other side, England refused to make, in order to save her continental allies, any maritime concessions necessary to our security. There was therefore no means of coming to an understanding. It is true that Lords Grenville and Grey (Howick) had, at the beginning of the year, formally signified the possibility of negotiating on the basis of *uti possidetis*, and if the cabinet had brought the same dispositions to the proposed congress of Copenhagen, there would have been no obstacle to forming a general peace; one of those ministerial revolutions which sometimes change the course of English policy, or at least seem to give it a new direction, had just proved that nothing was to be hoped from that source; perhaps this change even resulted from the declaration itself. Perceval declaimed strongly in the House of Commons against this pacific policy, and boldly declared that so long as I was at the head of affairs in France and had Talleyrand for councillor, there was no hope of a durable and honorable peace.* This enemy of our repose, applauded by the majority in England, instead of being recalled to sentiments more humane, was placed, a few weeks after, at the head of a new ministry which rivaled that of Pitt in the

* Talleyrand, having invested largely in Bernese funds, was at this time doing all in his power to effect a treaty of peace with England, by which he would have derived large profits from his investment. Availing himself of his official information on affairs of state, he was in the habit of speculating largely in the funds. These speculations sometimes had much influence upon his management of foreign affairs. At one period he was immensely rich, but in 1828, his fortune suffered considerably by the failure of a great Paris house in which he was interested.

exaggeration of its hatred to France and her chief. Canning was placed at the head of foreign affairs, and his opinions on this point were not less decided than those of Perceval.

These statesmen persuaded themselves that if they allowed me to consolidate the empire, which my recent successes had extended to the Vistula, England would soon be reduced to a power of the second order. Perhaps there were grounds for such fears. But they exaggerated my ambition, as well as the dangers that threatened them; this led them to demand certain concessions on my part, to secure what they were pleased to denominate the *repose of Europe*, but which really meant, the *triumph of England*. A patriotism, respectable in itself, but carried to excess, animated them against me, and forced me to oppose them in return. They believed me dangerous to England, and by their exaggeration, rendered it necessary for me to treat them as irreconcilable enemies.

Treaty of Bartenstein.—At the very moment when this ministerial revolution was destroying all hopes of peace, and while we were still disputing about accessories, Russia and Prussia formed a still closer alliance at Bartenstein, on the twenty-sixth of April, with the firm resolution of driving me behind the Rhine. Although they did not stipulate, as in 1805, to take from me Lombardy and Belgium, this treaty was intended to throw me entirely out of Germany, and to restore Holland to the House of Orange.

I repeat, once for all, a Russian should be Russian in his feelings, and a Prussian should be Prussian; the feeling is censurable and despicable only where men, influenced by private interest or personal animosity, seek to abase their own country and exert their power to attain this object. Always disposed to render justice where it is due, I confess that this treaty was much more moderate than the project of 1805, and was perfectly suited to the interest of these two powers. England hastened to accede to it. Canning even agreed to allow Prussia a subsidy of twenty-five millions, to recruit her army, and prepare the English expedition which was to make a diversion on the Elbe. If it was natural that Russia and Prussia should wish to remove me beyond the Rhine, it was also natural that I, victorious, master of Germany and allied to ten millions of Germans, should be unwilling to decamp like a coward, without even disputing for the influence which they wished to take from me. The sword alone could decide the question. Will my detractors dare to ascribe this prolongation of the war to my ambition? What would the French, what would posterity say of me if I had done otherwise? Could I surrender the whole continent, without any equivalent concessions from England? Would it not have been base in me to abandon Bavaria, Saxony, and Wurtemberg to the resentment of my enemies? To deprive the Turks of two of their provinces, which the cabinet of London had promised to the Russians, while the sultan, yielding to the councils of my ambassador, had just saved his empire from the influence of these enemies, and had announced his intention to redouble his vigor on the Danube? I have not always been moderate; but it is not at this epoch that they can accuse me of exaggeration in my pretensions. Let us say frankly, a spark of Pitt's genius still animated Perceval and Canning; and his system had constantly been not to make peace while France was mistress of Belgium, and influential in Holland and Italy. If he ever had consented to it, it had been merely to deceive us, as in 1802.

It is thus seen that notwithstanding all the declamations of my enemies, I always occupied the same political ground. They formed coalition after coalition to destroy my influence, and I sought to extend it, so as to secure and preserve it.

Operations in Pomerania.—While these great interests

were in agitation, I neglected no means to conciliate the Swedes ; it will be remembered that, in setting out for the Vistula, I had charged Mortier to observe them with the eighth corps. He had no difficulty in holding them in check ; the quixotic Gustavus IV., was not a very formidable enemy ; although he commanded brave soldiers, this petty war was much like that which the Swedes had formerly waged against Frederick the Great.

After two or three unimportant combats, Pomerania was occupied and Stralsund closed. I wished to end this contest, which was neither to the advantage of Sweden nor of me, and I wrote to Mortier to embrace the first opportunity to conclude a peace. Persuaded that the Swedes would not attempt any thing serious, and hearing of some sorties of the garrison of Colberg, Mortier deemed it best to direct his forces toward this point ; but the Swedes having driven before them General Grandjean who had been left to observe them, Mortier returned and repulsed them with loss at Anklam.

Negotiations with Sweden.—D'Armfeld, the moving spirit of the war, had been wounded in this affair ; the English no longer acted in accordance with the pleasure of the whimsical Gustavus ; his nation disapproved of a war in which they had no interest, and this inconstant prince ratified an armistice, signed, April eighteenth, by General Essen, with the same want of consideration which he had shown in declaring war, for this occurred at the very moment when the English were at last sending him succor. Mortier had followed my instructions too literally in checking his victorious career instead of pushing the vanquished enemy into Stralsund and capturing their great flotilla, which had been retained by bad weather in the Haff ; there would always have been time enough to sign an armistice.

But as the error had now been committed, it was necessary to make the most we could of it; I required that a month's, instead of ten days' notice, should be given before breaking the armistice, which quieted all fears of enterprises by England and the coalition on my rear, and gave me time to complete the reduction of Dantzic. I added to the letter which Mortier was to send to General Essen:

"I have nothing more at heart than the restoration of peace with Sweden. Passions may have dissevered us, but the interest of the people, which should form the rule of action of sovereigns, ought to unite us. In the present contest, Sweden is as much interested as France in the success of my arms: She will feel still more than France the effect of an increase of Russian power. Is it then for the destruction of Constantinople that the Swedes fight? * * * Since the invasion of Walachia, and Moldavia, and the last English expedition to Constantinople, are not the objects of the coalition sufficiently unmasked? Sweden is no less interested than France in having a counterpoise against the enormous maritime power of the English. In any event, Sweden can have nothing to fear from France, but every thing from our enemies. Accustomed by the traditions of our fathers to regard each other as natural friends, it would seem that there were still greater reasons for closer relations since the partition of Poland and the dangers that threaten the Ottoman Porte; as our interests are the same, we ought to be allies, or at least not enemies." I added to the Marshal:

"If the Swedish general refuse his consent to the proposed modification, you will be supported by Marshal Brune, who has received orders to second you, and will renew the invasion of Pomerania. It will be impossible for the enemy, without the assistance of this province, to keep a large number of cavalry in Stralsund. Moreover, by occupying Pomerania, you will greatly embarrass the king of Sweden, for he will compromise himself in the eyes of his people, by favoring a party so opposed to the true interests of Sweden.

"On the contrary, if M. Essen accedes to what is required by the emperor of the French, you will immediately send back to Dantzic, Marienwerder, and Thorn, the third and seventh mounted chasseurs and all the provisional regiments; you will establish your head-quarters at Stettin; you will canton your troops around Stettin, Demnin and Anklam; you will cause to be reconnoitred the banks of the Peene, the position of Demnin and the banks of the Trebel; and you will fortify and intrench, on your line, all the places susceptible of defense, so as to cut off all communication between Swedish Pomerania and the Prussian states. You will immediately direct your attention to the preparation of a siege-equipage for Colberg, the materials for which will be furnished from Stettin, Custrin, and Magdeburg; your *corps-d'armée* must be prepared, at any moment, to march either in the direction of Hamburg or on the Vistula. You will open a correspondence with our *chargé-d'affaires* at Copenhagen, and recommend to him to keep you advised of any movement of the English in the Sound, for their expedition, fitting out in the Thames, should always be an object of your surveillance. Also keep up a daily correspondence with Marshal Brune and the duke of Feltre, so as to form all your operations in concert. It is probable, from all information received from England, that the debarcation can not take place in less than a fortnight; by that time the divisions of Generals Boudet and Molitor will arrive from Italy at Magdeburg, and secure the rear of the army."

The additional articles which I had required were agreed to on the twenty-ninth of April, and Mortier came at once to the environs of Stettin and reënforced the blockade of Colberg. Considering the state of things in the north of Germany, this event was not without importance. England, who had long promised a still more efficacious succor than that of her subsidies, had at last prepared to keep her word. The new English ministry, anxious to distinguish itself by some brilliant affair, had already preluded this expedition by projects for uniting, on our rear, forty thousand Anglo-Hanoverians, twenty thousand Swedes, fifteen thousand Russians, and all the Prussians that could be collected at Stralsund. Without attaching too much importance to these projects, it is nevertheless true that this diversion, had it been made at the proper time, would have given me some embarrassment. The English are reproached, with reason, with having acted too late; although time was requisite for preparations for a distant expedition, which could not be combined till after my passage of the Vistula, still, there was no reason why they should not appear in the Baltic by the latter part of April. Already a strong Hanoverian legion, recently organized, had been placed at Stralsund at the disposal of the king of Sweden; the Prussians were assembling, at the same place, a corps of which they then had a nucleus of four or five thousand men; but they limited themselves to these insufficient preparations.

Army of Observation on the Elbe.—Persuaded that England would not fail to do all in her power to disturb our security in these countries, which had so long submitted to her influence, I had collected, as has before been said, a corps of observation on the Elbe. Two French divisions from Italy, under Boudet and Molitor, the Gallo-Batavian troops, with which my brother Louis had reduced Hameln and Hanover, and the Spanish corps of Romana which arrived during the month of March, forming, with some other detachments, an effective force of fifty thousand men, seemed to me more than sufficient to check any descent made with such heterogeneous troops. Marshal Brune, who took command of these forces, was instructed to defend the mouths of the Elbe, the Ems, and the Weser, to hold Swedish Pomerania in check, and particularly to guard Berlin, Magdeburg, Hameln and Stettin. If a landing should be effected by the enemy, Brune was to immediately unite these forces and to compel him to reëmbark; his first line was to canton between the Weser and the Oder; his head-quarters were to be at Schwerin, and the two French divisions, the *élite* of his forces, in reserve at Magdeburg. He thus held in respect Lubeck, Hamburg, Berlin, and even Amsterdam. Mortier left him, in addition, the divisions of Loison and Grandjean employed at Stettin and the siege of Colberg, and he directed himself with two others toward Dantzic.

Expedition of the English to Egypt.—The English ministry, which pleaded its want of land forces, when solicited for assistance by its allies, could find plenty of troops where its maritime advantages were concerned. At the moment when it was reluctantly engaging in the expedition of the Baltic, its arms experienced a repulse both in Egypt and at Buenos-Ayres. Piqued at their unsuccessful attempt on Constantinople, the English thought to avenge themselves on the banks of the Nile. Seeking to profit by the momentary interest which they had in sustaining Russia against the Porte, to get possession of this rich granary of the East, they hoped to succeed the more easily as they counted on the support of the Mamelukes and the peaceful inhabitants of the country, trampled under foot by the Pacha of Egypt. The project of the cabinet of London was to reëstablish the power of the Mamelukes, under the protection of the English, and to form with them an alliance which should secure to England the commerce of the country, and the political and military influence of all the Levant.

General Mackenzie, leaving Sicily with five thousand men, made a descent, on the fifteenth of March, at Aboukir, and entered into Alexandria by capitulation. General Frazer, coming from the Dardanelles with the squadron of Duckforth, landed with reënforcements, a few days after Mackenzie. He immediately detached two thousand men to gain possession of Rosetta and secure his junction with the Mamelukes. The Albanians of Mahomet Ali allowed the English columns to penetrate into the narrow streets of this city, assailed them in this *coupe-gorge* by a murderous fire, and forced them to retreat, with great loss to Alexandria. Frazer, feeling the necessity of putting himself in communication with the Mamelukes, who were said to be toward Elhammed, sent General Stuart again to Rosetta. But Mahomet Ali, descending the Nile with his flotilla, was near capturing him, and drove him back to Alexandria, with a loss of twelve hundred men. Frazer, defeated, and about to be himself invested, proposed the evacuation of Alexandria and Egypt, on condition of the surrender of the prisoners captured by the enemy. The Porte, indignant at this new attack, declared war against England, armed a squadron of nine ships, and sent it to the Dardanelles, where the Russian fleet of Admiral Siniavin had just replaced that of Duckforth, and taken possession, on the twenty-first of March, of the island of Tenedos.

Sieges in Silesia.—While my warlike preparations formed so strong a contrast with the calm that reigned in the cantonments of the two armies on the Passarge, I profited by the leisure afforded me by the enemy, to reduce all the works which were calculated to trouble our rear. The reduction of Silesia was continued with favorable results: Glogau, Breslau, Brieg, and Schweidnitz, had already capitulated; Neiss, Cosel, and Glatz were about to experience the same fortune; but there still remained for me to reduce Colberg, Grandentz and Dantzic. I besieged the latter and blockaded the two others.

Siege and Fall of Dantzic.—Dantzic, defended by General Kalkreuth and the celebrated engineer Bousmard, had a garrison of twelve thousand Prussians, and three battalions of Russians. The siege of such a place is an important enterprise. Marshal Lefebvre, with the tenth corps, composed of Poles, Badois, Saxons and some French battalions, were charged with this siege. Lannes was placed in observation, with the grenadiers of Oudinot; the fifth corps, which he had heretofore commanded, passed to the orders of Massena, and was reënforced by the Bavarian division of Wrede. The siege of Dantzic was begun on the first of April, and was pushed forward with vigor. The place was pretty seriously battered after the first of May, and asked for succor. The island of Oliva, defended by about a thousand Russians, was carried on the sixth.*

* The siege of Dantzic is, probably, next to Sebastopol, the most celebrated in modern times. The strength of the place, the obstinacy of the defense, and the scientific ability of the siege, all combined to give it great notoriety. Marshal Lefebvre commanded the forces, but General Chasseloup de Lobat, one of the ablest French engineers since the days of Vauban, directed the operations of the siege. The place held out for fifty-one days after the opening of the trenches. The impatient old marshal chafed under the slow operations of a regular siege, and was eager to make the assault. He also grumbled at the inexperience of some of his troops. But, Napoleon, who fully understood the nature of the operations as well as the impatient character of his marshal, took measures to restrain as well as to pacify him. His rebukes to Lefebvre are equally applicable to "petty cavilers" of the present day, who freely criticise military operations which they are incapable of understanding, and who recklessly urge the sacrifice of thousands of lives which could readily be saved by the application of that military science and skill which they pretend to despise. A general who ignorantly or uselessly wastes the lives of his soldiers for an object which can be attained by other means, is no better than a *murderer*, and should be held up to universal detestation. Those who urge him to such a course are accessories to the crime.

In answer to one of Lefebvre's despatches in which he exhibited his contempt for a science which he did not possess, Napoleon wrote: "You can do nothing but find fault, abuse our allies, and change your opinion at the pleasure of the first comer. You wanted troops; I sent you them; I am preparing more for you, and you, *like an ingrate*, continue to complain without thinking even of thanking me. You treat our allies, especially the Poles and the Baden troops, without any delicacy. They are not used to fire, but they will get accustomed to it. Do you imagine that we were as brave in '92 as we are now, after fifteen years of war? Have some indulgence, then, old soldier as

The Emperor Alexander had, at this epoch, gone from St. Petersburg to Memel, either to take command of the armies in person, or to be near the theatre of negotiations. He had just established himself at Bartenstein, and a council of war was convoked to devise means of rescuing Dantzic: a general attack against my army on the Passarge was rejected as dangerous. They adopted the project of landing, under the protection of the fort of Weichselmunde, a division of nine or ten thousand Russians, under the orders of Young Kamenski, and of seconding him with three or four thousand Prussians who were to advance by the tongue of land of Nehrung. It is rare that such partial and complicated debarkations ever succeed; this one failed. The Russians had but one means of attaining their object; this was to fall, the next day, on our line of investment. They hesitated, from the eleventh to the fifteenth of May, and then debouched from the camp of Neufarwasser. After an obstinate combat, General Schram was near being taken, when Lefebvre hastened to his assistance with a part of the siege corps. The combat was

you are, for the young soldiers, who are starting in the career, and have not yet your coolness amidst danger. The prince of Baden, whom you have with you (that prince had put himself at the head of the Badenese and was present at the siege of Dantzic) has chosen to leave the pleasures of the court for the purpose of leading his troops into fire. Pay him respect, and give him credit for a zeal which his equals rarely imitate. The breasts of your grenadiers, which you are for bringing in everywhere, will not throw down walls. You must allow your engineers to act, and listen to the advice of General Chasseloup, who is a man of science, and from whom you ought not to take your confidence at the suggestion of the first *petty caviler* pretending to judge of what he is incapable of comprehending. Reserve the courage of your grenadiers for the moment when science shall tell you that it may be usefully employed, and in the mean time learn patience. It is not worth while, for the sake of a few days, which, besides, I know not how to employ just now, to get some thousand men killed, whose lives it is possible to spare. Show the calmness, the consistency, the steadiness, which befit your age. Your glory is in the taking of Dantzic; take that place, and you shall be satisfied with me."

A very complete popular description of this siege is given by Thiers; but those who desire to examine the operations professionally, must consult the special reports made by engineer officers.

prolonged and still in favor of the Russians; but Launes, having hastened to the assistance of our troops, with the grenadiers of Oudinot, drove the enemy back into his camp. The Prussians, who presented themselves too late, regained Pilau. Kamenski did not venture to attempt any thing further.

Foreseeing that the enemy would attempt the rescue of Dantzic, I had ordered Mortier to leave Pomerania on the first alarm, and approach the siege; and Brune, with the army of reserve was to replace him as far as Stettin. The corps of Mortier, composed at that time of the divisions of Dupas and Dombrowski, having reënforced the besieging army, and Dantzic having no further hopes of succor, the place capitulated on the twenty-fourth of May, after having sustained fifty-one days of open trenches. This siege was honorable to both parties. Kalkreuth and Lefebvre rivaled each other in glory as also did the chief engineers and soldiers of the two armies. After the fall of the place, as Kamenski could do nothing further at the camp of Weichselmunde, he left this little fort to the defense of its garrison and reëmbarked.

Siege of Neiss and Glatz.—The same success crowned our arms in Silesia, where the campaign had been continued during the winter. Notwithstanding the considerable resources found in the places which had already been reduced, the siege of Neiss was a difficult operation. A garrison of six thousand men, intrenched even on the exterior of the place, required for its reduction a larger corps than that at the command of my brother Jerome. He had to furnish a corps of observation, to check the garrison of Glatz, where General Kleist attempted, not only to raise the siege, but also to surprise Breslau. Lefebvre Desnouettes succeeded in baffling the first of these enterprises, and, seconded by General Dumui, who commanded at Breslau, he also forced Kleist to renounce the second. Neiss, closely pressed, capitulated, on the first of June, and the garrison, reduced to about five thousand combatants, were made prisoners; we found in the places more than three hundred cannon.

Glatz, notwithstanding its strong position, surrendered on the fourteenth of June. The garrison, exhausted and discouraged by its enterprises on the exterior of the place, did not make the resistance that we anticipated. This capture completed the campaign of the ninth corps, in which Vandamme distinguished himself, and, with less than twenty thousand men, took, in eight months, six great places, one thousand five hundred cannon and near twenty thousand prisoners.

Hostilities Renewed.—During the three months of repose which we had enjoyed, the Russian army had received a division of infantry, and the entire division of guards under the orders of the Grand-duke Constantine, numbering thirty battalions and thirty-four squadrons, including the grenadiers; nevertheless the Russians could not bring into line more than one hundred and twenty or one hundred and thirty thousand men, including the Prussian corps of Lestocq, and that remaining on the Narew. But there was an army of reserve, formed of the depôts and numbering about thirty thousand men, which was advancing on the Niemen, under the orders of Prince Labanoff. The Emperor Alexander had taken up his quarters in the vicinity of his army, so as to attend to either negotiations, or military operations. His headquarters were at Tilsit; the court of Prussia was at Memel.

My army had also been joined by strong reënforcements in addition to the depôts for recruiting the regiments; it had received the divisions of Oudinot, Verdier, Dombrouski, and Dupas, which came from Dantzic; these belonged to the corps of Lannes and Mortier. I had put both the *personnel* and the *matériel* in the very best condition. The effects of the bloody scenes of Jena, Pultusk and Eylau, were now scarcely visible. The Poles had levied near twenty thousand men, forming two divisions, under Generals Dombrouski and Zayonschek. The seven corps of my grand army, forming nineteen divisions, besides the guard of Murat's cavalry, were estimated at one hundred and seventy thousand men. I had therefore, a decided superiority, after the arrival of the troops from Dantzic, which joined me previous to the arrival of Prince Labanoff.

To restore the equilibrium, and to form a good support for the first line, Benningsen had constructed a very strong intrenched camp near Heilsberg, in position to command the two banks of the Alle. It was composed of five great works, enclosed on three sides, and sixteen *flèches* or intrenched batteries. The main body of the army was between this city and Bartenstein; the right, under Tolstoy, between Launen and Siegburg; a corps, at the left, kept up the communication with that of Essen, who was still near Ostrolenka. The Cossacks of Platoff covered all the front. By means of the inappreciable advantage of the sea, the allies had made of Königsberg an immense depôt of munitions and provisions. The army was abundantly supplied with every thing; one hundred thousand fire-arms recently landed from St. Petersburg and London, were to be used in arming such Prussians as the king might raise, and also to supply the losses resulting from the war; more than one hundred vessels laden with munitions and provisions, were to supply every thing that might be wanted.

It was well enough to use Königsberg as a temporary depôt; but this place, resting as it does on the *cul-de-sac* of the Curishaf, was not properly situated for a strategic base; it would have been far better if the magazines had been taken up to Gumbinen. This fault influenced all the events of the war.

My army, though less richly supplied than the enemy, was, nevertheless, pretty well provided by the rich products of Old Prussia and the inexhaustible environs of Elbing and Dantzic.

Such was the respective situations of the armies on the return of the favorable season; the reduction of Dantzic, and the failure of negotiations, rendered it necessary for us to renew the contest. For some inexplicable reason, Benningsen, who had neglected to attack me while I was weakened by the absence of the corps employed in the siege of Dantzic, now advanced to make this attack, after the fall of that place, and previous to the arrival of his reserves. My army, fully reëstablished, occupied the following places: A Bavarian division at Warsaw; Massena on the Omuleff; a Polish corps of observation under Zayonschek at Neidenburg; Davoust at Allenstein, Hohenstein and Deppen; Ney at Guttstadt; Soult at Leibstadt and Mohrungen; Bernadotte in Holland and Braunsberg; Lannes at Osterode; Mortier on the lower Vistula, marching to rejoin me. The corps of Lefebvre (the tenth), was broken up, after the fall of Dantzic; a part formed the garrison of that place, and the remainder was given to the corps of Lannes and Mortier. The second corps was still in Dalmatia, and the ninth in Silesia. Germany was occupied by Brune with the army of observation.

Danger and Escape of Ney.—Benningsen formed the project of cutting off the corps of Ney, which in fact had advanced too far. On the fourth of June the Russian army put itself in march, and took position with its right near Wormdit, the centre at Arensdorf, and the left at Lannau; on its extreme right the Prussian corps directed itself toward Spanden. On the other side, a Prussian corps, coming from Seeburg, took position on the Alle, between Guttstadt and Allenstein. The next day this corps forced the passage of the Alle at Bergfried and attacked the right of Ney, while his left was attacked by the left of Benningsen, and the centre of the Russian army marched by Wolfsdorf to cut off his retreat. If the Russians had acted with vigor, they might have made themselves masters of the road from Guttstadt to Deppen, and have thus secured the destruction of Ney; but fortunately they manœuvred so leisurely, and my marshal, although attacked by triple forces, displayed so much energy, coolness and courage, that he had time to retire from Guttstadt to Ankendorf. On the same day, the right of the Russians and the Prussian corps made demonstrations on the Passarge. Doctoroff presented himself with two divisions at the bridge of Lomitten, which Soult's division defended with much firmness. The Russian General, after having vainly endeavored to seize the passage, fell back on his left, either because he had been too roughly handled by Soult, or because his orders had been merely to make a demonstration. He moved toward the *corps de battaille* which was near Guttstadt. The Prussians had been still less fortunate at the bridge of Spanden, where Bernadotte had collected his entire corps; he succeeded in repulsing the enemy, and was wounded on this occasion in the head. On the sixth the Russians fell, in three bodies, on Ney; the little lakes which covered his flanks, forcing the enemy to long and indirect marches, enabled this marshal to fall back on Deppen, notwithstanding he was menaced on all sides at the same time; he finally succeeded in repassing the Passarge at that place, after a contest in which he covered himself with glory.

Napoleon marches to his Assistance.—On the seventh, the enemy remained stationary opposite Deppen; I profited by this circumstance to unite my army. I rejoined Ney with the corps of Lannes, my guard and the reserve of cavalry; Mortier moved by forced marches on Mohrungen; Davoust connected himself with the right of Ney. I, at the same time, ordered Soult, who had assembled his corps at Leibstadt, to cross the Passarge at Wolfsdorf, in order to threaten the enemy's communications with the intrenched camp at Heilsberg and to force them to abandon, without resistance, the banks of the Passarge. We effected a junction with him, on the eighth, at Altkirch; Benningsen, not thinking proper to await us, put himself in retreat on Guttstadt, where he passed the Alle on the ninth, and regained his camp at Heilsberg by the right bank. The same day, Murat pushed to Glottau the Russian rear-guard which attempted to defend the approach to Guttstadt, where my army had just taken position. We followed the enemy the next day, descending the left bank of the Alle.

Chances of Napoleon's Position.—As the enemy had given me time to increase my army to one hundred and sixty thousand men before the arrival of all his reënforcements, it was evident that the chances of the campaign would be in my favor, if Austria should delay hostilities. It was, therefore, for my interest, to strike a quick and decisive blow. Benningsen in attacking Ney at Deppen, had merely anticipated me a day or two, or rather favored my views by coming out to meet me, for I had left Ney in his advanced position to induce the enemy to leave his intrenchments. The union of my forces around Guttstadt no longer permitting delay, I resolved, in my turn, to take the offensive.

The intrenched camp of Heilsberg, and the concentration of all the enemy's magazines at Königsberg presented two principal manœuvres to my choice. The first and most skilful was to execute a general movement, the right in advance, in order to establish my line between Bichoffstein and Heilsberg, the right toward Bartenstein and the left toward Guttstadt. This would have been the same manœuvre as that of Jena and Naumbourg against the Prussians, with still greater chances of success, since the Russian army, beaten on the left and driven back on the Lower Passarge and the Frish-Hoff, would have been thrown on the sea. Königsberg would undoubtedly have given it a refuge; but this place, shut in, as it were, on the west by the Baltic and on the north by the Curishaff, would have offered no issue to the beaten army; for I should anticipate them at Weklau as soon as they should attempt to put themselves in retreat. The second was to advance my right on the intrenched camp of Heilsberg, while fifty thousand men manœuvred by my left on Eylau, to menace the allies' line of operations, to force them to abandon their redoubts without combat, and to press them closely in their retreat so as to cut them up at the passages of the Pregel and the Niemen. This last plan was less advantageous than the first and was opposed to the rules of strategy, inasmuch as it compromised a considerable corps between the enemy and the sea. I nevertheless preferred it, because my left was already in that direction, and it would have been necessary, in order to manœuvre by my right, to describe a long curve around the Russian army, to uncover my communications with Thorn and Warsaw, and to throw myself into the woody and rough country on the right of the Alle. I must confess, however, that the first plan was more in conformity with military rules. One of the motives which contributed most to induce me to choose the second, was, that I had already remarked, at the epoch of the battle of Eylau, that Benningsen exhibited a pusillanimous uneasiness about Königsberg; and, as this was not a military point, I concluded that there was some particular motive for this, either of policy toward Prussia, or of the means of supplies. By depriving the enemy of his magazines, I should not only procure certain supplies for my own troops, which was an important consideration in these distant countries, but I should overturn the allies' entire system of operations. On the other side, it was possible that the march of Soult on Königsberg might decide the Russians to fall back on their right to cover that city, and I should still remain capable of throwing menacing forces on their left flank, to cut them off from the road to Tilsit. For these reasons, I neglected strategic principles and decided to advance by the left bank of the Alle on Heilsberg.

Battle of Heilsberg.—On the tenth of June, my van-guard met that of the enemy near Bewernick. After an obstinate combat, the Russians were beaten and driven back on their army. At nine o'clock in the evening we formed ourselves opposite their camp. I at first had the idea of attacking the left of the right wing of the Russians, posted on the left bank of the Alle so as to penetrate to Heilsberg and cut their army in two, and thus render its destruction inevitable. Although it was already quite late, I ordered Soult's corps to attack the intrenchments which covered the Russians on the side of Lawden and Langviese. Although I seconded Soult with the corps of Lannes and the fusileers of the Guard, the Russians still maintained their position; we only carried an outwork, from which their reserve afterward dislodged us. In less than three hours we had lost about six thousand men *hors-de-combat*.

By renewing the attack the next day, I should risk the loss of the corps engaged in it, and there was less reason for making this attack, as by moving on Königsberg I was certain of displacing the enemy without resistance. I hesitated a moment whether I would not march on Bischoffstein, with the corps of Ney and Davoust; the motives already given induced me to take the opposite direction. On the eleventh, at break of day, my army moved in two columns on Landsberg and Preuss-Eylau. A single corps was left before the camp of Heilsberg to cover my movement. I confess that this operation was not without its objections, for it exposed my communications, and the enemy, basing himself on the camp of Heilsberg might have operated on our rear, and enclosed us between his army, the Lower Pregel and the sea. But I knew Benningsen too well to fear this; so vigorous an operation was above his grasp, and I had every imaginable reason to suppose that, instead of attacking our communications he would retreat, in order to prevent his being anticipated on the Pregel. Moreover, I took good care not to pass Landsberg, so long as the enemy remained at Heilsberg; and if he had marched on my rear I should have made haste to assail him in the same manner as Davoust had moved against the Prussians at Auerstadt, with the additional advantage of having a superiority of numbers on my side. In the last extremity, I could have fallen back by Mehlsack on the Lower Passarge, and have escaped with the sacrifice of a mere rear-guard.

Benningsen retires.—But I had no need to resort to this, Benningsen fully justified my expectations; during the night of the eleventh, he passed to the right of the Alle, burned the bridges of Heilsberg, and commenced his retreat by Bartenstein, Schippenbeil and Friedland, on Wehlau; I then continued to advance with security toward the Pregel. On the twelfth, I arrived at Preuss-Eylau; on the thirteenth, Soult moved on Creutsbourg. The grand-duke of Berg and Davoust took the direct road from Preuss-Eylau to Königsberg. Lannes advanced to Domnau; he was supported by Mortier and Ney who moved to Lampach. The corps of Bernadotte, commanded by Victor, had left the Lower Passarge to join us by Mehlsack, and was also directed on Preuss-Eylau. Benningsen, having reached the heights of Friedland, had suddenly suspended his march on Wehlau. Piqued at seeing himself decidedly anticipated by us in the direction of Kõnigsberg, he resolved to himself pass the Alle offensively, in hopes of beating in detail, the different corps of our army. This movement was not contrary to the rules of the art, but it should have been executed with vigor and been limited to a series of partial combats, rather than a general battle. The Russian general had an additional reason for such a course, inasmuch as he was awaiting the arrival of a corps of twenty-six or twenty-eight thousand men, which Prince Labanoff was bringing from Tilsit, whereas I had no hopes of any further reënforcement.

Battle of Friedland.—Conformably to this plan, Benningsen, preceded by all the cavalry of reserve of Prince Galitzin, took the road to Friedland on the evening of the thirteenth of June. A regiment of our hussars, which had already occupied that city, was driven out the same evening. The fourteenth, at break of day, the Russian army passed the river, and deployed itself in the plain on the left bank. The corps of Lannes had arrived near Friedland; unable to dispute the plain with the enemy, it at least succeeded in maintaining itself in the village of Posthenen and the surrounding woods. Whatever course the enemy might take, it was for my interest to concentrate my forces on the right in order to bar the road from Allenbourg to Wehlau. For this purpose I had directed Mortier to the support of Lannes, and had advanced myself with the guard on Domnau, and also had ordered half of the reserves of cavalry and the corps of Ney to the same place. Victor received orders to move by a forced march to pass this city.

Learning at Domnau the true situation of affairs and the unexpected return of the enemy, I hastened to dispatch Mortier to Lannes' assistance, and ordered these two marshals to check the Russians as much as possible, to give me time to arrive with my guard and the corps of Ney and Victor. The position of the enemy in the bend of the Alle, offered too fair an opportunity to celebrate the anniversary of Marengo for me to suffer it to escape. Lannes and Mortier punctually executed what had been directed, by pivoting on their left to defend Heinricksdorf and cut off the road to Königsberg. The enemy admirably seconded my views. Instead of attacking us boldly, he spent five or six hours in firing and deploying, without advancing a step.

I at last arrived about one o'clock, followed at an interval of two hours by Ney and Victor. Murat with half of the cavalry and the corps of Davoust and Soult, being still engaged in their movement on Königsberg, I directed the first two to march in the direction of Friedland. Perhaps it had been well to await them, in order to acquire a decided superiority over Benningsen, and I should not have hesitated to do so had I believed that he would venture to pursue his march against me, and engage himself on the road from Königsberg in the direction of Abschwang. Reënforced by forty thousand men, and having been joined by my fine cavalry, I could have driven him into the marshy forests of Zehlau and Frischind, from which he would never have escaped. I had so well foreseen all the chances which had just offered themselves to me, that I had written to the grand duke of Berg as follows :

"The enemy is here in order to give battle with all his army. He at first thought to debouch by the road from Stockeim to Königsberg; now he seems to think only of receiving the battle which is about to commence. I hope that you will be already in Königsberg; and as the corps of Soult will be sufficient to guard that city, you will undoubtedly fall back with the rest of the cavalry and the corps of Davoust, on Friedland. This is the more urgent, as it is possible that the affair may still continue to-morrow. Endeavor, therefore, to arrive by one o'clock in the morning. If I perceive, at the beginning of the action, that the enemy's forces are too numerous, it is possible that I shall merely cannonade him to-day and await your arrival."

But after I had more closely reconnoitred this *coup-gorge*

into which Benningsen had engaged himself, and had reflected on the unenterprising character of my adversary, I deemed it best not to postpone the opportunity to punish him for his error. It will be seen that in this I was right.

Friedland is situated in the reëntering bend of the Alle; the curve opened in the direction toward our approach. The space included in this bend is cut in two by a small mill-stream and the lake formed by damning up the water for the use of the mills. The enemy's left, composed of four divisions under Prince Bagration, was between this lake and the Alle. The right composed of three divisions of Prince Gortschakoff and two-thirds of the cavalry, extended from the lake to the north into the plain opposite Heinrichsdorf. The enemy, in order to facilitate his communications had thrown three bridges across the Alle, immediately opposite the city and near his left wing. It was evident that to strike a decisive blow, it was first necessary to overthrow this left, in order to gain possession of Friedland and the bridges; for the right, extending three-quarters of a league from the city to the north, would be driven on the Alle and cut off. I instantly formed my plan from these facts. The dispositions dictated for the battle are worthy of a place here:

"Marshal Ney will take the right from Posthenen toward Sortlack, and will rest on the present position of General Oudinot. Marshal Lannes will form the centre, which will extend, at the left of Marshal Ney, from Heinrichsdorf to nearly opposite the village of Posthenen. The grenadiers of Oudinot, which now form the right of Marshal Lannes, will insensibly incline to the left so as to attract the attention of the enemy. Marshal Lannes will mass his divisions as much as possible, and by this means will be able to place himself on two lines. The left will be formed by Marshal Mortier, holding Heinrichsdorf and the road to Königsberg, and thence extending opposite the right wing of the Russians.

Marshal Mortier will not advance, as the movement will be made by the right, resting on the left.

The cavalry of General Espagne and the dragoons of General Grouchy, joined to the cavalry of the left wing, will manœuvre to injure the enemy as much as possible, when, pressed by the vigorous attack of our right, he shall find it necessary to fight in retreat. General Victor and the imperial guard will form the reserve, and be placed at Grunhof and Botkein, and in rear of Posthenen. Lahoussaye's division of dragoons will be under the orders of General Victor: that of Latour-Maubourg will obey the orders of Ney; General Nansouty's division of heavy cavalry will be at the disposition of Marshal Lannes, and will fight with the cavalry of the *corps d'armée* of reserve, at the centre. I will be with the reserve. The advance will be by the right, the initiative being taken by Marshal Ney, who will await my orders. The moment the right moves on the enemy, all the artillery of the line will redouble its fire in a direction best calculated to protect the attack of this wing."

About five o'clock in the afternoon the signal of attack is given, and everything is executed with admirable precision. Ney advances with intrepidity; the Russians defend themselves with equal bravery. The concentric fire of our artillery commits so much the greater execution as the enemy falls back on the city, where, crowded on several lines, he cannot move. To disengage themselves, a grand charge of cavalry is made against the right flank of Ney; but this Marshal, leaving to the dragoons of Latour-Maubourg the care of repelling this charge, precipitates himself on Friedland at the head of his divisions. This vigorous blow, sustained successively by the divisions of Dupont and the other troops of the first corps, decides the victory. The artillery of Senarmont and Ney scatter terror and death among the squadrons and battalions of the enemy, which, hemmed in by the river, the city and the lake, knew not how to escape from the gulf. It was sad to see these men uselessly slain in the terrible position in which they were placed. Benningsen, seeing too late his error, leaves Friedland and goes to the right bank of the Alle to rally some reserves and artillery so as to take our line in flank and suspend its movement.

Ney already reaches the head of the great lake and presses the enemy who is crowded in the entrance to the city, but he is here attacked with great bravery by the Russian imperial guard. The division of Bisson, abandoned by its chief, is driven back; that of Marchand is checked; a retrograde movement begins at the left; but the division of Dupont, rivaling its ancient comrades of the field of Montreuil, falls on the enemy's guard, and assisted by Marchand, pierces and drives them all back into the *cul-de-sac* of Friedland.

Nevertheless Bagration does not suffer himself to be discouraged by his difficult position. Being able to bring into action only a small number at a time, he continually relieves them by fresh regiments, who in turn are sacrificed.

The French divisions fight as furiously to force an entrance into Friedland, as the Russians do to maintain themselves there till their right can fall back. In the space of two hundred and fifty toises, sixty thousand men fight with the rage of despair, and seem to have sworn to conquer or die. Benningsen, hoping to save his material, orders the artillery to cross the river; the Russian infantry, unable any longer to support the contest, moves by platoons in disorder along the road to the bridges. Benningsen in vain endeavors to rally the wrecks on the other side of the Alle, and to repass the river offensively under the protection of one hundred and twenty pieces of reserve which he had stationed up the river. Nothing could arrest the impetuosity of the columns of Ney and Victor; and Bagration, having withdrawn his lost battalions, plunged into Friedland, and set fire to the bridges in order to check the ardor of our pursuit.

While we obtain this decisive success, Lannes and Mortier give occupation to the enemy's right, and even allow Prince Gortschakof to gain some successes, in order to draw him the more certainly into the snare which I have set for him, by permitting him to engage himself on the road to Königsberg. Warned too late, of the catastrophe of the left wing by the burning of Friedland and the stragglers who returned from that place, the prince forms the resolution to cut a passage, sword in hand. One of his divisions penetrates into Friedland, where a horrible *mêlée* is again formed with the troops of Ney. But the bridges are already destroyed, and Lannes and Mortier fall on the rear of the enemy, while Ney and Victor check him in front. Here the carnage becomes frightful, and there is every reason to expect the entire destruction of this half of the enemy's army. But none of the isolated corps of these brave men ever think of capitulating; they prefer to throw themselves into the Alle and to seek a ford even at the risk of drowning. They thus succeed in rejoining Benningsen. Even the artillery precipitates itself into the river; but only a small part is saved. The cavalry of their extreme right files along the left bank on Allenbourg where it crossed the river.

Benningsen had this day committed innumerable errors; in the first place, he should have fallen vigorously on Lannes when he debouched in the morning on Friedland; if he had not thereby secured the victory, he would at least have procured a suitable field of battle, and by turning on his left, so as to extend his right on Heinrichsfeld, would have preserved his direct line of retreat on Wehlau, without exposing himself to be driven upon the Alle. There was, in his conduct, a mixture of rashness and irresolution difficult to be reconciled.*

The Russians recross the Niemen.—The Russian army, enfeebled by the loss of about twenty thousand men *hors-de-combat*, sought only to regain its frontiers. On the fifteenth, it passed the Pregel at Wehlau, and took the road to Tilsit. The corps of Kamenski and of Lestocq which defended Königsberg, having learned the result of the battle of Friedland, evacuated this city and also retreated on Tilsit, hotly pressed by Davoust. On the sixteenth, Soult entered into the capital of Old Prussia, where we made immense captures; for, independently of considerable magazines, we found there more than one hundred thousand stand of arms, recently debarked from England, and also a large quantity of munitions. Murat, who had hastened to pass the Pregel at Tapiau as soon as he heard of the victory of Friedland, cut up the enemy's rear-guard, and his army, closely pursued by our cavalry, passed the Niemen, at Tilsit, on the morning of the nineteenth: the same day I entered that city.

They propose Peace.—The Emperor Alexander, who had arrived from Memel at the head-quarters of his army, being dissatisfied with England for having refused him the means of facilitating a loan of one hundred millions, and having promised for six months to make powerful diversions, without sending a single man, now offered me peace. Victorious in Turkey, but thus engaged in a double war, he had

* Alison estimates the Russian loss in this battle at seventeen thousand killed and wounded, and the loss of the French at nine thousand. These estimates are about as erroneous on one side as were those of the French bulletins on the other. From the best authorities that can now be procured, the Russians lost about twenty-five thousand men *hors-de-combat*, and the French about eight thousand. Alison says the Russians lost but seventeen guns, but Thiers, after a full investigation of all the authorities, says the French captured eighty pieces of cannon. Few prisoners were captured on either side, except the Russian wounded left on the field. A large number of Russians were drowned in crossing the Alle. These are included in the above estimates.

no immediate motive for sacrificing himself for Europe, which left him unassisted. He had undertaken this war for interests entirely distinct from those of the people who separated his empire from mine. As for me, I esteemed myself fortunate in terminating the war so advantageously; for Austria was at length beginning to assemble her troops.

Interview of Tilsit.—Our first interview took place on a raft in the middle of the Niemen. On approaching me, the Emperor Alexander remarked that he had no less complaints against England than I had. In that case, I replied, *peace is made;* and we will shake hands in sign of reconciliation. We afterward had several other interviews at Tilsit, where the Emperor Alexander established himself. His exterior was noble, gracious, and imposing; the quickness of his conception seemed to me great; he comprehended at a glance the most important questions. Like Francis I. and Louis XIV., in every thing, it might also be said of him that he was a knightly king (roi-chevalier). If he had lived in the same age with the conqueror of Marignan, he would incontestably have carried away the palm. It may have been good policy to represent him differently from what I saw him, and it is certain that his conduct in 1812 and 1813 was different from what I anticipated; I believed him quick, but I thought him weak. It was not easy fully to understand the character of this prince; even Labruyère would have been embarrassed in exactly defining him.*

Alison thus describes the interview of the two Emperors on the Niemen:

By direction of the French general of engineers, Lariboissière, a raft of great dimensions was constructed on the river Niemen; *the raft of Tilsit*, which will be recollected as long as the cage of Bajazet, or the conquests of Alexander. It was moored in the centre of the stream, and on its surface a wooden apartment, surmounted by the eagles of France and Russia, framed with all the possible magnificence which the time and circumstances would admit. This was destined for the reception of the Emperors alone; at a little distance was stationed another raft, richly, but less sumptuously adorned, for their respective suites. The shore on either side was covered with the Imperial Guards

I also saw at Tilsit a regiment of his guards; and I never forgot the sensation I felt on seeing them. Many men saw in this troop only disagreeable stiffness. I myself never admired automaton soldiers; I wanted such as could be acted on by proclamations; nevertheless, I was surprised at the precision and the *aplomb* of this infantry. I saw that an army so thoroughly disciplined, and of such extraordinary firmness, would be the first in the world, if to these qualities, it should add the electric enthusiasm of the French. Some time afterward, speaking on this subject with a connoisseur, I said to him: "My soldiers are as brave as it is possible for men to be; but they reason too much. If they had the impassible firmness and docility of the Russians, the world would be too small for me. The French soldiers love their own country too well to become Macedonians."

Peace concluded.—After fifteen days of conferences, peace

of the two monarchs, drawn up in triple lines, in the same firm and imposing way in which they had stood on the fields of Eylau and Friedland. At one o'clock precisely, amidst the thunder of artillery, each emperor stepped into a boat on his own side of the river, accompanied by a few of his principal officers; Napoleon was attended by Murat, Berthier, Bessières, Duroc, and Caulaincourt; Alexander, by the Grand-duke Constantine, General Benningsen, Prince Labanoff, General Ouwaroff, and Count Lieven; the numerous and splendid suite of each monarch followed in another boat immediately after.

The bark of Napoleon, rowed by the marines of his guard, advanced with greater rapidity than that of Alexander. He arrived first at the raft, entered the apartment, and himself opened the door on the opposite side to receive the Czar, while the shouts of the soldiers on either shore drowned even the roar of the artillery. In a few seconds Alexander arrived, and was received by the conqueror at the door on his own side; their meeting was friendly, and the very first words which he uttered, bespoke both the lacerated feelings occasioned by the conduct of the government of Great Britain during the war, his deep penetration, and clear perception of the ruling passion of Napoleon—'I hate the English,' said he, 'as much as you do, and am ready to second you in all your enterprises against them.' 'In that case,' replied Napoleon, 'every thing will be easily arranged, and peace is already made.' The interview lasted two hours, during which Napoleon exercised all the ascendant which his extraordinary talents and fortune, as well as singular powers of fascination gave him, while the Russian Emperor gave proof of the tact and *finesse*, as well as diplomatic ability, by which his nation, beyond any other in Europe, is gifted."

was signed, on the seventh of July, at Tilsit. It was honorable for the two nations who had fought with so much bravery; but the advantage was on my side. The empire acquired an immense preponderance by this peace. As the most obstinate of my enemies began to regard my cause as gained, how could I myself fail to think so?

Nevertheless this treaty found many detractors among the critics of the *salons*, who imagine that treaties are made as readily as decrees: Some reproached me with having too much humiliated Prussia; others, and this party was the most numerous, pretended that I ought to have united with the liberal party in dethroning Frederick William, whom I had made my irreconcilable enemy, by the spoliation of half his states. The prompt rout of the Prussian armies, and my brilliant reception at Berlin, had proved to me, it is true, that this war had not the assent of the mass of the people. It has been falsely concluded from this that I ought to have profited by the existing circumstances to give a democratic organization to Prussia. Even had it been in accordance with my principles to propagate a new revolution, I had every reason to apprehend serious obstacles on the part of neighboring powers, interested in opposing them. Russia would not have treated on such conditions, and Austria would have interposed an obstacle.

Prussia.—The system on which I had formed my empire was not at all to the taste of the old dynasties; but it was not necessary to conclude, as so many declaimers have done since the event, that it made inevitable a war of extermination between us. They are very much deceived who think that the house of Brandebourg saw in me only an agent of the Revolution; its conduct toward me for the preceding six years, the alliance of the court of Madrid, the conduct of the cabinets of Berlin and Copenhagen, sufficiently prove that the existence of my throne accorded very well with theirs. All my steps had tended to reconcile France to the institutions of her neighbors; and those who observed me ought to have appreciated the efforts which I made to reconcile the revolution with Europe. In constructing the royal authority of new elements, I wished to concede what was demanded by the spirit of the age.

To derive the greatest possible advantage from my position and my successes, and to give to the empire an auxiliary force calculated to secure its durability, I had to choose between three means: either to base my support on the nations themselves, or to treat with their existing governments, or to seek to conciliate both the governments and the people. The worst system of all, was to humiliate the kings and to cut up their states without doing anything for the people.

To base my support entirely on the mass of the people, it would have been necessary to scatter anarchy everywhere, and to destroy both the form and *personnel* of the existing governments. But this would have been the inevitable means of producing a war of extermination between my dynasty and every thing around me.

There was but a single moment in my whole career when I could have applied the third of these means in Prussia, and have attached to myself both the prince and the nation; this was the beginning of 1806. After the war had once begun, the thing was impossible. The court had thrown itself headlong into the arms of my enemies; the nation, oppressed by the war, felt its humiliation. In truth the people were anxious to adopt the institutions which governed in my empire; but they did not want revolutionary principles. The fault which had separated my interests from those of the house of Brandebourg had been committed; there was now only one way of reconciling us; this was, *to give to this monarch, states equivalent to those which he had lost,* and on this condition, to induce him to contract an alliance with me. All this might have been very well before the war, when the Presidency of the Confederation of the Rhine could have been offered to Frederick William; but after Tilsit, there was no way of doing this without sacrificing to him Hanover and Westphalia, or of conferring on him the title of king of Great Poland, not as a Prussian province, but as a separate state. After the intimate relations which had been formed between this prince and the Emperor Alexander, would it not have been imprudent to make such a donation? Would it not have been furnishing arms to my adversaries? Moreover, would Russia herself have recognized this kingdom? I leave it to diplomatists to decide this question; but although I have resolved it negatively, I should have preferred it to demagogic propagandism. In fact where has this system of propagandism ever served us? Certainly not in Italy, where all the country was in insurrection against us, except some patriots in the cities. If it procured us friends, it also made us enemies; and existing interests have always more arms for self-defense, than new interests have for acquisition. This system of propagandism has sometimes been useful as a counterpoise; it has never been either the cause nor the agent of our success.

Pichegru alone found it a powerful support in Holland. My victories were never so great as from 1805 to 1810, when I no longer carried to the people anarchy under the cap of liberty. I was certain to overcome resistance by reducing them to questions purely military. What advantage did I derive in Spain by taking the interest of the people against the abuse of fanaticism and despotism? The king of Prussia had already effected a demi-revolution himself, by promulgating a new law for military promotion without respect to birth; civil employments in Prussia were already open to all the citizens. Thus, with the exception of a few insignificant principles, equality of right was already established; what remained for me to give the Prussians? the agrarian law?

Condition of the Treaty of Tilsit.—But let us leave the field of conjecture and return to the treaty of Tilsit. Prussia had provoked the war; it was necessary that some one should pay its expenses; and, under the conviction that it was no longer possible to make her our friend, it was very natural that it should be imposed on Prussia. I therefore determined to reënforce my federative system at her expense; this was indispensable since I threw her into the ranks of my enemies, it was necessary for me to reënforce mine in proportion. I created the duchy of Warsaw as the basis of a project for the restoration of Poland; I augmented the Confederation of the Rhine by the kingdom of Westphalia, formed of the Prussian provinces between the left bank of the Elbe and Magdebourg, the states of the elector of Hesse-Cassel, and the duchy of Brunswick. This kingdom fell to my brother Jerome, to whom I afterward gave Hanover also; but the last was still reserved at Tilsit as the means of treaty with England. The Confederation of the Rhine had already been reënforced, as has been said, by Saxony, whose elector took the title of king, and of grand-duke of Warsaw; his grandfather had already occupied this throne, and the selection of this prince sufficiently announced my intention of ultimately restoring Poland.

Revolution at Constantinople.—It was in the middle of the conferences of Tilsit that I learned the new revolution which had precipitated Selim III. from a throne which he had just shown himself so worthy to fill. Such are the monstrous governments of the East, that the smallest event often overthrows the finest combinations and leads to incalculable catastrophies. The death of an old mufti, changing the entire face of the empire, proved to me that its policy was not to be relied on from one day to another. Selim sought to rid himself of the turbulent spirit of the degenerate Janissaries; he had seen the advantage of a corps of European discipline (the Nizzam-Geddites) who had distinguished themselves at St. Jean-d'Acre against us, and quite recently in Romelia. He wished to effect an insensible fusion of the Janissaries into this corps; we induced him to adopt this system, which was the only one that could give the Porte a means of repression against the undisciplined and unbridled soldiery, and against the insolent priests and ulemas, who made of this soldiery blind instruments of their own ambition. This was at once a political and military restoration.

The ulemas and the chiefs of the Janissaries, masters of the multitude, incited it against these changes; it was necessary to renounce the proposed fusion. But difficulties did not end here; the old mufti, a friend of the sultan, dying at this time, was replaced by one of those crafty and ambitious men, who make religion the means of intrigue and trouble, in order to rule the state. Soon the opinion of the multitude became more and more excited and exceeded all bounds; the mufti and the caimacan, profiting by the absence of the visir and the captain-pacha, who were with the army of the Danube, fomented an insurrection in the capital, seconded by an audacious adventurer, named Cabakchi-Oglou. This man placed at the head of the yamacks, soon became the arm of this vast conspiracy. The Janissaries, the artillerists, sailors and people, were all led away by the high sounding phrases announcing the pretended crime of Selim against the laws of Mahomet, the usages of the empire, and the privileges given to his predecessors; of that Selim, in a word, who had dared to form the project of assimilating them to infidels. They demanded the heads of all the friends of the Sultan who had seconded his impious projects; all were sacrificed. After two days of these threatening scenes, the mufti, interrogated by the conspirators, with all the charlatanism of pretended inspiration, declared that Selim could no longer reign, by the laws which he had despised and sought to change. The Janissaries loudly demanded his deposition ; he was imprisoned and replaced by his nephew, Mustapha.*

This catastrophe suspended, for the whole month of June, those immense preparations which the Porte had ordered for the expulsion of Michelson from the Principalities. According to the plan of campaign adopted by the advice of Sebastiani, two hundred thousand men, assembled at Schumla, were to pass the Danube near Ismail ; and, profiting by the detachments which had weakened Michelson, to cut him off from the Dniester or force him to regain, in all haste, the Padolia. Nothing of all this was yet executed ; Michelson, who had already evacuated Bukarest, returned there with audacity.

Projects on Turkey.—These revolutions, whose results on the policy of the Divan I did not yet know, disgusted me with an alliance on which no solid projects could be founded. Strenuous as I had formerly been in stipulating for the integrity of the Ottoman Empire, to the same degree did I now feel myself free from all obligations toward barbarians who were incapable of respecting their best princes.

* A counter-revolution took place in July, 1808, and Mustapha IV. was deposed; but the unfortunate Selim III. lost his life, and Mahmoud II. was raised to the throne. The Janissaries were the principal opponents of all reforms attempted by Selim III. and his successors, and produced several revolutions in the government. They were particularly opposed to the introduction of the European military organization into the Turkish army. Their last revolt was on the fourteenth of June, 1826, when the Sultan and Hussein Pacha, at the head of the grand seignor's troops, repulsed the rebels, burnt their barracks, and put many of them to death. A proclamation was issued on the seventeenth of June, abolishing the corps forever, and pronouncing a curse upon the name.

This corps was first organized about the year 1389, from captive slaves. After long years of severe discipline, it became the terror of other nations, and finally of its own government.

A conquering tribe descending from the mountains of Natolia for the invasion of the Greek Empire, these Turks are Tartars, encamped in Europe; they have nothing European. It is in vain to praise the services rendered by them to France by their different attacks on Hungary, and diversions against the then all-powerful house of Austria; in these aggressions there was nothing based on the interests of European policy. They fell upon Hungary and Austria, as they formerly fell on Romelia. Once only did France arm them in favor of Poland, in an interest which was still their own. Our manners, our usages, our religion, all are in formal opposition to these barbarians.

Convinced that if they were driven back into Asia, it would be a benefit to the human family, I gave the Emperor Alexander to understand that I would not fail to coöperate in this noble enterprise. I judged Turkey too much by European States; this revolution, combined with the anarchy which reigned in all the pachalics, and which seemed to tend to an emancipation from the Porte, made me feel that the Ottoman Empire was about to fall. I might gather a rich harvest in her ruins; master of Corfu and the Ionian Isles, I might pretend to the possession of Albania, the Morea, the islands of the Archipelago, provinces rich in mines, and forests of good ship-timber, and furnishing a good nursery of excellent seamen. I should thus secure my influence in the Levant; I should prepare immense maritime means; who knew but the glory of restoring Greece was reserved for me?

Stipulations in the Treaty of Tilsit.—But as this subject might lead to discussions and postpone our reconciliation, the basis of which was already laid, and as I could not immediately effect the partition of an empire with which I was connected, if not by formal treaties, at least by close relations and mutual conveniences, we postponed the question with the understanding that it should be discussed at some other time. It was agreed that the present state of the Ottoman Empire should be provisionally maintained, and that no ulterior changes should be made but by mutual consent. I tacitly consented that the Russians should continue to occupy the Principalities as far as the Danube; I was to occupy Prussia so long as the provisional state continued.

We were to propose peace, in concert, to our reciprocal enemies; Russia to offer her mediation to England, and I to the Turks; if our propositions were rejected, we were to act together for the same common object. An eventual treaty provided in part for the rejection of peace by the English. Russia was to force Sweden to close her ports; I was to effect the same in Denmark, Portugal and the States of the Pope; Spain, who had already closed her ports, would also adopt the system of reprisals ordered by the Berlin decree; thus putting the English under the ban of Europe. I promised the Emperor Alexander not to augment the Duchy of Warsaw, and to do nothing further toward the restoration of Poland.*

* The following eloquent remarks on the treaty of Tilsit are extracted from Thiers' Consulate and Empire:

"Never had greater lustre surrounded the person and the name of Napoleon; never had greater apparent power been acquired for his imperial sceptre. From the Straits of Gibraltar to the Vistula, from the mountains of Bohemia to the North Sea, from the Alps to the Adriatic, he ruled either directly or indirectly, either personally or by princes who were some of them his creatures, the others his dependents. Beyond were allies or subjugated enemies, England alone excepted. Thus almost the whole continent was under his sway; for Russia, after resisting him for a moment had warmly adopted his designs, and Austria found herself forced to suffer them to be accomplished, and even threatened with being compelled to concur in them. England, in short, secured from this vast domination by the ocean, was about to be placed between the acceptance of peace and a war with the whole world.

"Such was the external appearance of that gigantic power: it had in it enough to dazzle the world, and it did actually dazzle it; but the reality was less solid than brilliant. A moment's cool reflection would have sufficed to convince one's self of this. Napoleon diverted from his struggle with England by the third coalition, drawn from the shores of the ocean to those of the

Such in substance was the treaty of Tilsit, on which has been formed so many romances. It has been pretended that I spoke of restoring the eastern and western empires, prom-

Danube, had punished the house of Austria by taking from it, in consequence of the campaign of Austerlitz, the Venetian States, the Tyrol, Suabia, and had thus completed the territory of Italy, aggrandized our allies of South Germany, removed the Austrian frontiers from ours. So far, so good—for, to finish the territorial emancipation of Italy, to secure friends in Germany, to place new spaces between Austria and France, was assuredly consistent with sound policy. But in the intoxication produced by the prodigious campaign of 1805, to change arbitrarily the face of Europe, and instead of being content to modify the past, which is the greatest triumph given to the hand of man, instead of keeping up for our profit the old rivalship of Prussia and Austria, by advantages granted to the one over the other—to wrest the Germanic sceptre from Austria without giving it to Prussia; to convert their antagonism into a common hatred of France; to create, by the title of Confederation of the Rhine, a pretended French Germany, composed of French princes, to whom their subjects had a natural antipathy, of German princes, unthankful for our gifts, and after rendering, by this unjust displacement of the boundary of the Rhine, war with Prussia inevitable, war impolitic as it was glorious, to suffer one's self to be carried by the torrent of victory to the banks of the Vistula, and on arriving there to attempt the restoration of Poland, having on one's rear Prussia, vanquished but fuming, Austria secretly implacable—all this, admirable as a military work, was, as a political work, imprudent, extravagant, chimerical.

"With the aid of his genius, Napoleon upheld himself at these perilous extremities, triumphed over all obstacles, distance, climate, mud, cold—and completed on the Niemen the defeat of the continental powers. But, at the bottom, he was anxious to put an end to this daring expedition, and his whole conduct at Tilsit betoken that situation. Having estranged for ever the heart of Prussia, which he had not the good idea to attach to himself for ever by a signal act of generosity, enlightened respecting the sentiments of Austria, feeling how victorious soever he might be, the necessity for making himself an alliance, he accepted that of Russia, which presented itself at the moment, and conceived a new system of policy founded on a single principle—the concurrence of two ambitions, Russian and French, to do whatever they pleased in the world—a mischievous concurrence, for it behoved France not to allow Russia to do everything, and above all not to allow herself to do everything. After having aggravated by the treaty of Tilsit, the deep ranklings of Germany, by creating in her bosom a French royalty which must cost us in men, money, animosities to overcome vain counsels, all that those of Naples and Holland already cost us; after having half reconstituted Prussia, instead of restoring or destroying her entirely; after having, in like manner, half reconstituted Poland, and done everything in an incomplete manner, because, at these distances time pressed, the strength began to fail, Napoleon made irreconcilable enemies, impotent or doubtful friends, raised, in short, an immense edifice, in which

ising to aid Russia in the conquest of Constantinople, provided she would consent that I, or my family, should possess Italy, Spain and Portugal; and that taking a map of Europe I myself traced out the line of demarcation, following the river Oder, thence directly across the rapids to the Danube and the Black Sea, giving all east to the Russians and taking the west as my own empire. I may have used some high sounding phrases in presence of a young sovereign, but these pretended projects are too absurd for comment.

everything was new from bottom to top. an edifice run up so rapidly that the foundation had not had time to settle, the mortar to harden.

"But, if every thing is censurable, in our opinion, in the political work of Tilsit, brilliant as it may appear, all is admirable, on the contrary, in the conduct of the military operations. That army of the camp of Boulogne, which, carried with incredible dispatch from the strait of Calais to the sources of the Danube, enveloped the Austrians at Ulm, drove back the Russians upon Vienna, finished by crushing both at Austerlitz, having then rested for some months in Franconia, soon recommenced its victorious march, entered Saxony, surprised the Prussian army in retreat, broke it up by a single stroke at Jena, pursued it without intermission, turned it, took it to the last man on the shores of the Baltic; that army which, diverted from north to east, ran to meet the Russians. hurled them into the Pregel, then exhibited the unheard of spectacle of a French army quietly encamped on the Vistula, then, suddenly disturbed in its quarters, left them to punish the Russians, reached them at Eylau, fought, though perishing with cold and hunger, a bloody battle with them, returned after that battle to its quarters, and there, encamped again upon snow in such a manner that its repose alone covered a great siege, fed, recruited, during a long winter at distances which baffle all administration, resumed its arms in spring, and, this time, nature assisting genius, placed itself between the Russians and their base of operation, compelled them, in order to regain Königsberg, to cross the river before its face, flung them into it at Friedland, and thus terminated by a splendid victory, and on the banks of the Niemen, the longest, the most daring expedition, not through defenseless Persia or India, like the army of Alexander, but through Europe, swarming with soldiers as well disciplined as brave—this is unparalleled in the history of ages, this is worthy of the everlasting admiration of men, this combines all qualities, celerity and slowness, daring and prudence, the art of fighting and the art of marching, the genius of war and that of administration, and these things, so diverse, so rarely united, always opportune, always at the moment when they were needed to ensure success. Every one will ask himself how it was possible to display so much prudence in war, so little in politics. The answer will be easy,—in war Napoleon was guided by his genius, in politics by his passions."

The peace of Tilsit was unexampled in the annals of France; who could expect that it would find detractors? such might well be found in Germany and in England; but it was reserved for evil Frenchmen to revile the finest monument of national glory.

CHAPTER XI.

FROM THE TREATY OF TILSIT TO THE BEGINNING OF THE WAR IN THE SPANISH PENINSULA.

Results of the Campaigns of 1806 and 1807—Origin of the Continental System—Its general Plan—Its Influence on Commerce—On Industry—This System leads to War—Its Influence on State Policy—On Maritime Relations—Measures requisite for its Execution—Mediation offered by Russia to England—English Expedition against Denmark—Preparations of the Danes for Defense—Capture of Copenhagen and the Danish Fleet—Brune takes Stralsund and Rugen—Russia declares War against the English—Intercession of Austria—Negotiations respecting Turkey—Distribution of New Titles of Nobility—Suppression of the Tribunat.

Results of the Campaigns of 1806 and 1807.—The war with Prussia had produced extraordinary results; I hardly knew how to dispose of the power which it gave me. Since their departure from Boulogne, two hundred thousand Frenchmen had been paid, fed, and clothed, at the expense of the enemy; more than four hundred millions of contributions in money and supplies had been levied on the occupied countries; the treasury had received a part of this, and the expenses of our budget, reduced by the entire support of the army, had not employed one half of the funds which had been assigned to it. A short time before, I had sold Louisiana in order to procure money; in returning from Austerlitz, I had found the treasury empty, and the bank on the eve of bankruptcy. Two years had scarcely elapsed since this crisis, and I now had a year's revenue in advance, in the coffers of the state, and a considerable reserve in the vaults of the Tuileries; while the pamphleteers, in English pay, were proclaiming throughout Europe that my power would soon terminate for want of finances.*

Origin of the Continental System.—But if my resources were great, a proportionally vast field was open for their employment. The epoch of the treaty of Tilsit was the apogee of my glory and power, for I there laid the basis of a great system which was calculated to consolidate them. This system, properly called *Continental*, has never been perfectly understood.

However great the immediate advantages of this system, I hoped for one still greater in forcing the English to peace; for the British colossus had heretofore been but feebly affected by the increase of my power; it regarded this increase as a temporary evil which would touch England only indirectly. Maritime peace was henceforth the only object of my wishes, and I explained myself to the Emperor Alexander in such a manner as to leave no further doubt on the subject, by intrusting him with the care of procuring it for the world by his powerful intervention. To prove that my desire on this

* The following brief summary of the condition of French finances at different periods, is copied from Thiers:

"A vulgar sign, but a true one, of the disposition of minds, is the rate of the public funds in the great modern states which make use of credit, and which, in a vast market, called Exchange, permit the sale and purchase of the titles of loans which they have contracted with the capitalists of all nations. The five per cent. stock (signifying, as every body knows, an interest of five allowed for a nominal capital of one hundred), which Napoleon had found at twelve francs on the eighteenth Brumaire, and which afterward rose to sixty, got up, after the battle of Austerlitz, to seventy, and then passed that point to reach ninety, a height at that time unprecedented in France. The disposition to confidence was even so strong, that the price of this stock rose still higher, and toward the end of July, 1807, reached ninety-two and ninety-three. Previously to the time of the assignats, when a fondness for financial speculations did not exist; when the public funds had not yet made the fortune of great speculators, nor had, on the contrary, brought ruin on the legitimate creditors of the state; when the value of money was such that it was easy to find in solid depositories an interest of six or seven per cent.—it required immense confidence in the established government to cause the titles of the perpetual debt to be accepted at an interest of five per cent."

subject was sincere, it will be sufficient to look for a moment at the situation of the two parties and the evident interest which I had in such a course.

The burning of Toulon, the naval battles of Ouessant, of Cape St. Vincent, of Camperdown and of Trafalgar, the surrender of the Batavian fleet in the Texel, and the disaster of Copenhagen, (which remains to be described), had ruined, for twenty years, all the continental navies. England had no further rivalry to fear; the use she made of this power is but too well known. A long peace was requisite to reconstruct maritime arsenals, to rebuild ships, and to train sailors by voyages on the ocean.

Although France had lost her most important colony, she still might raise up sailors by her commerce with the vast Spanish possessions, and with India through the Isle of France; Holland still preserved the Moluccas, and her relations with China and Guiana. Spain had still more ports and extent of coast in the two hemispheres, than all Europe united, and much more than she required to form sailors for her merchant ships. The Americans were developing themselves from day to day, and the greater their increase, the more intimately were their interests connected with France. If I had a positive maritime interest in desiring peace it was no less to my interest on the continent; my power could not be further extended without injury to its solidity; it was necessary to render it invulnerable by binding it together, with institutions of reciprocal advantages to all the parts of this immense edifice. To render peace durable, it was necessary that neither party should have any thing to regret; but this was not possible; a truce for a year or two would have profited England only, and have ruined our commerce, by engaging it in distant enterprises. In order to obtain the complete and durable peace which we desired, it was agreed that Russia should propose her mediation for peace, and, if

England should persist in rejecting it, Russia should accede to the Continental system.

Its general Plan.—This system which has been so unjustly decried without being understood, we will now proceed to examine; it may be divided into two distinct branches:—the one political, and the other commercial or maritime.

Its Influence on Commerce.—In its commercial relations, two essential points of view were to serve me as guides; the first, to so cripple the English commerce as to deprive the ministry of the means of *subsidising* the continent and of continuing the war; the second, to oppose their manufactures by developing ours. For this purpose it was necessary to open channels for our products and to close them to the enemy, that is, to exclude the English from the markets. Many partial measures had already been taken for this purpose, but they amounted to nothing, so long as no general system was adopted for placing these rulers of the seas under the ban of Europe. I had given the prelude to this system in my Berlin decree, in 1806, and the finishing stroke in the Milan decree of 1807. This system of legislation was an outrageous one, but necessity and the example of my enemy forced me to it. Decrees alone were not sufficient, it was necessary to isolate England from Europe and to ruin her commerce. In this respect the Continental system only partially performed its object, because the war in Spain opened to the enemy the most important outlets for her products.

Its Influence on French Industry.—With respect to industrial products this system led to important results. A great empire requires not only a general direction for its policy, but its economy must also have a similar tendency. Home industry requires a channel or road, like every thing else, in which to move and advance. But France had no such channel till I marked out one by giving to her the Continental system.

The economy of France, before the Revolution, was directed to colonies and exchange commerce. This was then the fashion. She had the greatest success. Some have ventured to say that this success had no other results than the ruin of the state finances, the loss of our credit, the destruction of our military system, the loss of consideration abroad, and the ruin of our commerce at home. These are just so many absurdities! It is not colonial wealth and commerce of exchange that have produced such sad results; but a debilitated administration, and factious *parlements*. Fine harbors and rich merchants have no more prevented agriculture from flourishing in France, than they have in England; and the kingdom was so far from being ruined under Louis XVI., that it sustained twenty years of wars and revolutions, and prospered all the time.

All nations have been enriched by this colonial and commercial system, and France especially owed to it her splendor. But the war had utterly destroyed this system; the sea-ports were ruined; no human power could immediately restore to them what the Revolution had destroyed. It was, therefore, necessary to give some other impulse to the spirit of trade, in order to restore life to French industry. The only means of doing this was to deprive England of her monopoly in manufactures, and to direct to this the general tendency and economy of the state. This required the Continental system in all its force; nothing less could answer the purpose, for it was necessary to offer an enormous premium upon fabrics before capitalists could be induced to make the requisite outlays for the construction of large manufacturing establishments.

The result proved the correctness of my views, I transferred the seat of industry across the channel, and it has made such great progress on the continent that it fears no rivalry. If France wishes to prosper, let her retain my system, merely changing its name. If she desires ruin, let her recommence her maritime enterprises ; the English will destroy them at the first outbreak of war. I was forced to carry the Continental system to extremes, because it then was my object not only to benefit France, but also to injure England. We could receive colonial products only through the English ministry, for it naturally controlled all the flags that engaged in colonial trade. It was, therefore, necessary to import as little as possible ; and the best means of accomplishing this was to impose enormous duties on such products. The political object was accomplished ; the state finances were benefitted ; but the French ladies were disconsolate, and they sought to avenge themselves on me for thus cutting off their luxuries.

Every day's experience proved the benefits of the colonial system, for the state prospered notwithstanding the burthen of war. The imports were well regulated ; credit on a par with the interest of money ; the spirit of improvement showed itself in agriculture as well as manufactures ; villages were built up anew, like the streets of Paris ; the roads and canals facilitated the interior movement ; some new improvement was invented every week ; I caused sugar to be made of beets, soda of salt, indigo of pastel ; the improvement in the sciences kept pace with that in the arts. In England, on the contrary, a few merchants enriched themselves, but the industrial mass suffered ; the notes of the bank lost a third and almost one half their value, for a pound sterling was worth in exchange only thirteen francs. The injury to England would have been still greater if Spain had entered into my system as I had hoped, and if the unexpected revolutions in Spanish America had not opened valuable markets to the English. Although its execution was imperfect, and had much fallen short of its intended object, it nevertheless would have been madness to renounce this system at the very moment when it was bearing fruit: it was necessary to strengthen it and to give it a wider career of emulation.

This System leads to War.—The obligation which now rested on me to persevere in this system, and the necessary continuance of the war by England, influenced the political condition of the continent. From this moment the matter assumed a more serious character. The question involved the prosperity and almost the existence of England. The war became popular with the people. The English no longer entrusted their protection to foreigners; they now took the matter into their own hands, and again appeared with strong armies on the continent. They were to have for auxiliaries all those whose interests were momentarily affected by my system, and this class was large. If a great maritime commerce is one of the first elements of wealth and prosperity, the freedom of the seas becomes the most necessary and valuable of all things, for every nation on the globe. This freedom of the seas was the main object of my Continental System; but people who preferred their present enjoyments, could see, for the moment, only the closing of their ports; and the cessation of their traffic; future benefits were scarcely considered. This explains the general hatred which was unchained against my system. Not only were all the coast countries tired of the war and the sacrifices it imposed on them; this feeling extended even to the heart of the continent. The cloths of Silesia and the fabrics of the confines of Bohemia went no longer to Cadiz, to be carried by Spanish flags to Mexico. The North no longer sold its grains to Holland, or purchased wines of us. The silks of Lyons could reach Prussia only by land; England and Sweden were reached in trade, only by Archangel. The true cause of this evil was the maritime despotism of an insular power, which had the means of placing so many obstacles to the general welfare of the continent. I had now grappled with this colossus; but the people whom it oppressed, instead of momentarily submitting to sacrifices in order to second my efforts, imputed to me all the evils from which I was seeking to deliver them; so true is it that great national policy is above the understanding of the merchant and stock-jobber.

Its Influence on State Policy.—The political branch of this Continental system offers, like the commercial branch, two points of view of equal importance; the first consisted in effecting with the neighboring powers, by means of alliances, treaties and leagues, what I had effected in France by decrees—the exclusion of English commerce; the second consisted in preparing, by the same alliances, the maritime and military means for attacking more directly the British colossus, when the favorable moment should arrive. We could attack in India by means of Russia, Persia, and Turkey; we might reach it in the Antilles, from Spanish America and the United States. Finally, we could attack it in Europe, by the union of all the states interested in overthrowing its maritime despotism.

The treaty of Tilsit had not absolutely provided for all the combinations conducive to this result; but it had, nevertheless, done much in that direction. Since the English refused to respect neutrals, it was necessary that no one should be neutral; every one had necessarily to decide for England or against England; our engagements, made on condition that this power rejected the mediation of Russia, would oblige the maritime nations to act in concert with us. Spain was at war with the English; Turkey had just declared against them; Italy, with the exception of the court of Rome, which still held out, was subject to my laws. Prussia had just broken with them. There was then only Portugal, Sweden and the Pope to bring to terms, in order to entirely interdict to them all access to the continent, for we hoped that Denmark would hasten to join our system.

Austria, indeed, offered more difficulty, but she had only the single sea-port of Trieste. From Venice I could control all vessels approaching that port; and the Seven Isles rendered me master of the Adriatic. Moreover, Austria would hardly expose herself to a war with Russia and France for relations that concerned her less than any other continental power; she had neither colonies to regret nor products for maritime exportation. I could give her promises to indemnify her for any losses. If I should finally enter into the project of the partition of the Ottoman Empire, Servia and Bosnia might serve as the price of her condescension. I determined to bring her into my Continental system.

Its Influence on Maritime Relations.—In case England should refuse the Russian mediation for peace, it would be necessary not only to close against her all access to the continent, but also to turn against her all the resources of the maritime powers. Europe could still oppose to her one hundred and eighty ships of the line, viz: sixty French, forty Spanish, twenty-five Russian, fifteen Swedish, fifteen Dutch, fifteen Danish, and ten Portuguese. In a few years this force could be increased to two hundred and fifty. By the aid of these means and our immense flotilla, it was not impossible to conduct a European army to London. One hundred ships, employed in the two hemispheres, would draw away a great part of the British naval forces, while eighty of the best vessels, united in the channel, might secure the passage of our flotilla and avenge the outraged law of nations.

Such was the fundamental principles of my system, which writers in English pay have taxed with folly; the want of success of the project resulted, perhaps, from faults committed in its execution with respect to Spain. How is it possible to judge fairly of a project which was not adopted till the end of 1807, and failed the following year by the misfortunes which opened to the English on the Peninsula and the American continent? Had it not been for the war with Spain, the whole continent of Europe and all the Spanish colonies would have been interdicted to English commerce; the naval resources of all the continental powers would have been directed against England; I should have resumed my project of a descent from Boulogne with much greater chances of success.

Measures for its Execution.—The first means of reaching my object, in this double political and commercial relation, was to occupy militarily all the maritime countries where England had great influence, and where no sincere accession would be given to our system. Sweden, Portugal, and Rome were of this class; Denmark was to be invited to accede to this system, and, in case of her refusal, to be occupied like the others. England, who had eyes and ears everywhere, and whose gold discovered the most profound secrets of foreign cabinets, was informed of these dispositions as soon as they were made. Instead of yielding to the tempest, she prepared herself to master it.

Mediation offered by Russia.—In the meantime the emperor of Russia had hastened to send to London the offer of his mediation for peace, announcing that he had agreed with me, that I, on my side, would accept it, provided that England did the same within a month from the ratification of the treaty. The cabinet of London consented to the mediation, but would make no reply to the proposition till it should see the secret articles of the treaty of Tilsit! It was in vain objected, on the side of Russia, that these articles were eventual, temporary; that the emperor could not communicate them, inasmuch as he had promised secresy, but that they were in no way prejudicial to England, since they ceased to have any force the moment the cabinet of St. James decided on peace. The matter rested here, when the news of the English attack on Copenhagen filled Europe with alarm.

English Expedition against Denmark.—The great armament so long promised to the coalition was just ready to sail for the Baltic when peace was signed. Perceval and Canning deemed the moment opportune to employ this imposing force, now useless on the continent, against Denmark, who had opposed the pretensions of England, but was at peace with her. If a debarkation on the continent was impossible, such was not the case with the island of Zealand, where they could attack Copenhagen in spite of our legions, whose passage the English fleet might intercept by the Belt. The expedition was, therefore, directed against that city, and its success was deemed the more certain, because Denmark, surrounded by belligerent troops on the side of Pomerania and Mecklenberg, had directed all her attention and forces on the side of Holstein, in order to secure her territory from insult.

The cabinet of St. James alleged, as the motive of this unjust aggression, its knowledge of the secret conditions of the treaty of Tilsit, in which we (France and Russia) had stipulated the conditional closing of the ports of Denmark, and the exclusion of the English from the continent.

A fleet of twenty-nine ships, twelve frigates and five hundred transports, set sail, on the twenty-seventh of July, entered on the fourth of August, a port in the Sound, and a port in the Belt, and landed an army of thirty-two thousand men, including the Hanoverians before sent to Stralsund. Lord Cathcart commanded this expedition. Under him was Sir Arthur Wellesley, afterward Lord Wellington. This conqueror of Schindiah and the Mahrattas, recalled from India by the laws of his country, here performed his first service on the European continent. An immense equipage and select troops furnished these chiefs the means of a successful enterprise. Jackson was sent to Christian VII. to propose to him a close alliance with England, and to demand the surrender of his fleet, to be taken to English ports, as a pledge of his sincerity! It was a repetition of the infamous demands made upon the Turks, but supported, this time, by more powerful means. The King, the Prince Royal, and the two Bernstofs, had too high a regard for their own dignity to accept what the Turks had repelled with indignation. If England had denounced the stipulations of Tilsit, and proposed to Denmark to join her in the defense of her territory, declaring war against her in case of her refusal, this step would have been more natural; but to impose on her the obligation of committing an act of base cowardice, was rather too much! On vague rumors, and a mere suspicion of what had taken place at Tilsit, the English were about to assail a government which had armed itself on the shore of the Trave, to oppose us.

Preparations of the Danes for Defense.—The Danish government, though taken unprepared, showed itself no less noble than in 1801. The Prince Royal, who was in Holstein, flew to Copenhagen, through the midst of the English cruisers, induced the king to retire to Gluckstadt on the continent, confided the defense of Zealand to General Peymann, organized the provincial militia for the succor of the capital, then returned to the army of Holstein to hasten its arrival. During the communications between the authorities of the two parties, and while the English were constructing and arming their land batteries, these militia, numbering about ten thousand advanced toward Kioggo; but being surprised there on the twenty-ninth of August, by twelve thousand Anglo-Hanoverians, they were beaten and dispersed.*

* This attack upon Copenhagen, without any previous declaration of war, and without any just cause of complaint against the conduct of Denmark as a neutral power, has been condemned by every impartial writer on that event. The English themselves do not attempt to justify it on any other ground than that of *expediency*,—a word so frequently employed to cover injustice, dishonesty and crime, by states as well as individuals.

The reply of the Prince-Royal to the demand of the English to surrender into their hands his entire naval force, was a noble one: "No example is to be found in history of so odious an aggression as that with which Denmark is

Capture of Copenhagen.—The efforts of the English negotiator and generals having failed to accomplish their object, they declared, on the second of September, that they would bombard the city. General Peymann had only a small number of troops of the line, but the bourgeoise militia of Copenhagen, had taken arms with the same enthusiasm as in 1801. But this force could do nothing against the thunders of the enemy's fleet and land battalions; this beautiful city was soon set on fire; in three days, six hundred houses became a prey to the flames, and a capitulation was the only means of saving the city from total destruction.

In the mean time the Prince Royal had hastily assembled the army cantoned in Holstein, and marched it to the coast of Fionia. Vain hope! The passage of the Belts was cut off, the capital had already fallen, and the English had carried away their fleet of eighteen ships and twenty-one frigates or brigs. Not content with despoiling all the maritime arsenals, they destroyed the Danish shipyards and all the utensils and machines used in building; then, with their important but odious trophies, they returned to the Thames. The exasperation of the Danes was such that the Prince Royal sent an order to General Peymann to burn the squadron rather than surrender it. But the officer who carried this order was taken in his attempt to penetrate into Copenhagen. Far from being discouraged by this misfortune, the king of Denmark indignant at such treatment, swore desperate war against the English, closed his ports against them, ordered the cessation of all relations with them, and

menaced; more honor may now be expected from the pirates of Barbary, than from the English government."

The injury to Copenhagen before the surrender was very great. The principal churches and public buildings were in ruins; eighteen hundred houses were destroyed; fifteen hundred inhabitants lost their lives, and a vast number were wounded. About three thousand five hundred pieces of artillery were captured, and the prize money distributed to the British troops was about four million and eight hundred thousand dollars.

seized upon British subjects and property throughout all the kingdom. This venerable prince never returned to his capital, but died shortly afterwards at Rendsbourg, and it is thought that the chagrin he felt at these reverses contributed to accelerate his end.

Assuredly, if the interest of state is sufficient to legitimatize such an aggression, and if the cabinet of London can, on this principle of great state policy, justify itself in the eyes of Europe, it would have been just, at least, to treat my enterprises with more indulgence than has been done; for no one of them was so unpardonable as this, and none but were as necessary for the interests of my empire as this was for England.

Brune takes Stralsund and Rugen.—As soon as I heard of the approach of the enemy's squadrons, I directed Brune to do every thing in his power to assist the Danes. After the peace of Tilsit, it was no longer for the interest of Sweden to remain in close alliance with England against France and Russia combined; this was to expose herself to certain ruin. But Gustavus IV., consulting only his passions, and influenced by the success of the English against the Danes whom he hated, did not fear to brave the threatening thunders, by himself breaking the armistice of Schlatkow. It is said that the promise of Norway and a part even of the Danish territory, led him to adopt this extravagant resolution.

I ordered Marshal Brune to get possession of Stralsund. This place, easily supplied by sea, was capable of a long defense. Chasseloup was charged with this siege, the means being supplied from the arsenals of Magdebourg, Berlin and Stettin. The attack, begun on the fifteenth of August, on three fronts, was pushed with uncommon activity. The recollection of the fine defense of this place by Charles XII., whom Gustavus pretended to imitate, was a powerful motive for him to hold out to the last extremity; but this prince possessed only the rashness of his ancestor, not his genius. The Swedes complained moreover, of the obstinacy of their sovereign. Abandoned by the English who had concentrated their forces in Zealand, and touched by the remonstrances of the magistrates, he ordered the place to be evacuated, and Brune took possession of it on the twentieth of August, finding four hundred pieces of cannon and the fortifications untouched. Fifteen days after, the island of Rugen was also ceded to us, in virtue of a capitulation requiring the Swedish army to retire to its own country and the fleet to leave the coasts of Germany. Stralsund was of no use to me for a continental war, but if I restored it to the Swedes it might be made a place of debarkation for the English; I therefore directed Brune to dismantle it.

Russia declares War against the English.—The affair of Copenhagen was the most insulting answer that could be given to the Emperor Alexander's offer of mediation. Justly indignant, he declaimed with energy against this infraction; but all his efforts being unable to prevent the spoliation of the fleet and the arsenals, it only remained for him to break off all relations with England; which he did by his manifesto of the seventh of November. After a long enumeration of griefs, the cabinet of St. Petersburg broke off all communication with England, recalled its legation, interdicted all relations between the two countries, proclaimed the principles of the armed neutrality, and declared that it would reëstablish nothing without first obtaining satisfaction for Denmark; it finally closed with these words:

"When the emperor shall be satisfied on all pending points, and especially on that of peace between France and England, without which no part of Europe can hope for real tranquillity, His Imperial Majesty will then willingly resume with Great Britain the relations of friendship, which, under the circumstances, the emperor has already preserved, perhaps, too long."

England replied by specious arguments, but without manifesting any sincere desire for an accommodation. War was now inevitable.

Intercession of Austria.—The cabinet of Vienna had already offered its mediation when the continental war was at its height in Poland. Invited to enter into the general league, it thought best to add its influence to that of Russia to induce England to make peace. If she should accept the proposition, it was thought at Vienna that this alone would dissolve the formidable league established under my influence. Two or three years of maritime peace would overthrow all the supports of this league, for it would then have no object. If, on the contrary, England should refuse, and Austria should be drawn into a rupture, the cabinet of Vienna flattered itself that it would obtain, on my part, a just indemnification; and to stimulate this expectation, I had already proposed to Francis I. such parts of the Turkish provinces as he might desire. Consequently the Count of Stahremberg, Austrian minister at the court of St. James, made strong efforts to induce the English cabinet to make concessions.

Negotiations respecting Turkey.—In the meantime matters took a more favorable turn for us at Constantinople than I had anticipated, which placed me in an embarrassing position in regard to Russia. The factionists who had dethroned Selim soon disputed among themselves for the spoils. The mufti triumphed over the caimacan by the aid of this same Cobakchi who, from an obscure chief of Yamacks, became for a time the regulator of the empire. Sebastiani was sufficiently adroit to secure his support, so that he soon exercised over Mustapha part of the influence which he had had over Selim. The issue of the enterprises of the English against Egypt, and of the naval combat of Lemnos, was calculated to increase this ascendency. As soon as the war with England had been formally declared, the new captain-pacha, Seyd-Ali, desirous of distinguishing himself, made sail with a squadron of nine ships, passed out of the Dardanelles, and, on the first of July, offered battle to his adversaries near Lemnos. The engagement was warm; the Russians, better instructed in naval tactics and better disciplined, broke the enemy's line, captured a vessel, and forced the captain-pacha to return into the Dardanelles; but having suffered themselves, they returned to Corfu, where they soon learned of the peace of Tilsit and of the armistice of Slobodza.

Colonel Guilleminot, sent to the army of the vizer to negotiate this armistice, had concluded it on the twenty-fourth of August. Michelsen was dead; his successor agreed to two articles which the Emperor Alexander rejected. Nevertheless the evacuation of the Principalities had commenced; the Turks violated the armistice by passing the Danube at Galacz, and by executing some Moldavian authorities established by the Russians. The latter, informed of the refusal of the emperor to ratify the armistice and of the infraction of the treaty, promptly reoccupied the left bank of the Danube.

But the treaty of Tilsit had completely changed the policy of the cabinet of London in regard to Russia and the Porte; it immediately ordered the evacuation of Alexandria, and attempted to reëstablish its relations with Turkey. Lord Paget endeavored to be admitted at Constantinople; but Sebastiani succeeded in procuring his rejection. On the other hand, the Turks had accepted my mediation. I therefore was obliged to decide upon the course I was to pursue. The good dispositions of the Divan had somewhat calmed my resentment against the persecutors of Selim. Sebastiani, whose opinion I had asked respecting a partition, opposed the project with specious arguments; should I renounce it, it would then be for my interest to act as mediator in order to conciliate the interests of the two nations from which I could derive equal advantages against my irreconcilable enemy, either to close the Black Sea, or to open to ourselves the gates of the East. I felt that, perhaps, I had gone too far in my conversations at Tilsit; I directed Savary, who was on a mission to St. Petersburg, to enter into explanations respecting the future fate of Moldavia and Walachia, and in regard to their evacuation, which the Turks insisted upon as a preliminary to any negotiations.

The Emperor Alexander opposed to him my promises; the Chancellor Romanof objected on account of the effect which this evacuation would have on public opinion, which was already very unfavorable to the treaty of Tilsit; the cession of these two Principalities was the only satisfaction which they could give to the nation for the sacrifices which this treaty had imposed. The position was becoming delicate. If the expulsion of the Turks from Europe often excited my imagination, as an enterprise both chivalric and philanthropic, I also felt that state policy rendered this project somewhat difficult. I thought that the care and profit of it should not be left to Russia alone; and that if I did not participate in it, I ought not to encourage it. On the other hand, I was of opinion that, with the concurrence of these two powers, we could close the Black Sea and the Levant against the English. To attain this great object, I could not sacrifice the Porte to Russia, nor could I fully and openly espouse the cause of the Turks against Russia, with whom I had just so intimately connected myself at Tilsit.

Statesmen will comprehend the difficulty of attaining my objects with means so heterogeneous. The cabinet of London, it is true, had succeeded, in 1799, in effecting this monstrous union of opposing elements, but all had then a common object—the prevention of our establishing ourselves in

Egypt—and all old resentments were hushed till that object could be accomplished. But my position was very difficult; I could only propose my good offices to bring about a peace. This, however, was no easy matter; the Emperor Alexander persisted in demanding the Principalities, and the Turks refused to discuss the subject, so long as the cession of these provinces was spoken of. It was to be feared that the mere proposition of abandoning the Principalities would throw the Divan into the arms of England, although this power had promised them to Russia in 1806. In state policy, the past is forgotten, and only the present is considered. The entire year was passed in discussions on the single question of the place of negotiations; Russia wished to have them conducted in Moldavia; and I preferred to treat by myself at Paris. My object was to gain time, till I had executed my projects on Rome, Portugal and Spain. If these projects should succeed, I should then be better prepared to pursue toward Russia the course which might seem preferable.

Distribution of New Titles of Nobility.—Before relating what took place in these countries, it may be well to say a few words in regard to France and the new nobility which I had just instituted. I was induced to this measure by powerful motives.

The scenes of Jena, Auerstedt, Pultusk, Eylau, Heilsberg, and even the victory of Friedland, had terribly thinned the ranks of my veterans of Boulogne; only the souvenirs of them existed in the regiments. The skeletons (*cadres*) were filled with young soldiers. I thought to stimulate them to new exertions by giving a just recompense to their predecessors for the glory acquired by so much courage and resignation. Moreover, the position of my throne required that I should leave to my successor a respectable class, interested in its maintainance. If a nobility be a doubtful support of thrones, and if it be true that nobles and priests are as factious as plebeians, at least this is not applicable to a new dynasty sustained by a nobility of its own creation.

Equality of ranks, in an old state demoralized by luxury, is a monstrous idea; and, as I have said before, I had resolved to destroy this deplorable result of the Revolution; but, in establishing social supremacies which were demanded by good morals and good sense, I sought to maintain *equality of rights*, without which there is only abuse and injustice. The institution of my nobility could not injure this *equality of rights*. The right of transmitting from father to son the souvenirs of services rendered to the state, is derived from the principle of property, and is nothing more than justice. Why is it permitted to transmit, in this way, wealth, often unjustly gained, and not to transmit the most valuable of all riches—honor?

The establishment of an hereditary nobility was calculated to reconcile, in time, New France with Europe and with Old France. It was substituting a nobility acquired by illustrious services, for one which was founded only on feudal rights. All Europe was governed by nobles who were armed against the French Revolution, and we found them an obstacle wherever we sought to introduce our influence. It was important to bring this contest to an end. To secure the fusion of the two nobilities, I wished to reconstitute the old; I was ready to stipulate that any family which had had among its ancestors a Marshal of France, or a Minister, should be susceptible of obtaining Ducal letters; an Admiral, a Lieutenant-general, an Archbishop, would have established claims to the title of Count, etc. It was sufficient to constitute the necessary *majorats*. This historical nobility would have combined the past, the present, and the future. A Montmorency would have been a duke, not because he was a Montmorency, but because one of his ancestors had been Constable. Every citizen who faithfully served the state, could aspire to the same grade and to the same title. This idea, like that of the Legion of Honor, was essentially liberal; the people attached to it no other meaning than that of reward for services rendered. Every one could merit it by services; all could obtain it at the same price; it was offensive to no one.

The spirit of my empire was a movement upwards—an elevation. Such, indeed, is the character of all revolutions. This spirit pervaded the whole nation; it had taken up arms in order that it might rise. I placed at the head of this movement, and as its object and reward, great recompenses. They were the result of public gratitude. They were to be kept in conformity with the spirit of equality, for the lowest soldier could obtain them by great deeds.

The statutes of March 1st, which accorded titles, were promulgated and produced a great sensation in France as well as in the army. I have never had the slightest reason to regret this measure. Perhaps the nominations were made too much in mass, and some of them without due consideration. If I had at first named only the marshals, and a hundred distinguished generals and colonels, reserving to myself the right of granting new titles and dotations, either after a a battle, or every year at some great national festival, I should have possessed a strong means of stimulating powerful exertions; but this would have produced dissatisfaction, and my object would not have been so well accomplished. Nevertheless, I repeat it, the distribution was too general, and it was intrusted too much to deputies. The secretaries of Berthier became the dispensers of glory; they appointed by the Imperial Almanac, and there were found among the elect, the names of colonels who had been killed a year or two before; certain generals, through accidental or intentional errors, received double dotations. This depreciated, in public estimation, one of my finest institutions and one of my noblest conceptions.

The Faubourg of St. Germain did not fail to ridicule these nobles of new creation. Even the army was less pleased with the measure than I had anticipated. Some attached little value to titles against which they had contended with so much success; they pretended to accept them merely as an act of obedience; others regarded them as a burden difficult to be borne; and the nomination being made by grade, it was looked upon as a system rather than a personal distinction. The same objection had been made to the Legion of Honor. But this latter had a very different object; it was intended as a distinction for all kinds of merit; those who had gained this distinction, had an incontestable right to it; it was not a favor. It must be confessed, however, that after an extensive distribution of this cross, I ought to have instituted one purely military. This I thought to do by instituting the order of Trois-Toisons, a project which was afterward abandoned.

There are great differences in the several European systems of reward for public services. All have their abuses. Austria and England are sparing in their use; Russia is prodigal. The best is a medium between these extremes. I abandoned the order of the Trois-Toisons, because the plan was objectionable. Ney, Davoust and many other brave generals who were not present at my three entries into Vienna, Berlin, and Madrid, but who had covered themselves with glory at a distance of fifty leagues, would have been excluded; this would have been unjust. Moreover, this institution would have awakened the disagreeable recollections of these powers which had now become my allies. But I might have instituted an order of merit exclusively military, in three classes, like the Legion of Honor; this would have been more acceptable to the army.

Suppression of the Tribunat.—During this year the *tribunat* was suppressed.* Having already lost its consideration by the elimination of its most distinguished members, this assembly was of no advantage to the progress of state affairs. The legislative body was sufficient for the discussion of projects of laws, and for afterward voting for their adoption or rejection. The senate, as an upper house, preserved the initiative of all great changes in public institutions, and a control over the measures of the lower house. It was indeed a mute government, but experience had somewhat

* The following history of the French Tribunat is copied from the Encyclopædia Americana:

"The French constitution of December 15, 1799, projected by Bonaparte and Sièyes, committed the legislative power, though more in appearance than in reality, to a body (*corps legislatif*) of three hundred men, and a *tribunat* of one hundred members chosen by the conservative senate, from the three lists of candidates proposed by the departmental colleges. To the three consuls was reserved the right of initiating laws; to the *tribunat*, that of deliberating on subjects thus proposed, and to the legislative body that of accepting or rejecting measures thus proposed by the first, and discussed by the second. The members of the council of state, as the mouth-pieces of the government, had a considerable influence in each body. The *tribunat* had also the privilege of expressing its wishes, and making representations to the government, and sometimes ventured to exercise this right. A *tribun* was to be twenty-five years old, and have a yearly income of fifteen thousand francs. The *tribunat* was renewed every five years, by the reëlection of one-fifth of its members yearly. The last voice of freedom in the *tribunat* was Carnot's speech in opposition to the election of Bonaparte, as emperor, in 1804. By the *sénatus-consulte organique* of May 18, 1804, its general meetings were abolished, and it was permitted to meet only by sections, of which there were three (for legislation, home affairs, and finance). In 1807, the *tribunat* was suppressed."

Many have supposed that the suppression of the Tribunat was virtually a prohibition of the liberty of discussing the laws prepared by the government. Such was not the case. It was simply a transfer of the right of discussion to the legislative body, which, under the constitution of 1799, voted silently and without any discussion whatever. By the present change that body recovered the faculty of speech, and was permitted to discuss the *projets de lois* submitted by the government. A part of the members of the suppressed Tribunat were transferred to the legislative body, and the others provided with places in the various administrative departments. The details of these changes are very fully given in Thiers' Consulate and Empire.

disgusted us with the declamations of the tribune. France in 1814 and in 1815, has shown whether I was right in distrusting large deliberative assemblies, where passion rules more than reason, and which are always basely servile in flattering authority, or visionary and imprudent in opposing it.

CHAPTER XII.

AFFAIRS OF SPAIN AND PORTUGAL; FROM THE BEGINNING OF THE PENINSULAR WAR TO THE CONVENTION OF CINTRA.

Affairs of Spain—Napoleon decides to occupy Portugal—Treaty of Fontainebleau—Junot occupies Portugal—Dissensions in the Royal Family—Talleyrand urges a War with Spain—Affairs of Italy—Napoleon's Interview with Lucien—The Milan Decree—Difficulties with the Pope—Napoleon's vast Designs in Italy—Projected Transfer of the Holy See to Paris—Occupation of Rome—Annexation of Tuscany to France—Difficulties in the Royal Family of Spain—The French occupy the Spanish Fortifications—Alarm of the Spanish Court—The pretended Project of removing it to Mexico—Political Explosion in Spain—The Revolution of Aranjuez—Murat enters Madrid—Napoleon's Instruction—Interview with the Spanish Court at Bayonne—He resolves to place a New Dynasty on the Throne—Objections to Napoleon's Plans—His Reasons for adopting them—Operations of Murat—Insurrection of the Second of May—Spanish Junta convoked at Bayonne—Napoleon's Conduct toward Ferdinand VII.—General Insurrection in Spain—Moncey driven from Valencia—Insurrection in Aragon—The Army of Galicia advances on Valladolid—Joseph proclaimed King of Spain—Dupont capitulates at Baylen—Beginning of the Siege of Saragossa—Retreat from Madrid—Romana flies from Denmark—Errors of the Campaign—Junot's Position in Portugal—General Interests of this Country—Sacrifices imposed on the Portuguese—General Insurrection in Portugal—Landing of Wellington and the English Army—Junot evacuates Portugal—Military Operations in the North of Europe.

Affairs of Spain.—It is time to direct our attention to the Iberian Peninsula, where a frightful revolution was about to take place. The negotiations opened with Portugal, in consequence of the treaty of Tilsit, did not prove successful; I expected this, and my measures were prepared to terminate the matter with this vassal of England. Relying on the weakness of Godoy, I also had good reason to count on Spain, and determined to attach her more irrevocably than ever to my interests.* For this purpose it was necessary to give a new basis to our relations, so as not only to induce her to adopt the Continental system with all my commercial regulations, but also to secure myself from any new hesitations on her part.

The famous and imprudent proclamation of the Prince of Peace had proved that this power adhered to France from fear, rather than from that strong community of interests which had presided at the family pact of 1762, and the treaty of St. Ildefonso. If she made the least retrograde step from the system which she had heretofore followed, I might expect at any moment to see her in the arms of England. What would then have been the result of all the efforts which I had made for the last ten years?

It is true, as has already been said, that the cabinet of Madrid had some reason for complaints respecting the Balearic Isles, and that the battle of Trafalgar had already disposed them to regret this alliance. The English party had daily gained strength since these events; of this I was

* English and Spanish historians state that Napoleon's attempt to subjugate Spain was planned at Tilsit. On the contrary, there seems to have been no such design on his part; he was drawn into it step by step by the political events which occurred from time to time. Thiers, who has had an opportunity to examine unpublished French and Spanish documents on this subject, says: "I declare that all the historians who have represented the origin of Napoleon's designs upon Spain as dating so far back as Tilsit are mistaken; that all those who have supposed that Napoleon assured himself at Tilsit of the consent of Alexander to what he projected respecting Madrid, and that he was in haste to sign the peace of the North, in order to return the sooner to the affairs of the South, are equally mistaken. At Tilsit Napoleon settled nothing but a general alliance, which guaranteed the adhesion of Russia to all that he should do on his part, on condition that Russia should be suffered to do what she pleased on hers. At this period, he did not at all consider it urgent to interfere in the affairs of Spain; he was full of resentment on account of the proclamation of the Prince of Peace, promised himself to express his sentiments upon it some day, and to secure himself, but thinking at his return of nothing but imposing peace upon England, by threatening her with complete exclusion from the continent, and of making use of the cabinet of Madrid to bring the cabinet of Lisbon into his projects."

not ignorant. All who resided in the sea-ports, or who had an interest in Spanish America, wished for peace with England. My difficulties with the Pope influenced the opinion of the clergy. Nevertheless, public opinion was still on my side, and all the public animadversions fell on Godoy. Although he had repaired his error toward me by sending the corps of Romana to the north, I nevertheless felt convinced that I could not venture to count too much on the continuance of his blind devotion.

These extraordinary threats of the cabinet of Madrid had the advantage of discovering to me the precipice, not before perceived, but whose depth I now might sound. Not only my Continental system, but still more, my maritime system, would fall, if Spain should ever join the interests of England. I had reason to fear this sooner or later, and especially so, since what had just occurred. Not only was the prosperity of France warmly interested in this, but also my own dynasty. If Charles IV. had abandoned the Bourbon interest in France, what guarantee had I that his successor would do the same, and that Godoy would not renew the foolish enterprise of 1806? What would become of me, if, while in the heart of Poland with all my forces, a French prince, assisted by one hundred thousand Anglo-Spaniards, should present himself at Bordeaux? Even supposing that there was no danger of such an attempt during my life, what a powerful motive would be left for future troubles, if even, after my death, the Peninsula should become the point of support for some new Pretender, assisted by England! It was the lever of Archimedes which would overthrow my empire.

If I had at first intended to dethrone the Spanish branch of the Bourbons, and this had been my only object, I should have profited by my alliance at Tilsit, and the grounds of complaint afforded by the proclamation of the Prince of Peace, to openly declare war. This would have been the most loyal course, and one which best accorded with my character; but it would have produced precisely what I wished to avoid; at the first sound of cannon, all the ports of Spain and Spanish America would have been open to the English, and the English influence would have been established for a long time at Madrid, Cadiz and Mexico. An idea, much less chivalric, but much more expedient, naturally presented itself to my mind; this was to secure for ever my ascendency and my influence in the Peninsula by ceding Portugal to Spain and demanding of her in exchange the provinces between the Pyrenees and the Ebro. *This was all I could desire to completely secure my control even to the heart of the monarchy, to make it dependent on me, and to break forever the English connection with Portugal, and consequently with Spain.**

Napoleon decides to occupy Portugal.—Portugal presented itself naturally as the first step for attaining the object of my enterprise. England had reëstablished here all her influence and her monopoly. The first step taken in accordance with the treaty of Tilsit to oblige the Prince-Regent to enter into this grand alliance, had no other results than to confirm England respecting the tenor of the secret articles of this treaty. It was to London that the Prince-Regent went to ask what response he should make to my

* Several historians, Spanish, Portuguese and English, have stated the determination of the Prince Regent to emigrate to Brazil, was fixed by the British ambassador's communicating to him a decree of Napoleon in the *Moniteur* of November 11th, "*that the House of Braganza had ceased to reign.*" Alison repeats this story, but says the ominous line appeared in the *Moniteur* of November 13th. Thiers says that no such phrase can be found in the *Moniteur* of these or any posterior or anterior date. But in an article of the *Moniteur* of the twelfth, commentating on the conduct of the English at Copenhagen and Constantinople, it is remarked, that these English intrigues in Portugal, if persisted in, might produce the downfall of the House of Braganza. It is quite probable, however, that Lord Strangford did make the statement, as represented, in order to influence the Prince Regent to leave Portugal.

summons! I had judged, by the negotiations of 1801, the interest taken by the cabinet of St. James in its relations with this country, since the mere approach of General Leclerc's army had done more to decide them to sign the preliminaries of peace than any thing else that took place at that epoch in Europe.

I knew, therefore, that the occupation of Portugal would give a marked blow to British commerce and British policy. The same lesson of the past convinced me that the Prince-Regent, yielding to the rule of necessity, would promise for the moment whatever I might desire. But we could never count on his sincerity, for his course was already determined on; he would prefer to transport his residence to Brazil rather than enter frankly into my alliance. He had been preparing himself for this for the last four years, and avowed it formally by his proclamation of the second of October. When the storm threatened him more nearly, he indeed offered to close his ports to the English; but so little dependence was to be placed on his promises, that two days after, (October 22, 1807,) his envoys signed, at London, a more close alliance with England! It was evident that he merely wished to gain time enough to secure the emigration of all his court, with the archives and the superior employees of the government. Moreover, the mere expulsion of the British flag had not prevented, under a borrowed flag, Portugal from being used as an English colony by English factors established in Portugal, and by companies having the exclusive trade in the wines of Oporto. I, therefore, demanded the expulsion of the English, and the confiscation of their property and merchandise. The Prince Regent, who had not the same motives for hatred and vengeance as I had, could not agree to these conditions; had he promised, his people would not have suffered him to accomplish it.

The formal refusal of this prince determined me. I saw

that it required a power as formidable as mine, to effect an entire change in the future relations of Portugal. I decided on the partition of this kingdom, and the expulsion of the House of Braganza. There was, it is true, more violence than justice in this measure; but I hoped from it the eternal expulsion of the English from the Peninsula; an immense result for the accomplishment of my projects, and for the future greatness of my empire. Of course I had the same right to this usurpation, as the English had to burn Copenhagen and carry off the Danish fleet. If they did not keep that country, it was merely because they had not forces sufficient to maintain themselves in it. The formal occupation of the kingdom of Portugal enabled me either to dispose of it at my pleasure, or to exchange it for Etruria and the provinces from the Pyrenees to the Ebro; it might moreover serve as an introduction to the eventual occupation of Spain itself.*

Treaty of Fontainebleau.—The better to attain my objects, I proposed to the cabinet of Madrid the partition of Lusitania. A treaty to this effect was concluded at Fontainebleau on the twenty-seventh of October, 1807. It procured me the possession of Etruria, and the Infante of Parma received in exchange the province of Minho; Godoy, the Algarves, and Alentejo; the remainder was to be sequestered till peace, and Charles IV. proclaimed emperor of the (Spanish) Americas. The court of Madrid entirely adopted my

* This is not good logic. The conduct of the English at Copenhagen, did not justify the seizure of Portugal by the French. The only tenable ground for justifying the invasion of Portugal was, that by the long dependence of this government upon England, and its entire submission to English dictation, Portugal had become a mere vassal state, and had thereby lost her rights as a sovereign and independent power. She, therefore, could not, in a war with England, claim the rights of a neutral state. There can be no doubt that Portugal at this time was as much under the dominion of England as any of her dependencies in Asia, Africa or America, and had about as little claim to the rights of neutrality. But great conquerors, like Napoleon, pay little regard to the forms or principles of International Law.

'views; it not only granted a passage to our troops, but placed a corps of the élite at my disposal in order to secure the success of the enterprise.

Junot occupies Portugal.—At the approach of the army commanded by Junot,* the Prince Regent promised everything that was desired of him; but such had always been the case. Nevertheless my lieutenant, having orders to occupy Portugal at all events, continued to advance. The terrified court embarked for Brazil, and left me its kingdom, by transporting a European dynasty to an American throne.

Informed of this project by the proclamation of the second of October, I had directed Junot to make all haste to prevent the embarkation; but my declaration of November fifteenth, announcing that *the House of Braganza had ceased to reign*, inserted too soon in the Moniteur, reached Lisbon, by way of London and the sea, in eight days.† The Prince Regent, dethroned by my decrees, was relieved from further uncertainty respecting the course he should take, and deemed it prudent not to await the approach of my troops. He embarked on the twenty-seventh of November, and took with him a treasure of five hundred millions, and a fleet of eight ships, three frigates, four brigs, leaving behind five ships, five frigates and twelve schooners, which he was unable to take away. Contrary winds retained them two days in the

* Andoche Junot, duke of Abrantes, was born in 1771, at Bussy-les-Forges. He first studied law, but afterward entered the army, and at the siege of Toulon was made Napoleon's secretary. Just as he had finished a dispatch during this siege, a shell which fell near him covered him with dust. Turning to Bonaparte, he coolly remarked: "This comes just in time, I wanted some sand to dry my writing." This gave the general a high opinion of his courage, and he appointed him aide-de-camp. He accompanied Napoleon to Italy and Egypt, and served in most of his campaigns, receiving numerous wounds. For his early success in Portugal he received the title of duke of Abrantes, but his subsequent operations proved his utter want of capacity to command a separate army. In 1812, he commanded the eighth corps and distinguished himself at the battle of Valoutina. He died in 1813.

† *Vide* Note on page 353.

Tagus ; our troops were within two leagues, and the next day entered Lisbon.

Junot had marched with such precipitation that he had crossed, without the slightest precaution, the sterile country from Alcantara to Castelbranco and the frightful mountains which separate this city from Abrantes, where his army was near perishing. He reached Lisbon with only two or three thousand men, who resembled spectres more than conquerors. This rapidity was requisite to prevent the emigration of the government. Junot deemed this object so important that he entered Lisbon with only a feeble escort, and even fired at the departing squadron with the Portuguese batteries, so great was the terror which preceded him. He nevertheless was too late, and this imprudent and precipitate march contributed not a little to our ulterior reverses in this country, by exhibiting to the Portuguese our young and famished conscripts as adversaries not very formidable,—a first impression which was never effaced. The history of the miseries endured by this army would have turned me from my projects, if I had not been entirely deceived respecting the character of the nations which I wished to subdue.

While Junot was thus making his adventurous march to Lisbon, the Spanish General Taranco took possession of the provinces of the Douro, and the marquis of Salano penetrated by Alentejo to Evora and Setuval ; a Spanish division under General Caraffa, had followed Junot to Lisbon.

Dissensions in the Royal Family of Spain.—At this epoch, domestic quarrels of a scandalous nature disgraced the family of Charles IV. The Prince of Peace, abusing his influence, humiliated the heir to the throne ; and the latter, seeking shelter from the vexations of the favorite, authorized by his father, had asked of me the hand of a princess of my house, with the hope of securing my protection. Unfortunately, I then had at my disposal none but the daughter of Lucien

Her father had so ill conducted himself toward me that I could hardly reward him for it by giving a throne to his daughter, over whom he would exercise more influence than I could. Moreover I had no great confidence in this step of Ferdinand. This prince had married, as his first wife, the daughter of Queen Caroline, of Naples, the most implacable of my enemies; I knew that this connection had influenced his political sentiments, and that his hatred to Godoy had alone caused his proposed connection with France.

Nevertheless, the false steps recently taken against me by the favorite and the demand of a princess of my house by Ferdinand, was sufficient proof that the hatred of this prince was susceptible of change; he called me in his letter, *the great man of the age.* But was this step of the prince of the Asturias legal? An hereditary prince, who, without the consent of his king, establishes relations with a foreign dynasty, is the most guilty of state criminals. I deferred answering him. It was necessary first of all to have some explanations with my brother Lucien.

Talleyrand urges War against Spain.—Talleyrand, whose pride equaled his ambition, had left, at the end of 1807, the department of foreign affairs, in the quality of Vice-Grand-Elector, an office which had been created for him, as that of vice-constable had been for Berthier. A base jealousy actuated this vain diplomatist, and a question of the antechamber made him leave a post where he had more importance and power, in order not to suffer the proximity of a rival whom he detested. Skillful in directing an intrigue, Talleyrand was a man of business rather than a statesman. He had an easy and luminous way of presenting things. His work suited me, and I did all I could to turn him from the ridiculous change which he solicited. He was replaced by Champagny.

At the time of the ordinary trip to Fontainebleau, and of

the dissensions in the royal family of Spain, he had already begun to regret having left the ministry; he was tired of inaction, and thought that I might consent, perhaps, to give him a kind of supreme control over our foreign relations, and also allow him to retain his new dignity. With this object he overwhelmed me with memoirs, notes, and conversations, tending to prove that I had only to show myself with thirty thousand men to subjugate Spain. Europe was strangely deceived in this matter, for it deemed him, on his own word, to have opposed the war.

Affairs of Italy.—Far from adopting his views, I wished to begin by securing to myself the line of the Ebro, and then to wait the course of events. After the signature of the treaty of Fontainebleau, I repaired to Italy. I had several objects in view in this journey; I hoped that my presence in this country might decide Austria to enter frankly into our grand alliance against England. This object was accomplished, for the cabinet of Vienna soon directed Count Stahremberg to quit London, if his mediation should be rejected; and in fact this embassador left England the early part of February. Moreover I imposed on the Pope, and made him enter into an Italian Confederacy like that of the Rhine, composed of Naples, Etruria, the kingdom of Italy, and the states of the Pope, under my protectorate.

Interview with Lucien.—I afterward wished to come to explanations on the proposition made by the prince of the Asturias. Lucien had been embassador to Madrid, and was well acquainted with this court; by placing his daughter* on the throne, he would have been able to serve my policy; but I demanded, as a pledge of his obedience, that he should separate from his wife whose conduct was far from irreproachable and who had lived with him publicly as his mistress.†

* This daughter was by Mademoiselle Boyer, Lucien's first wife.

† This was the widow of the banker Jouberteau, whom Lucien had married

I wished to ally my brother to one of the greatest sovereign houses in Europe. And the act of obedience which I required would have been in my estimation a sufficient pledge of his future sentiments, and have redoubled the honor of my family. We had an interview at Mantua. Lucien consented to the marriage of his daughter, but refused the conditions which I made to a reconciliation; I had everything to apprehend from a brother who gave to Europe this dangerous example of scorning my wishes; of a madman, who was sacrificing to his base inclinations the throne of Spain, and the destinies of France; a deplorable blindness, since it had great influence on my own disasters as well as those of Spain!!

The celebrated Milan Decree.—It was on my return from this interview that I issued my famous Milan decree, in reprisal for the new pretensions of England. When near the accomplishment of my grand system, I received the British Order in Council of November 11th, declaring *that all countries occupied by our troops, or excluding the English flag from their ports, should be considered in a state of blockade; and that every vessel destined for such countries, should be subject to visit, stopped in the open seas, taken to English ports, and made to pay such an imposition as should be fixed by law of Parliament.*

This was subjecting our commerce and that of Europe to an infamous tax, since it admitted a kind of suzerainty, and right of control in the English over all foreign goods crossing the high seas; this was stamping the seal of infamy on all powers which should willingly submit to such a code. I opposed to it the Milan decree of December 17th. It declared:

1st. *That every vessel which should conform to the British Order in Council, should be denationalized, treated as an*

at the end of 1803. This marriage greatly enraged Napoleon, and was the foundation of the misunderstanding between the two brothers.

English vessel and a good prize, whether taken in the ports of the continent, or captured on the high seas.

2d. *That the British Isles should be declared in a state of blockade, on land and on sea, and that any vessel sailing to or from these islands, or their colonies, should be a good prize.*

Thus one abuse led to another, in this fatal career in which we were urged by our bitter hatred; nevertheless, this corsair legislation would have resulted in the detriment of our enemies, had it not been for the lamentable event which opened to the English the ports of Spain and of Spanish America.

Difficulties with the Pope.—At this epoch a quarrel, not very serious in appearance, but which might, however, have led to serious results, took place between me and the Pope. Since the *articles réglementaires* which I had added to the concordat, or rather, since the return of Pius VII. from my coronation without having obtained the restitution of the provinces as he had hoped, the Holy See had commenced a little underhand war, which had become the most bitter at the epoch of 1805. The court of Rome complained that, in its temporal relations, I had required it to enter into this Italian confederation.

An English and Russian squadron was then preparing to effect a landing in Calabria and even in Naples. The French *corps-d'armée*, placed in the *presqu'ile* of Otranto, would have been lost if the Pope had consented, through worldly ambition, to ally himself with *heretics*. I demanded of the Holy See that it should receive a garrison in Ancona, and conclude an offensive and defensive alliance against the coalition, with the viceroy of Italy and the king of Naples. It refused to do this.

After the peace of Presburg, a French army entered Naples, and it became more necessary than ever for me to communicate with my army through the Roman states. In the mean time, without troubling himself with the condition of Austria, the Pope had surrendered himself to English councils. Agents were exciting the people to revolt; every where from Ancona to the frontiers of Naples, they murdered our soldiers. General Bentinck had organized a focus of insurrection in Sicily, and his great laboratory was in Rome. I warned the Pope of this, and summoned him to close his ports to the enemies of France, to drive them from Rome, and to frankly make common cause with us. I renewed these demands at the time of my journey to Milan, and my proposition for entering into the Italian confederation was no better received. The Holy See responded by menaces which would hardly have been pardonable in the time of Gregory VII. This was to completely annul my position in Italy, and to permit a handful of degenerate Romans under the monastic yoke to oppose all that I could do to aggrandize this peninsula; such a state of things could not continue.

Lombardy already began to appreciate the efforts which I was making for the regeneration of that country. The army was naturally the main object of my care; no means were neglected to revive a military feeling in this people, debased by three centuries of foreign domination; I revived the love of glory by constructing great monuments. The Forum-Bonaparte, an enterprise worthy of the Romans, was to be built on the ruins of the citadel of Milan. The project had been traced out by the celebrated Antolini, but its execution was deferred till peace; in the mean time a magnificent arena and a circus, which would have done honor to the most glorious era of Rome, were raised in a portion of this same ground. The superb triumphal arch of the Simplon, projected on the avenue of Domodossola, was to carry to the remotest ages the memory of the campaign of the St. Bernard, and the resurrection of the Italian Republic. Measures were also taken to encourage letters. Some have reproached me with having imposed chains on literature, or with having degraded it to such eulogies as I ordered; this is absurd; to repress abuses is not to oppose an obstacle to *belles-lettres* under a glorious reign; and if eulogies were pronounced upon the great things which I undertook, it was because there could be no better theme for letters than in celebrating immortal works.

Napoleon's vast Designs in Italy.—I moreover had vast designs on Italy. This long *presqu'île* with Sardinia, Corsica, and Sicily, presented a sea-coast of not less than one thousand two hundred leagues; it had once ruled the world by its armies, and it seemed not the less intended by nature to rule the seas. Too narrow and deep for a continental power, it did not offer the necessary surface for manœuvering easily on either slope of the Apennines; the invading armies have always been obliged merely to attack the defensive forces in front. An enemy, coming from the north, and making himself master of Rome on the one side and Pesaro on the other, would be in quiet possession of all the country in his rear, for the Italian army driven back into Calabria, could only act by debarkations. As a maritime power, on the contrary, Italy would be formidable.

The Genoese and Venetian sailors for three centuries disputed the commerce of the East, and they would have played a much greater part, had not their country been divided up into twenty smaller states. Magnificent roadsteads, like those of Spezzia, Tarentum, Cataro, Ragusa; considerable ports, as Genoa, Leghorn, Naples, Ancona, Venice, Ragusa, Corfu; an abundance of sailors; a proximity to Macedonia, Bosnia, and Albania, whose vast forests furnished the finest ship-timbers; and to Hungary from which copper could be obtained with facility:—such are some of the innumerable advantages presented by Italy for equipping large fleets. Time and money were only necessary to equip, in this country, a naval force of fifty ships and as many frigates, and, in concert with Spain, France and Holland, to put an end to English supremacy.

Transfer of the Holy See to Paris.—The first step toward the regeneration of Italy, was to put an end to the temporal power of the Pope. The possession of the Roman States was essential in order to connect Naples, that is eight millions of southern Italians, with the kingdom of Italy, Tuscany, Genoa, Piedmont, Cisalpine, or the eight millions of northern Italians. To take possession of the Roman States, and still leave there the spiritual power of the Pope, was a difficult matter, as it would have been forging arms against myself. I found a unique and admirable means of attaining my object, in executing a double project which would leave me free arbiter of the Roman States, and at the same time reënforce my authority by all the influence left to the Holy See in Europe. This was to transfer the head of this church to Paris, and afterward to unite the people of Italy as a single nation.

It was with this object, and on the news of the agitation which reigned at Rome, that I resolved to make an end of the matter. A few days after my victorious entrance into Vienna, and four days previous to the battle of Essling, I issued my decree, annexing Rome and the States of the Church. What immense results would have sprung from this project, if I had succeeded in it? I should have rid the empire of all ultramontane intrigues; I should have procured for it, by the influence of the Pope, a great ascendency over the Catholics of Poland, Hungary, Ireland, Spain and Portugal. And by retempering the descendants of the ancient Romans, and putting them in the same mould with the Neapolitans, and Lombards, I might make Italy a respectable maritime power, since she would have as much coast and as many ports as France. The Pope would also have gained more than he lost by this project, for instead of being a petty prince of Italy, he would have become the second personage in Europe.

Occupation of Rome.—Perhaps I committed an error in hastening too much the execution of this design. It was important for me to spare the Pope as much as possible, at the moment when I was dealing my blows in Spain and Portugal; but, drawn on by the moral effect produced on me by the hostile course of the Roman Pontiff, at the moment when the alliance of Tilsit gave him up to my discretion, I ordered, at the end of January, 1808, a corps of six thousand men to enter Rome, and I demanded the cession of the Marches, and a frank adhesion to the Italian league. The Pope, proud of being placed on his own field of battle, thought to defend his temporal power by replying to me with the thunders of the church. Briefs,* bulls, complaints, menaces, were redoubled. His brief of March 27th, 1808, especially, held language to which I was little accustomed; it threatened me with excommunication, I replied to it by a decree annexing Ancona and the Marches to the kingdom of Italy.

Annexation of Tuscany to France.—These partial reunions were, as I have said, only a prelude to a more vast design; some weeks after, having given a part of the Roman States to the kingdom of Italy, I pronounced the reunion of Tuscany and the duchy of Parma with France. The treaty of Fontainebleau had given me this country in exchange for a part of Portugal. It was important for me to hasten to take possession of it, and, by transporting the limits of my empire to the Ombrone, I should give a more solid basis to my influence over Naples.

* A *brief* is distinguished from a *bull*, in being more concise, written on paper, sealed with red wax, and impressed with the seal of the fisherman, or Peter in a boat. A *bull* is more ample, written on parchment, and sealed with lead or green wax.

Napoleon renounces the Alliance of Ferdinand.—I returned from Italy to France more indignant than ever with Lucien, and very little disposed to satisfy the wish of Ferdinand. I had not so replied to him; this was a fault with which posterity will reproach me, although it was not exclusively mine. It was the result of circumstances. *But what would have been said of me, if, justly distrusting Ferdinand and his counsellors as I did, I had moreover placed Lucien, in the quality of his father-in-law, at the head of the opposition against me?*

Ferdinand arrested by his Father's Orders.—Events soon became so complicated as to render it uncertain what course I ought to pursue. Godoy, hearing of the proposition which Ferdinand had made to me, to marry a princess of the imperial family, and of the conferences which this prince had had on the subject with the embassador, Beauharnois, thought that his own existence depended on his preventing this union, which would secure the triumph of the heir to the throne, on whom he had cast so many indignities. Trembling at the consequences of such an event, he induced Charles IV. to consider this intrigue as a serious matter, and to have his son tried, as a state criminal, by the high court of the Council of the Indies and of Castile; he was made prisoner in the palace, (October 29), and there was every probability that this prince would experience the same fate as the unfortunate Don Carlos, who was condemned by Philip II. I succeeded in saving him; Charles IV. pardoned his son; but proceeded against his counsellors.

Napoleon occupies the Spanish Fortifications.—The occupation of Portugal required a line of posts across Spain; this arrangement accorded very well with my views. Under pretext of sustaining Junot, I had pushed Murat on the Ebro, with fifty thousand men. Duhesme entered into Catalonia as if merely to cross and rejoin Murat. He succeeded in placing garrisons in Figuièras and into the citadel of Barcelona; Murat also succeeded, by subterfuge, in garrisoning Pampeluna and St. Sebastian. I shall not undertake to justify these steps, though they will appear less censurable, if it be remembered that these places were to fall to me in the projected exchange of Portugal for the provinces of the Ebro. By occupying them I wished to prevent all idea of resistance on the part of the Spaniards, and to more easily remove all scruples that might oppose this exchange; history had taught me that, in great enterprises, success justifies the means; the result of my enterprise was to be so immense that I sacrificed every other consideration to its success. I deemed myself the more certain of becoming the arbiter of Spain, as the *élite* of the Spanish army was with Romana, near Denmark, and twenty-five thousand men had just entered Portugal with Junot. An unexpected revolution soon gave a different aspect to affairs.

Alarm of the Spanish Court.—There being no further reason for delay, and Portugal being agitated by the rumor of a partition, I directed Junot to take possession of the whole country in my name. This step was a natural prelude to the projected cession, for before ceding away a country, it is necessary either to establish a claim to it, or to gain possession of it as a right of conquest. This apparent violation of the treaty of Fontainebleau was a thunder-clap to Godoy and his partisans, who did not comprehend its motive. Combined with the clandestine occupation of the fortresses, this measure discovered to him the abyss which was opening beneath his feet. He remembers his proclamation; the trial of Ferdinand, the marriage project, and trembles at being exposed to my vengeance. He persuades Charles IV. that I am going to treat him as I had done the Prince-Regent of Portugal. With this idea he induces him to transfer the court to Seville, where he can defend himself on the left bank of the Tagus, or, if beaten, fly to America.

Project of removing it to Mexico.—Godoy has been accused of contriving with me the removal of the royal family to Mexico, the same as the family of Braganza had taken refuge in Brazil. Two circumstances will be sufficient to demonstrate the folly of these allegations: the 1st, is the importance attached by England to the departure of John VI. to Rio Janeiro, and her interest in having Charles IV. imitate his example: the 2d, is the opposition made by my embassador, Beauharnais, to this departure. I, indeed, blamed him for it afterward, but the course he pursued is proof that no such project had been previously concerted; I merely reproached my minister for not allowing them to execute this unexpected resolution, which would have simplified this question and rendered me absolute arbiter of Spain, instead of plunging me into the inextricable embarrassments of a revolution.

If the emigration of Charles IV. to America had been my original object, it might very properly be imputed to me as a fault; I knew too well the hazard of presenting myself to the Spaniards as the arbiter of their destinies, bringing, as its first pledge, the separation of their colonies. The progress of affairs might lead to this result; but it never entered as a basis in my projects. As an alternative, I should prefer to see the Bourbons in Mexico than in Madrid. Moreover, it was possible that Charles IV., placed on the throne of Mexico, might connect himself by a good treaty with the mother country, and that this vast transatlantic empire, revivified, under a direct and concentrated government, might at least sustain the independence of its flag and of its commerce. If I attained neither of these two objects, I might at least give a strong impulse to the interior of Spain, and give her more vigorous institutions, in order to direct all her energies to a maritime war. *At all events, it is certain that, if England preserved the universal empire of the seas, America would sooner or later fall into her dependence, but, the only means of disputing this empire with her, was to secure the resources of Spain. If, by the aid of these resources, I should succeed in reëstablishing the maritime equilibrium and the liberty of commerce, the emancipation of Spanish America would profit French industry as much as the English.*

Political Explosion in Spain.—Be this as it may, the news of the departure of the court to Seville, spread through Spain, became an electric spark, which occasioned a sudden and terrible explosion. Public opinion in this country had not kept pace with the rest of Europe. The lights of intelligence had not penetrated either the highest or the lowest class, but was confined to the middle classes of the petty nobility, men of the robe, and the secular clergy. These felt the degradation of their country and blushed to obey a government which was conducting it to its destruction. They were called liberals.

Revolution of Aranjuez.—The rumor of my projects, amplified and interpreted to suit party passions, set every thing into fermentation. The monks, fearing for their influence, deemed themselves lost, if my government should be extended to Spain ; for the catholicism of the concordats was not what suited them. The liberals felt the humiliation of their country ; all thought to prevent its ruin by a conspiracy.

In the night of the nineteenth of March, 1808, the people of Madrid go in a crowd to Aranjuez and demand the head of Godoy ; the army, and even the body guards, as at Paris, place themselves at the head of the revolution. The Prince of Peace, concealed in a granary, escapes from search ; happily for him, he was not discovered till afterward, and they then satisfied themselves in securing his person, after having maltreated him. The old king, frightened by the cries of the multitude, and the insinuations of the conspirators, abdicated in favor of his son. The Spaniards gained nothing by this change, for the son whom they placed on the throne would have conducted matters no better than his father. But they rid themselves of an execrated favorite, and this was much in the eyes of the multitude, who do not look below the surface of things.

Murat enters Madrid.—Murat, on hearing of the troubles at Aranjuez, immediately directed himself on Madrid with thirty thousand men who were cantoned in Castile; he entered this capital on the twenty-third of March. A few days after, Charles IV., recovering from his stupor, and incited by Godoy and the queen, retracted his abdication, and declared that it had been drawn from him by force. He cared little about the crown, but much about its being given to his son. This entrance of Murat into Madrid was an imprudent and premature step. The grand-duke of Berg flattered himself that he should be placed on the throne of Charles V., and his desire to accomplish this object hurried him on, without reflection, to whatever seemed calculated to hasten this desired event. So far was I from having decided to change the dynasty, that, only a few days before this news reached me, I had remitted to Eugenio Isquierdo (the Spanish embassador), the basis of a treaty, *ceding to Charles IV. all Portugal, for an equivalent territory between the Pyrenees and the Ebro; I guaranteed to him the rest of his monarchy on condition that he opened the ports of America to French ships and French commerce.*

I was aware that this alienation of four provinces might meet with some difficulties; but by being already in possession of them, the main obstacle was removed, for, on the one hand, I would only ask for provinces which I already possessed, on the other, offer a more than equivalent indemnity from territory already in my power. This was the secret object of my occupation of a part of the kingdom, and of the presence of Murat in Castile.

Napoleon's Instructions to Murat.—Nothing better proves the correctness of my views in this affair, than the letter which I wrote to Murat, on the twenty-seventh of March, on learning the revolution of Aranjuez:

"To the grand-duke of Berg: I fear that you deceive me on the situation of Spain, and that you are yourself deceived. The affair of the nineteenth of March has signally complicated events; I am in great perplexity.

"Do not believe that you are attacking an unarmed nation, and that you have only to show your troops to subjugate Spain; the revolution of the twentieth of March proves that there is still energy in the Spaniard. You have to deal with a new people; they have all the courage, and they will have all the enthusiasm, which is met with among men who are not worn out by political passions.

"The aristocracy and the clergy are the real masters of Spain; if they fear for their privileges and for their existence, they will make *levées en masse* against us which may render the war interminable. I have partisans; if I present myself as a conqueror, I shall have none. The Prince of Peace is detested, because he is accused of having given up Spain to France; this is the complaint which has served for the usurpation of Ferdinand; the popular party is more weak. The prince of the Asturias has none of the qualities requisite for the head of a nation; but this will not prevent that, to oppose us, they should make a hero of him. I do not wish that any influence should be used toward the personages of this family; there is never any use in making ourselves odious and in influencing passions. Spain has near one hundred thousand men under arms; this is more than enough to sustain with advantage an interior war; divided on different points they can serve as a nucleus for the total rising of the monarchy.

"I present to you the general views of such obstacles as are inevitable. There are others which you will meet. England will not fail to take advantage of this occasion to multiply our embarrassments. She daily sends dispatch-vessels to the forces which she keeps on the coast of Portugal, and in the Mediterranean she is enrolling Sicilians and Portuguese.

"As the royal family have not left Spain for the Indies, nothing but a revolution can change the state of this country; and perhaps of all Europe this country is the least prepared for such a change. The men who see the monstrous vices of this government and the anarchy which has taken the place of legal authority, are few in number; the majority profit by these vices and by this anarchy. In the interest of my empire, I can do much good for Spain. What are the best means of doing this? Shall I go to Madrid? Shall I exercise the act of a grand protectorate in pronouncing between the father and son? It seems to me difficult to support Charles IV. on the throne. His government and his favorite are so unpopular that they cannot sustain themselves for three months. Ferdinand is the enemy of France; this is the reason of their making him king. To place him on the throne will serve the factions, which, for twenty-five years, have labored for the ruin of France. A family alliance would be a feeble bond. Queen Elizabeth and other French princesses have perished miserably, when they could be immolated with impunity, to satisfy atrocious vengeances. I think that nothing should be precipitated; that we should take council from the events which shall follow. It will be necessary to strengthen the *corps-d'armée* on the frontiers of Portugal and to wait. * * *

"I do not approve of the course of your Imperial Highness in thus precipitately taking possession of Madrid; you should have kept the army ten leagues from this capital. You have no assurance that the people and the magistracy will recognize Ferdinand without a contest. The Prince of Peace must have partisans in the public employments; there is, moreover, an habitual attachment to the old king which may produce results. Your entrance into Madrid, by disquieting the Spaniards, has powerfully served Ferdinand. I have given orders to Savary to go near the new king to learn what is passing. He will concert with V. A. I.; I will hereafter advise what course is to be pursued. In the meantime I have marked out the course which I deem it proper to direct.

"You will not compromise me to an interview in Spain with Ferdinand, unless you deem the situation of things to be such that I ought to recognize him as king of Spain; you will conduct yourself respectfully toward the king, the queen and Prince Godoy. You will exert yourself in their favor, and render them the same honors as heretofore. You will regulate your conduct in such a way that the Spaniards shall be unable to divine what course I intend to pursue; it will not be difficult for you to do this, as I myself even do not know.

"You will give the nobility and clergy to understand that if it should become necessary for France to interfere in the affairs of Spain, their privileges and immunities will be respected. You will tell them that the emperor only desires to improve the political institutions of Spain in order to place it in keeping with the present state of civilization in Europe, and to rescue it from the rule of favorites. . . . You will say to the magistrates and to the *bourgeois* of the cities, to the men of intelligence, that Spain has need of a new government; that she requires laws to guarantee the citizens from the arbitrary rule and usurpations of feudal rights; and institutions calculated to stimulate manufactures, agriculture and the arts. You will describe to them the present tranquil and prosperous condition of France, notwithstanding the wars in which she is engaged; the splendor of her religion, as reëstablished by the concordat, which I have signed with the Pope. You will demonstrate to them the advantages to be derived from a political regeneration; order and peace at home, and consideration and power abroad. Such should be the spirit of your speeches and your writings. Do not take any abrupt step. I can wait at Bayonne; I can pass the Pyrenees, and fortifying myself on the side of Portugal, can carry on war from that side.

"I shall attend to your individual interests; banish them from your thoughts, Portugal will remain at my disposition. Let no personal project occupy your thoughts or influence your conduct; that will only injure me, and yourself still more than me.

"You are too hasty in your instructions of the fourteenth. The march you prescribe to General Dupont is too rapid; on account of the events of the nineteenth of March, certain changes are to be made. You will make new dispositions; you will receive instructions from my minister of foreign affairs.

"It is my order that discipline the most severe be maintained; no pardon for the smallest faults. Have the strictest regard for the inhabitants; the churches and convents will be especially respected. The army will avoid all rencounters with the corps or detachments of the Spanish army. Let not a particle of powder be burned in this way. Let Solano pass Badajos. Let him be watched; so arrange the marches of my army as to always keep it some leagues distant from the Spanish corps. If war should be kindled, all will be lost. Policy and negotiations must decide the destinies of Spain. I recommend to you to avoid any explanations with Solano, or any other of the Spanish generals and governors."*

* As this letter so entirely differs from Napoleon's instructions of the twenty-seventh and thirtieth, it has been pronounced by some a forgery. It, however,

In reading these instructions, no one will accuse me of having inconsiderately engaged in a foolish enterprise. I wished to place my relations with Spain beyond the caprices of a favorite and the intrigues of the English party; I deemed a change to be for the interest of all, but I wished it with the assent of the Spaniards themselves. I wished to commence by connecting the ancient dynasty more closely to my system.

Napoleon meets the Spanish Court at Bayonne.—The ascension of Ferdinand to the throne, rendered necessary on my part new combinations; to the motives of hatred which this prince might already have toward the former protector of Godoy, I had just added a cause of complaint, not less evident, by the silence which I had kept on his propositions of marriage. It was now necessary either to attach this prince to myself, or to dispose of his throne, by restoring it to his father or by giving it to one of my brothers. To the first I felt opposed; chief of a new monarchy I had no inclination to encourage palace-revolutions; the other two had also great inconveniences. In this perplexity I resolved to go to Bayonne to see for myself what course I should take.

I at first had an idea of going to Spain, for the old court was urgently entreating me to come to its assistance, and to rescue it from the abyss into which it was plunged. It was unwilling to live at any price under the domination of Fer-

bears indubitable evidence of being the production of the emperor. Thiers has examined the question with great patience and industry, and concludes, from all the evidence, that it is genuine, that it was dated March 29th, but was never delivered. The date it has usually borne, is the twenty-ninth. It certainly could not have been written on the twenty-seventh. Between the twenty-seventh and the thirtieth, Napoleon was still undecided in regard to the course to be pursued toward Spain. This letter must have been written during that interval. But having determined upon his course, after receiving, on the thirtieth, Murat's letter of the twenty-fourth, this one of the twenty-ninth was recalled.

dinand, and asked for the most modest asylum in France as a special favor, wishing only to be rid of the cares of the throne and the presence of a son whose faults it exaggerated. I resolved upon a conference with this court. I also gave Ferdinand to understand that I desired to confer with him on the grave position in which the revolution had placed him. I thought that, not to place him in my presence or that of his father, they would induce him either to revolt or to fly to America; he did neither the one nor the other. After having conferred the regency on the council, with his uncle Don Antonio as president, he set out to meet me, thinking to find me at Vittoria. Not finding me there, he resolved to push on to Bayonne, notwithstanding the discouraging letter which I had sent him. Undoubtedly the treaty made with Isquierdo contributed to quiet his counsellors with regard to my intentions on the Spanish monarchy; the entire cession of Portugal seemed to them a sufficient pledge for these intentions. It therefore only remained for Ferdinand to gain his suit personally, and he flattered himself that this could be gained without difficulty by his protestations.

My detractors have accused me of forcing him to leave Vittoria for Bayonne. This had been an absurd fault; it would have given me the appearance of a felony without any advantage. I was not displeased that he came, for I had promised him an interview; but I should have preferred to have him take the part of embarking. So far was it from necessary to employ force to bring him to Bayonne, that he was on the point of asking the aid of French troops against those who wished to prevent him.

He resolves to place a new Dynasty on the Throne of Spain. —I had no sooner conferred with him and his counsellors than I saw how ignorant they were of their own situation. They had determined on nothing; they never had any foresight; they pursued their policy like blind men. I immediately saw the danger of leaving Spain in such hands; before a year had elapsed it would have been in the hands of the English. I then decided to provoke an abdication and to place one of my brothers on the vacant throne.

The thing was easy enough with the father, for he had resolved not to again place his feet within a kingdom where he was continually exposed to the excesses of an exasperated multitude; the queen asked for nothing but the favorite. Arriving at Bayonne, some days after his son, he repeated that his abdication had been forced from him; he required that Ferdinand should restore to him the crown, which was done on the first of May; four days after, the father ceded to me his rights on Spain, from the sole fear that his son might succeed him.

The history of the Atridæ offers nothing more disgusting than the hatred which animated the king and queen of Spain against their son; and the latter, goaded by ill-treatment, returned this sentiment with interest. I expected no very serious resistance, for the revolution of Aranjuez was not, as has been imagined, the result of a great national movement. It was merely the affair of a coterie—a palace revolution—the expulsion of an unpopular vizier. It in no respect resembled the origin of the French Revolution. Nevertheless the feelings of the nation had been put in effervescence; this might produce disagreeable results, and the several parties were already flattering themselves to be able to turn it to their own profit. The men who wished a change in Spain were agreed only on one point; this was that they did not desire such a revolution as ours; some desired a capable government, an authority which would sweep away the rust that covered their country, in order to give it consideration abroad and civilization at home; others, and they were the most powerful, wished to substitute a confessor in place of

Godoy, and to restore, in all its lustre, the rule of the clergy; others again wished to augment the influence of the grandees at the expense of the favorite and of the monarch.

I could satisfy the first, by seizing the revolution where they had now brought it. It was necessary to give to Spain a dynasty, at the same time strong and free from prejudices. Mine united these qualities. Every thing seemed to promise that Spain, to avoid anarchy, would accept a sovereign who should present himself armed with a powerful lever. It would, by this means, enter into my system without resistance and without war. By ending with Spain as I hoped, I should accomplish the three great objects of my reign; *I should secure to France the most important maritime alliance; I should be relieved from all the embarrassments of a reaction; I should give solidity to my edifice; I should regenerate another of the finest portions of the globe.*

Objections made to Napoleon's Plans.—I do not pretend that these reasons have seemed satisfactory to all; since the turn which affairs took, they have by some been severely censured. These objections may be summed up as follows:

1st. That I was already deriving all the advantages which I could hope from Spain, since her fleets and armies were already at my disposal, and her ports open to my commerce.

2d. That one of my brothers, even supposing that he should be recognized on the throne of Spain, would be unable to do as much for me as Charles IV.

3d. That in any state of the question it would be impossible to close all access to clandestine commerce in Spain and America; and if it were possible, it could be done more successfully by the old dynasty than by a new government, which would be under the necessity of making concessions to commerce in order to make partisans. (The conduct of my brother Louis, in Holland, would seem to prove the correctness of this).

4th. Even supposing that the threatening proclamation of the Spanish government, in 1806, was a sufficient indication of its secret intention to quit my alliance at the first favorable occasion, it was, nevertheless, certain that it would persevere in this alliance so long as my position should be respectable on the continent.

5th. That an ally of such importance, however vacillating it might be, was certainly better than an irreconcilable enemy.

6th. That by a war we might lose every thing, but would gain nothing; in a word, that it was both dangerous and wrong to attack a government that was already doing every thing that I desired.

7th. That should the Spaniards make resistance to me, the scission of America would become inevitable, and these territories would thus pass under the control of the English.

His Reasons for adopting them.—All these arguments were specious; they would have been just if I could have reckoned, on a continuance of our existing relations with Spain; but it has been shown that nothing was less certain, and that it was precisely to render these relations certain and lasting, that I formed my projects.

But if my object was simple and suited to the interests of my empire, the means of attaining this object were difficult and complicated. A formal declaration of war, based on the hostile proclamation of the Prince of Peace, was no longer possible when Ferdinand came to Bayonne; I could not proclaim myself the defender of Charles IV. and sacrifice, at the same time, both the favorite and Ferdinand, for Charles would not have remained three months on the throne. Moreover, it was not the question to render the war less easy by siding with this party or that, but to avoid war, for even its declaration would have been a calamity. I feared this most of all things; for if I had not been persuaded that it was possible to avoid it entirely, I should have recognized Ferdinand without hesitation. My instructions to Murat are sufficient proof of this.

If, on the contrary, I should succeed in inducing the son to renounce, as easily as his partisans had induced his father to abdicate, then sixty thousand men, supported by a powerful party, had been sufficient to ensure our possession, and the rupture would not take place. I did not leave Ferdinand long uncertain of his fate; I represented to him that the interests of France and Spain were that they should always remain united against England; that he was surrounded by the enemies of France; that he was, perhaps without being aware of it, at the head of this party; that the Bourbons of Spain would never entirely forget that their family had once possessed the throne of France, and that on this account the alliance so necessary to the two states would never be solid; that his father Charles IV. had abdicated the crown in my favor, and that it only remained for him to follow his father's example. After some hesitation he resigned.

Such was the origin of the war in Spain, and such the reasons which guided my conduct in undertaking it. The just complaints which I had to make against Spain, the contemptible nullity of its government, the grand results which I should have obtained from it, if I had succeeded in my project, may serve to explain the motives of this project, as posterity will justify the views of Catherine II. on Poland. I have been reproached with the means which I employed to ensure success. Nevertheless, my conduct has not been so tortuous in this affair as appearances have led some to suspect; it appears more ambiguous, because I myself changed my views after the revolution of Aranjuez and the interview of Bayonne. The skin of the fox but ill fits the lion; and I have never sought to disguise myself in it.

Operations of Murat.—I was not long in being undeceived respecting the results of this step. All the month of April was passed in petty hostilities between Murat, who was hoping for this throne, and the council of regency left by Ferdinand VII. on his departure from Madrid. The grand-duke of Berg flattered himself that he would put an end to these difficulties by obtaining from Charles IV. the title of Lieutenant of the kingdom, at the moment that he resumed the reins from the hands of his son. Strong in this authority, Murat thought that he had now only to take possession of the provinces, and accordingly detached Marshal Moncey on Valencia, and Dupont on Cadiz. He went to work more rapidly than I wished; he was eager to reign.

Insurrection of May 2d.—On leaving Madrid, Ferdinand had announced his intention of going to Vittoria, where they persuaded him that I would meet him. No sooner was his departure decided on than the report spread through all parts that the prince, surrounded by French troops, had been constrained by force to take this course. A deep agitation, the precursor of an eruption, propagated itself thenceforth even to Madrid. To incite the people still more, it was added that the Infante Francis de Paul, the only one of the royal family left in the capital, was to be carried away into France. At this news, all Madrid rises; Murat, assailed by a furious multitude, is obliged to employ grape-shot to prevent being overcome by them. Our columns, encamped around Madrid, penetrate into the streets, where a furious combat takes place. Our soldiers immolated in the first success of the populace, incite their comrades to vengeance; all citizens found armed are slain. These scenes of terror continue till night, which, with its shadows, veiled the execution of the most guilty of the leaders of this emeute.

Spanish Junta convoked at Bayonne.—On learning this deplorable massacre, I immediately saw all its consequence;

to retreat was not now possible. I hoped to gain a decisive success by assembling a grand national junta. I demanded of the regency constituted by Ferdinand, to designate, by the councils of the kingdom, the one of my brothers whom it preferred for its sovereign; it selected, of its own choice, Joseph, then king of Naples. A junta of one hundred and fifty of the most notable of the Spaniards, taken from the three orders, was assembled at Bayonne to discuss, in concert with me, the constitutional act which was henceforth to govern the kingdom.

The discourses made in this august assembly are an historical monument, remarkable, and calculated to confound all the conjectures on the secret motives which caused minds to change *so promptly*. The dukes of Infantado, of Ossuna, of Fernando Nunez, of Hijar, and Delparque, made no scruple in promising to Joseph the same attachment which they had always shown to their legitimate princes. On the sixth of July, the junta recognized him as king, and proclaimed the constitutional act which fixed his powers and the succession to the throne, and also contained numerous principles of reform.

There remained no legal power in Spain to oppose this change of reign. The old king was grateful to me for having taken the throne from his rebel son, and went to repose first at Campeigne, and afterward at Marseilles. His son was taken to the Chateau of Valençay, where the necessary preparations were made for his reception as a dethroned king. This chateau belonged to Talleyrand, who, far from opposing the choice made of it for his royal guest, even offered to make him take the oath to the new constitution and to Joseph!

The Spaniards could not abide their old king; he left neither regrets nor *souvenirs*; but his son was young, his reign offered some hopes; he was unfortunate, and they made a martyr of him. They imagined everything in his favor;

the liberals cried out for national independence; the monks exclaimed against illegitimacy and impiety. All the nation took arms under these two banners.

Napoleon's Conduct toward Ferdinand VII.—It has been said "that I was wrong in putting this young king in sequestration at Valençay, and that I would have done much better by leaving him on the throne and sacrificing Godoy. He had not failed to make discontents; factions would have increased, and soon begun to war against each other; I should have acquired the title of protector of the old king, by affording him an asylum. The new government would not have failed to compromise itself with the English; I should have declared war against it, both in my own name and in the quality derived from the powers of his father. I should, in this way, have made war with the support of a powerful party. Spain would have confided to her army the care of her defenses, and, after it had been beaten, the nation would have submitted to the right of conquest. They would not have thought of murmuring at this, because in disposing of a conquered country I would only have acted according to established usages, and because she would have seen in me the man who had delivered them from Godoy."

All this had been well enough, if I had not feared even the idea of war, certain that the English were ready to collect all the fruits of it. In default of this system, I could still have returned to the project of the marriage of Ferdinand VII. with a princess of my family; and if I had not a little too much reckoned on the facility of the execution of my new design after Ferdinand had left his kingdom, I should not have failed to adopt this course.

If I had possessed the gift of reading the future, I should have adopted this step, but I thought that, the result being the same to them, the Spaniards would accept, without hesitation, a change of dynasty which the position of affairs rendered inevitable. I acted too abruptly in this second period of the enterprise, because I neglected the gradations, and, not satisfied with giving them a king, I also announced myself as a reformer. No country had more need of reformers; but those who fed on abuses, were thus made my opponents, and these were the most influential mass. The monks especially, and the high clergy, fattening on the public distresses, made it a duty to oppose me. Demagogues railed at the constitution as despotic, because it was wise, and gave the necessary guarantees to the throne; the priests rejected it, because it imposed limits to their influence; the grandees of Spain, divided in opinion, thought it gave them too little power. All interests and wounded self-loves, rose in insurrection, and, pretending that I had dispossessed the old dynasty in a way offensive to all Spaniards, refused to recognize that which I had put in its place. It resulted from this, that no authority was any where recognized, or rather that it sprung up every where. The nation *en masse* deemed itself charged with the defense of the state, since there was no army or authority to be intrusted with this defense. Each man took upon himself the responsibility of it. I had against me anarchy with all its resources; I had an entire people on my hands.

General Insurrection.—At the very moment that I was flattering myself to have my projects sanctioned by the deputies of the Spanish nation, convoked at Bayonne, this entire nation rose in insurrection, as if to confound my hopes. The cannon of the second of May, was still echoing through Spain, when the report was circulated that Ferdinand had been forced to abdicate the crown, and was imprisoned; that this prince had not only protested against this violence, but had also appealed to all brave Spaniards to save the kingdom. A thrilling proclamation, fabricated by our enemies, is addressed, in the name of the captive king, to the Aragonese and the faithful Asturians who defended the cradle of the monarchy; this confirms the rumors. In an instant Spain is on fire; Valencia, Seville and Cadiz revolt, the French squadron at anchor in the latter port is captured. The Captain-general Salano, who had covered himself with glory in fighting against us in 1794, on the eastern Pyrenees, but who had since then followed the army of Moreau as a volunteer, accused of protecting the French, is massacred. At Seville and at Valencia the same scenes are repeated; here the captain-general is torn in pieces; the French, established in great numbers in this latter city, are massacred or put in irons, and their property given up to pillage. A junta of government is installed at Seville, and arrogates to itself the powers conferred on the provisionary council and that of Castile and the Indies, to govern the kingdom in the absence of its sovereign. The province of the Asturias also creates a junta, and through its chief, demands the assistance of England. Another junta in the east demands the assistance of Austria, and, as if in remembrance of the War of the Succession, offers the throne of Spain to the Archduke Charles. Admiral Collingwood sends a frigate to Trieste for him, while England officially recognizes Ferdinand VII. The energy extends with electric rapidity from one end of the kingdom to the other; each province, and each city, however unimportant, has its junta, where all objects of public interest are tumultuously discussed; all Aragon rises; and the inhabitants of Saragossa, after having thrown in prison all the captains-general whom they suspect, decree, by unanimous acclamation, the general command to Palafox, a young officer, twenty-eight years of age, who has escaped from Bayonne, whither he had followed Ferdinand, and whose decided character is in unison with the general opinion. Catalonia imitates this example, and Duhesme is soon shut up in Barcelona, and cut off from all communication with

France. Even at Valladolid, in the centre of our cantonments, the junta which organizes itself there, issues a proclamation worthy to figure, from its frightful energy, with the discourses of Barrère of the twenty-third of August, 1793.

The movement was so general and so spontaneous, that I have never been able to explain it; but as it had its origin in the populace, I have reason to believe that it was the result of a vast conspiracy formed by the clergy. But, what is very remarkable in this sudden revolution, is, that it offers the anomaly of republican demagogues and religious fanaticism acting in concert for the independence of the nation, and the deliverance of the legitimate sovereign. Between them there is no dissension, no suspicion, no civil war, and, except a few hundred victims massacred at the first outbreak, all the fury of the people turned against us. Never was a national movement more complete or more extraordinary than this. The Romans, selling the ground on which was encamped the army of Hannibal, exhibited less energy than the Spanish nation in these grave circumstances.

At no period of the French revolution was France so near ruin, and at no period did she exhibit so much energy. In 1792, when the Prussians entered Champagne, the National Assembly had already had two years to confirm its authority, to organize more than three hundred thousand good troops, and to place the frontiers in a formidable state of defense. In 1793, when, after the battle of Neerwinden and the defection of Dumouriez, France saw her northern frontier invaded, the war of La Vendée extending its ravages, the south agitated by the federalists, she was saved by the force of the revolutionary government; but the power given to this deçemvir-dictatorship, far from being the work of the nation, was the conception of a few men of energetic character, placed between victory and death. The mass of the French disapproved of these measures, and took up arms only to escape the guillotine. There is, therefore, no resemblance in the two cases. If Paris had been occupied by the Austrians, would the terrible law of the fifth of September have produced the same results? There is reason to doubt it. In fine, the movement of France was more regular, more military, more imposing; that of Spain was more extraordinary.

The monarchy was militarily occupied; its capital in my power; the legal government captive; the frontier defenses surprised; the army scattered in Holstein, Portugal, and in the maritime ports closed against England; this army had not more than sixty thousand men. Notwithstanding this sad state of affairs, not a Spaniard despaired of the kingdom; some faithful friends, sent by Ferdinand with his protestation, were sufficient to raise in all the provinces the cries of vengeance and death. The entire nation was in motion; if they did not fly to their colors, as they did in France in 1793, it was because the Spaniard abhors the restraints of military discipline; but each one is indignant, is excited, and swears to defend his fireside till death.

Such was the nation which three centuries of political nullity and apathy had so degenerated under the yoke of the monks, and which my agents compared to the Neapolitans. To what cause must we attribute this enthusiasm of the Spanish people? Was it patriotism, or offended pride? Where are the heroes of this war? With the exception of Palafox and Alvarez, who merit this title? Far from me be the thought of depreciating the gallant and the generous; but I seek the causes of an extraordinary event, and I confess myself unable to find them. The sudden resuscitation of a whole nation, plunged for ages in a torpor, is always connected with a thousand incidents which escape the most profound observation. It requires the pen of a Tacitus to trace the picture of this revolution; but let it not be too long delayed; for, in time objects become discolored, and take the hues which a skilful writer knows so well how to give them.

But let us return to our subject. On all sides the levies are multiplied; the troops of the line are increased; the provincial militia organized; soon Spain will have an army of from one hundred and twenty to one hundred and fifty thousand men, supported by the whole nation in arms. These events must soon destroy the communications and prevent the junction of my *corps-d'armée*, for they are dispersed over an immense surface, and their total force does not exceed seventy thousand men.

Moncey driven from Valencia.—Moncey was marching with six thousand men on Valencia, where he flattered himself with being sustained, in case of need, by the division of Chabran which he called from Tortosa; but Caro disputed its approach with a corps of troops of the line and peasants. After some success, Moncey failed in his feeble efforts against the walls of this capital. Destitute of heavy artillery, cut off from all communication with Chabran, and reduced to five thousand men, he very reasonably determined to regain Madrid by a different route from that by which he had come.

The centre and the north of Spain, occupied by the *corps-d'armée* of Bessières, are a prey to insurrection like the extremities of the kingdom, and here it is more dangerous, since it threatens the line of the Ebro and our communications. St.-Ander, incited by its bishop, Logrono, bý a stonecutter, are the theatres of partial revolts, the precursors of a general movement; the insurgents of the north have established themselves as far as Reynosa. Valladolid, rises in its turn. The captain-general, Cuesta, carried away by the universal movement, puts himself at the head of two thousand soldiers and five or six thousand insurgents. Galicia, which was not yet occupied by us, is entirely at the disposal of the authorities which are established there. Here, as elsewhere, all the male population from seventeen to forty years of age, are required to take arms.

In the mean time, Bessières, established at Burgos, has pushed Verdier on Logrono; Lasalle goes to burn Torquemada. Merle puts himself in march on St.-Ander, when the movement at Valladolid obliges Bessières to check him; the marshal hastens to march against Cuesta, posted militarily at Cabezon, and dislodges him, after a slight combat. Our troops enter Valladolid on the twelfth of June; Lasalle pursues and sabres the insurgents. Cuesta retires to Benevento, Bessières returns to Burgos, after having withdrawn the arms from Valladolid; Merle then resumes his expedition against St.-Ander, forces the passage of the mountains, presents himself before the city, and enters it on the twenty-third of June.

Insurrection in Aragon.—Our success is not so easy in Aragon, where Palafox justifies the confidence reposed in him. Destitute of troops of the line, the entire province takes up arms; old soldiers serve as a nucleus for the army; officers of artillery fly hither from Pampeluna and Madrid, and engineers from the school of Alcala. I order General Lefebvre-Desnouettes to march from Pampeluna with three thousand Poles and the same number of French, to destroy this germ of resistance. Palafox marches toward Epila against him at the head of six thousand insurgents; after a few discharges of artillery and musketry, the Polish lancers overthrow them in an instant, and with great carnage. Saragossa is nevertheless disposed for a vigorous resistance. The most suitable convents are transformed into batteries of two tiers; traverses and coupures are constructed in the streets; the male population prepare with energy to bury all beneath the ruin of their houses. A first attack succeeds in penetrating the city, when it is found impossible to take the place. I cause a siege equipage to be collected from Pampeluna; but a whole month passes before they can begin a regular siege.

The Army of Galicia advances on Valladolid.—In the mean time the storm increased in the west. The junta of Oviedo had received promises of assistance from England, and embarkations were preparing in all the ports of Great Britain. Fifty thousand fire-arms were immediately sent with Colonel Doyle to encourage the levies of Galicia which assembled at Lugo, and were reënforced by the corps of Taranco from Portugal. The exasperation of these troops was carried so far as to massacre the respectable General Filangieri, who had been designated to command them, and whose only crime was his having given offensive advice. This army, debouching on Astorga under the orders of Blake, united on the Esla to that of Cuesta, and advanced on Medina del Rio-Seco, with thirty-five thousand men, and thirty pieces of cannon. Bessières, hearing at Burgos of this threatening assemblage, and being timely reënforced by Mouton's division of troops from Poland, decided to march against the enemy, though inferior in numbers by one half.

Joseph proclaimed King of Spain.—At the same time the junta which was assembled at Bayonne, adopted the constitution of the kingdom, on the sixth of July, and proclaimed my brother Joseph, as it were in derision, king of Spain and of the Indies. This constitution, modeled after that of the empire, and preserving strong powers for the executive, contained all the generous principles which were calculated to secure a better future to Spain; it does much credit to the duke of Bassano, who was one of its principal framers; but the reforms contained in it contributed not a little to augment the number of our enemies. It was too liberal for the monks, and not enough so to satisfy the radical party.

Joseph entered Spain at the moment that Bessières was marching to meet Cuesta and Blake. If these were victorious, the fate of our army in Spain had been sealed; for they would have been in possession of our line of retreat, and all had been lost. The rencontre took place the fourteenth of July at Medina del Rio-Seco; the Spaniards, formed in two lines too great at an interval, were impetuously attacked in front by Merle and Mouton, while Lasalle charged them in flank. The first line was broken and routed; the second now took the offensive; while Mouton received its attack in front, the division of Merle assailed it in flank and spread terror and death everywhere. This victory, which procured us four thousand prisoners and fifteen pieces of cannon, and saved the army, was glorious, for the Spaniards fought with courage, but without experience. Generals Guilleminot and Mouton distinguished themselves.

Joseph arrived at Madrid, preceded by the news of this sad victory over the people whom he was called to govern. Bessières, though reënforced, did not pursue the enemy's generals between whom there was much discord; he might easily have advanced into Galicia, and even have shown my victorious eagles on the banks of the Portuguese Douro, so as to disengage Junot, who was then attacked by numerous enemies. But, perhaps, it was fortunate that he did not do this, for the bloody check which we received a few days after at Baylen, had probably turned against us the momentary success which had conducted this marshal to the gates of Coruña.

Dupont capitulates at Baylen.—Dupont had been detached on Seville and Cadiz, to reduce these two important places. One half of his *corps-d'armée* being employed on secondary expeditions, he passed the Sierra Morena at the head of only eight thousand men; reaching Andujar about the first of June, he carried the bridge of the Guadalquiver at Alcolea, after having beaten a corps of twelve thousand men under General Echevari, and carried Cordova by a *coup-de-main* on the seventh of June. He was seconded by the division of Wedel, which had at first been destined for another expedition, but had afterward received orders to join him. Dupont, hearing at Andujar that at the order of the supreme junta at Seville, all the south of Spain was rising; that Solano's troops of the line, returned from Portugal, and joined by the garrison of Cadiz and the regiments dispersed in Andalusia or at the camp of Saint Roche, formed a mass of forty thousand men, deemed his mission impossible, and waited behind the Guadalquiver for further orders and reënforcements. Savary, to whom Murat in his illness had momentarily confided the command, having directed him to keep in rear of the Guadalquiver so as not to draw the fire of the insurrection on this side of the Sierra-Morena, Dupont had taken position at Andujar and directed Wedel to guard Baylen, so as to cover himself on the side of Baeza, when Castaños presented himself with his army before him, and manœuvred to gain his left. Dupont, who had shown so much presence of mind and vigor on the Mincio in 1800, and before Ulm in 1805, is here completely confused; he demands one of Wedel's brigades. The latter repairs to Andujar, on the sixteenth of July, with his entire division, leaving at Baylen only a detachment under General Gobert. Castaños sends there twelve or fifteen thousand men, under the orders of General Reding; the ford of Mengibar, on the Guadalquiver, is forced; the enemy penetrates between our divisions, and sustains this movement. Dupont imagines that he can avoid the embarrassment by ordering Wedel to return to Baylen, to dislodge the enemy, and after securing this post, to again join him at Andujar, whence he was to fall, in concert with him, on the divided corps of the enemy. But if such was really the project of Dupont, since Wedel was already united with him, why again separate and send him away to Baylen? Why not attack the enemy, with his united forces, first at Baylen and then at Andujar, if Castaños should venture to cross the Guadalquiver? The position of Dupont was about the same as mine at Castiglione, in 1796, when the enemy took possession of Brescia, on my communications; he should have followed my example, and first beaten the corps which threatened his retreat and then have overthrown the other.

Dupont committed the fault of dividing his forces at the critical moment, and his lieutenant committed another not less grave. Wedel, finding Baylen evacuated by the troops of Gobert, who had been wounded in fighting Reding, went as far as Carolina to rejoin him, thus enabling the enemy to reoccupy Baylen after his passage. The entire corps of Reding established itself here without obstacle. Dupont, hearing of this event, determined, too late, to march on the same point himself, and to open a passage; he made three or four fruitless attempts to accomplish this on the nineteenth; his attacks were repulsed. He flattered himself that Wedel, hearing the sound of his cannon, would return, and that their combined efforts would restore the victory. Vain hope! Instead of learning the return of his lieutenant, he learned that Castanos had taken advantage of his departure from Andujar, to get possession of that place and to send, in pursuit of him, a strong division under General La Pena. Dupont, seeing himself surrounded and repulsed, proposed a treaty of evacuation. Reding referred him to the general-in-chief, Castaños, at Andujar, but consented to a suspension of arms.

I had charged the inspector-general of engineers, Marescot, to follow Dupont to Cadiz, and to examine the fortifications of this place where I supposed my troops would enter without opposition. This general, being personally acquainted with Castaños, having been engaged with him in marking out the frontier line after the peace of Bâle, offered to go and negotiate with him, in hopes of obtaining better conditions. This was on the twentieth of July.

In the mean time Wedel had returned to Baylen, had attacked Reding and captured some cannon and six hundred prisoners. Reding, now placed between two fires, in the position that he had thought to put Dupont, succeeded in extricating himself by announcing that an armistice had just been concluded. After being assured of the truth of this assertion, Wedel, established himself above Baylen, and waited for orders. The report of a treaty, or rather of a capitulation, spread among the soldiers who had been so recently victorious, and whose courage had been restrained by the orders of their superiors. These brave men became indignant and mutinied; they wished to renew the attack and pierce even to Dupont and save him at least from the disgrace of a capitulation, by securing his retreat. Their assembled officers assented to the project, and one of them was despatched to the general-in-chief for his authorization; but he replied that he could not authorize an attack at the moment when they were treating for an honorable capitulation, and while an armistice still existed.

The division indignantly withdrew to Carolina. The Spaniards demanded that the general-in-chief should make it return to Baylen, threatening to attack him if this was not instantly executed. The position of Dupont was certainly critical; he had just deprived himself, by his refusal, of the coöperation of Wedel; he could no longer hope for that coöperation, except by perfidiously charging the officer who should be sent to direct his return, to concert, on the contrary, an attack with this general. If such a course was repugnant to Dupont, and he preferred trusting himself to Spanish loyalty (which he should have distrusted in these times of revolution, when even their own generals lost their heads for exhibiting the least sign of moderation toward the French), how could he decide to treat for troops who had an open line of retreat on Madrid? Was he ignorant, that even among the Turks, the Grand Vizier in such circumstances, has a right to treat only for himself? Dupont had but one course to pursue; he should have signified to Reding and Castaños, that a general surrounded by an enemy can give no orders to one of his lieutenants who has an open retreat; that if they demanded of him so humiliating a step, it only remained for him to conquer or die, and to immediately give the order for battle. He would, perhaps, in that case have been made prisoner on the field; but then he would have fallen like a brave man. I should not have reproached him for his other faults. Instead of this, he had the weakness to obey the injunctions of Castaños, and thought to cover his responsibility by stipulating that his division should be regarded as prisoners and transported to France, but not to serve till regularly exchanged; that the division of Wedel should defile with its arms, and deposit them in stacks, till the moment of their embarkation for France. Fifteen thousand Frenchmen were thus to lay down their arms, when the half of them were free to retreat on Madrid, and only thought of vengeance and battle!! *

* We extract the following interesting passages from Thiers' Consulate and Empire on this capitulation.

"At length, on the twenty-second, that fatal capitulation was brought from Andujar to Baylen, to General Dupont. He hesitated several times before he signed it. The unhappy chief struck his forehead and flung down the pen; then, urged by those men who had all been so brave under fire, and who were all so weak out of fire, he wrote his name, once so glorious, at the foot of that document, which was destined to be the everlasting torment of his life. Why had he not fallen at Albeck, at Halle, at Friedland, or even at Baylen? How deeply he regretted it subsequently, before judges who inflicted on him a dishonoring condemnation! * * *

"Such was that famous capitulation of Baylen, the name of which, in our boyhood, rang in our ears as frequently as that of Austerlitz or Jena. At this

It is well known how the Spaniards violated this capitulation, and how, under the pretext of reprisals for my conduct toward them, they threw these unfortunate men into the

period, the ordinary persecutors of misfortune, judging of that deplorable event without knowledge and without pity, imputed to cowardice and to anxiety to save the wagons laden with the spoils of Cordova, the terrible disaster which befel the French army. Thus it is that the baseness of courtiers, ever rancorous against those whom power gives it the signal for immolating, is accustomed to judge! There were many faults, but not a single infraction of honor, in that deplorable campaign of Andalusia. * * *

"A serious error of Napoleon's in regard to Spain, a military position ill-chosen by General Dupont, too great delay in changing it, an ill-planned battle, false movements of General Wedels, demoralization of generals and soldiers—such were the causes of the cruel reverse of Baylen. All that has been said in addition is mere calumny. The long file of baggage, it has often been repeated, brought upon us all our misfortunes. Supposing that a general had been capable of so stupid a calculation as to sacrifice his honor, his military profession, the marshal's baton that was reserved for him, for a few hundred thousand francs, a sum far inferior to what Napoleon gave to the least favored of his lieutenants, eight or ten wagons would have carried all the pretended riches of Cordova in gold and silver-plate, and the question related to several hundred carriages, the extraordinary number of which was evidently occasioned by the moral state of the country, in which not a sick or wounded man could be left behind. At last, as we have seen, those famous baggage wagons were plundered, and the chest of the army carried off; it contained not more than three or four hundred thousand francs. All that can be said, in short, is, that General Dupont, intelligent, capable, brilliant under fire, had not the indomitable firmness of Massena at Genoa and Essling. But he was ill, wounded, exhausted by a heat of forty degrees; his soldiers were boys, worn out with fatigue and hunger; disasters followed close upon disasters, accidents upon accidents; and if we sound this tragic event to the bottom, we shall see that the emperor himself, who placed so many men in a false position, was not in this case the most irreproachable. Still we must add, for the interest of military morality, that, in these extreme situations, the resolution to die is the only worthy, the only salutary resolution; for certainly, on General Wedel's arrival, the resolution to die in the attempt to cut a passage through Reding's division would have enabled the two parts of the French army to join, and to get triumphantly out of the scrape, instead of finding themselves humbled and prisoners. By sacrificing on the field of battle one-fourth of the men who afterward died in a cruel captivity, one might have transformed into a triumph the most signal of the reverses of that extraordinary period."

But if Dupont's conduct at Baylen was less blamable than was supposed at the time, and if Napoleon treated him and his officers with undue severity, his course of conduct after the restoration fully justified every thing that had previously been said or written against him. From a pretended friend of Napoleon, to whom he owed all his wealth and position, he became his most bitter

pontons, where most of them perished from want and despair.

This sad catastrophe taught Europe that we also might be forced to surrender our arms; it ruined, for a long time, our affairs in the Peninsula; it exalted even to frenzy, the enthusiasm of our enemies. Dupont and Marescot, who had negotiated this treaty, were arrested on their return to France, and kept as prisoners till my first abdication. I had ordered them to be tried, as an example. This trial lingered along without being brought to a close; it has been said that I feared the issue; there certainly was no reason for this. If Admiral Byng was condemned for not having conquered at Port Mahon, what punishment was not merited by those who signed a treaty which was near causing the destruction of all our troops in Spain?

The desperate position in which Dupont had been placed was certainly a fault; he might have been taken; this would have been a misfortune; but he ought at least to have caused himself to be taken, like Francis I., at Pavia. A general-in-chief, to save an entire army, may sign treaties of evacuation, as Melas did at Marengo; he secured the safety of seventy thousand men at the price of some fortresses; but a lieutenant-general, commanding a portion of an army, ought never, under the vain pretexts of humanity, to sign capitulations in

enemy and denounced him in terms of unmeasured animosity. Thus it often is, that weak men, unjustly accused of offenses of which they are not guilty, smarting under the accusation, commit the very crime of which they are accused; General Dupont was tried by a high Court of Honor, each of the members giving his separate opinion. Three copies of the proceedings of this court were made and ordered to be deposited, one in the depôt of war, one in the senate, and one in the High Imperial Court. Smarting under the sentence of this Court of Honor, Dupont procured an ordnance from Louis XVIII., directing the destruction of the three copies of the proceedings. Two were destroyed, but the third could not be found, as the "High Imperial Court" was never organized. Fortunately this has been preserved, and it furnishes the best defense extant of his conduct at Baylen! If it had rested with him, he would have destroyed his only possible justification in the eyes of posterity.

an open country, to preserve some battalions more to his country; these capitulations, far from being advantageous, on the contrary, compromise the entire army, and the moral influence acquired by ten years of victory. Dupont tarnished in this operation, in a moment of weakness, a career made illustrious by decided talents and brilliant feats of arms.*

* The violation of the capitulation of Baylen by the Spaniards, was one of the many disgraceful acts of that government and people during the Peninsular War. The following is Thiers' description of the march of Dupont's army to Cadiz:

"The French troops were immediately marched off for San Lucar and Rota, where they were to be embarked for France in Spanish vessels. Their route was made to avoid the two great cities of Cordova and Seville, in order to withdraw them from the popular fury, and lay through the less important towns of Brijalance, Ecija, Carmona-Alcala, Utura, and Lebrija. In all these places the conduct of the Spanish populace was atrocious. Those unfortunate French, who had behaved like brave men, who had made war without cruelty, who had suffered, without revenging, the massacre of their sick and wounded, were pelted with stones, and often attacked with knives, by men, women, and children. At Carmona, at Ecija, the women spat in their faces, and children flung mud at them. They trembled with rage, and, though disarmed, were more than once tempted to take a terrible revenge, by seizing such as they could lay hands on and making weapons of them; but their officers restrained them, in order to prevent a general massacre. Care was taken to make them pass the night outside villages and towns, and to collect them in the open field like droves of cattle, to spare them still more cruel treatment. At Lebrija, and in the towns near the coast, they were stopped and doomed to tarry, upon pretext that the Spanish vessels were not ready. But they soon learned the cause of this delay. The junta of Seville, governed by the lowest demagogue passions, had refused to acknowledge the capitulation of Baylen, and declared that the French should be detained prisoners of war, under various pretexts, all illusory, and false even to impudence. One of the reasons alleged by this junta was, that they were not sure of obtaining the consent of the English to the passage by sea—a false reason, for the English, notwithstanding their animosity, manifested a generous pity for our prisoners, and, as we shall see, soon suffered other troops, which they would have been greatly interested in detaining, to pass by sea. Our officers addressed themselves to the captain-general, Thomas de Morla, remonstrating against this unworthy violation of the law of nations, but received from him only the most indecorous answers, to the effect that an army which had violated all laws, divine and human, had forfeited the right of appealing to the justice of the Spanish nation.

"At Lebrija the furious populace broke, in the night, into a prison, in which was one of our regiments of dragoons, and slaughtered seventy-five, of whom twelve were officers. But for the clergy, they would have put all of them to death. Lastly the generals, who had committed the serious fault of separating

Siege of Saragossa.—While this was passing in the south, the siege of Saragossa was prepared with all the activity which the nature of the country and the obstacles to be encountered

themselves from their troops, in order to travel apart with their baggage, were severely punished for having thus withdrawn themselves. No sooner had they arrived at Port St. Mary, with their wagons exempt from examination, than the people, unable to contain themselves at the sight of those vehicles, crammed, as they said, with all the riches of Cordova, fell upon them, broke them in pieces, and plundered them. Men belonging to the Spanish authorities were not the last to assist in this pillage. But, though these wagons contained the whole of the savings of the officers, and even the chest of the army, no more was found in them than eleven or twelve hundred thousand reals, according to the Spanish newspapers themselves, that is to say about three hundred thousand francs. That was the whole result of the sacking of Cordova. The French generals had well nigh been slaughtered, and they escaped the fury of the populace only by throwing themselves into boats."

Alison says that for the "violation of the capitulation no sort of apology can be found." * * * * * "Instead of being sent by sea to France, the soldiers and regimental officers were crowded together into the hulks of Cadiz, where, such were the privations and misery to which they were subjected, that very few remained at the conclusion of the war. Dupont, the officers of his staff, and all the generals, were permitted to return to France, but the remainder, nearly eighteen thousand in number, were kept in lingering suffering in their dismal captivity, and with the exception of a few who accepted service under the Spanish government, and took the first opportunity to desert to their beloved eagles, and those contained in one hulk, who overpowered their guards during the night, and contrived to float her across to the lines of their countrymen, three years afterward, during the siege of Cadiz, hardly any ever revisited their native country. This frightful act of injustice was as impolitic as it was disgraceful."

The translator has not found, in the whole course of his military and historical reading, an example, among civilized nations, of conduct so utterly disgraceful as this of the Spanish authorities and the Spanish people toward the French troops who were included in the capitulation of Baylen. Every obligation imposed by international law, and every obligation of military and national honor, as well as the solemn stipulations of the convention, and the common laws and usages of war, were violated. Alison, while he condemns the acts of the Spanish authorities, seeks to clear the skirts of the British government from all responsibility in this matter, by quoting the opinion of Sir Hew Dalrymple, given at the time, that Spain was bound to carry out in good faith the conditions of the capitulation, by sending the prisoners to France, and the offer to transport them in British ships. But unfortunately for the reputation of Mr. Alison as an historian, and for his government, there is abundant proof that the English authorities not only connived at, but actually advised the Junta of Seville to retain these French prisoners of war in this terrible and infamous captivity. Even as late as 1811, when the commander, Suchet, after

would permit. Lefebvre-Desnouettes was reënforced by Verdier, who took the command. I charged my aide-de-camp, Lacoste, with the direction of the siege. But eight or nine thousand men were insufficient to invest a city of seventy thousand on the Ebro; communications were kept up between Saragossa and the surrounding country. All our means were concentrated, on the fourth of August, to batter in breach the convent of Santa Engracia, and the gate Del Carmen. The breach being practical, the assault was made, the two posts carried, and our soldiers spread through the city. They already deemed themselves masters of the place, when the defenders, concentrated in the Corso, fell on them, a part in deep column, a part scattered through all the houses, on the terraces of the roofs, the windows and the balconies, whence they poured on us a shower of balls. Our troops were driven back to the posts which they had carried, with the loss of a thousand men.

Retreat from Madrid.—The news of the disaster of Baylen rendered these efforts useless. Joseph having just entered Madrid, was forced to evacuate it, in order to concentrate his forces behind the Ebro, and await reënforcements. Generals Lefebvre-Desnouettes and Verdier, constrained to

the fall of Tarragona, overlooking the violation of the conditions of the convention at Baylen that these French prisoners were to be sent by sea to France, offered to exchange his Catalonian prisoners, the best soldiers in Spain, for those taken at Baylen—men utterly ruined in constitution by their cruel captivity—and when the Spanish general was willing to accept the proposition, the Regency, at the request of Wellesley, the British envoy and brother of Wellington, peremptorily forbade the exchange; and the French prisoners therefore remained, says Napier, 'a disgrace to Spain, and to England, for if her envoy interfered to prevent their release, she was bound to insist, that thousands of men, whose prolonged captivity was the result of her interference, should not be exposed on a barren rock, naked as they were born, and fighting for each other's miserable rations to prolong an existence inconceivably wretched."

It was by such conduct as this that England earned her appellation of *Perfidious Albion!*

raise the siege of Saragossa, fell back on the Tudela, and united with Moncey, who formed our left.

Romana flies from Denmark.—To cap the climax of this strange war, the half of the corps of Romana, which had been imprudently left on the coasts of Holstein in communication with the English, embarked, unknown to Bernadotte, and landed on the coast of Biscay.

Errors of this Campaign.—Three errors were committed in this first period of the expedition to Spain, which compromised its success, if in other respects the success was possible. The first was, in not having sacrificed Godoy to the general hatred, by causing Charles IV. to send him into exile; the second, in having sent into Spain only raw conscripts; the third, in not having paid liberally for the support of my troops, as they were quartered in the country, even in not having required all of them to encamp out. The Spaniard is proud and detests trouble; the quartering of troops on him seems to him insupportable, on account of his pride and his interest; for the Spanish people are penurious and generally poor. Some millions expended *à propos*, had probably weakened the discontent. Our troops lived by requisitions which were promised to be paid, but these promises were never worth the ready money. This means alone was, of course, insufficient to insure the success of the enterprise; but order, discipline, and exact distributions would undoubtedly have diminished the hatred and resistance; they would have secured the mass of supplies, and have doubly reacted on the military operations. I had given all the orders necessary for this purpose, as is shown in my instructions to Murat; but the events did not allow us time to establish magazines every where, and, after the insurrection broke out, the thing was impossible.

Position of Junot in Portugal.—There was wanting only one more misfortune to complete the ruin of this expedition;

and of all those which befell our arms, the least probable actually occured; Junot had fallen beneath the blows of the English in Portugal. In fact, this general was ill-suited for a mission so delicate; endowed with much activity, bravery and energy, he stained these qualities by rudeness of manners and harshness of character. It required an administrator supple, adroit, insinuating; if a man like Suchet had been there, at this epoch, he would have created for himself a party. Undoubtedly the thing was not one of the easiest, or at least it could not have been durable; for here the question was not a simple change of dynasty, but the entire existence of Portugal. Although my projects on this country were suited to my system against England, of course it did not suit the Portuguese that I should threaten the loss of Brazil, the total closing of their ports, and a reunion with Spain. I, therefore, was not deceived with respect to this matter; I did not expect to succeed, except by force.

General Interests of Portugal.—We had, in the intelligent class of Portugese, partisans, who saw, with regret, their country used as a British province, for the profit of the English, and who desired reforms. Portugal, on whom nature had apparently exhausted her favors, intersected by mountains whose smiling aspects yield in no respect to the most renowned localities of Switzerland and Italy, favored by a superb climate, tempered at different zones by the progressive elevation of these same mountains, possessing the finest ports and the richest colonies of Europe—Portugal, I say would have been the real El Dorado, had not the monks degraded the people, and the English prevented the development of their industry. We might free her from both these evils, and many people would have rejoiced at it, for they were not indifferent to the dependent situation in which this country had been placed toward England. England purchased her wines and her fruits, but poured in upon her, the products of her own manufactures, and thus carried away all the profits, and all the specie of the country. Nevertheless, there was no country better able than Portugal to live independent of others. If her people, placed under so fine a sky, had applied themselves to industrial pursuits, the population of their cities would soon have been doubled, and the manufacturing portion of this population would, by furnishing the agriculturists the products of their labor, have consumed the fruits, and the wines of Oporto, without resorting to the British islands and paying so dearly in return. Brazil alone, vivified by an industrial mother-country, would have been sufficient for the consumption of these wines.

Sacrifices imposed on this Country.—But the introduction of such a system required half a century; and the Portuguese saw, for the moment, in their separation from England, only the closing of their ports, the interruption of all commerce with Brazil, the loss of the only outlet for their territorial produce, and the privation of all objects of manufacture necessary for habitual consumption. Add to this the hatred of the clergy, the fanaticism of the people, the contributions levied in money and supplies, the expense of military quarters to which they were unaccustomed, and, finally the rumored project of a partition which threatened the existence of a proud nation, and it will appear less astonishing that the public feeling changed so suddenly. The annunciation of the projected partition produced a general fermentation. The taking possession in my name, which was done on the first of February, occasioned an explosion, and it was necessary to resort to force to restore order. Nevertheless we succeeded in disbanding one half of their army, and in taking the other part, under the marquis of Alorna, into my pay and sending it into France under the title of the allied contingent.

These measures made matters still worse, and the cessation

of all exterior commerce completed the despair of the Portuguese. The Spaniards in that country, informed of what was occurring in Spain, added to the elements of the tempest. The divisions of Taranco and of Solano evacuated the provinces which were to have fallen to Spain in the partition, seizing all the French that they could, in the passage. Junot could no longer regard those who remained as auxiliaries, for their soldiers and ours were at war. It was necessary to strike a blow of vigor, and disarm the division of Caraffa, which had been united with our troops.

General Insurrection in Portugal.—The departure of the Spaniards was the signal for insurrection in all the provinces which they left; but they waited for the succors promised by England before organizing open resistance; but as soon as these appeared, the restrained torrent burst forth only the more furiously. Oporto had only waited for this to raise the standard of independence. A junta or regency, established under the presidency of the bishop, hastened to London to demand assistance, by the aid of which they flattered themselves that they would be able to deliver the kingdom. The disbanded regiments were reorganized and the militia called out. Junot, hoping to impose on them, detached General Loison from Almeida on this city; but on ascertaining the certainty that his means were insufficient, this general decided to fall back on Almeida, before being surrounded. He here received the new order to repair to Lisbon, and commenced his march by Guarda and Alcantara on Abrantes.

Junot, justly uneasy at the events which were threatening him on all sides, thought to prepare for the danger. The landing of an English division near Faro, at the extremity of the Algarves, had just occasioned an universal rising. Every where our feeble detachments, scattered through the kingdom, are assailed; nevertheless, with the exception of a single battalion taken at Faro, all succeed by their good conduct in effecting a passage. Maransin brings away from the Algarves, as by a miracle, a thousand men, and sacks Beja, where the insurgents oppose his march. Even at Lisbon they take up arms; all the banks of the Mondego are in arms; the mountaineers even descend toward Abrantes and Santarem; a Spanish division, debouching from the Guardiana, threatens Kellerman at Elvas, foments insurrection even at Evora and Estremoz, and forces the recall of this general on the Tagus.

Under these critical circumstances, Junot decides to assemble all his means and to hold Lisbon as long as possible, then to open a passage by Elvas to rejoin Murat at Madrid or Valladolid. Loison, on his return to Lisbon, is detached on Leyria against the insurgents of Coimbra; but Kellerman having already attacked them with success, the presence of Loison is deemed more necessary at Evora, where the support of a Spanish division had caused a threatening insurrection. He marches there at the head of four thousand men. The enemy, confident in numbers, ventures to meet him outside the city; he attacks them with impetuosity and defeats them with great loss; they return within the walls. Loison summons them to surrender, but they refuse; he then prepares for an assault. In the midst of the tumult, the Spaniards, established near the gate of Elvas, succeed in effecting their escape, but not without sensible loss. The attack continues on both sides; finally our soldiers penetrate into Evora, where a frightful butchery is continued for several hours. The fight goes on from street to street, and from house to house; every one taken in arms is massacred without mercy. The city is completely sacked; and our soldiers, wearied with the carnage, capture some two or three thousand prisoners, the remains of eight thousand militia and armed citizens. This bloody execution secures to General Loison a sad celebrity in these countries; it, for a moment, causes terror throughout Portugal; but not being followed up by farther victories, it eventually becomes a motive of reprisals and vengeance in the irascible heart of the Portuguese.

Landing of Wellesley with the English Army.—The succors promised by England were not long in making their appearance. The cabinet of St. James had made great preparations on the first invitation of the Spanish juntas. Sir Arthur Wellesley, who had distinguished himself at Copenhagen and in the Indies, had embarked for Galicia; but difficulties being made in regard to his reception at Coruña, he soon came to Portugal where he united at first fifteen thousand of the best English troops. He was soon followed by fifteen thousand more under Generals Moore and Dalrymple, the latter taking the command.

Learning the spirit which animated the Portuguese, and certain of a powerful support, Wellesley (whom we shall hereafter designate by the title of Lord Wellington), resolved not to await his chief, but to win for himself the glory of delivering Portugal. Having landed, on the second of August, at the mouth of the Mondego, he passed this river at Coimbra and marched toward Leyria.

Junot defeated at Vimiera.—His calculation was correct. Junot, forced to watch the entire population of Lisbon, to defend the forts and batteries of that city, and to guard the disarmed Spaniards, could oppose him with only ten or twelve thousand men, and even for this he was obliged to wait for Loison's arrival from Evora. In the meantime General Laborde opposed the English with three thousand men, and even had the audacity to receive battle at Rolica, where he fought with glory against quadruple forces, and retired only after having caused the enemy great losses. Loison having arrived, Junot marched against the English general who had united sixteen thousand men, exclusive of the Portuguese.

But, defeated at Vimiera on the twentieth of August, and surrounded by innumerable enemies, Junot deemed himself fortunate in signing at Cintra a treaty of evacuation more honorable than that of Baylen. At least this was respected. One of the vexatious results of this convention was the loss of the Russian squadron under Admiral Saniavin. It had held the Archipelago since the campaign of 1805, and after the declaration of war by Russia against the English, had taken refuge in the Tagus. Compelled to partake the fate of our arms, it was sequestered till peace; the equipments only were restored to Russia.

Dalrymple, who had just arrived, signed this convention, and incurred the blame of England for having allowed to escape a prey, still more secure than that of Baylen. Even Wellesley was recalled to London to render an account of his conduct, and it required all his talents and the credit of his family to save him from disgrace.

On the other hand, Junot incurred from me the reproach of having left too many troops to guard Lisbon and Santarem, and the left bank of the Tagus, and of having attacked Wellesley in parallel order on the centre instead of turning his left by a movement at night. Nevertheless, supposing Junot had acted according to my wishes and had driven Wellesley back to the mouth of the Mondego, the arrival of the troops of Moore and Dalrymple, the general rising of the Portuguese, and the state of affairs in Spain, would have cut off all hope of retreat. Under these circumstances I was compelled to regard as fortunate a treaty which restored to me an army whose loss seemed certain.

Military Operations in the North of Europe. — While these things were occurring in the south, Russia had declared war against Sweden, which still persisted in remaining in the paws of the English leopard. The impetuous descendant of Charles XII. had resisted all our efforts to induce him to declare war against the English. Some say that he pursued with chivalric obstinacy, the course which he had imposed on himself after the death of the Duke d'Enghein, which had involved us in hostilities; others think that the catastrophe of Copenhagen and the hope of gaining Norway retained him in his connection with the cabinet of St. James. England paid him subsidies; the Swedish flag was allowed to float on the seas, by submitting to the British code. Gustavus deemed this order of things advantageous to his commerce and conformable to his principles. So long as he exposed only Pomerania and Stralsund, this system may be accounted for, but, after the declaration of the Emperor Alexander, it is difficult to conceive how he could venture to contend against the two greatest powers on the continent.

The cabinet of St. Petersburg had for a century coveted Finland, an important province at the very gates of the imperial capital, and which was more precious to Russia than to Sweden, as the latter was separated from it by the gulf of Bothnia and the deserts of the polar regions. The ninth of February, 1808, notwithstanding the excessive cold, General Buxhowden entered Finland at the head of twenty thousand Russians. After some insignificant skirmishes, he gained possession of Helsingfors, left a corps of observation before the important place of Sweaborg, and fell back on Tawasthous, in order to anticipate the enemy at Wasa, and to cut him off, if he should attempt to defend Abo and the coast. These dispositions effected a part of the desired success. If the roads and the snows did not permit him to reach Wasa before the enemy, they at least accelerated his retreat and prevented the occupation of all the provinces, by forcing him to retire in disorder on Sweaborg.

Buxhowden had in the mean time reduced the forts of Schwartholm and Kangout, and blockaded Sweaborg on the ice. This Gibraltar of the Baltic, which can give an asylum to the largest fleets in the world, is built on seven rocky islands which close the entrance to the gulf of Helsingfors. As an anchorage, a fortress and arsenal, this maritime establishment is inferior to no other. The channels are a little difficult for large squadrons, but for the forces employed in the Gulf of Finland, it leaves nothing to be desired. Admiral Cronstadt, commanded there about three thousand troops of the line and as many Finland militia. After a blockade executed on the ice of the gulf and a *simulacrum* of bombardment which continued from the eighth to the twenty-fifth of March, he basely surrendered the place at the very moment when the approach of spring gave him reason to expect to be freed by the melting of the ice from the siege on the water side, and when the success of the Swedes at Brahestadt over the division of Touczkof, might have changed the state of affairs on the land. He defiled on the twenty-fourth of April, and surrendered himself a prisoner. This important conquest secured to the Russians two thousand pieces of cannon, and a considerable amount of stores, besides the prisoners and an impregnable fortress. It was now impossible for the Russians, whose numbers were increased to forty thousand men, to be driven from Finland.

My own forces in the north were not inactive ; recognizing the difficulties to be encountered by the Russians in turning the gulf of Bothnia, I resolved to second them by threatening Gustavus in the centre of his power, in directing my army to enter Zealand in concert with the Danes. The English fleets could not keep the sound in the winter, and only a few hours were requisite to make a descent on Scania. The bare possibility of such an event would force the Swedes to guard this coast and thus effect a useful diversion for our allies, even if it did not force the obstinate Gustavus to yield to the imperious law of state interest. Bernadotte, who had replaced Brune, entered Zealand at the head of thirty thousand men including one of the Spanish divisions of Romana* ; the other division had remained in Fionia and Holstein with other French troops. The English hearing of this event, and fearing that we might treat Sweden and her fleet as they had the Danes, hastened to dispatch General Moore with ten thousand men to Gothenbourg, (May the 17th). The events in Spain induced the English government to recall this corps in order to employ it more usefully in the Peninsula. We have seen that it arrived in time for the deliverance of Portugal, and we shall soon meet it again in the plains of Castile.

* Romana (Marquis de la) was born in the Island of Majorca. He was of illustrious descent and received a very liberal education. Having early entered the army, he served with distinction in the campaigns of 1793 and 1795. In 1807, he commanded the Spanish division of ten or twelve thousand men in Zealand and Jutland. Learning there the events at Madrid, he entered into negotiations with the commander of the British fleet, and in August, 1808, embarked with most of his forces for Coruna. From this time he took a prominent part in all the operations of the Peninsular War, till his death, which occurred in January, 1811.

CHAPTER XIII.

AFFAIRS IN SPAIN AND PORTUGAL IN 1808; NAPOLEON'S CAMPAIGN IN THE SPANISH PENINSULA.

French Reverses in Spain—Military Preparations of Austria—Difficulties and Chances of Napoleon's Position—Conference of Erfurth—Napoleon goes to Spain—Supreme Junta—Position of the Spanish Forces—Napoleon at Vittoria—Character of the War—Plan of Operations—Affair of Burgos—Defeat of Blake at Espinosa—Battle of Tudela—Battle of Sommo-Sierra—Napoleon enters Madrid—The English advance from Portugal—Napoleon marches against them—Moore retires on Coruña and Romana on Orense—Battle of Coruña, and Embarkation of the English—Lefebvre on the Tagus—Victor defeats Infantado at Ucles—Operations in Catalonia—St. Cyr recaptures Rosas and succors Barcelona—Affair of Cordedeu—Victory of Molino-del-Rey—Victories of Cappellados and Walsch—Second Siege of Saragossa—Soult sent to Portugal—Departure of Napoleon for Paris—Intrigues of Talleyrand.

Results of the French Reverses in Spain.—At the news of the catastrophe of Baylen, Europe was as much convulsed as though I myself had sustained a complete defeat, and my empire had been shaken to its foundation. Austria and Prussia made no efforts to conceal their joy; all my enemies were in raptures, and there were few countries where I had not a goodly number of them. Austria had been impatient to repair the losses which she had sustained in the last three wars. Count Stadion, who was then Prime Minister, was a man of talent and one of my most formidable enemies.

Military Preparations of Austria.—As soon as the news of the insurrection of the second of May, and of the rising of the provinces, had proved to him that the occupation of Spain would be attended by an effusion of blood, he ordered (June 9th,) the organization of the *landwehr*, which, in a short time, would put the army on a respectable footing. Republican France had given to Europe the example of great national levies, and it is astonishing that Austria, in 1805, did not resort to this means, the only one that can save a state in times of great danger. The Archduke Charles, president of the Council of War, applied himself with great industry and activity to the reorganization of the army of the line; that of the *landwehr* progressed with no less rapidity. I heard of these military preparations while at Bayonne, and demanded explanations of Count Metternich, then minister at Paris. He replied with commonplace remarks on the necessity of placing the military institutions of Austria on the same footing as their neighbors. Bavaria not only adopted the system of conscription, but she organized her militia on the basis of the national guards of France, which put her in condition to march to the field a hundred thousand men. The alleged motive was specious; I was not duped by it. Affecting, nevertheless, an entire confidence, I invited the princes of the Confederation of the Rhine to form an encampment with their contingents.

Difficulties of Napoleon's Position.—But I was not altogether easy about the part that Europe might take; nor was I less embarrassed about the course which I myself ought to pursue. I had arrived at the decisive epoch in my career. My position was a delicate one. I had evidently mistaken the character of the war in Spain; and what immense advantages might not England derive from this error! I could reëstablish my affairs only by going there in person, or by sending there a great part of my army. Whatever course I might pursue, I should risk upon the continent every thing that I had accomplished during the last ten years; I should give to Austria an opportunity to resume the sceptre of Germany, and perhaps that of Italy also.

His Chances.—The new interests which I had created in

the Confederation of the Rhine formed a powerful counterpoise to the cabinet of Vienna. A hundred thousand Frenchmen aided by the Confederates, would be sufficient to oppose all its efforts. But if Prussia, which had much to avenge, should arm against me, she might decide the question. My alliance with Russia was, therefore, my most reliable resource, at least for preventing war by holding Prussia and Germany in check. But could I count on this alliance when its effects would be to ruin the maritime commerce of Russia? Fortunately, at this moment, the open and frank conduct of Alexander and the sagacity of Caulaincourt removed all doubts from my mind as to the course I was to pursue.

We had agreed at Tilsit that I should occupy Portugal; but not that I should dispose of the throne of Spain. Alexander might not agree to what had been done; he had not recognized my brother Joseph as king, and Count Strogonoff, his minister at the court of Madrid, had received no instructions on the subject. Caulaincourt seized the fit occasion to ask the emperor to give me a pledge of his favorable dispositions by recognizing my brother. Alexander felt that a refusal might destroy all that had been done at Tilsit; he unhesitatingly accepted the proposition, and this recognition, which I did not hope to obtain without making some concessions to Russia, proving to Europe the intimacy of our relations, gave me all the advantages of a victory, for it imposed on my enemies.

Nevertheless, it was only a preliminary step toward extricating me from my difficulties; I had now to choose between two chances of final success in my Spanish enterprise. The first consisted in withdrawing the army of Murat to the Pyrenees, and sending back Ferdinand to Madrid, at the same time declaring, *that I had only intended the regeneration of the nation by vigorous institutions, but that I would now abandon it to its own fate, inasmuch as it did not desire my assistance ;* the second consisted in forcibly carrying out my project of regeneration, and intrusting the peace of the continent and my dearest interests there to my ally, the Emperor Alexander. The first seemed the more prudent course ; but the fear of a retrograde step which might destroy the prestige of my invincibility, and more than all, the certainty that Spain would throw herself, *à corps perdu,* into an alliance with England, induced me to prefer the second. I had undertaken this enterprise, not merely through ambition, but because it was necessary to me in sustaining the maritime contest in which I was engaged, and moreover was important in taking from the Bourbons their last support in Europe. This double motive was sufficient to determine my choice. I confess that there was a little temerity in intrusting the fate of my empire to Russia, and the vulgar, who always judge superficially, will blame me for it. But the plausible reasons already cited determined my course ; moreover, I thought that eighty thousand men of my old troops would, with the fifty thousand already there, suffice for the subjugation of the Peninsula, and the levy of a double conscription would place my army in Germany on the same footing as it was before this great detachment. I said to myself, moreover, if Austria feared to declare against me after Pultusk and Eylau, how could she venture to do so after Russia had joined me ? I was not so simple as to suppose that Russia would prefer my interests to her own, or that, should I experience reverses, she would repair them. But I knew that a power having self-respect does not immediately pass from the position of an ally to that of an enemy. It was sufficient, for the present, that Russia should feign to render me the promised assistance ; time and a preliminary success was of great importance to me at this juncture ; with time and a nation as active as the French, all things are possible.

Short-sighted politicians, looking only at the result of the enterprise, have found fault with my course, without at all comprehending the chances of my position. Of course it would have been better to recognize Ferdinand as king and give him a princess of my house, than to drive him from the throne with an armed force; but the war once begun, how could I abandon Spain and Spanish America to the English leopard? To judge by the event, I admit that it would have been more prudent to withdraw my army on the Pyrenees and leave Spain under the yoke of its monks; civil war would soon have burst out. But who could have foreseen the difficulties which I encountered? and what statesman could, with *sang froid*, have seen the commerce of Vera-Cruz, of Lima and of Cadiz, take its way to the Thames—the infallible result of this retreat? To save Spanish America, it was important to resuscitate old Spain, and give her a fleet and an army; and, to accomplish this result, it was necessary that the garb of a monk should no longer rank first in the state; it was indispensable to reform public feeling and remodel national institutions. To accomplish this object it only required a firm hand and strong will.

Conference of Erfurth.—Having decided to go myself to the Peninsula, I thought I ought first to confer with my powerful ally, on the position of our affairs in Europe. We met at Erfurth about the middle of September. I there exposed to Alexander my intentions with respect to Spain; I explained to him my plan of rescuing America from the English, and of afterward striking, by Turkey and Persia, a mortal blow at their possessions in India. Alexander had views sufficiently extended to appreciate my project; but he also knew that it would require time to execute it, and that I had too many obstacles to encounter in Europe to make any progress, if he should make the least opposition. He was willing that I should engage in this Peninsular contest, for his empire would profit by any turn which affairs might take. This policy was wise and natural, *for to know how to wait and profit by time and opportunity, is every thing in politics.* I proposed to leave him Moldavia, Walachia and Finland; he promised to guarantee the state of Europe as had been decided at Tilsit, and our defensive alliance was made more close. Before separating, we resolved to renew offers of peace to England, and we addressed in concert, a pressing letter to George IV., urging him, for the sake of humanity, to put an end to the war. But the cabinet of St. James, little pleased with this direct appeal to the feelings of the sovereign, answered evasively. It was evident that the war in Spain and the report of the great Austrian levies had raised too high her hopes of success, to expect from her a moderation which she had not shown after the treaty of Tilsit, when her cause had been abandoned by the rest of Europe. Now, however, she might very well prefer the chances of war, for they were all in her favor. Nevertheless, I felt quite confident of a continental peace, for the emperor of Austria had just contributed to remove my remaining doubts and fears. This prince, after having unsuccessfully attempted to get Metternich admitted into the conferences of Erfurth, wrote me a letter from Presburg, on the eighteenth of September, by Baron Vincent, in which he expressed his desire to maintain peace. I believed him, because I thought Austria not strong enough to contend with France and Russia united; that she had put a good grace upon the recall of Count Stahremberg and the rupture with the English; and especially because I felt capable of defeating her, should she take a fancy to renew the war.

Napoleon sets out for Spain.—Having no farther uneasiness about the peace of the continent, I directed the dissolution of the camps of the Confederation of the Rhine, and resolved to set out immediately for Spain with my guards, preceded by three corps of my old army, those of Ney, Mortier and Victor. I had no idea that a city populace, who, with the militia and a few soldiers of the line, had driven away the conscripts of Murat, could a long time hold out against soldiers that had defeated the finest armies in Europe. I was far from foreseeing that a sublime despair would pervade all classes of a nation which had been painted to me in unfavorable colors, but which, in its misfortunes, showed itself equal even to the Romans. Such resistances do not belong to our age; and they almost induce us to believe that fanaticism is a stronger motive than patriotism and glory.

Supreme Junta of Aranjuez.—The retreat of Joseph from Madrid had given the Spaniards an opportunity to centralize the action of their government, by naming a supreme junta; but instead of sending deputies direct from the provinces, with powers proportional to the dangers to which the country was exposed, the provincial juntas sent two of their members to the central junta, restricting the powers of these members so as to preserve, as much as possible, their own authority. The supreme junta assembled in the palace of Aranjuez, under the presidency of Count Florida Blanca, a venerable statesman, whose name carried with it the public confidence. The selection was a remarkable one, as Blanca's old attachment to the French alliance ought to have caused him to be suspected. A council of war, in which figured Generals Castaños, Morla, and the marquis of Castellar, directed all the disposition for the levies and the defense of the kingdom; the repairs and armaments of the fortifications, the disposition of the resources of the kingdom, and the succors sent from England. Tarragona, Tortosa, Gerona, Badajos, Cuidad-Rodrigo, were put in a state of defense; works were also ordered at Saragossa and at Valencia.

Position of the Spanish Forces.—The Spanish forces were formed into four armies. On the left, Blake with the army of Galicia, forty-five thousand strong, had passed Bilboa, and was now marching on Mondragon, with the intention of debouching in rear of Vittoria; in the centre, the army of Estramadura, of twenty thousand men, commanded by Count Belvedere, occupied Burgos; on the right, Castaños, with the army of Andalusia, of thirty thousand men, extended along the Ebro from Calahora to Tudela; and Palafox, at the head of twenty-five thousand men of the army of Aragon, occupied the left bank of the Aragon. Besides, the Spaniards had a corps of reserve of ten thousand men, in advance of Madrid. In Catalonia, General Vives was blockading Duhesme in Barcelona. Finally, an English army of thirty thousand combatants, coming partly from Portugal by Salamanca, and partly from Coruña, was to unite at Valladolid under the orders of Moore.

Napoleon joins Joseph at Vittoria.—I repaired, in November, 1808, to the head-quarters of my army at Vittoria. The corps of Moncey formed its left wing at Taffala, extending along the Aragon; the corps of Ney was at Vittoria; that of Soult at Miranda and along the Ebro; the corps of Victor was on the march from Vittoria to Orduna; at the extreme right, the corps of Lefebvre occupied the heights of Durango; my guard was with me at Vittoria. The corps of St. Cyr which had assembled at Perpignan, penetrated into Catalonia to relieve Duhesme at Barcelona. I still expected the corps of Mortier and that which Junot had brought back from Portugal after the convention of Vimiera; but I felt strong enough already to take the offensive with what troops I had in hand.

Character of the War.—In forming my plans for subjugating Spain, I had to choose between regular and methodical operations, and a war of a more irregular character. By the first system, provisions must be carried in the suite of the army, or be regularly purchased and paid for from the inhabitants. No great detachments could be made to regulate the administration of the provinces, or to pursue the insurgent corps to the fastnesses of the mountains. In fine, effecting a military occupation of Spain without its subjugation. By the second, war would be made to support war. To march rapidly against all organized masses, living from day to day, upon the local resources, as we had done in Italy, Austria and Prussia, sparing our reserves for the occupation and pacification of the conquered provinces—this mode promised more prompt and decisive results. The individual losses, rendered still more disastrous by the flight of the civil authorities, caused by this method, made us numerous enemies. Nevertheless, in spite of these unavoidable excesses and the vengeance taken by the insurgents in reprisal, we should finally have succeeded in restoring order and peace, had it not been for the English coöperation, the position of Portugal flanking our line of operations, and the advantages which her maritime ally derived from her eight hundred leagues of coast. By sacrificing three or four hundred millions of money for the subsistence of my troops, and devoting two whole years to overrunning Spain, it is possible that the first method would have succeeded. By maintaining good order and discipline among my troops, and by distributing the money necessary to support them among a people poor and interested, would have gradually made us many partisans. We could then have offered them, with a firm and just hand, the olive or the sword. But great as were the advantages of this system, it must be confessed that its application was very difficult. The thing had been very easy with an army of fifty thousand men, as was done by Vendôme under Louis XIV.; then three quarters of the nation were for us and for Philip V. But we had now almost the entire nation in arms against us; we could not suppress such an insurrection, and at the same time oppose the Anglo-Portuguese, with less than two hundred thousand men; but how was it possible to make regular provision for this number in a country where there was no means of organizing administrative authorities whose requisitions would be respected? Suchet and Soult partially succeeded with this system for a time, with small forces and in a more favorable part of the country. By the second system I had always succeeded; it led more directly to the destruction of the enemy's armies; and avoided the enormous drafts upon the treasury of France which would have been required, under the other system, for the armament, clothing, and support of two hundred thousand armed men in a foreign country. It will be said, undoubtedly, that only a year's advance from the French treasury would have been required, as, at the end of that time, regular contributions could have been levied and collected in Spain. Nothing can be more absurd; those who know the difficulties experienced by the Spanish government in collecting sufficient for its ordinary expenses will agree with me, that it would have been impossible for King Joseph to effect with that impoverished nation, what Charles III. failed to do in the glorious epoch of his reign, and the golden age of unhappy Spain. To these motives, quite sufficient, we must add, that the war was not popular enough with the French, to justify any great sacrifices by France. Besides, the want of navigable rivers, good roads and suitable means of transport, rendered problematical the possibility of moving a sufficient quantity of stores in an insurgent country. I, therefore, determined to adopt the same course that I had already pursued with so much success. It caused great excesses, but this was rather the fault of the chiefs who tolerated them. Had I succeeded, I should have indemnified the mass of the people for their losses, by the sale of the great wealth of the clergy, which would have rendered the Church more dependent on the government, and caused a more just division of the riches of this world; thus, the evils of the war would have been forgotten in the happy triumph of public and private interest over that of an ambitious and exclusive clergy.

Plan of Operations.—Having determined to carry on the war of invasion upon the same principles by which I had gained success in former campaigns, I prepared to attack the Spaniards with our accustomed impetuosity. My plan of campaign was marked out by the faulty positions of the hostile forces. Their centre, too weak to oppose a serious resistance, would be easily overthrown; then the two wings, separated and turned, would be in a very critical situation. The army of Blake, in particular, having ventured past Bilboa, might be entirely cut off and driven into the sea. Unfortunately, the aged Lefebvre, urged forward by the impetuous ardor of youth, did not even wait for my arrival at the army before attacking Blake, whereas he should have manœuvred to retain him in advance of Bilboa. On the thirty-first of October, Blake had been driven from this city which was now occupied by our troops. The seventh of November, Lefebvre attacked him again at Guenes, and obliged him to fight, retreating on Espinosa.

On the other hand, the events of Baylen had given me a higher idea of the resistance to be opposed by the Spanish troops in line, and as the road from Bayonne was my only communication, I did not wish to penetrate too far beyond the Ebro, before having secured this route from the enterprises of Blake. I had sent, for this purpose, the corps of Victor, to reënforce Lefebvre, with directions to push the army of Galicia as soon as Soult and my guard should be in position for piercing the centre. The two corps of my right performed their task, but more rapidly than anticipated.

Affair of Burgos.—Ignorant of this premature success, I did not yet despair of being able to turn Blake. On the tenth of November, Soult marched on Burgos. The army of Estramadura was broken by the first shock of General Mouton's division and a detachment of cavalry. It lost twelve colors, twenty-five cannon and three thousand prisoners. The rest were dispersed. Master of Burgos, where I established my head-quarters, I hastened to direct Soult on Reynosa, in hopes of there anticipating the army of Galicia, while the three divisions of cavalry were thrown on Medina-del-Rio-Seco to cut off from Zamora the English who, it was said, were assembling near Valladolid.

Blake is defeated at Espinosa.—Blake directed his march on Espinosa-de-los-Monteras, which lies on the direct road from the Ebro to St.-Ander; he flattered himself to thus cover for some time the great road that leads from Burgos to this sea-port, the road which runs to Reynosa where the Spanish army had collected the mass of its material. Re-enforced by the corps of Romana, which had just returned from Denmark, Blake established himself before Espinosa, having in rear the ravine of the Trueba. Such a position would of course render an attack difficult, and a defeat disastrous. Victor arrived here on the tenth, and immediately directed an attack. Our troops had not been able to transport their cannon through the mountains, while Blake had brought some pieces from St.-Ander; but, in spite of this advantage, the corps of Romana, placed on an advanced plateau, was overthrown by the division of Pactod, driven into the ravines, and partially destroyed. Night put an end to this first combat. The next day Victor resumed the attack. The enemy took position in a bend of the Trueba to the south of Espinosa, having this little village in rear of its left flank; an absurd position where the slightest check must become disastrous; it was a repetition of the defeat of Friedland, with the difference that, having Spaniards instead of

Russians to deal with, the rout and confusion were the more complete.

Deceived by the attack of the night before, Blake believed that our main efforts would be directed against his right, and therefore concentrated his *élite* at that point. Victor, on the contrary, threw General Maison against the left; he routed this wing, and pursued it pell-mell upon the bridge of Reynosa, which was the only one in the enemy's possession. The Spaniards of the right and centre, formed *en-masse* in squares, threw themselves into the Trueba, and the most horrible confusion ensued. A part fled on the St.-Ander road; others took that of Vilarcayo, and fell into the hands of General Sebastiani who had marched in that direction; the greater part fled to Reynosa.

In this battle Blake lost about ten thousand men killed, wounded and prisoners. If the movement of General Maison had been directed upon the right instead of the left, the whole Spanish army, thrown back on St.-Ander, would have been forced to lay down its arms. Blake passed Reynosa on the morning of the twelfth, and Romana, finding the wrecks of his army in the most deplorable condition, was obliged to throw himself, by the high mountains at the head waters of the Ebro, into the kingdom of Leon, in order to collect and recruit his exhausted forces. He reached there with scarcely fifteen thousand men. A single day's delay in Victor's attack, and this army would have been utterly annihilated. Soult, instead of continuing the pursuit through this horrible country, took the road from Reynosa to St.-Ander, overran this province, taking a large number of prisoners, the guarding of which he intrusted to the division Bonnet, and then descended upon Leon.

Castanos and Palafox beaten at Tudela.—We still had on our hands the armies of Castaños and Palafox, which were united at Tudela. Reënforcing Ney with the division

Dessolles. I ordered him to march from Aranda by Soria on Agreda, in order to turn these armies. Lannes, at the same time, was dispatched from my head-quarters, to put himself at the head of Moncey's corps near Logrono, and attack them in front. Ney reached Soria on the twenty-second. Lannes had passed the Ebro the night before, by the bridge of Lodosa, and was now marching by Calahora on Tudela. On the morning of the twenty-third, he arrived in front of the enemy's line. This army, composed of the conquerors of Baylen and the defenders of Valencia and Saragossa, was the hope of Castile; counting in all forty-five thousand combatants, it formed a line of battle about two leagues in extent. Palafox, with the Arragonese, formed the right, the Valencians and the Castilians the centre, and Castaños the left, which rested near Cascante. Lannes had not more than half their numbers; but as soon as he saw, on the morning of the twenty-third, the extent of their line, he commenced the attack by throwing the division of Maurice Mathieu on the centre, and that of Lagrange on the left. Sixty pieces of cannon protect these attacks. The Spanish line is pierced; the cavalry of Lefebvre-Desnouettes penetrates the opening, and falls with impetuosity on the infantry of the right wing, fighting as though determined to revenge the affair of Saragossa; the Arragonese, attacked at the same time in flank and in reverse, take to flight. The haughty conquerors of Baylen fall back before Lagrange; assailed in front and rear by Maurice Mathieu, they retreat along the Tarragona road; Palafox had taken the road to Saragossa. Thirty pieces of cannon, three thousand prisoners and as many enemies *hors-de-combat*, were the fruits of this victory. But I had hoped for still greater results; although the movement of Ney was a little too well understood to be concealed from the Spaniards, still I hoped that the Castilian pride would prompt them to await battle, and that once engaged with Lannes, Ney might arrive in time in their rear to destroy them. Lannes here committed the same fault as Victor at Espinosa; he attacked a day too soon. It is possible, however, that, had he delayed, the enemy might have retired unharmed, which would have been worse than this incomplete success. But Ney did not accomplish all in his power; he marched too slowly. Arrived, on the twenty-second, at Soria, he halted there to collect his troops and gather news of the enemy. It was proposed to him at the heights of Almazan, to take by this city the road to Calatayud, a point that he could easily have reached before the enemy. In fact, the position of Ney was a little embarrassing; if he directed his course from Osma by Almazan upon El-Amunia or Calatayud, he would gain more securely the road to Valencia, but, at the same time, would, by increasing the distance between him and Lannes, expose the latter to be defeated without the possibility of succor. If Ney, on the contrary, should march by Soria on Agreda, he could not prevent the enemy from moving directly on Tarragona and Calatayud. Ignorant of what was actually taking place, he remained at Soria, and allowed the enemy time to escape.

Malevolence, which would blast and destroy every thing, has imputed this delay of Ney to his jealousy of his colleague. It is but too true that my marshals were not always free from this passion, so fatal to an army; but Ney was incapable of pushing it so far as to defeat a concerted operation; moreover, in this case, the half of the honor of success would have belonged to him, as he would have captured all the prisoners and trophies.

Thus, the two decisive operations of the campaign, counteracted by fortuitous circumstances which it was impossible to foresee, prevented me from destroying, at a single blow, the two armies on which Spain placed most reliance. The war, without doubt, would have still continued; but what a difference would there have been in succeeding events, if Castaños and Blake, captured with all the skeleton of good troops, had left the kingdom without any other defense than the local rage of an unbridled populace.

Battle of Sommo-Sierra.—Having defeated and routed the Spanish armies of the right and left, I could now advance with security on Madrid. I passed the Douro, on the twenty-ninth, at Aranda, with the corps of Victor, my guards and the cavalry, and the next day reached the foot of the Sommo-Sierra. Ten thousand Spaniards, of the corps of reserve, defended this position, almost impregnable, on the great road from Burgos to Madrid. Closed in by steep rocks on all sides, it could hardly be approached except by the road. Our infantry attacked it in vain, both to the right and left; as the enemy's cannon enfiladed the road, an attack in close column became exceedingly destructive to our troops. I then threw upon these batteries the brave Polish lancers of my guard; the first squadron, suffering severely from the murderous fire, hesitates; others come to their support; galloping up the steep sides of the mountain, and falling upon the cannon, they capture them, and put to flight the Spanish infantry, who, astonished at so much valor and audacity, retreat in disorder on the road to Madrid. This feat of arms, one of the most brilliant of all my campaigns, covered the Polish lancers with glory, and won for them the title of "the most intrepid."

Napoleon enters Madrid.—We passed the defile, and on the second of December, I established myself on the heights that overlook Madrid. I had with me only thirty thousand men; the capital was defended by more than forty thousand armed forces under General Morla, one of the most intelligent men in Spain. But in truth, one half of these were peasants just collected together, or the undisciplined inhabitants of

Madrid, and I counted much upon the panic produced by my success. In this I was not mistaken. Notwithstanding the noisy boasting of this multitude, a few cannon shot against the old walls of the Retiro led to the capitulation of Madrid; I entered the city on the fourth.

Ney, at first directed on Saragossa, was to be replaced there by Mortier, and, in the mean time, he was to leave that place to the care of Moncey's corps; he now received orders to join me at Madrid with his sixth corps. I passed it in review on the heights of Chanmartin, and made it enter Madrid with great pomp. The superb appearance and martial air of this corps, formed a strong contrast to the conscripts of which the first army of Spain was composed. Lefebvre left Biscay, and also marched for the capital; Soult marched upon Leon to observe Romana and the English; a new corps under the orders of Delaborde, formed of the wrecks of the army of Portugal, passed the Pyrenees and directed itself on Burgos.

I had more than once observed the influence which the fall of its capital exercises upon the submission of a state; and I resolved to profit by the fall of Madrid, to influence the minds of the Spaniards.* I determined to adopt no half

* In speaking of the capture of Madrid and the importance of fortifying the capital of a state, Napoleon, in his Memoirs, dictated at St. Helena, vol. ix., uses nearly the following language:

If Vienna had been fortified in 1805, the battle of Ulm would not have decided the fate of the war. Again, in 1809, if this capital had been fortified, it would have enabled the Archduke Charles, after the disaster of Eckmuhl, by a forced retreat on the left of the Danube, to form a junction with the forces of General Hiller and the Archduke John.

If Berlin had been fortified in 1806, the army routed at Jena would have rallied there and been joined by the Russians. If Madrid had been strongly fortified in 1808, the French army, after the victories of Espinosa, Tudela, Burgos, and Sommo-Sierra, would not have marched toward that capital, leaving in rear of Salamanca and Valladolid, both the English army of General Moore and the Spanish army of Romana. If Moscow had been fortified in 1812, its conflagration would have been avoided, for, with strong defensive

measures with the clergy; I had, during my short sojourn at Madrid, sufficient proof of the part they had taken in the revolution, to remove all doubts on this point, if any had previously existed. Repelled by the Church, I had no hope of gaining the attachment of its implacable ministers—a class of men more disposed than any other in Spain to uphold existing abuses. In spite of their well-known influence, I was persuaded that there existed in Spain a numerous party of men wise enough to second the reforms that could be made, particularly in the monastic orders. I tried to rouse the patriotic desires of this party. I knew that the numerous class of magistrates and notaries, these veritable *ulemas* of the Spanish monarchy, aspired to a more liberal organization. It was through this intermediary class that I hoped to act upon the mass of the nation. I caused to be sent to me a deputation of the notables of Madrid. More than twelve hundred of the most distinguished individuals of the different classes and corporations of the capital, with the corregidor at their head, came to compliment

works, and the army of Kutusof encamped on its ramparts, its capture would have been impossible.

Had not Constantinople been well fortified, the empire of Constantine must have terminated in the year 700, whereas the standard of the Prophet was not planted there until 1440. This capital was, therefore, indebted to its walls for eight hundred years of existence. During this period it was besieged fifty-three times, but only one of these sieges was successful. The French and Venetians took it, but not without a very severe contest.

Paris has often owed its safety to its walls. In 885 the Normans besieged it for two years without effect. In 1358 the Dauphin besieged it in vain. In 1359 Edward, king of England, encamped at Montrouge, devastated the country to its walls, but recoiled from before it, and retired to Chartres. In 1429 it repulsed the attack of Charles VII. In 1464 the count of Charlerois surrounded the city, but was unsuccessful in his attacks. In 1472 it repulsed the army of the duke of Burgundy, who had already ravaged its precincts. In 1536, when attacked by Charles V., it again owed its safety to its walls. In 1588 and 1589 it repulsed the armies of Henry III. and Henry IV. In 1636 and several succeeding years, the inhabitants of Paris owed their safety to its walls. If this capital had been strongly fortified in 1814 and 1815, the allied armies would not have dared to attempt its investment.

me at my head-quarters at Chanmartin. Never did a more solemn assembly present itself before a conqueror to recognize his power. I profited by the occasion to proclaim my intentions with respect to Spain, and replied to their address in these terms :

"I am pleased with the sentiments of the city of Madrid. I regret the ills that have befallen it, and I am very happy in having been able, under the circumstances, to save it from greater misfortunes. I am impatient to take measures to tranquillize all classes of citizens, knowing the injurious effects of uncertainty upon the people.

"I have preserved the religious orders, limiting the number of monks ; there is not a sensible man who will not agree with me that they are too numerous. Those who are called to this vocation by the grace of God will remain in their convents ; as to those who have inconsiderately, or from worldly motives, adopted it, I have established them in the order of secular ecclesiastics. With the surplus wealth of the convents I have provided for the wants of curates, the most interesting and useful class of clergy. I have abolished the inquisition, a tribunal denounced by all Europe, and repugnant to the feelings of the age. Priests should direct the conscience, but can exercise over citizens no exterior and corporal jurisdiction.

"I have obtained satisfaction for myself and for my nation ; vengeance is complete ; it has fallen on ten of the principal criminals ; entire and absolute pardon is granted to all others. I have abolished the rights usurped by the nobility in times of civil wars, when the kings were too often obliged to surrender their rights in order to purchase their own tranquillity and the repose of the people. I have abolished feudal rights, and every one can now establish inns, bakeries, weirs and fisheries, and give free scope to their industry, only observing the laws and regulations of the police. The egotism, wealth and prosperity of a few, do more injury to your agriculture, than the heats of the dog-days. As there is but one God, there should be in a state but one justice; wherefore all special jurisdictions, being usurped, and contrary to national law, have been abolished. I have also made known to all persons what each has to fear and what each may hope.

"As to the English armies, I will drive them from the Peninsula. Saragossa, Valencia, Seville, shall be reduced either by persuasion or by force of arms; there is no obstacle capable of retarding, for any length of time, the execution of my wishes. But what I can not do is, to constitute the Spaniards a nation, under the orders of the king, if they continue to be imbued with the spirit of opposition, and of hatred to France, which English partisans and the enemies of the continent have instilled into their minds. I can not establish a nation, a king, and Spanish independence, if that king is not certain of the affection and fidelity of his subjects.

"The Bourbons can never again reign in Europe; the divisions in the royal family were fomented by the English. To drive King Charles and his favorite from the throne was not what the duke of Infantado, the instrument of England, wished; papers recently taken in his house prove what the real object was; it was British preponderance that they wished to establish in Spain. Insensate project! which could have led to no other result than an endless war and the shedding of oceans of blood. No power under British influence can exist upon the continent; if there are any who desire it, their desire is folly, and will, sooner or later, cause their ruin.

"It would be easy for me, and I may be compelled to govern Spain, by establishing a viceroy in each province. But I will not refuse to concede my rights of conquest to the king, and to establish him at Madrid, when the thirty thousand citizens of this capital, the ecclesiastics, nobles, merchants, lawyers, shall manifest their sentiments and their fidelity, set the example to the provinces, and make known to the people and the entire nation, that the happiness of all depends upon a king and a liberal constitution, favorable in its provisions to the people, and opposed only to the egotism and haughty passions of the aristocracy.

"If such be the sentiments of the thirty thousand inhabitants of the city of Madrid, let them assemble in the Churches and on the Holy Sacrament take an oath, not with the mouth alone, but with the heart, and without any jesuitical restriction, *to be true to the king, and to love and support him.* Let the priests from the pulpit and in the confessional, the tradesmen in their correspondence, the lawyers in their meetings and discourses, inculcate these sentiments among the people; then I will relinquish my rights of conquest; then I will place the king on the throne, and take pleasure in showing myself the faithful friend of the Spaniard. The present generation may differ in opinions; too many passions have been excited; but your descendants will bless me as the regenerator of the nation; they will mark my sojourn among you as memorable days, and from these days they will date the prosperity of Spain."

These words, promulgated through all Spain, and accompanied by proclamations and decrees reducing two-thirds of the monastic orders, only irritated the resistance of the clergy, without making me a single partisan. The nobility, threatened in their feudal rights and *seigneurial* jurisdictions, were only the more bitter in their opposition; finally, the *Escribanos*, ill satisfied with the destruction of an order of things which multipied law suits, deemed it their duty to pronounce, for certain vague hopes which they did not appreciate, the vengeance inspired by a sense of insulted national honor.

Posterity, more disinterested and impartial, will decide that the views contained in these proclamations were the only ones which could rescue Spain from the gulf into which misfortune had precipitated her ; she will some day regret having rejected these wise and salutary measures. But the mass of the nation, incapable of understanding my language and of appreciating its meaning, docile to obey the impulses it received, repelled them with indignation. Ten years afterward, they received with enthusiastic joy, then condemned to death and dragged upon the hurdle, those Spaniards who had ventured to follow in my footsteps, and to proclaim these salutary measures. There is a time for all things !

The English advance from Portugal.—During all this time the English army had remained stationary. Its operations had been ill-combined ; the faults were attributed to Lord Castlereagh, who directed the department of war in utter ignorance of the art. Moore was a very distinguished officer, but he committed many errors ; he debouched from Portugal by Salamanca, and sent his material by Badajos, as if it could not have followed by Almeida. General Baird was to join him with a corps which was to land at Coruña ; but he was delayed some twelve days for permission to disembark his troops—a permission which the Spanish officers were unwilling to give. He finally effected his landing on the twenty-eighth of November, and directed his march on Astorga, at the time I entered Madrid. Moore, forced to wait at Salamanca for his material and half of his army, finally decided to march on Valladolid. The news of the bloody checks experienced by his allies induced him to decide rather hastily to retreat ; but on hearing that the Spaniards had announced their intention to redouble their efforts in the defense of Madrid, he renewed his plan of marching on Valladolid. It is a singular and almost unaccountable circumstance that, although in the midst of a friendly population, he did not learn the surrender of Madrid till the fourteenth, and even then by an intercepted dispatch of ours, containing at the same time information of the position of Soult on the Carion. The Spaniards had concealed this event, either through their national pride, or on account of dissatisfaction. The public voice accused the English general of tardy, irresolute movements; he thought to calm public opinion by forming the project of capturing the corps of Soult. He left Toro on the twenty-second, at the head of thirty thousand English troops, for Sahagun. Romana, with the Spaniards, was to push from Leon to the north of Saldana, and fall on Soult's right, while the English should turn his left, by crossing the Carion. To secure the success of this project, it was necessary that the English should take the road from Palencia on Herrera; but they feared to separate themselves too far from their line of retreat, and preferred to march directly to Sahagun.

Napoleon marches against them.—Hearing of this march of the English, I immediately resolved to operate on their rear, in order to cut them off from Portugal and the ports of Galicia. For the security of Madrid, I established on the Tagus the corps of Lefebvre and Victor, the first at Talavera, and the second at Toledo; a part of my cavalry remained at Madrid. I, myself, with my guards, the corps of Ney, the division of Dessolles, and the remainder of the cavalry, left the capital on the twenty-second, and marched on Tordesillas, where I crossed the Duero on the twenty-fifth. This direction was good; that of Toro might perhaps have been preferable. Ney, yielding to good advice, was on the point of taking from Arevallo the road direct to that city; perhaps we might have anticipated the English at Benevento. This was the decisive point of the two lines of retreat on Coruña and Portugal. My positive order to go to Tordesillas dissuaded him. This would have been of no importance, if we had marched from there direct on Benevento, but the fear that Soult might be engaged alone with the English caused me to incline a little too much to the right on Medina-del-Rio-Seco, where I arrived on the twenty-seventh of December. General Laborde, who had just arrived in Castile with the old corps of Junot, received orders to join me by Valladolid; Soult had already called him upon the Carion.

Moore retires on Coruna.—The following days I continued my march to take the English in reverse. Moore was too prudent to fall into the snare. On hearing of my advance with a considerable force from Madrid on Leon, he renounced his projects against Soult; and, on the twenty-fourth, instead of marching from Sahagun to Carion, he fell back on Benevento, where he took position, on the twenty-sixth, in rear of the Esla, at the junction of the roads to Salamanca, Madrid, Leon, and those leading to Galicia. The vigilance of the English general having defeated my projects, it only remained for me to profit by my superiority in numbers to push the enemy warmly, while Soult sought to turn his left, by moving from Leon on Astorga. This movement completed the separation of the corps of Romana, which took the road to Orense. On the second, Moore left Benevento, and hastened his retreat by Astorga and Lugo on Coruña; a single brigade took the road to Orense. I followed only to Astorga; for I deemed it useless to fatigue all the troops which I had with me, by marching them to the extremity of Galicia, and the corps of Soult was sufficient for the pursuit of the English army, already broken and much weakened. Nevertheless, I took the precaution to direct Ney to follow Soult near enough to render him assistance in case of need. With the remainder of my troops I took the road to Valladolid.

Battle of Coruna.—The English rapidly retreated to

Coruña, where they expected to embark. Their fleet was at Vigo; a contrary wind would have caused them the greatest embarrassment. Happily for them, the road to Coruña traverses from Astorga to Lugo a defile of thirty leagues formed by very high mountains. A feeble rear-guard was sufficient to protect the road, and the country was such as to preclude all possibility of manœuvring on the flanks. This prevented Soult from cutting off the enemy's march; and Ney, encumbered in the defile in their rear, could do nothing. This was the more to be regretted as the English army, having nothing prepared on this line, was destitute of every thing, and reduced to a frightful condition by the forced marches which it made without any necessity. They hamstrung the horses of their cavalry and train, and abandoned three or four thousand stragglers and sick, without ever having their line of operations threatened. Whatever may have been said of it, this retreat of Moore was, in reality, nothing less than a flight. It is not easy to conceive why the English were unwilling to defend Coruña. Of course it was not a Gibraltar; but it might have resisted an enemy who had only light artillery; honor required a defense; besides there was the sea by which the place could be provisioned, and by which, in case of necessity the army could retire. This operation of which the English have boasted, is incomprehensible to me, and without a parallel in history.

Having reached Coruña, the English army to gain time for the embarkation, put themselves in order of battle in front of the city; this gave us time to overtake them; Soult began the attack on the sixteenth of January; he had twenty thousand men, and the English about the same numbur. The battle was well contested but indecisive; General Moore was killed,* and Baird and Paget each lost an

* Sir John Moore was born at Glasgow in 1761, and at the age of fifteen, entered the army as ensign. In 1790, he was made a lieutenant-colonel, and

arm. The British troops exhibited great firmness, which strongly contrasted with the disorder and precipitation of their retreat, in which their only embarrassment was a want

was wounded at the siege of Colvi. In 1796, he accompanied Sir Ralph Abercrombie to the West Indies, as brigadier-general. In 1799, he was sent to Holland, and subsequently engaged in the expedition to Egypt. In October, 1808, he landed in Spain at the head of the English forces, and fell at Coruña, January 16th, 1809, mortally wounded by a cannon ball.

Napier thus describes his death and character:

"Sir John Moore, while earnestly watching the result of the fight about the village of Elvira, was struck on the left breast by a cannon shot; the shock threw him from his horse with violence, but he rose again in a sitting posture, his countenance unchanged, and his steadfast eye still fixed upon the regiments engaged in his front, no sigh betraying a sensation of pain. In a few moments, when he was satisfied that the troops were gaining ground, his countenance brightened, and he suffered himself to be taken to the rear; then was seen the dreadful nature of his hurt. The shoulder was shattered to pieces, the arm was hanging by a piece of skin, the ribs over the heart were broken, and bared of flesh, and the muscles of the breast torn into long strips, which were interlaced by their recoil from the dragging of the shot. As the soldiers placed him in a blanket his sword got entangled, and the hilt entered the wound; Captain Hardinge, a staff-officer, who was near, attempted to take it off, but the dying man stopped him, saying, '*It is well as it is, I had rather it should go out of the field with me;*' and in that manner, so becoming to a soldier, Moore was borne from the fight. * * *

"He was carried to the town by a party of soldiers; his blood flowed fast, and the torture of his wound increased, but such was the unshaken firmness of his mind, that those about him, judging from the resolution of his countenance that his hurt was not mortal, expressed a hope of his recovery; hearing this, he looked steadfastly at the injury for a moment, and then said, '*No, I feel that to be impossible.*' Several times he caused his attendants to stop and turn him round, that he might behold the field of battle, and when the firing indicated the advance of the British, he discovered his satisfaction, and permitted the bearers to proceed. Being brought to his lodgings, the surgeons examined his wound, but there was no hope, the pain increased, and he spoke with great difficulty. At intervals he asked if the French were beaten, and addressing his old friend, Colonel Anderson, he said, '*You know that I always wished to die this way.*' Again he asked if the enemy were defeated, and being told they were, observed, '*It is a great satisfaction to me to know we have beaten the French.*' His countenance continued firm and his thoughts clear, once only, when he spoke of his mother, he became agitated, but he often inquired after the safety of his friends, and the officers of his staff, and he did not even in this moment forget to recommend those whose merit had given them claims to promotion. His strength failed fast, and life was just extinct, when, with an unsubdued spirit, as if anticipating the baseness of his posthumous calumniators, he exclaimed, '*I hope the people of England will be satisfied! I hope my*

of provisions; an important lesson, which proves the difficulties of carrying on a war in a disorganized country, where it is impossible to live by requisitions. Nevertheless, the

country will do me justice!" In a few minutes afterward he died, and his corpse wrapped in a military cloak, was interred by the officers of his staff in the citadel of Coruña; the guns of the enemy paid his funeral honors, and Soult, with a noble feeling of respect for his valor, raised a monument to his memory.

"Thus ended the career of Sir John Moore, a man whose uncommon capacity was sustained by the purest virtue, and governed by a disinterested patriotism more in keeping with the primitive than the luxurious age of a great nation. His tall, graceful person, his dark, searching eyes, strongly defined forehead, and singularly expressive mouth, indicated a noble disposition and a refined understanding. The lofty sentiments of honor habitual to his mind, being adorned by a subtle, playful wit, gave him in conversation, an ascendency that he always preserved by the decisive vigor of his actions. He maintained the right with a vehemence bordering upon fierceness, and every important transaction in which he was engaged increased his reputation for talent, and confirmed his character as a stern enemy to vice, a steadfast friend to merit, a just and faithful servant of his country. The honest loved him, the dishonest feared him; for while he lived he did not shun, but scorned and spurned the base, and, with characteristic propriety, they spurned at him when he was dead.

"A soldier from his early youth, Moore thirsted for the honors of his profession, and feeling that he was worthy to lead a British army, hailed the fortune that placed him at the head of the troops destined for Spain. As the stream of time passed, the inspiring hopes of triumph disappeared, but the austerer glory of suffering remained, and with a firm heart he accepted that gift of a severe fate. Confiding in the strength of his genius, he disregarded the clamors of presumptuous ignorance, and opposing sound military views to the foolish projects so insolently thrust upon him by the ambassador, he conducted a long and arduous retreat with sagacity, intelligence, and fortitude; no insult disturbed, no falsehood deceived him, no remonstrance shook his determination; fortune frowned without subduing his constancy; death struck, but the spirit of the man remained unbroken, when his shattered body scarcely afforded it a habitation. Having done all that was just toward others, he remembered what was due to himself; neither the shock of the mortal blow, nor the lingering hours of acute pain which preceded his dissolution, could quell the pride of his gallant heart, or lower the dignified feeling with which, conscious of merit, he at the last moment asserted his right to the gratitude of the country he had served so truly. If glory be a distinction, for such a man death is not a leveller!"

This campaign of the English has been most severely criticised, and the general, who conducted it, was, at the time, made the subject of the most unmerited and unreasonable abuse. Sir John Moore was not a great military genius. This was never claimed by himself, nor by his friends for him. But he was a brave, honest and sensible man, and withal a great general, far above

English maintained their principal position, and, the night after the combat, effected their embarkation. The Spaniards, discouraged and few in number, did not even attempt to defend the places of Galicia. Coruña capitulated on the twentieth, and some days after, the important place of Ferrol surrendered to Soult without resistance In the capture of this place we took seven ships of the line and three frigates, besides a considerable number of vessels undergoing repairs. Romana at first retired toward Orense, and afterward regained the Asturias.

Lefebvre on the Tagus.—The news of my departure from Madrid in pursuit of the English, had revived the courage of the wrecks of the army of Andalusia which were collected at Cuença, under the orders of the duke of Infantado, and

the majority of those who have commanded armies and conducted campaigns. He did not succeed! A crime which has no pardon and no mitigation in England and the United States. In other countries, a general's character is judged by his plans and the use he makes of the means at his command. Not so in England, at least in Moore's time. He *must* succeed, whether furnished with means or not. In this respect we copy the English pretty closely; success, not merit, is the criterion by which popular opinion at first decides. Defeat, unless of a party favorite, is followed by unmeasured condemnation and abuse.

Perhaps the history of the world scarcely furnishes a parallel to the abuse which was heaped upon Moore for this retreat, which was entirely unavoidable, and well conducted. The party press of England seized upon it as a topic for political animadversion, and the furtherance of party schemes. Every thing was misunderstood and misrepresented. Personal and party abuse was the order of the day. The opposition thought, by Moore's failure, to weaken and break down the administration, let the consequences to the country be what they might. Many were led even to the very verge of treason. But time, which ultimately separates the true from the false, and vindicates the right, has rescued Moore from his slanderers, and placed his name high on the rolls of fame; while his detractors are utterly forgotten. Napier most ably vindicated his character and military conduct, and the verdict of history has, in the main, supported Napier's opinion. On the contrary, his enemies, who so profusely abused him in the public press of England, have sunk so deep into obscurity, that they can only be reached by the resurrectionary trumpet.

It is a singular fact, that not one of those who abused Moore and opposed the war, ever afterward attained any rank or consideration in England. An important lesson to those who, for interests of party, cease to be patriots and become half-way traitors to their government and their country.

of the army of the centre which was behind the Tagus, under General Galuzzo. The fourth corps under Marshal Lefebvre, prepared to repel this latter army. After having surprised the passage of the Tagus at Almaraz, Lefebvre drove back upon Merida the enemy, who were much scattered along an immense line. General Galuzzo was forced to collect the fragments of his army behind the Gaudiana.

Victor defeats Infantado at Ucles.—The duke of Infantado, expecting to find Madrid defenseless, advanced, at the end of December, from Cuença on that capital. The duke of Belluna, who was cantoned about Toledo, met him half way. The rencontre took place at Ucles, on the thirteenth of January; the division of Villatte, falls on the enemy as soon as it arrives; that of Ruffin, having lost its road, debouches, by unexpected good fortune, behind Ucles, and also falls suddenly on the enemy's rear. The hostile forces are completely routed, more especially the newly levied troops which form the great mass of their army. Eight or ten thousand prisoners, and thirty pieces of cannon, are the trophies of this easy triumph. Unfortunately, Latour-Maubourg's division of dragoons, which had followed the first corps, did not arrive in time to take part in the combat; otherwise, not a single battalion of Infantado's army would have escaped! Victor, after pushing the enemy on Cuença and exploring that province, fell back on Madridegos and Consuegra.

Operations in Catalonia.—Our affairs in Catalonia took a turn not less brilliant in appearance, but much less fortunate in results. This province, whose inhabitants had immortalized themselves by their resistance to Philip V. in 1709, is the most warlike in Spain. Its steep mountains present great difficulties in military operations, and especially in the supplies of an army, for it produces very little grain, and the cattle, on the first alarm, are driven away by the inhabitants into the mountains. Add to this, that its cities occupy sites strong by nature, and made still stronger by the resources of art. Its frontier population, composed of contrabandists and smugglers, is well suited for war. The news of the success of Baylen, exaggerated, as is usual with the Spaniard, had electrified all Catalonia. The people every where ran to arms. Duhesme, who commanded at Barcelona, feeling the necessity of opening a communication by Gerona, invested that place. After two unsuccessful attacks, executed with more courage than skill, he was reënforced by the division of Reille, and directed his operations more in accordance to rule; but allowing himself to be surprised, on the tenth of August (1808), by General Caldagues, who succeeded in supplying the place with provisions, he was finally forced to retreat. Reille regained Figueras with four thousand men; Duhesme had great difficulty in reaching Barcelona with seven thousand, where he was besieged by the enemy.

I now assembled three new divisions on this frontier, forming about twenty thousand men, and ordered St.-Cyr to take the command, directing him to effect a junction, as soon as possible, with Duhesme; but Berthier, who was incapable of doing any thing without my special instructions, took no administrative measures for providing this corps with the necessary supplies. It was composed of the Italian division of Pino, the French division of Souham, and of Tuscans, Neapolitans, Valencians, etc.

The retreat of Duhesme had inflamed the ardent Catalans; the supreme Junta sent them the troops of Minorca and reënforcements drawn from Valencia and Grenada, under the command of the Swiss General Reding. The ports of Tarragona, Tortosa, Palamos, and Rosas, afforded every facility for rendering this province impregnable. They formed there forty battalions of *miguelets*;[*] and it was estimated that seventy thousand men, in all, took up arms for the common defense, exclusive of a multitude of peasants, and of women, who, animated by a holy ardor, often bore arms in the defense of their ramparts. General Vives took the command in this province, and the English squadron under Collingwood cruised along the coast to second him.

St.-Cyr succors Barcelona.—In order to succor Barcelona, and supply that place with provisions, it was necessary first to capture Gerona and Hostalrich, the only points by which supplies could be conveyed. This seemed impossible in the face of so many difficulties; nevertheless St.-Cyr, judging that it would be dangerous to advance towards Barcelona while Rosas remained in the power of the English and insurgents, who might at any time cut off his communication with our frontier, determined to lay siege to that place. It is due to this general, to say, that this decision was contrary to my orders, which, under the circumstances, he was perfectly justifiable in disregarding. The English, under Cochrane, sought in vain to sustain the place, and the Spanish army to effect its rescue. The garrison, numbering three thousand men, abandoned by the squadron of its allies, was obliged to capitulate on the sixth of December.

St. Cyr, now yielding to my pressing instances, advanced to the succor of Barcelona. This was a difficult task. The marquis of Lusun, having retired from Aragon and Cerdaña, assembled under Gerona a corps of ten or twelve thousand men. It was necessary to leave him behind, for even should we attack him with success, it would be impossible to pursue him on the upper Fluvia without deviating from the object of the expedition. The marquis of Vives commanded from twenty-five to thirty thousand men around Barcelona, which place he was closely investing. Gerona and Hostal-

[*] Armed mountaineers of the Pyrenees.

rich obstructed the only road, so that neither cannon nor caissons of munitions could be transported. St.-Cyr might, therefore, find himself on the Bezos surrounded by twenty-five thousand good troops and a multitude of militia and miguelets, without having the means of sustaining two combats. Setting out from the Abispal by Valdreras, he succeeded in turning Hostalrich and getting through the important passage of Tordera and the defile of San Celoni, where one-half of the army of Vives might have formed an impenetrable barrier.

Affair of Cardedeu. — On reaching the plateau between Llinas and Cardedeu, on the sixteenth of December, St.-Cyr at last encountered Vives there formed to close the passage. He attacked him with impetuosity, completely routed his troops, captured all his cannon without losing one of our own, and then marched in triumph into Barcelona. This enterprise, which was conducted with rare precision, did great honor to St.-Cyr.

Victory of Molino-del-Rey. — Deeming it necessary to profit, without delay, by this victory to annihilate the regular corps of the enemy's army which had rallied behind the Llobregat, in order to cover Tarragona, St.-Cyr attacked Vives, the twenty-first of December, broke his right wing, and drove it back on the left. All took to flight, throwing away their arms and baggage. If they had held out a little longer, turned and out-flanked as they were, they would have been completely destroyed. As it was, they lost only twelve hundred prisoners, but we captured fifty pieces of their artillery. According to strict strategic principles, the attack should have been made on the left of the Spaniards, so as to drive them back on the sea and the marshes of Gava. It is true that their artillery and best troops were concentrated on this wing, in order to defend the bridge of Molino-del-Rey; but was it not possible to debouch by Pelleja on Moscaro, and, if this operation had succeeded, would there have been a single Spaniard left to carry to Tarragona the news of the destruction of their army? The difficulty of the ground is the only reason that can be given for the attack on the right. I know very well that strategic movements are of little avail against Spanish insurgents; but when there is a considerable corps of regular troops to deal with, and an opportunity occurs to manœuvre so as to throw them back upon the sea, it is always well to attempt it.

Victories of Capellados and Walsch.—So far from allowing itself to be discouraged by these reverses, the junta of Catalonia, established at Tarragona, threw Vives into prison, and supplied his place by Reding, an officer of valor and energy. Exposed to every privation, St.-Cyr, nevertheless, maintained himself with tenacity, till the month of February, between Barcelona and Tarragona. At this epoch Saragossa was closely pressed by Lannes. Reding having received reënforcements from all sides, deemed it the proper time to resume the offensive, hoping to be able, should he succeed in driving St.-Cyr from Catalonia, to fly to the assistance of Aragon. If Reding had understood strategy as well as he did fighting, he might here have played an important part. A slight success on the right flank of St.-Cyr, would have paralyzed his whole corps; but Reding thought his superiority authorized him to envelop our troops. Forming four columns several leagues apart, he marched to the right with the *élite* of his forces on the direct road to Vendrel, while his left under Wimpfen, was to descend from Lacuna and Igualda on Villa Franca. This was a double fault; Reding should have allowed St.-Cyr to move on Vendrel and Tarragona, while he himself was defiling with thirty thousand men on Capellados and Martorel, so as to turn our right and cut us off from Barcelona. St.-Cyr took the wisest course which could be adopted in such a case; he concentrated his forces on the centre at Lacuna, the sixteenth of February, overthrew his adversary's centre at Capellados, and drove it back on Cervera and Manresa. To complete his task, St.-Cyr drew back from the right toward the left (from Igualda on San Magi), so as to repeat on the enemy's right wing the operation he had just executed on the centre. Souham was to coöperate by effecting his junction at Villa Rodona; but the difficulty of sending orders prevented him from obtaining the desired result from this movement. Nevertheless, the junction was effected, and a French corps took possession of Walsch. Reding thought, by an inverse movement, to connect himself by Monblanch with the troops of Wimpfen near Igualda. He thus found himself cut off from the division which he had left in advance of Tarragona, and resolved to attack our troops and reëstablish his communication. St.-Cyr marched to encounter him; the meeting took place on the twenty-fifth of February, near Alcover. The enemy's defeat was complete; Reding, who was himself wounded, regained Tarragona, after losing more than three thousand five hundred men *hors-de-combat*. The handful of braves who gained these brilliant victories were, nevertheless, subjected to great want and its attendant maladies. The enemy repaired his losses by the continually increasing animosities of the population.

Second Siege of Saragossa.—Success, though much better contested, had also crowned our arms in Aragon; the modern Numantia, half buried in its own ruins, had capitulated. It will be remembered, that after the battle of Tudela, Palafox had retired upon Saragossa with thirty thousand men. A multitude of peasants, driven before our columns, had also taken refuge there. An ancient tradition made this city an object of peculiar veneration; it was the sanctuary of the Virgen-del-Pilar, the palladium of Spanish liberty, and all were resolved to save it or to die in the attempt. Priests, monks, citizens, peasants, as well as the military, were inflamed with unbounded enthusiasm. Never were so many different passions directed to the same object. Pride, patriotism, fanaticism, national and military honor—all the most powerful motives of human action were put in play to render the defense a desperate one.

Marshal Moncey had given to Junot the command of the third corps which first began the investment. Mortier had joined it with the fifth corps after Ney had received orders to move on Madrid. Marshal Lannes was placed in command of this army, and directed to proceed to the siege; General La Coste, my aide-de-camp, and Colonel Rogniat* directed the engineers, and General Dedon commanded the artillery.

Situated in one of the most fertile plains, with a population of sixty thousand inhabitants, Saragossa is built partly of brick and partly of granite; though not regularly fortified, it is surrounded by a thick wall. Since the first siege they had strengthened the weak parts of this wall, erected parapets, and constructed barricades across the streets, so that the wall being forced, a new enciente as it were, would be formed in each street; the place was well armed with one hundred and eighty pieces of cannon. Moreover, after the first siege, the English general, Doyle, had gone to Saragossa, levied a corps of troops, and furnished a large number of English muskets and military munitions for arming the Arragonese. The houses, being principally constructed of ma-

* Joseph Rogniat was born at Vienne, in 1767, and entered the service at the beginning of the Revolution. He served under Moreau, in 1800, as captain of engineers. He served in the campaigns of 1805, 1806 and 1807, and was made a colonel after the siege of Dantzic, in which he rendered valuable aid to General Chasseloup Laubat. In the Peninsular war he directed several important sieges, and was promoted to the grades of brigadier-general and general-of-division. In 1813, he directed the defenses of the capital of Saxony, and in 1814, commanded at Metz. He was afterward made lieutenant-general, and employed on important works of fortification. He was the author of several valuable books on military and political subjects.

sonry without the use of wood, rendered the usual incendiary projectiles utterly useless. It would, therefore, be necessary to resort to a bombardment, or to attack the place by mines, should the enemy not be forced by assault to capitulate. Both means were finally employed. Houses were attacked and defended like so many bastions in a regular fortress; and buildings, blown up by the mines, still found defenders who furiously disputed the scattered fragments. It would require the pen of a Homer to describe the heroic scenes of this siege, where art and well-directed courage finally triumphed over the strength and energy of despair. They disputed the possession of their houses, story by story, defending the rooms, the cellars, and the terraces, like so many demilunes, covered-ways, and counterscarps. The garrison multiplied its numbers; each point of attack was sustained by peasants and armed citizens who assembled at the sound of the tocsin in the different quarters to serve as a reserve. When an isolated post was not defended in a manner to suit the pleasure of the mob, the unfortunate officer who commanded, was either massacred or sentenced to be shot.

At the end of two months, the enciente of the city had been carried in many places, and one-fourth of the houses reduced by sword and torch. The population, half buried in their cellars, had been swept off by a horrible epidemic. Fifteen thousand soldiers and thirty thousand inhabitants had perished by fire, pestilence and famine; and when the place capitulated, it presented to our brave army, seized with admiration and horror, the aspect of a vast charnel-house. Palafox, who was sick, had given the command to a distinguished French emigrant (St.-Marc), but the latter soon threw his weighty responsibility on a junta of defense. This junta, yielding to the clamors of the majority, consented to capitulate, notwithstanding the opposition of fanatics who wished still to prolong the defense. My aide-de-camp, Lacoste,* had directed the siege till the moment of his death; Dedon was still spared; Lannes had distinguished himself, as he always did; as also had Mortier, Suchet, and the intrepid Gazan. Our loss did not exceed five thousand men. Manes of so many brave men! Providence had made you friends and allies, but a deplorable political error forced you to slay each other!

Soult is sent to Portugal.—I had hoped that England would be so disgusted with the catastrophe of Moore, that she would make no new efforts in the Peninsula; and my first idea was to avenge Junot by placing my eagles anew on the towers of Lisbon. The Portuguese army, a part disbanded, and a part sent into France, no longer seemed in condition to dispute our entrance. The return of our victorious troops, announcing a superiority which no force could oppose, seemed calculated to give confidence to our partisans and to induce them to declare boldly for our cause. Although they were not the most numerous party, they nevertheless counted in their ranks men high in public esteem.

The feeble part taken by the Portuguese previous to the defeat of Junot, deceived me respecting the state of feeling in the interior of the country, where exasperation was afterwards raised to the highest pitch. The English army, to which alone I had attributed the loss of Portugal, had disappeared at Coruña, and I flattered myself that my chances of success were better than before. My calculations proved erroneous, because my enemies displayed greater resources than I had supposed. The Prince Regent of Portugal had even outdone Barrère and the Committee of Public Safety, in his measures for national defense; he had ordered, by the

* Count N. Lacoste was an officer of the corps of engineers, and rose to the rank of colonel, in the campaign of 1807. He distinguished himself at the siege of Dantzic, and was made aid-de-camp to the Emperor, with the rank of general-of-brigade. San Genis, the chief engineer of the defenses of Saragossa, fell at nearly the same moment as Lacoste.

decree of December 11th (1808), a *levée-en-masse* of all men between the ages of eighteen and sixty years; every individual refusing to march against the enemy, was to be shot; every village that did not oppose all possible resistance, was to be burnt. There is no parallel to this in the code of 1793.

Beresford,* who had been made a Portuguese marshal, was entrusted with the general command. He organized twenty-four regiments under English pay, and with English officers for all grades above that of captain. Other regiments, entirely Portuguese, were also organized at the same time. The regular militia, instituted some half century before, and the reserve, known under the name of *ordonanzas*, were all put under requisition. A regency, composed of the Patriarch of Lisbon, the Marquis de Las Minas y do Monteyre Mor, was invested with unlimited powers, yet subordinate to the English general, who was the true dictator of the monarchy. Moreover, General Craddock, who remained English governor at Lisbon, on the departure of Moore, had received reënforcements, among which was the division of Mackenzie. The English sought to introduce this division into Cadiz, under the charitable pretext of defending that place from our troops, from whom, however, it was not in the slightest danger! But the Spaniards were not to be duped by such a pretext; and Mackenzie, very properly refused admission into a place from which it had been as impossible to eject him as from Gibraltar, resumed his anchorage in the Tagus.

* Sir William Beresford served with distinction in the Peninsular war, and was afterwards made a baron of the United Kingdom. For his services in Portugal he received the titles of Duke of Elvas and Marquis of Campo Mayor. The Prince Regent of Portugal made him generalissimo of his armies, but the severity with which he punished a conspiracy of General Freyre, in 1817, against the British domination in Lisbon, rendered him so odious to the Portuguese, that the Cortes afterwards dismissed him. In 1826 he again appeared at Lisbon, at the head of the British forces sent to quell the rebellion

Soult received orders at Ferrol to march on Lisbon with the second and eighth corps, whose effective strength a month before was near forty thousand men, but which had been reduced by sickness and losses during the campaign, to about twenty-four thousand. I hoped that these troops, reënforced by ten thousand convalescents and seconded by the corps of Victor who was to descend the Tagus, and the division of Lapisse who was to debouch toward Almeida, would suffice for the subjugation of a kingdom which I considered already nearly disarmed.

Departure of Napoleon for Paris.—I had not yet received any news from this expedition into Portugal, when important matters recalled me to France. Austria was arming in great force; and I inferred that there must be some grand project forming against me in Germany and in the north of Europe. I set out from Valladolid for Paris, about the middle of January.

In leaving the Peninsula, I was greatly embarrassed in selecting a successor. Joseph did not understand the art of war; but his title gave him command over the marshals who were unwilling to obey the orders of any one of their colleagues. He had remained with his court at Vittoria; and I was undecided about sending him back to Madrid, when a deputation of the grand functionaries of the state came to formally request his return. This request resulted from the fear of the Spaniards, lest they might be conquered and the kingdom dismembered; but the throne of my brother and the constitution of Bayonne, would at least be a guarantee of the integrity of their monarchy. This deputation decided me; and my brother made his formal entry into his capital at the very moment when I was entering the gates of Paris, January 22d. I left him in command, giving him Marshal Jourdan for an adviser; the conqueror of Fleurus had a name; he alone had commanded a hundred thousand men;

this would necessarily give him influence. I must confess that my choice was not a fortunate one ; Jourdan was a good soldier, but his system of military operations was erroneous ; he was a good administrator, laborious and methodical ; but he was incapable of giving motion to this vast machine. Indeed the task was exceeding difficult, on account of the contentious spirit of the marshals, the almost utter impossibility of communicating with the different *corps-d'armée*, and the necessity of covering the capital. To ensure success, it was necessary first of all, to keep constantly united a force sufficient to fall day and night on the English, without being troubled about Madrid ; but, with a king at head-quarters, seeking to control a vast kingdom, this was a difficult matter.

Nevertheless, at the time of my departure from France, I left my brother great chances of success.; for in three months I had greatly advanced our cause ; the destruction of three Castilian armies, the occupation of Madrid, the overthrow of Moore, the fall of Saragossa, the defeat of Vives and Reding, the occupation of Galicia, the assault of Oporto—had struck Spain and Portugal with terror. The English division left at Lisbon under Craddock, was already preparing to follow the wreck of Moore's army, as soon as Victor should advance by the valley of the Tagus. It seemed to require but the slightest effort to complete the enterprise. This appearance, however, was deceitful. In a couutry so vast, where the slightest thing may be converted into a serious obstacle, the absence of a firm and *single* directing mind must necessarily be felt sooner or later ; and obstinacy which forms the distinctive trait of the Spanish and Portuguese character, was calculated to eventually wear out the unconnected efforts of my lieutenants.*

* Napier's account of this campaign and his criticisms on the operations, are well worthy the attention of the military student.

Intrigues of Talleyrand.—On my return to Paris, I was not a little surprised to find the capital full of rumors on the inconveniencies of the Spanish war, and on the pretended counsels of Talleyrand, which would have prevented it, had they been followed ! I had good reason to be astonished and indignant at so incorrect a rumor, the object of which was too evident to be misunderstood. I now saw what I had to expect from a man who could lend himself to such an intrigue. I should probably have undertaken the war in Spain without his advice, but certainly his counsel contributed not a little to draw me into it. Deeming it best not to resort to too severe measures against him, I contented myself with reproving him in presence of the deputation of all the great bodies of the state, who had come to welcome my return to the Tuileries, reproaching him with these untrue stories which could have originated only with himself. I had already had occasion to observe his want of principle in pecuniary matters, and especially in the affairs of the princes of Germany and of the house of Orange ; but I had not deemed him capable of such an act as this. The rather severe reproof which I here gave him, was not the cause of the war which he declared against me, but it was the signal for hostilities.

CPSIA information can be obtained
at www.ICGtesting.com
Printed in the USA
LVHW101340160422
716387LV00003B/110